THE WC
WITH A MAN IN
HER HAT

P. J. Anderson

Nine Lives Editions UK

The author would like to thank Bob Hook and Sally Driscoll for reading and commenting on the first draft of *The Bogle from the Bladder of Hell.*

First published February 2018.

Second edition: *Nine Lives Editions UK*, 2019.

Follow the author on Goodreads.

ISBN: 9781099161063

CONTENTS

This book is in memory of 'Granny Delahunty', a woman who struggled against enormous odds and passed down through the generations her kindness and humanity and the ability to laugh in the face of adversity.

The War of Bill's Will

Prologue

It starts with the land and ends with the land. You're born, live, love if you're lucky, and die on it and then everyone fights over it. It's a story that's as old as the soil itself and the bones buried deep within it.

Ben O'Leary and Liam O'Reilly were each thirty years old and built like bears, with woolly red hair and beards so alike they could have been twins. They were bright as their sea blue eyes but stubborn as bulls and each had an unshakeable conviction that he was in the right and the other was as wrong as the devil himself. They stood like chieftains on the rocky crag that looked down on the fertile valley far below and made a deal, an escape from the war of their lawyers and the Battle of the Will of Bill. They'd fought to a draw with every legal ploy they could muster and their solicitors' fees were eating so many holes in their wallets that anything put in would just as soon fall out.

It had all started when their common godfather, old Bill Murphy, died without marrying. He left all of his land to the nearest he had to a son and heir, which, from a choice of the two of them, he decided was Ben. The problem for Liam was that, compared to Ben, he had spent twice the time helping look after the old man in his last year or two and had, so he thought, been promised all of the land himself. He challenged the will as soon as it was read therefore. All manner of peculiar circumstances around its signing and many amendments quickly emerged, leading to a long and complex legal duel. But half of the legal arguments for the resolution of the will's many problems pointed in Ben's direction, while the other half were in favour of Liam. The result was a deadlock that threatened to be unbreakable and to bankrupt the two protagonists if they kept fighting a battle that neither could afford nor win.

That was where the Wisdom of Solomon, as supplied by Sean O'Donnell, stepped in. Sean, a man as tall as the stories he liked to tell, was the uncle of both men who, to each other, were now sworn enemies. He was a kind and modest man in his early fifties, a gentle giant, with a face with a permanent smile. He had a credibility with each that guaranteed their attention when he suggested a way out of the impasse, given that both refused to countenance any deal whereby the land would be split between the two of them. To Ben he said exactly the same thing as he had done to Liam,

"My solution is this and you can laugh it down if you like, but it has a certain attraction for a man like meself who likes a bit of a punt on the ponies. There is a storytelling competition at Mullahy's Rock every June and a tradition of betting on the winner, which is a twin delight I can never resist – I've even told a couple of stories meself. Why don't the two of you come with me this year? You don't have to speak to each other if your heads are still as stubborn as before – just sit through the stories and bet on the winner at the end. The judges will announce how each tale has been ranked when they give their verdict. Whoever's bet is closest to the winner wins the land. It'll be a game of skill and judgment and the fairest and cheapest way I can think of for resolving the otherwise irresolvable. So what d'you think?"

As noted before, while stubborn to the point of stupidity, the two were otherwise bright and 'bright' included a love of stories and all the different ways of their telling. While the company of one had no appeal for the other, the prospect of a low cost resolution to their otherwise endless and highly expensive dispute was persuasive and after only a little thought and caution both agreed to Sean's proposal. They shook hands on the matter on top of the Kerry mountain that looked down on the land in question and through such silent means avoided the need to speak.

Mullahy's Rock was a local nickname for a crag that overhung a flat, lush green valley, within which sat a ribbony river, a small, squat village and a pub so old that Moses was rumoured to have once popped in for a pint. The annual story telling festival swelled the population to twenty times or more its normal size and put the pub in danger of exploding walls, given the disparity between its capacity and the numbers that entered its doors at the end of each day. Sean, Ben and Liam motored down together in Sean's monster of a camper van, with Ben sat at the front and Liam self-positioned so far away from him at the rear that he was as much on the outside as the inside. When they joined the ranks of other happy campers at the site set aside for the audience Sean and Ben slept inside the vehicle while Liam erected his own tent a good ten feet away. To Sean it seemed that he was only short of a moat, high towers and a row of bloodthirsty archers to ensure completely his separation from Ben.

Following a hearty breakfast of egg and sausage without the sausages, given that a dog from an adjoining tent the size of a house stole them out of the frying pan while Sean was brewing the tea, the three made their way over to the main marquee. After checking that the programme remained as originally advertised, Sean sat his charges down, one either side of him to avoid the risk of unpleasantness. He said,

"Now gentlemen, there are loads more storytellers performing here than are in the competition, which is just a small part of the festival. We need to be careful that we attend only the acts that count for the prize so that we keep our minds focussed on the point of the exercise. You need to weigh up every word and sentence and the skill of its use while keeping a sharp eye also on how well or not each tale goes down with the audience. Use every means and measure that you can think of to estimate the chances of each performance winning and then, when it's all complete and ready for judging, you must place your bets and see which of you comes closest. That, as we have agreed, will be the final decision on who gets the land. As your uncle, I expect whoever is the loser to uphold the traditions of the family and accept the result, whatever it may be. It would be my ideal – and your forebears' delight - if the winner would offer to share his prize with the loser, given that you are both cousins. But I must admit, given your joint determination on the matter, I'm not optimistic about such a fair and logical outcome."

At that point a clown on a unicycle rode into the tent handing out leaflets about the tale he would be telling at midday.

"Gimmicks, gimmicks, too many gimmicks," Sean muttered. "Keep it simple and let the words weave their magic on their own, that's my motto. He's not in the competition so you can forget him, he's just a sideshow. I know all of the tellers that are here this year in the sense that I've seen each perform at least a couple of times before, so I can give you a quick run down on each and what to expect before they start."

"You'll only give us any guidance when we're both together – nothing will be said when one of us is in the jacks or anywhere else than here?" Liam asked.

"I will indeed," Sean replied. "No word will pass my lips when one of you is absent so that the help that each of you gets from me is exactly the same. With the stakes as they are there must be no room for misunderstanding or mistrust."

"That's right enough, all or nothing means all or nothing and we need to be sure it's fair," Ben replied. He looked directly at Sean as he spoke so as not to be thought to be softening his attitude a little and sharing his words with Liam, although the leaden emphasis on all or nothing was a message clearly aimed at his adversary. Its dour and uncompromising tone was not well received by his cousin, as Sean noted out of the corner of his eye. In fact if a face was to be read – and the reading of faces was a skill for which Sean was famous – then alarms and sirens should have been beeping and shrieking in every molecule of the air between the two contestants. Whatever the two chieftains may have agreed by their shaking of hands on top of the mountain, one at least looked unlikely to accept a result that went against him. What then might follow was difficult to gauge, given that each was as strong as an ox and not afraid of flexing their muscles where peaceful means failed to settle deep disputes.

Sean began to feel increasing doubts as to whether the course he had set the two potential warriors on was the wisest remedy for their ill tempered disagreement. He had set Plan A in motion, but he was acutely aware that, by hook or by crook, he would need to come up with a Plan B to replace it should its wheels come off and the whole shebang shoot over the cliff. Preferably it would be a more sophisticated option than his having to use brute strength to separate two would be combatants. His thoughts were interrupted by the sudden sounding of an ancient post horn, followed by a Tannoy announcement that the first two festival sessions would be starting in half an hour. Ben said,

"They forgot to say which of these two is in the competition Uncle Sean."

"It's Jimmy Delaney with a little opener called the Bogle from the Bladder of Hell," Sean replied. "Although when I say little I should really say massive in so far as his tales are always five times as long as short and it's a miracle he can remember so many words at one go. There's a generous two hour maximum limit put on all the performers and Jimmy'll often as not push things right to the last permitted second. As the whole point of this year's exercise is for the tellers to come up with something new there's only going to be a limited amount I can tell you about what to expect with each performance. One thing I do know is that they've all been told to let their characters speak for themselves. Over descriptive narratives will not go down well. So that's a big giveaway about how the judges will be thinking – you'll need to see how well the tellers succeed in doing that. As for Jimmy, he's a man who likes the more comical kind of a tale, but with a dark edge, so whatever he serves up today is likely to be of a similar ilk."

"And his and all the other tales can be as traditional or non-traditional as the teller likes – the only iron rule being that they must all be set in Ireland and include the divil or divilish behaviour?" Liam asked, having heard the people in the next tent to his saying as much at breakfast and wondering if they were as correct as they seemed to think they were on all known matters in this and every other universe besides.

"That is indeed almost correct," Sean replied. "They can

include the divil himself, or characters of such devious intent they may as well be the divil. They can be told with diabolical wit or be about the diabolically witless, or a mixture of both. In the interests of spiritual diversity and those offended by the very thought of telling tales about Him Downstairs, however, angels of a more virtuous kind can be used instead. The Grim Reaper is also allowed for those who prefer his particular charms to those of your more conventional kinds of divils and angels. It all means things can be painted with a very broad brush, but that being said there will be whims and preferences among the judges that could well tip the balance in favour of one type of tale rather than another."

"And how do we find out how that balance is likely to be tipped uncle?" Ben asked. "Do you know anything about the panel and what each of them tends to like and dislike?"

"That I don't," Sean replied, "but one thing I have observed over the years is that judges seem reluctant to veer too far away from what went down best with the audiences. Most like a drink or two at the end of things and there's not much pleasure in a bar full of unhappy people scowling you down into your boots now is there? As I said before, one of the things I'd keep my eyes on closely would be how well the tales go down with the bums on the seats."

"Maybe it's time for us to get our bums on seats ready for Jimmy Delaney," Ben said to Sean, without as much as a sideways glance at Liam. "If he's a popular man we need to get ourselves into the venue in good time."

"A popular man he is if previous years are to go by, so yes, you're right, we all need to get ourselves moving," Sean replied, with a noticeable emphasis on 'all' and a nod and a smile at Liam. If there was to be an attempt by one cousin to isolate the other he was determined to tip the balance back and include them both.

Jimmy Delaney was a sight in himself. Six foot two with a rug of red hair that looked as if it might have absconded from the back of a cat, he had twinkling emerald eyes and a smile that was a mischievous laugh waiting to happen. He knew half of the people already planted in the semi-circular rows of seating that spread out from the stage and his booming baritone voice filled the competition tent as he exchanged quips, pleasantries and memories of festivals past with one or another of them. Sean exchanged a friendly nod with him as he came in and led his two recalcitrant charges to the best of the few remaining seats. Ben remarked on how Jimmy's bright red shirt was an anarchy of cloth in need of an iron. It seemed to swirl and flail like the sails of a ship as his expressive hands whirled through the air while he gestured and spoke, leading Sean to muse on how much he was a performance in play even before his tale had begun.

The tent was a veritable Babel of excited laughter, gossip and conversations so numerous that each was fighting the other for the ears of the listeners by the time a large brass bell of a gong was struck three times by Fierce Betty Nolan, the compere for all of the competition tales. Her commanding gaze had turned noise to silence and smiles to stone by the time the resonant echoes of the third of her gargantuan chimes had disappeared into the air all around. She said,

"Thank you for the attention of your ears ladies and those few of us present who may be called gentlemen. We start off the competitive section of this year's storytelling festival with a tale from Jimmy Delaney, which has never been performed anywhere else before. It's called the Bogle from the Bladder of Hell and - seeing as we're five minutes late in starting - I'll hand over to him without any further delay."

"Thank you Betty," Jimmy boomed and beamed, ignoring her unsubtle reprimand for overstaying his time in the audience chatting, "this is indeed a premiere for this most curious of stories. I'll just say a little bit of what it's about and then get on with things - there's fearsome and comical clergy and fearsome and comical all kinds of stuff, but with a dark shadow of repentance demanded hanging over all. There's magic, mayhem and murderous intent. There are strange forces at work and ridiculous ones as well and often times it's difficult to tell the one from the other – in fact seventy per cent of the tale may be as ridiculous as meself. So, before I tie meself in any more verbal knots, let's head straight off to County Galway to meet and greet that most interesting of gentlemen, *The Bogle from the Bladder of Hell!"*

The Bogle from the Bladder of Hell

Jimmy Delaney's Tale

Time it was when the sun rose before the moon. Stars kept to their proper hour and birds slept in obedient unison between dusk and night's drowning in the bitter dawn.

But this was not a day with any respect for tradition. In a quiet inlet of drying Galway seaweed, McMahon, flat out on his back and baffled, was convinced that the daylight was where the darkness should be and that he would have to do something about it.

Too lost in the philosophy of drink and concentration, he failed to notice the slow purr of a coasting, fierce looking BMW, its wheels grinding their way through the gravel of the dirt track that ended near the sea's edge behind him. Mesmerised by the picturesque sight of a ruined boathouse, reflected in the becalmed waters some little way off, the emerging driver was himself as unaware of McMahon as only the besotted can be. Drinking in the sun-drenched silence like a man who has just been released from a lunatic asylum, he dragged his enormous camera apparatus from the car and started to head excitedly towards the water's edge.

The shimmering image of the boathouse had him as firmly in its grip as if he saw in its place instead the soft alluring flesh of a virginal mermaid. What he found in his way was the decidedly un-virginal flesh of McMahon.

"What the hell's your game you whale footed clown?" the apparent heap of old sack yelled from the middle of its seaweed strewn place of repose. Its enraged tone was justified somewhat by the fact that the photographer had just trodden on the two parts of its anatomy that it valued most.

"Streuth," the occasioner of the violent assault gasped, "I didn't realise there was anyone inside your coat."

"Indeed?" McMahon enquired. "So the coat, I assume, was wearing itself. That, by any standards must make it an unusually intelligent piece of cloth."

"I'm sorry," the still startled aggressor offered, without sincerity or compassion, "I just didn't see you. Nothing broken by the looks of things."

"An Englishman, I might have known. You've been thrown out of the country for a lifetime or more and you're still jumping on the poor innocent bones of the Irish."

"If you call the fact that my father emigrated from here because he couldn't earn enough of a living on his small farm 'being thrown out' then you have a very peculiar view of things," the affronted photographer replied. "And if he was 'thrown out' as an Irishman, perhaps you'd care to explain how he was magically turned into an Englishman in the process of leaving."

The human coat grunted and hauled itself up into a sitting position. Dusting itself down it said,

"The very act of travelling across the water can change the unwary into all kinds of things. Turning English is only the most disturbing of the possibilities. I saw the whole business with me own eyes when I visited me brother in that heathen land ten years ago or more. By the time we reached Holyhead half the Irishmen on the boat would have sung every bar of God Save the Queen if you'd have asked. It was a terrible experience, terrible."

"And how many bars d'you think you managed?" the photographer asked.

"Think? There's no thinking about it. I found every one, from the Boar's Head to the Boilerman's Arms - and that's a dive I can tell you."

"I meant of God Save the Queen."

"Did you indeed," the coat said with twinkling eyes, "you see how the difference in culture makes even the one same language into two different things?"

"As you well appreciate," the photographer continued, his fiercely competitive streak driving him into a duel, "the fact that you've admitted that you were on the said boat means there's a fifty-fifty chance that you must have turned as English as any of the other Irishmen present and that despite your abuse, what we may well have here is a conversation between two Englishmen or no-one at all. That's not even to begin to mention the fact that Holyhead is in Wales."

McMahon considered the matter for a moment, then said,

"If that's the case I'll plump for no-one. The alternative is too worrying to contemplate. And if there's no-one here then there's a car without an owner that I'd like to give a home. Merciful Mary, are those the keys I see hanging in mid-air as if they might be attached to an invisible hand. If you'd care to pass them over here I'll do the necessary and look after the poor little orphan as if it were me own."

"Being no-one myself I am of course unable to oblige," the photographer replied, "and you being as equally non-existent, would be incapable of taking hold of the things even if they were somehow to pass between our two non-presences."

McMahon allowed a flicker of a smile to pass across his greasily bristled face.

"Well, you're either a considerable philosopher or a man who's had several times more of the hard stuff than is safe to drive and I'm in no fit state to make a judgment on the matter. Go on, take your picture of the Ireland you want to see before that large feller of a cloud over there swallows the sun."

"What cloud?" the Englishman asked. "The sky's as clear as a virgin pool."

"The one just sitting behind the horizon," McMahon replied. "Being an ordinary sort of mortal you won't see it for a moment or two. It has the most peculiar of shapes, something like an anvil with a beard. It'll take the light for a good ten minutes, by which time your mood will have changed and there'll not be half the pleasure in the photograph that you'll get by acting now."

"Oh really," the Englishman said with deep scepticism. "Do you by any chance see any flying pigs following upon the heels of this strangely bearded anvil cloud of yours? Or are those something that will only pass over when my back is turned?"

Apparently nonplussed, McMahon said, "Would you like something to eat, some sausages perhaps?"

"Ah, so the pigs will be coming ready sliced?" the Englishman enquired. In reply, McMahon pulled a string of five sausages out of his delicately removed left boot, followed by a frying pan, a decent sized camping stove and a large and clearly very heavy bottle of gas. Considering the size of the boot, which was hardly large enough to guarantee the exit of a hand or foot that managed for any purpose to gain entrance, the Englishman concluded that all was not necessarily as one might expect it to be. Far above he heard a strange and unpleasant combination of grunts and the repeated breaking of wind, together with the slow and ungainly thrashing of what sounded like wings. Not wanting to cast doubt on his sanity, within his own mind at least, he refused to believe the evidence of his eyes and ears and asked,

"What in God's name is that?"

Hardly bothering to raise his gaze from the already sizzling sausages, McMahon replied,

"That's a flying pig if I'm not mistaken and there behind's the cloud I warned you of."

Looking gingerly up, the Englishman saw what indeed was the clearest resemblance to an anvil and a beard that he'd ever seen in a cloud. The crazily zigzagging airborne pig in front of it was something he preferred to believe was an optical illusion. Suddenly, the unlikely bestial aeronaut decided that enough was enough and after a breaking of wind that would have put a thunderclap to shame, gave up any further attempt at flight. The desperate flapping of wings ceased and an eerie silence followed as it plummeted headlong towards terra firma. Paralysed with awestruck horror, the Englishman nearly jumped out of his skin when instead of the sickening thud he'd been expecting, a loud splash erupted some two hundred yards or more away.

"An intelligent animal," McMahon remarked, "it chose its spot well. I must confess my ignorance as to whether or not pigs can swim, but it at least has greatly reduced its chances of immediate oblivion. Even a few seconds more of life can be a superior experience to a more premature destruction."

Recovering his composure slightly, the Englishman said,

"If you know so much - about the things that are coming over the horizon and the existence of impossible forms of animal...," here he paused a bit to keep hold of his sanity in the face of the threat to the same that his own words and experience now presented, "then how is it that you don't know whether or not pigs can swim?"

"Oh like any man, there are many things between heaven and earth that leave me baffled and confused Mr. Ryan, even with so many years now between us and the blasting of the first man into space," McMahon replied.

"Oh really," Ryan replied, "then how is it that you even know my name without asking?"

"Did I use your name now? Well, isn't that amazing and me not even knowing that I did."

McMahon reached into his boot again and pulled out two large dinner plates and a complete set of cutlery. Laying it all out on the ground, he began to serve up the sausages, and to Ryan's astonishment, two half platefuls of potatoes and peas. He motioned to Ryan to seat himself. As he obeyed, the Englishman said,

"Just who or what on earth are you?"

"I'm McMahon, a simple man of the countryside and a lover of strong stout - in good Christian moderation of course."

"Come on, what's your game? You're no country bumpkin," Ryan said. "How do you do these tricks - is it some kind of hypnosis that you're using?"

"Hypnosis you think?" McMahon mused. "To tell you the truth I couldn't even hypnotise a flea, never mind a man."

Ryan tried a fork-full of potato to establish the reality or otherwise of the meal that lay before him. He said,

"Then how do you do all of this - you're not telling me these are natural occurrences."

"Now that all depends on what you mean by natural," McMahon replied. "Would you call a conjurer's trick natural for example?"

"You're saying you're a conjurer?"

"Well, a kind of one. A lot of what I do you'd call magic I suppose, so conjurer would seem a very reasonable sort of title."

Finding the contents of his plate to be as real as anything his stomach previously had digested, Ryan said,

"Reasonable perhaps with regard to the endless contents of your boots, rather reminiscent of the old bunnies out of a hat routine I concede. But I've yet to meet a conjurer who could predict the shape and arrival of a cloud that was invisible at the time - or materialise a flying pig upon demand. All of that seems to me much more in the realm of the supernatural."

"Does it indeed?" McMahon said thoughtfully. "Yes, I suppose to some things might seem that way. However, I'm sure someone supernatural would prefer to perform far greater miracles than making a poor innocent of a pig airborne by its own volition. And besides, there's no definite evidence connecting meself to the unfortunate animal - I never promised its appearance and the whole event may well have been entirely coincidental to my, or your, or indeed both our presences. For all an objective observer might know, the little creature might have made its most unusual flight even if we had both been pot-holing miles away in darkest Siberia."

"And pigs might fly," Ryan murmured, his voice trailing off as soon as the 'igs' of 'pigs' had left his lips and the complete inappropriateness of the phrase had sunk in like a lightning bolt.

He looked nervously in the direction of the distant pool, half expecting to see the unnatural animal scuttling frantically along the ground, its wings beating hopelessly as it tried one more time to perform a task for which probably only an elephant is less well suited.

"I'll show you a thing or two. If you want that is," McMahon said. "There's far more interesting sights that one can call extraordinary than that of a flying pig. Far less dangerous as well - just think what would have happened here if the overweight little darling had decided to fall out of the sky over our heads."

"What kinds of things do you have in mind?" Ryan asked. McMahon thought for a few moments, then said,

"I'll show you the truly marvellous and the truly stupid. But most of all, I'll show you the truly marvellous in the presence of the truly stupid."

Neither man exchanged another word between the swallowing of the next mouthful and the completion of the meal, Ryan keeping in the space between his own ears his dark suspicions that the 'truly stupid' might be himself. At length, the serious business of eating dispensed with, McMahon washed the various utensils within the gently lapping waters of the Atlantic and returned them all from where they had come. Ryan sat quietly chewing a twig while trying unsuccessfully to work out how the effortlessly accomplished trick was performed. McMahon said,

"Right, if I'm going to be showing you what you want to see we'd better be off. Just turn the vehicle round and let it follow its nose, it'll get us there soon enough."

"Are you sure it's necessary for me to drive at all?" Ryan asked with mild sarcasm. "Wouldn't it be better if I just sat in the back and let the car do all the work?"

McMahon acted as if he hadn't heard and proceeded to settle himself into the passenger seat. Reaching deep into a pocket, he inexplicably produced a large bottle of tomato ketchup and took a long, slurping swig. Ryan slung his camera bag none too delicately into the back and got in. Driving to where the dirt track ended in a T-junction, he was about to ask whether he should go left or right when the wheel seemed to make its own decision and his hands followed its inclination effortlessly to the left. He had the same experience at every turning or junction thereafter, the car leading him smoothly up high into the strange, bare rockscape of the Burrens. Given Ryan's normal preference to drive without any regard for the life or limb of others, all for the sake of his own adrenaline-junkie love of speed, such a leisured progress was a frustrating and annoying experience.

Finally, at the point where he began to wonder whether McMahon had transported them both magically to another planet, so extra-terrestrial and unfamiliar was the bald whiteness of their surroundings, the car swung gently onto the burnt grass verge at the side of the road and he obediently braked and switched the engine off.

"Where to now?" he asked Mc Mahon. "We appear to have reached the top of the world, so presumably whatever it is you intend to show me is near by."

"Over the wall," his guide commanded while simultaneously removing himself, his coat and all its strange contents from the vehicle. "Come on, follow me and watch your ankles on the stones. The ground's terrible treacherous up here, so put your feet only where mine have been. It's easy for the careless to break a bone or two."

The two men scrambled over the stone wall that separated the road from the sparse vegetation on the other side and proceeded with due caution up and over the two nearest hill tops. As they scrambled up the third McMahon said,

"When we get near the top we'll have to start crawling on the old bellies. If either of us are seen it'll ruin the whole thing."

Breathless from the exertions of the venture, Ryan felt it too much effort to ask what it was that would be ruined and decided simply to wait and see. When McMahon dropped down, soft belly against hard rock, he followed suit and the two slithered uncomfortably up onto the breeze-touched top.

"There," McMahon said, pointing to the valley below. Following his gaze, Ryan saw a strange gathering of about three hundred men, women and children, all brightly clothed in red, green and orange flowing robes. The assembly, about two hundred yards beneath them, could be heard chanting. Everyone was sitting down, holding hands and seemed to be staring at something high above. Looking up in the certain expectation of having the remainder of his sanity destroyed by the sight of another flying oddity, he found only that there was nothing at all to see, not even anything that would pass for a cloud in the vast blue silence of the sky.

"Who are they and what are they looking at?" he asked McMahon.

"Shh! Keep your voice down," the conjurer whispered. "They're a bunch of the largely sane engaged in an act of the grossest lunacy."

He looked knowingly at his companion as if this lone piece of incomplete information would be understood instantly in all its implications.

"What do you mean?" Ryan asked blankly.

McMahon gave him a brief look of incredulity.

"Well, to start at the beginning, as we seem to be missing the middle at the very least and most certainly the end as well, what you see before you is a group of mostly sober American citizens, all belonging to the Reformed Church of Christ and the Second Coming. Through an unfortunate typing error in the particular version of the bible which they use - an error to which the drunken old sod of a printer has never owned up I might add - they are convinced that on this day, in this place, the good Lord is going to produce a miracle in the sky. Being ridiculously unaware that the sky, like themselves, is itself a miracle, they are in dire need of something marvellous that they haven't seen before. And in that sense, while being in many ways intelligent, they are extremely stupid."

"The daft I can see anytime," Ryan pointed out, "but what I don't see is the extraordinary."

"And neither do they," McMahon replied, "such a terrible shame to see so many disappointed people."

Raising his hand in an attempt to dislodge a fly that had gone pot-holing in his ear, Ryan accidentally knocked a bun sized stone over the edge down towards the expectant worshippers below.

"It's a sign, the Lord is coming!" one of the gathering shouted, running forward to try and catch what he was sure would turn out to be as revelatory as the tablets entrusted to Moses. Unfortunately, the sign appeared to be one of the Lord's displeasure, as it struck him a sharp blow on his big toe and bounced spectacularly into the cooking pot full of oxtail soup in the centre of the circle, spattering all around with an unheavenly gift of greasy brown liquid.

McMahon forced his handkerchief violently into his mouth in an attempt to stop his laughter from exploding outwards for all to hear. When more or less recovered he said,

"Now what shall it be? Something special don't you think. When somebody's given me so much real pleasure I find it difficult not to want to return the favour. How about an echo or two of Fatima - the sun dancing in the sky, colour changes etc.? No, that mightn't go down too well upstairs, appearing to take the mickey out of an accepted miracle and all that. That's not the game at all. How about an early visit from the moon...there, see what I mean, a good full harvester if ever there was one."

Surprised but not astounded by the new heavenly arrival, Ryan said,

"A joint appearance by the sun and the moon is hardly an unprecedented event. Look, they've not even seen it yet. You'll have to be a bit more adventurous."

In the back of his own mind was the thought that, it being now rather late in the day, this could indeed be a quite natural phenomenon.

"You're right," McMahon said. "There's not a one of them that's looking in the right direction. Some fine tuning is in order, a slight pitch to the right I think."

This time Ryan was amazed. The moon slid in a graceful arc from one side of the sky to the other, becoming simultaneously twice as bright as any moon he'd seen before and appearing to trail smoke behind it as it went. A loud cry of awe and celebration went up from the crowd below and several started jigging up and down in uncontrollable bouts of excitement. McMahon laughed softly to himself.

"It would be a shame not to let them have some fun in the middle of such a miserable world. I suppose I'd better make the little round feller do a couple of party tricks. A few circles around the sun perhaps and a dance across the mountain tops."

What followed defied any frame of rational reference to which Ryan might have recourse. The dislocated satellite did exactly as McMahon had predicted, whizzing round and round the sinking sun and leaving a spectacular spiral of black smoke in its wake. Several of the assembled worshippers of the gospel according to St. Typing Error became so dizzy in watching the spectacle that they fell over. Then the clearly over-energised planet made a swoop for the most distant mountain top and started doing what could only be described as a full blown Irish jig above and around it. Leaving behind another ethereal pall of smoke, it then leaped across the sky to the surrounding hill tops and gave a repeat performance on all except the one where the two secret onlookers lay.

"Ah well," McMahon remarked at length, "all good things must come to an end. We'd better leave them a little message, just to put the record straight."

No sooner had he finished speaking than the moon shot high up into the sky and started writing in large smoke letters directly above. The message was clear and embarrassing for all to see. At precisely the moment when the assembled devotees had become convinced that their long years of belief in 'the special day of Burren revelation' had been vindicated by a heavenly sign, they were confronted with the news that,

"Your bibles are all wrong folks. Page 1096 is a typing error. Hope you enjoyed the show - couldn't bear to see you disappointed. So long!"

"I'm not so sure about me command of the American vernacular, but the sentiments are right don't you think?" McMahon said. Looking down at the stunned gathering below, Ryan said,

"Just who on earth are you? Am I in the company of a devil or an angel or what?"

"Divils and angels? Rather outdated ideas for an Englishman to be holding in the godless present aren't they?" McMahon asked.

"Just what kind of terms do you propose that I use to describe a man who spins the moon around the sun and writes messages in the sky?"

"That's an interesting question. If it's suggestions that you're wanting, then I'm your man. I'm always good at these types of games. Now we've had 'conjurer' already haven't we, but clearly you find that rather inadequate, otherwise you wouldn't have asked the question in the first place. I've already said I didn't think much of 'hypnotist'. How about 'illusionist', more appropriate don't you think? A conjurer is someone you think of when sleight of hand's the matter of concern. When the whole trick's up in the sky there's little the hands can do about it. A much grander scale of deception altogether. Yes, I think illusionist is the word we want. Are you happy with that now? I wouldn't want to be thinking that it was only me that was satisfied."

"To put it bluntly," Ryan said, "I think you're lying through your teeth. I'd run as far away from you as I could if I didn't have more than a slight suspicion that I'd be turned into a frog in the process. All this business of playing the true traditional Irish countryman is nothing more than a ruse. I'm not sure if you're in any sense a normal human being at all. Come on, you've played with me long enough, just what is it that you are?"

"First you say I'm not of me native country, then you tell the rocks and me and anyone else who cares to listen that I'm not even possessed of me common humanity. Do you think there's anything that you might have left out in your hail of unwarranted English insults?"

"You may have had me fooled before but it's not a fool you fooled," Ryan replied, feeling at once foolish for such gross overuse of a single word and its derivatives.

"If I were you and you were me," McMahon replied, "I'd think I'd known you for far too short a time to make any judgments whatsoever about your person. I'd think, 'I've seen him do this and I've heard him do that and there's not a bit of it that seems to fit in with what he says about himself. But I'm thinking all of this in the terms of me own logic without waiting to see if any of mine is the same as his. What if it's simply that our logics are different? If I give the poor man time and try and understand the logic of his own head I might well find that that is the solution to everything.' You see, what I'm saying is this, you've known me for one afternoon and have jumped to a lifetime of conclusions. Is that a wise and sober way for a man who has a whole month of holiday left to make a judgment?"

"You mean you intend taking the holiday with me?" Ryan asked in stunned horror.

"Don't look so mortal terrified," McMahon replied, "it's not as if I'll be sleeping in the same bed or room even. I'm a past master at the art of the makeshift nap. Your car will make a most comfortable hotel."

"Look, what is it you want with me?" Ryan asked in desperation.

"Want? There's nothing I want," McMahon said. "It's what I can show you that's much more to the point. You'll have a much more interesting time with me than without."

"Do I have any choice in the matter?" Ryan asked.

"To be honest and it's honest that you want me to be, no. Not that I mean that unpleasantly, or that there'll be any dire consequences if you try one or another way to escape the virtue of me company. It's just that I'll always be here if you see what I mean. Driving off and leaving me at the roadside would simply mean that you'd have the displeasure of finding me waiting wherever it was that you were going. You see, I am a most difficult person to get rid of. Not that you'll want to be rid of me after a day or two. Given time, you'll come to find me the most convivial of company. And there's things you'll see with me the like of which you'd never dream of on your own."

"That's what I'm afraid of," Ryan muttered. "How am I going to keep my sanity if you follow me all over turning normality upside down without offering a word of reasonable explanation to help me live with it? I'm a simple man who came here for a peaceful holiday - and solitude."

"You're neither simple nor in need of solitude," McMahon replied. "You're here because you've just sold your father's house after his death and caused a major rift with your sister. You used an error in the making of his do-it-yourself will to keep nearly all of the money for yourself and leave her with barely enough to buy a set of curtains. You thought a month on the other side of the water would allow things to calm down a little and as your holiday was due off you went and here you are."

"How d'you know all that?" Ryan asked, astonished.

"Just call it a bit of logical deduction," McMahon replied, "I'm just like Sherlock Homes. With your capacity for making enemies at the drop of a hat you'll be in desperate need of a friend to get you out of all of your messes on this little trip you're on."

"No, no, no, I don't want you with me, everything that you say and do is weird and weird is not what I do. I'm not listening to any more of this and I just want you to find someone else to play your mind games on," Ryan hissed. "I don't know how you do any of this stuff and how you found out about the house, but I want you and me to go our separate ways. You can say what you like but I'm not listening to another word you say."

"If I was your mother, God rest her blessed departed soul, you still wouldn't listen, but you know very well that what I've just told you is the truth. Mind you if I was your mother you wouldn't have any of me company to worry about because I'd most definitely be arrested. A great hairy chested mammy with five o'clock shadow and size twelve shoes on her hooves would be seen as some kind of criminal imposter, a bank robber in disguise perhaps, that no self-respecting upholder of the law could ignore.

Not that such a thought is of any relevance to present matters of course."

"It might help me a little bit if you could take all of this rather more seriously, to just listen to what I say and then take yourself as far away as possible," Ryan said icily.

"But only a little," McMahon replied, "so small an amount that neither I nor you with both our heads combined would be able to distinguish between its presence and its absence."

"Look," Ryan said, "will you at least tell me why you've chosen me for all of this. There must be hundreds of more suitable people who'd be perfectly happy to see the world turned upside down without asking any questions or expecting to get any answers. I'm someone who gets very frustrated with people and things I don't understand and I don't understand any of this in the slightest."

"You've been chosen because ultimately you will understand. We've a journey to go on you and I and when it's finished you'll have the Wisdom of Solomon. There can't be many who have that kind of experience on their holidays."

"And what will I do with this extraordinary wisdom that you're offering?" Ryan asked.

"That's something you'll need the Wisdom of Solomon to determine," McMahon said, "and as you are not yet possessed of such a gift you'll just have to wait until you are for an answer. Come on, let's get back to the car before these poor assembled lunatics spot us and we have to explain the inexplicable."

"And where is the car supposed to be going if I might be so bold as to enquire," Ryan said.

"Well and there's no reason to doubt the matter, it's under the clear impression that it's off to Limerick. And if that's the case, there are very reasonable grounds for assuming that our destination is one and the same. So the answer to the question that you did ask and to the one you didn't is Limerick."

"And what if I decide to spend the night somewhere different?"

"And indeed you can, although I would just mention the slight drawback that you would have to make the journey to whatever place you have in mind on foot. The vehicle has most definitely decided that Limerick is the place for the night."

The two men got in the car and drove off. Ryan determined that he would avoid the indignity of being dictated to by a motor vehicle and followed the signs for Galway city religiously. Given that he spent a good hour and a half doing so and thereby heading entirely in the opposite direction to the car's alleged preference, he was somewhat surprised to end up in Limerick. The look of innocence on McMahon's face was not convincing.

"And where in Limerick is it going to let me stay, this so supremely clever vehicle?" Ryan asked.

"Oh we're off to the Cathedral of St. John I do believe," McMahon replied, "we've someone to meet before we worry about your hotel."

The car duly led them down a quiet road by the riverside, with a shimmering view of King John's forbidding castle opposite, over a bridge and through a succession of grey streets to the grey church itself and its great grey spire. They pulled into a little square and walked over to the cathedral.

"Well, we're here," Ryan said, "where's this person we're supposed to meet?"

"We'll find him in the grounds," McMahon replied. "Come on don't look so English and untrusting."

Ryan duly followed his confidently striding companion into the distinctly uninspiring Cathedral car park. The two stood in expectant silence for a moment. Ryan had the feeling that they were being surveyed. Looking across towards the road he spotted a dishevelled face scrutinising them through a gap in the hedge. As their gaze met, the face hurriedly withdrew itself and its owner scuttled into the grounds to join them.

"Would either of you be having the price of a cup of tea?" the voice of hope personified said.

"And how much is the price of a cup of tea may I ask?" McMahon said.

"The price? Twice the price of nothing."

"Now that's a shame," McMahon replied, "because nothing is all I have. I'll have to give you the tea instead."

Thrusting his hand deep into his pocket he pulled out first a teapot, then a jug of milk, followed by three cups and saucers. After distributing all the relevant utensils and pouring each person, including himself, a cup of very hot tea, he put the pot and the jug back in his pocket and proceeded to drink. The poor disbelieving beggar looked as though he would swallow the cup as well as its contents as he bolted the latter in one gulp and scuttled hurriedly away and out of sight.

"That's what I should have done when I first clapped eyes on you," Ryan remarked sourly.

"It would have been of little use," McMahon replied, "wherever you'd have gone I'd have been there before you."

"So where's this gentleman we're supposed to meet, or was that him?" Ryan asked.

"He'll be out in a minute," McMahon replied.

"Out of where? The place looks pretty well closed to me."

No sooner had he spoken than the main cathedral door was flung open and a dishevelled looking individual in his early thirties was ejected, none too gently, by the scruff of his neck.

"The sick and the poor can lay their weary heads on me pews if they've nowhere else to go but I'm not having a heretic and a blasphemer within the four walls of God's holy house. Go on, get out of me sight and stay out of it!"

The words were those of a muscular, elderly priest who gave them suitable emphasis by banging the door shut with enough violence to make the spire topple and the buried dead break wind in mortal terror. The banished unfortunate surveyed his audience with sad, resigned eyes and shuffled over to them, his shoes, made more from holes than leather, impeding his every step.

"Another bad day?" McMahon asked, clearly knowing the gentleman with some degree of familiarity.

"As bad as terrible can be," he replied.

"Is there nowhere that will put you up?" McMahon asked.

"Oh, the guards will probably oblige if I loiter somewhere suspiciously enough."

"This is Mr. Ryan. He's come to swop his shoes."

"What?" Ryan asked, dumfounded.

"It's very simple, you give yours to him and he gives his to you and it's over and done with."

"Mine for his? That's very kind of you, but I really think yours will be the better fit. There's no comparison between the size of our feet."

"They're exactly the same," McMahon replied, "the two of

you could exchange your feet as well as your boots and neither would know the difference. Now come on now, we mustn't delay, there's a moment of ripeness for the changing of shoes and this is it."

"I tell you what," Ryan said to the poor man more without shoes than with, "I'll give you the money for a new pair and keep my own, how's that?"

"No, no!" McMahon spluttered. "The state his feet are in a pair of shoes that needs breaking in would feel like his toes had been wired to the mains. Give him yours and you'll give him bliss. Can you deny bliss to a man who's had a life full of insults?"

Ryan looked at the unfortunate, whose sad eyes seemed to be getting sadder the more he procrastinated. More in rage at being so demanded of than any genuine sympathy, he tore his shoes off and handed them over. The man thanked him with a smile that seemed simultaneously to fill Ryan's pockets with imaginary gold and his ears with a chorus of summer day birdsong. Ryan felt annoyed that the gold was only a trick of the mind and imagined fitting the birds with silencers to their beaks. Handing over his own flea bitten shoes in return, the allegedly heretical tramp smiled again and then sat down to ease on the supple English leather that he held as reverentially as if it were a new born babe.

"Come on," McMahon said, "it's time we were off."

"Really," Ryan muttered as far under his breath as he could so the seated unfortunate wouldn't overhear, "is there not an item or two of my clothing that you haven't given away yet? My trousers perhaps, or the shirt off my back?"

Bidding what was clearly a temporary farewell to his now happily re-shod friend, McMahon propelled the Englishman gently away.

"What a terrible moaner of a feller you are," he said. "I hand you on a plate an act of charity that would save a thousand souls and still you complain. I give you the chance to go to bed for once in your life with the warmth of the knowledge that you'd actually done something solid to help someone and all you do is ask if I'm after your trousers. If the good Lord himself offered you a seat in paradise you'd turn him down unless you had a written guarantee of a cushion to go with it. You're a hopeless case Michael Ryan, hopeless."

"Does that mean you'll leave me alone then?"

"Unfortunately for both of us, no. The more hopeless you are the more I have to stick with you."

The two men returned to the windblown square and lowered themselves once more into the fierce looking BMW that Ryan had customised to emphasise his devil may care approach to driving and to frighten other motorists into submission. They drove off in search of a place of repose for the night, Ryan's experience by now causing him to not even think about where he would go. The car, he knew, would make all the decisions. Its choice, however, gave him serious cause for concern. After a ten minute or so drive through the city, it stopped outside the most dark and miserable looking excuse for a hotel that he'd ever seen. It seemed more devoid of light than even the night that had wrapped itself quietly above them in an impenetrable quilt of cloud.

"I'm not staying here," he said firmly.

"Why on earth not?" McMahon asked innocently.

"What d'you mean, 'Why on earth not?' Look at it - it's more like a mortuary than a place to stay. I want a bed for the night, not a marble slab."

"Marble is it? Now yours will be a grand corpse by the sound of it. Have you never heard how good it is to get some practice in for an eventuality before it happens? A night on a slab would stand you in marvellous stead with the business of death. You'd have a handy lead over all the other corpses that kicked the bucket at the same time as yerself. You know, it's amazing how many people choose to drop down dead without even the slightest rehearsal for the event."

"Death is a far and distant event to a man of my age and something that I find best forgotten about until the hour approaches - and dead or alive, I'm not going to spend the night here," Ryan repeated firmly.

"Oh dear," McMahon said. "Well, we'd better just drive off and look for somewhere else. But you're very unwise in thinking yourself immune from the Grim Reaper on grounds of age – you can be carted off at any hour of night or day and if your mortal soul hasn't readied and purified itself in time it could be a downwards plunge into the divil's kitchen for the heathen likes of your good self. Part of me job is to make you ready in time, otherwise you'll fall into the divil's arms as helplessly as a little lamb."

"Really?" Ryan hissed, trying the ignition. "I think I'd prefer to remain an ignorant heathen and enjoy myself rather than be purified as you call it and lose all the fun of the fair."

To his relief the car offered no resistance and responded instantly to his anxious prodding of the accelerator. Released now, it seemed, from the calmness that had been the car driving itself, he careered and skidded around for another ten minutes before he screeched all four tyres while turning into a comfortingly suburban street of large, staid and respectable looking houses. Taking control once more, the car decelerated rapidly and pulled slowly into the kerb. Stunned by its unwarranted interference he looked across at the building that hid quietly below the dim hotel sign opposite. He couldn't believe his eyes. The street was most definitely different - as unlike the previous one as anything could be - and yet the hotel was exactly the same.

"Is there a problem?" McMahon enquired.

"You know damn well there is," Ryan replied. "Look, just what kind of a game is it that's being played here?"

"What are you getting so agitated about?" McMahon asked. "If you don't like the place let's try another."

"Which will, of course be exactly the same, even if I find it sitting alone in the middle of the country covered in cow shit."

"Did I say that? There's never a man that knows anything until he takes the trouble to find it out. Now why don't we just have a go at finding somewhere else and see what happens?"

Ryan re-started the car and roared away from the kerb with a criminal and angry disregard for the life and limbs of himself or anyone else in sight. He ignored every subtle urging of the steering wheel and was under the firm impression that finally he had regained control of the vehicle. It was going where he alone wanted it to. After twenty minutes of taking any turning he fancied he saw a row of hotels and screeched to a triumphant halt outside them.

"There! I've beaten the damn thing!" he shouted. "Whichever one of these has a vacancy, that's it. That's where I'm staying."

Slamming the car door defiantly he strode over to the nearest hotel, only to find that it was full. Each of the next five was the same. Just at the moment when his heart had sunk so far within his being that only a well bucket might retrieve it, he found that the last of the row had a vacancies sign. It was then that his hope collapsed, almost simultaneously with the moment of its rising. It was exactly the same hotel that he had already tried to avoid twice before.

He heard a thud behind him. He turned round to see McMahon unloading his suitcases from the back of the car.

"Just thought I'd give you a hand," the smiling owner of the hand in question said. "Shall I take these in for you?"

"Why not," Ryan replied, "no doubt you know your way around."

"And what, may an innocent man ask, is implied by that?"

"A good question," Ryan replied, "and one I might well ask myself."

"Indeed?" McMahon said. "Then if you're asking yourself and I'm asking yourself there's two of us puzzled by the same conundrum with neither likely to get an answer. If all matters of enquiry had proceeded along the same lines the whole of humanity would still be sitting around in animal skins unable to solve a single one of the problems of creation. And as no-one would have discovered the arts of building there would be no hotel here for you to complain about. D'you see, your whole life has been blighted by the mischievous solvers of problems, the logical men who went too far and answered the questions they asked?"

"Is it me or you or both of us that you're taking the mickey out of, or is that another unanswerable question?" Ryan asked.

"The only question that's unanswerable is the one that's never asked," McMahon replied.

"And what is that?" Ryan enquired resignedly.

"That's an unanswerable question," McMahon said.

"But you've just said there's only one unanswerable question."

"Indeed I did and as it's the question that's never asked that you've just asked then I've made no contradiction of meself."

"But how can it be the question that's never asked if I've just asked the damn thing?"

"Have you never heard of the Law of Carvalius?" McMahon asked. Taking Ryan's grim silence as a no, he continued, "Carvalius showed that all things that are two are really one and that nothing that is in one piece can be two things. He did this through a series of experiments conducted entirely in the dark and without anyone, including himself, being present. The results were the opposite entirely of what he'd expected, so he reversed them twice, multiplied them by themselves and triple inverted the answer. A most wonderful piece of mathematics, which proved conclusively the veracity of all such claims as the one so hotly disputed by yourself."

Deciding firmly that the retention of his sanity was preferential to further lunatic debate, Ryan strode determinedly into the hotel foyer which, until now, he'd been so keen to avoid. To his great surprise, what had seemed so dingy and unpromising outside was of a truly palatial appearance within.

"Puzzled?" McMahon enquired impishly. "Have you never before been familiar with the simple, ancient truth that that which is the most desperate on the surface is frequently the most beautiful beneath? And what if I don't see the manager coming to greet you in person."

Ryan was stunned to see the same tramp to whom he had so recently donated his shoes graced by clothes of such elegant wealth that the sale of only one item would most surely have raised enough to dress an average man ten times over.

"Good evening sir," the apparition said, "if you would be so good as to sign in at the desk I will get one of the porters to carry your baggage up to your room. It is ready for you as soon as you would like to go up."

"Haven't I just seen you in the cathedral grounds?" Ryan spluttered.

"Possibly sir, quite possibly, I do quite frequently take my evening stroll in that direction. I hope sincerely that you find everything here to your satisfaction. Perhaps you would like to relax for a few minutes after signing in by taking a seat in the Tulip Lounge? We are having a little wine and champagne tasting for our guests this evening and you should find the experience extremely refreshing. Now, if you'll excuse me, I must go and see how the chef is progressing with various matters."

Turning to McMahon, Ryan found he was looking at thin air. Presumably his very peculiar friend had headed back to the car which, as he had threatened earlier, was to be used as his bed for the night while, uninvited, he turned the Englishman's expedition into a holiday for two. Considering the startling variety of miraculous acts that McMahon had shown himself capable of so far it was a puzzle as to why he didn't also conjure up a nice comfy room for himself in the hotel itself and stay in that instead of the car. Ryan began to fear that there was something his weird companion knew about this hotel that he wasn't telling him and as this thought grew within his mind so did a parallel sense of foreboding.

While he was contemplating all of this a porter was in the process of loading his baggage, which seemed mysteriously to have grown by the addition of at least two extra suitcases and a leather bound trunk, onto a trolley. The glossy faced and Brylcreemed counter clerk stood smiling behind the register, pen invitingly in hand, and a string quartet could be heard through an open door, drawing out the opening bars of a Vivaldi piece which he couldn't quite place.

Other than standing and feeling extremely foolish, there seemed to be little else to do than sign in and see what other strange surprises were waiting for him. Once he had scratched his name into the book, seen the luggage safely into his room and tipped the porter, he decided to investigate his surroundings a little before going to bed. He didn't like to think what might be lurking in the extra suitcases that had appeared from nowhere and decided he would delay opening them until after he'd had a strong whiskey to fortify himself. He took the lift back down to the ground floor and marvelled at the Tardis-like nature of the building, which from the outside looked very modest in size, but was huge inside. There was clearly some kind of social gathering going on in the Rose Lounge, the largest of the rooms that led off from the foyer and he wandered over to take a peek and see what was happening. As he approached the doorway he could hear a babble of English Hooray Henry voices and asked a harassed looking waiter who they were as he came out of the room with a tray full of empty glasses and champagne bottles.

"The sons of entitlement," the man said with some

exasperation. “It’s some riotous club of posh Oxford types who’ve hopped across the pond on a ferry and they’re getting to the point where there’s a danger of them wrecking the joint. I’m just off to warn the manager. I wouldn’t go in if I were you.”

Ryan decided to take his advice, but couldn’t resist sticking his nose through the doorway just to see what was going on. The room, its exquisite decoration of flowered silk wallpaper and beautifully carved panelling bathed in a warm, rich, yellowish glow, was impressively large and swimming in red faced young gentlemen in dinner jackets, several of whom seemed out of control of themselves. It looked like something out of Jeeves and Wooster and reminded him of everything he found most archaic about ‘the other island’ from which he came. Presumably they were all here for a bit of hunting, fishing and rioting before going back to their privileged lives preparing to be the next generation of bankers and politicos. Suddenly a highly inebriated voice, so rich in plumminess that it dripped juice onto the carpet, rang out across the room,

“That man in the doorway, yes, him, that’s the wretch that sacked my brother Charles! Grab him!”

Startled, Ryan looked hard at the man and then spotted the family resemblance. Of course, Charles Wright, that must have been his brother, the man he sacked simply to balance the budget of his section within O’Reilly Construction and gain a bonus at the end of the year for so doing. Bitter and twisted Charlie must have pointed him out to his pugilistic looking younger brother, he must have been the anonymous face that helped him clear his desk when he left, someone who hadn’t even registered on Ryan’s consciousness except as a shape at the time. And now here he was with all his hale and hearty chums, built like rugger players to a man, half cut with every form of alcoholic indulgence that could be imagined – and after his blood. Ryan decided that the safest strategy would be to exit stage left but, on turning round, found his path blocked by a young gentleman the size of a mountain. If the man still denouncing him loudly from the other side of the room was Charlie’s brother this certainly wasn’t Charlie’s aunty. The mountain said,

“Terribly sorry old chum, but this doorway seems to be blocked.”

He started pushing forwards, with Ryan involuntarily being propelled in a backwards direction by the mountain's giant hands that were now glued to his shoulders. Simultaneously a slow handclap started and soon built to a threatening thunder. At the point where Ryan was within punching distance of Charlie's displeased brother, the mountain spun him around so that the two stood face to face. Charlie's avenger grabbed him by the lapels and said,

"Well, well, well, it really is him. You won't remember me, you didn't even bother giving me a glance when I helped poor old Charlie fill his boxes and carry them out. But you'll remember me after tonight old chum – you're on my territory now, not yours, my rules not yours and my rules say you're going to pay for being a slimy little toe rag. How say you fellow revellers, should our friend here pay small time or big time – or very, very big time?"

As one the assembled inebriates roared,

"Very, very big time!"

"Right," the avenger said, "bring me that large bowl of trifle from over there - and all the ice cubes from the champagne bucket."

What followed was a fate worse than the fires of hell. Unable to utter any sound more distinct than a muffled scream, Ryan found a messy and freezing surfeit of the materials demanded being poured down the front and back of his neck, an experience in itself akin to jumping stark naked into ten feet of sub-zero porridge. Then his shoes were removed and each sock was stuffed with enough ice to fill the North Pole twice over and build an igloo as a bonus. His feet were then violently reinserted. As he wriggled and squirmed and danced around in fierce discomfort, his arms being held all the time so he couldn't free himself from any of the freezing ice that bit into his person like a Pekinese with a grudge twice its size, the avenger shouted,

"Right, that's enough dancing for the night, we won't waste any more time on a complete waste of space, let's feed the blighter to the lions."

Ryan's whole person was immediately upended and he was carried, gasping, over to an open window. With a complete absence of ceremony he was pushed out, with only the slightest of drunken grips being kept on the icicles that had replaced his ankles.

"Now then," his chief tormentor boomed, "let's see if we've got the right window. Yes we have indeed, down there's the flower beds we saw being filled with a lorry load of manure when we arrived. You can let go of him now chaps."

Fortunate not to end up with a broken neck, Ryan discovered that the Rose lounge was named as such due to the fact that it overlooked a garden full of the things. That was after he slid out of the wheelbarrow into which he had been so mercilessly dropped and landed on a collection of the deadly thorns of the aptly named 'Invincible'. Before that he had discovered, face first, the large quantity of manure that filled the wheelbarrow itself. The one at least served to take his mind off the other. Just to add to his discomfort, a couple of large flower vases were emptied of their contents over his head to the accompaniment of an evil cackle of highly satisfied malicious laughter. The window was then shut and the curtains drawn and the vanquished unfortunate was left in the darkness, a sad and embittered figure not knowing whether to concentrate most on holding its offended nose or pulling thorns out of its trousers, but with the single, clear desire to get its hands round the throat of McMahon.

After what seemed like an eternity of groping his way through rose garden, refuse bins, brambles and a surprise patch of stinging nettles, Ryan finally found his way back to the street. Creeping up on the long shadow of his car with the determined stealth of a madman, an approach that was in perfect accord with his trifle and manure covered appearance, he waited until he was no more than a foot away from the vehicle, then sprang forward and ripped open the passenger door. All his two wildly lunging hands succeeded in grabbing was themselves, however, there being not the slightest trace of McMahon or anyone even faintly like him.

"You can't expect me to be sitting there like a sackful of cabbage waiting for an enraged lunatic to come and throttle me in me sleep now can you?" a voice from behind said. Ryan turned to see his prey standing a safe six feet away.

"That was all your doing! You used your bizarre powers to manipulate the car's steering so that I ended up in that hotel - you deliberately lured me to a fate worse than death," he thundered. "I'm covered in crap, icicles and trifle and the thorns in my arse make it feel like it's been sewn together by a one-armed seamstress - and it's all your fault!"

"Now, now, let's not be too hasty in talking about my faults," McMahon said reproachfully. "It was simply me honest duty to remind you of some of your own, most particularly the little matter of your self-serving ruthlessness in the way you've dealt with some of the people who've worked for you, or with you. There was no harm at all in reminding you that, even if we put aside the considerable matters of right and wrong, such ways of doing things can bide their time and bite you up the bum, in your case quite literally. Had you not treated that man's brother in the way you did, none of the crap that's landed on you, or that you've landed in, would have happened. Now you can't deny that those are lessons of the greatest of value to draw from your experience and that in me own humble way, I've been your teacher as well as your friend. The experience you've just had will stop you from repeating similar errors and might even save your rotten soul to boot."

"Experience? Is that what you call it?" Ryan thundered. "If everyone 'learnt' as a result of experiences like that the homicide rate would quadruple overnight. How would you feel about being four times dead by morning, because at this precise moment in time I feel like four times strangling you! You said I would see things in your company that no normal man could hope to see - you didn't tell me you were going to hand me over to my worst enemies so they could drop me arse over elbow into a heap of crap."

"Alright, if you're so offended by me good intentions, tell me any experience you'd like to have to make up for what's happened and I'll see what I can do."

"You could put me in a room full of tap dancing monks in black stockings and it wouldn't make up for what you've done to me," Ryan hissed, while simultaneously wondering why on earth he'd ever want to be in such a room and how the idea came into his head in the first place.

"Oh, you never know a thing until you try it," McMahon replied innocently. No sooner had he spoken than Ryan found himself crashing down onto a hard, cold wooden bench. Looking round in shock, he observed that he was in what looked remarkably like a monastery refectory, with several rows of highly scrubbed benches and tables distributed evenly around the shadowy, grey-stone floor. The only illumination seemed to come from two or three bare electric light bulbs in the middle of the room and two haphazardly arranged clusters of candles at either end. Before he had time even to pinch himself to find out whether he was dealing with reality or some bizarre dream, a strange, echoing, rhythmic, tap-clattering sound started to advance down the corridor that led to the room. As in the case of the flying pig, he knew precisely what was on its way without wanting to look to confirm the impossibility of his suspicions. He began to sweat in a desperate and growing doubt about his own sanity as the clickety-clack-clack-clackety-click-clickety-clack-click-clack of the advancing feet grew rapidly closer.

Suddenly, just at the point where he felt he wanted to leap through the nearest window and flee, the heavy oak door burst open and his worst suspicions were confirmed. At least forty overweight monks danced vigorously in, each clackety-tap-tapping in unison with the others and each sporting black fishnet tights beneath the swirling, thrashing cover of their robes. They did a couple of boisterous circuits of the room, their specially adapted tap-dancing sandals seeming to move even faster than the feet within them. This was followed by a brief but spectacular solo performance by the abbot, who unfortunately thrust one foot into a half-full cleaning bucket at the end and fell heavily onto the tail of the monastery cat. The little creature did an impromptu little tap dance all of its own and then sank its claws firmly into the abbot's shins.

Despite the haunting, desperate harmony of the cries of the cat and the perpetrator of the assault on its tail, both of whom were now engaged in a most ungodly wrestling match upon the floor, the show clearly had to go on. As one the rest of the company leaped up onto the tables and started to do a Hollywood-perfect rendition of 'Happy Feet', followed by a succession of Ginger Rogers and Fred Astaire numbers, as loosely adapted for forty tap dancing celibate monks. As Ryan looked up at the unimaginable spectacle of fat, hairy legs in black nylons thrashing around on the heavily vibrating tables, he couldn't decide whether the most bizarre aspect of what he was seeing consisted of the dancing itself, the decidedly un-monastic nature of the tights, or the weirdly smiling faces which the monks maintained throughout the performance as if they were auditioning for a job at McDonalds.

The spectacle lasted for a good hour, at the end of which Ryan was holding his head in his hands, a shadow of his former self and quite unable any more to distinguish reality from illusion. For a finale, the monks pirouetted up into the air with a breathtaking, simultaneous leap, spun three times on their journey back to the floor and landed with unplanned precision, each on the feet of his neighbour. There followed an embarrassing minute or two of forty madly hopping monks performing an unintended parody of a tribal dance while holding gingerly a set of highly painful toes. The now recovered abbot restored order with a loud commanding bawl. The monks instantly fell into line, military style. Each holding onto the hips of the man in front, they clack-tap-tapped their way through the door and back down the corridor again, the echoes of their frenetic dancing gradually fading away to a whisper.

"Now," McMahon's all too familiar voice said, "how was that? Has it made up for the little episode with the thorns?"

Ryan turned round to hurl at the owner of the voice a look of studied contempt. He said,

"You've really given the game away now haven't you? At least I know it's not some kind of an angel that I'm dealing with. Nothing from heaven would have brewed up that kind of perversion. And what's more, I can smell booze on your breath! Come on, what are you, some kind of Faustian fool who's sold his soul to the devil, or the man himself? It's no good looking so fierce either, I'm past the point of being afraid."

McMahon sat down with a sigh on the nearest bench. He said,

"I suppose you're right. The game would appear to be up. I never was very good at this type of thing. You see, the truth is that I'm a Bogle, a half fallen angel with one foot in purgatory and the other in hell. There's only two of us in existence. When Lucifer was cast down into the depths with all his diabolical fellow exiles, God decided that I and me fellow Bogle weren't quite as bad as the rest. So he decided to suspend final judgment and give us something of a second chance. I've got an opportunity to redeem meself you see, a passageway out from the bladder of hell. That's why I'm trying to do the best for you, showing you things that will help your blackened, selfish soul improve itself and bringing the chance of a redemptive act or two your way. If I manage the savin' of your soul, having failed miserably to salvage hundreds of others through all the centuries of human history, mine might still be forgiven as well. You're pretty much me last chance in fact. But the problem is I'm a terrible man for the old temptations and that's what's caused all me failures before. I couldn't resist the business with the swopping of yer shoes - or the little lark with all those monk lookalikes. But such things are a small price to pay for both of us if the ultimate prize of me company is a fast track to paradise instead of a plunge into Hades don't you think?"

"One man who chooses to give no warning of the likely dropping of another head first into a barrow load of crap is about as interested in the saving of souls as a pimp in a Dublin brothel!" Ryan rasped through a mouth still half full of unmentionable substances. "A Bogle you may or may not be, but a hypocrite you most certainly are!"

"What a great harvest of bitterness this little adventure in the hotel has sown in you," the Bogle said. "If it's any consolation, the whole business was an illusion, just like the moon that thought it was a dancer, the pig that flew and everything else. See, it's all gone, the trifle, the dung and even the pain. You're exactly the same as before. And what's more, to make up, I'll give you a night in the best hotel you can find anywhere in or near Roscrea."

"There's no vacancies," a passing stranger remarked.

"There are now, for tonight at least," the Bogle said. No sooner had he spoken than Ryan, freshly de-dunged and trifle-free, found himself standing in a large, plush, hotel foyer, with nothing more threatening than potted plants and a distant reception desk in sight. The Bogle hadn't managed the transition quite so smoothly, having materialised in the gents with one foot firmly down a lavatory bowl. It emerged into the foyer with a distinct squelch in its walk.

Ignoring it completely, Ryan sat down on a convenient chaise longue and retreated into deep contemplation. Failing to raise any kind of reply or even the faintest sign of recognition from him, the Bogle squelched its way into the bar and ordered itself a stiff drink. It was on its third glass before Ryan came in to confront it again. He sat down next to it and looked it straight in the eye. He said,

"Ridiculous as it might seem in such a time of technology and science, I can only conclude that I have no reason to doubt your claims as to who, or what you are. There's no other explanation that can both fit the facts and allow me to keep my sanity. But that doesn't make you any more palatable a companion and it's quite obvious to both of us that it's you that's more in need of spiritual help than me. I wouldn't have thought that an obvious tendency towards alcoholic over-indulgence - or, even more to the point, your little magical flights of fancy into such perversions as tap dancing monks in black stockings - are going to do you very much good at all with whatever's left of your 'second chance'. I may well be a little in need of spiritual help, but by comparison your own soul must be at desperation's door."

His last words caused the Bogle to almost choke on its drink. He continued,

"In short, you're much more in need of reform than me. My solution to all of this is that we do a deal. I'll take you in hand and help you clean up your act if you'll help me answer some of the questions about existence that have puzzled us ordinary mortals since time began. That way you'll find your way back into heavenly favour and I'll be a lot more capable of dealing with the baffling contradictions of life."

"And maybe become rich and famous as well?" the Bogle added. "Don't think I can't read your mind when I need to. You see, there it is again, that same old weakness, gross selfishness, just as I said before. Your first thought is always what you might get out of a thing, without a breath of concern for anyone else. There's no hope of you helping me unless I first help you with your own corruptions. And even if I did eventually agree to let you in on a few of life's little mysteries - and I don't guarantee that that would be the case - then you must understand that God has His own official secrets act. There's a definite limit to how much I could tell you. There are many things that, even if I tried to reveal them, would merely leave my lips as silence. A Bogle, you see, is as much subject to censorship on such matters as an angel in heaven."

"And what are the criteria for that which can't be told and that which can?"

"Very simple," the Bogle replied. "There are some things which can't be revealed to mortals without the very revelation ending their mortality. As God's plan is that mortality should only be ended by death, He would have to either wipe such revelations from your mind as soon as they were given to you or instantly take you from this world into the next. That is why, even if you were to do a Dr. Faustus and sell your soul to the divil in return for all life's secrets, you would either obtain nothing forbidden by God, or, if you did, descend straight into hell upon receipt."

"So how much would I be likely to learn - anything at all?" Ryan asked.

"Well, providing you accepted my help with the wickedness of your soul and I then decided to let you in on one or two of the curiosities that so concern you, I would say that while you would be no nearer to being able to end much of the suffering and stupidities of the world, you would at least be a man more at ease with the complexities of his own existence."

"But if you're so far away from heaven yourself, how can you help me in any useful way with the supposed 'wickedness' of my soul?" Ryan asked.

"Ah, but you forget," the Bogle replied, "because I used to be an angel I know the wisdom of angels. It's just that I'm not very good at putting it into practice meself. 'Lacking in backbone,' God said when throwing me out. So if I can give you spiritual wisdom and you can give me backbone, then the one will indeed save the other. So if it's a 'deal' you want, something that guarantees from me the delivery of what you so curiously desire, then that's the kind of arrangement I might be interested in - I might be prepared to let you in on an odd secret or two then. But I'll have to have a drink or two to think about it first."

"Then, if you accept, this drink must be your last excess," Ryan declared. "From hereon, if our deal's to work, you'll have to take all things in moderation."

"Including advice from the likes of sinful mortals like yerself," the Bogle muttered beneath its breath. To Ryan's untutored eyes, it seemed remarkably as though the glass which now was filled never became unfilled, despite the repeated sips the Bogle took from it. After an hour, with no clear indication from his strange companion as to what his decision might be, he took his person to the reception desk and from there to bed.

The morning came as a considerable surprise. Ryan found that his superbly comfortable bed of the night before had been transformed into stinking straw. What's more, he was woken by the bizarre sensation of his face being licked by a being unknown, which proved, upon the opening of his eyes, to be an affectionate horse. Pulling himself upright with a mixture of puzzlement, alarm and disgust, he found himself to be in a stables. Hearing loud and uncivilised snoring coming from the adjoining stall, he looked over to see the Bogle flat out and bedraggled, with an empty bottle in its outstretched hand. Seeing also a convenient pail of water at his own feet, he poured its contents liberally over his curious companion. The result was a desperate panic as the previously beatific slumberer tried to grapple with the cold, wet mystery that had descended into its left ear at such an unreasonable velocity.

"Jaysis wept! What's happening? What's going on? The ark! Get me to the ark!"

"Dreaming of old Noah were we?" Ryan asked sourly. "Might I enquire just how it is that a being that is capable of so many spectacular party tricks - and is allegedly an ex-angel to boot - needs to sleep like a poor honest mortal?"

"So it's you, you're the criminal who drowns the innocent while they sleep. Has it never crossed your mind that part of the sentence of hell - to which I am partially subject - is to suffer all the tiresome pains and weaknesses of the humanity from which most of its occupants have come? It's the same for a Bogle as anyone else. Angelic origins are no get-out for the likes of me."

"Fair enough. Perhaps you might also explain how we seem to have been transported from 'the best hotel anywhere in or around Roscrea' to a stables."

The Bogle dragged itself up and supported itself unsteadily on the stable partition. Scratching its unshaven chin it said,

"Good question, a very good question. A lack of precision I think is the problem here. I said we'd be there for a night didn't I. What I forgot to provide for was the fact that technically at least, as soon as the clock strikes twelve you're into the morning. You see, to avoid all the business of hunting through hotel guides and all of that stuff I invoked a magical 'best hotel' precisely on this spot, which normally being a stables, reverted to its former state at midnight on the dot. Yes, it's a lack of precision that's been the problem. I've made a right couple of Cinderellas out of us haven't I?"

"But why on earth stick your magical hotel in the same place as a stables?" Ryan thundered.

"Why indeed?" the Bogle muttered. "A slight problem with the geography of things would seem to be the answer. But…"

"Who's there?" a thundering voice demanded from behind the stable door, which swung violently open to reveal a large, ungentle looking stable master with a shotgun the size of a cannon gripped firmly in his bear-like hands. Seeing the empty bottle still hanging on for dear life in the Bogle's uncertain grasp and the desperate, unshaven and straw-covered state of the two trespassers, he jumped at once to the most logical and un-Christian conclusion.

"Drunks and horse thieves! The two scourges of civilisation wrapped into one and split between two! You'll be the renegades who stole Roscrea Lass last week no doubt - came back for more and were too drunk to escape, that's it, isn't it! Well you're out of luck, the pair of you, it's gun law not Garda law that we use for horse thieves here. You can kiss your drunken arses goodbye because I'm about to blast them into kingdom come!"

"No, wait! We can explain!" Ryan shouted.

"Really?" the man mountain said, his gun aimed ready for the kill.

"You see this gentleman here is a Bogle, not quite a devil and no longer an angel, or something like that and we were…"

"How exceedingly interesting, I'm pleased to meet you Mr. Bogle. I should of course introduce meself. Me name's Squellor and I'm about to give you both a bucketful of buckshot, now would the two of yous please bend over as I've got a busy day ahead of me and I'd like to get this over with as soon as possible."

"No, please, you don't understand," Ryan protested.

"Bend over!" Squellor roared. "If you don't do as I say immediately it'll be two arsefuls each you get instead of one. Do it! Now!"

Whimpering and desperate, Ryan did as instructed.

"And you too!" Squellor roared at the Bogle.

"I will, I will," the Bogle replied, "I have a terrible back and can never bend over for more than a few seconds at a time, so as soon as you've shot me friend here I'll be glad to oblige."

"Right, that's two arsefuls each for the both of you!" Squellor boomed, unleashing the first blast from his gun simultaneously.

To Ryan, everything thereafter seemed to occur in slow motion. The expected agony in his behind never materialised. What, through his legs, he saw instead was the buckshot stop miraculously a good twelve inches from its target, then do an about turn and head back from whence it came. It stopped again just in front of Squellor, did a U-turn round him, then shot with full force into his own backside. The resulting astonished and agonised roar was so loud that one of the horses took fright and bolted out of its stall, knocking the unfortunate Squellor into a neatly piled heap of manure by the side of the door as it did so. The poor man was reduced in an instant from being an angel of death to the most piteously gibbering sight that mortal man could ever wish to cast eyes upon.

The Bogle straightened its dishevelled person with quiet dignity and marched out to safety past the felled giant. Ryan, still in a state of shock from the sound of the gun blast, followed him numbly. No sooner had his feet trodden two boot marks in the muddy stable yard than a bucket of ice cold water cascaded over his head, soaking him from head to foot.

"That's to give you a dose of your own medicine and to get you out of the state you're in," the Bogle said mischievously. Ryan shuddered, shivered, yelled and danced with rage as the icy fingers of the water crawled over every inch of his already cold anatomy. An uninformed bystander would undoubtedly have mistaken the whole performance for a spontaneous display of traditional folk dancing skills by an expert devotee of the art.

"Right! That's absolutely it!" he screamed. "I've had it up to here with you. I want you out of my life now, for good and none of your damned ifs or buts. Spending a night in a stable is one thing, being terrified out of my wits by some lunatic with a shotgun is another. I don't care whether you're a Bogle, an angel or what, from now on I don't want to see you within a million miles of my person! You're a disaster in every possible way and several more impossible ones besides. Just stay away from me and let me have the remains of my holiday in peace!"

The Bogle looked clearly startled.

"But if I don't follow you around I can't do the good deeds that I had planned for the benefit of both our souls."

"Don't you see?" Ryan raged. "Everything you do backfires. You've got a history of it - right from the time you backed the wrong horse and sided with the devil! You're a flop, an incompetent, a supernatural buffoon! Making me permanently enraged isn't going to do either of us any good, spiritual or otherwise. The best thing you can do for both of us is just leave me alone - or get a professional on the job, get a proper angel to stand in for you. Let's face it, you're just a ham-fisted amateur with a few clever party tricks up your sleeve."

The Bogle looked quite crest-fallen, never having received such a dressing down since the day God took away his angel status and booted him out of heaven. To be so criticised by a perfect divinity he could live with. After all, only God could hope to come up completely to His own standards of good behaviour and to be told one had fallen short in this regard was not entirely surprising. But to be informed that one was a complete failure by a mere mortal and to have one's faults so comprehensively enumerated by the same inferior category of being was more than any ex-angel could be expected to cope with.

"Are you sure you really mean this?" it said forlornly. "Some terrible things will happen if I'm not with you to help out."

Ryan didn't even bother to enquire what the Bogle meant by such a statement. He said simply,

"And some terrible things will happen if you are with me won't they? With your record it's more than likely that the things that happen with you around will be infinitely worse than those that occur in your absence. I can forgive many things in life but you're not one of them. I've had enough of you - your sick jokes, your self-seeking party tricks, your spineless drinking, but most of all your complete and utter bloody incompetence!"

The Bogle looked even more depressed by this damning evaluation of its talents. It said,

"Very well, but don't say I didn't warn you. If you change

your mind just call my name and I'll be there."

"Fortunately I don't know your name, or at least your real one," Ryan hissed.

"Oddsockk," the Bogle muttered.

"Well, odd socks to you Oddsockk," Ryan growled and stalked off to hunt down a bus back to Limerick to pick up his car.

When he finally made it back he found that the vehicle had somehow moved itself to a clump of trees half a mile away. Too wearied by prior experience to even begin to ask why he roared back onto the road and drove south like a madman, determining to get as far away from the disastrous Bogle as possible and spend the rest of his holiday in Cork.

Even after a good half hour's drive he was still doing twice the speed a sane and considerate man would contemplate. Approaching a village whose name he didn't even notice he made no attempt to slow down. Equally, the road beneath his wheels made no attempt to compensate for the rain that had flowed steadily throughout the night, and a cow that was in the process of wandering through the main street in the company of its owner and its peers made no attempt to change its lifelong habit of walking in idiosyncratic zigzags from one side of the road to the other. The result was a horrendous and desperate screeching of the BMW's tyres as a terrified Ryan slammed the brakes full on. The vehicle slewed wildly across the road, narrowly missing the cow but finding a decidedly unsympathetic lamp-post with unerring precision. Miraculously and undeservedly unhurt, apart from a cut to his forehead and forearm, Ryan shook uncontrollably from head to foot for the second time in the same day. The car had wrapped itself so efficiently round the lamp-post that it looked like the two were locked in fond embrace. There were several unwelcome hissing noises coming from the engine compartment. A little crowd rapidly gathered and a muscular arm wrenched open the banana shaped door.

"How are you in there?" the owner of the arm asked.

"I'm ok," Ryan replied.

"Your back's alright and you can move everything?"

"Yes, yes, my back's ok," the object of concern said.

"Well you're a lucky man and a bloody eejit for coming into town so fast. It's not only the cow you could have killed. Come on, let's get you out."

After being both treated and admonished by the local doctor and spending an uncomfortable hour with the local police, Ryan went round to the garage where the car had been towed.

"You'll not be going very far in this for a while," the extremely overweight proprietor said. "You're lucky I'm a specialist in accident repair. It'll take a good ten days to get all the bits and get the thing back to good as new - and that's assuming we can sort out the little matter of the insurance payment. Have you anywhere to stay?"

Ryan shook his head morosely.

"Well, providing you don't mind a lively house, my sister puts up visitors for a reasonable rate. She's the best cook you'll find round here if you're fond of your stomach."

He scrawled the address down on a piece of oily card and handed it to Ryan. The latter thanked him, and after retrieving his suitcases from the rear of the stricken vehicle, set off in search of the highly recommended sister.

The house, when he found it, looked anything but lively. It was a reasonable sized terrace dwelling with a facing of pebbledash grey and windows that looked uncannily like eyelids about to drop off to sleep. He rang the doorbell. What followed could only be described as the unleashing of an avalanche.

"Hello, my brother rang to tell me you were coming, you'll be Mr. Ryan. I'm Mrs. O'Dredlin. Come in."

No sooner had Mrs. O'Dredlin spoken than four human bullets shot out, each in pursuit of the other.

"Come back here at once, all of you!" she shouted. "Bridey O'Dredlin, let go of Thomas' ears! John, will you stop trying to pull Sian's hair out of her scalp. Come on now, all of you, back inside this minute! I'm terribly sorry Mr. Ryan, they're my sister's children – I'm looking after them for the afternoon while she's at the hospital."

No sooner had the miniature rioters returned indoors than Mr. O'Dredlin came out, accidentally treading on the cat's tail in the process. The little creature's appalling scream of protest was followed by instant deep-clawed vengeance on the nearest human leg, which, unfortunately for Ryan, happened to be his. As he hopped about wildly on one foot, Mr. O'Dredlin apologised profusely for his suffering and then, mounting a bicycle a full size too small for the length of his legs and the enormity of his bottom, wobbled off.

"I do wish Sean wouldn't try to travel by bike," Mrs. O'Dredlin sighed, "the poor man has no sense of balance on two legs never mind two wheels. If ever there was a man unsuited to run a bicycle shop it's him."

As if to confirm her doubts her unfortunate husband completely mismanaged the graceful arc he was attempting to take from one side of the road to the other, hit the kerb and flew spectacularly over the handlebars and into a waste skip on the pavement's edge. Ryan made as if to go over and help him.

"Don't worry," Mrs. O'Dredlin said resignedly, "he never hurts himself. If he doesn't fall off his bike at least twice in any week I begin to think he's ailing for something. In his case, the repeated falling off a bicycle is the sign of a healthy disposition."

Sure enough, Mr. O'Dredlin hauled himself out of the skip, dusted himself down and then continued on his way on foot, the dreaded bicycle being wheeled gingerly at his side.

"Right, it's safe to come in now," she said.

"Hello Mary!" a voice shouted. Looking round, Ryan saw a ferocious looking middle aged-priest approaching rapidly down the street.

"Hello Frank!" she replied. "Will you come and have a cup of tea?"

Ryan was struck by the fact that the priest appeared to be creaking metallically as he walked. His step was measured but definitely forced and uncomfortable.

"My father was like that," he said.

"Like what Mr. Ryan?" Mrs. O'Dredlin asked.

"He had a bad leg too."

"Bad leg? Oh Frank doesn't have a bad leg, that's his chastity belt. He always wears it to keep his mind from the occasions of sin. Has done for years. Makes them himself you know, one type for women, one for men. He's the only cousin I've got who's any good with his hands. If you're in need of a belt just ask him, he might be able to fit you up off the shelf. Frank, come in dear. This is Mr. Ryan, the man who had the accident this morning. He's going to be staying with us for a few days."

“Pleased to meet you Mr. Ryan,” the priest replied, “I’m Father Delaney. Are you a Catholic?”

“Well, sort of, my family always has been,” he muttered embarrassedly.

“D’you hear that Mary, you’ve got a sort of Catholic staying in the house. That’s what comes of living in England you see Mr. Ryan, it’s a house of sin beyond all salvation. It’s full of ‘sort of’ Catholics. We must have a talk sometime while you’re here. We’ll see if we can’t send you back a ‘sort of’ saint.”

As they advanced in single file down the dark, narrow hallway, something short but otherwise large loomed ahead, sailing in the opposite direction.

“Mother, this is Mr. Ryan, the guest I was telling you about. Mr. Ryan, this is my mother.”

The old lady looked up at the visitor knowingly.

“I thought you’d end up here,” she said. “You can’t run away from things just like that you know young feller.”

Before he could ask her what she meant, she’d sailed off into the lounge and disappeared from view. Mrs. O’Dredlin led the convoy forwards into a small, cosy dining room.

“There, now the two of yous just have a little sit down and I’ll put the kettle on. I’m sure you’ll find lots to talk about.”

After a good two minutes of deafening silence Ryan decided unwisely to try and break the ice.

“I hear you make chastity belts as a hobby,” he said.

“Hobby!” the priest thundered. “I’ll give you hobby you English heathen. What I do is work, God’s work, for the salvation of souls like yours. The fruit of my hands becomes the legitimate means by which Catholic couples wishing to preserve their virginity before marriage might do so. At this very moment, besides meself, there’s ten young godly men and women walking around with their chastity as safe as Fort Knox.”

“Ten indeed,” Ryan said. “But how can you be sure that they’re actually wearing the belts?”

“Ah, that’s the clever bit,” the priest said. “First, I’m the only one with a key for each and every belt and should any determined sinner ever manage to extricate themselves without my say so, there’s the Delaney clank. All the belts have it - if I meet a one of them coming down the street and they’re not clanking at least as vigorously as meself I'll know instantly that it's a weakened soul that's approaching me. It's the ultimate in foolproof devices. Will you let me fit you up for one while you're here? It could be your first step back on the road to salvation."

"No, no thank you," Ryan replied, "I've had no occasion for the sinfulness that worries you for some time."

"Better to be safe than sorry," the priest warned, "I could take a fitting now and have you fixed up by tomorrow lunchtime. You could be the pioneer who takes the Delaney clank over to England."

"No, thank you anyway, but I've enough problems at the moment without starting to clank as well," Ryan said as politely as he could. Mrs. O'Dredlin came in with the tea just in time to save him from further discussion of the matter. No sooner had she served her guests than the doorbell rang and a sallow faced, stringy haired man of an ill looking forty or so was ushered into the room by the grandmother.

"Hello Mary," he said, "have I missed Sean?"

"You have indeed, he's just gone back to the shop this very minute. Mr. Ryan, this is my brother Seamus, he's a publican if you're a moderate drinking man in the evenings."

"I could certainly do with a beer or two after all that's happened today," Ryan said. No sooner had he spoken than Seamus went three shades paler than before, and clutching his stomach with both hands, rushed out of the room and into the lavatory, from which violent retching could be heard for a full minute afterwards.

"Is he ok?" Ryan asked, not knowing what else to say.

"He'll be as right as rain in a while," Mrs. O'Dredlin replied. "It's just that I know it's strange for a man of his profession, but you must never mention the word 'beer' when he's around. It always has the same effect. All the locals know the problem and avoid the use of such a term like the plague. It stems from when he spent a couple of years in England, you see. He found some of the more commercial kinds of beer so bad that a single use of the word stirs up all the old memories like a volcano in his stomach. If you want a drink ask for a stout, a whiskey, a gin or whatever you like, but for the poor soul's sake, try and hold yourself from saying anything that even rhymes with beer."

"I'm terribly sorry...," Ryan offered, with a characteristic lack of any genuine concern for the man or anything else other than himself, but was unable to finish his hypocritical apology due to an enormous roar from somewhere to the rear of the house.

"You try sticking your paws up above ground again and I'll chop your bollix off you little furry bastard!"

"That'll be Sergeant Throttler home for his dinner. He's having terrible trouble with moles at the moment. It's a useful deterrent to burglars having a terrifying policeman living next door to you do you not think Mr. Ryan?" Mrs. O'Dredlin said.

"Throttler by name, throttler by nature," the priest murmured darkly, "that man will fry in hell for the violent thoughts he harbours against God's creatures."

"I can understand him getting annoyed at moles," Ryan said cheerily, trying to keep the conversation steered firmly away from the terrible wrong he had just done to Seamus the sickly publican, "I was driven mad by a plague of the things on my lawn last year."

"With the sergeant, the mutilation of moles would just be the beginning of it," Mrs. O'Dredlin said in a voice so low that, had it taken a solid form, the unwary could have tripped over it.

"What do you mean?" Ryan asked. "He seemed perfectly normal when he took my statement this morning."

"Some things are better not asked about," said the granny, who seemed to have an ethereal ability to float in and out of the room without being noticed. Before Ryan could ask why some things shouldn't be asked about, or more particularly, why Sergeant Throttler shouldn't be asked about, Seamus stuck his head through the doorway, a sight so drained that it seemed as if his face had been siphoned of blood, and announced his return to the pub. Having delivered a sympathetic and apologetic goodbye, Mrs. O'Dredlin returned her attention to Ryan.

"We've two other guests besides yourself. There's a Protestant aunt of mine from the North, Mrs. Quinn and a gentleman from Dublin, Mr. O'Rourke. Mr. O'Rourke's here for a week and my aunt is here for the summer. Mrs. Quinn lived in England for years - she was very fond of your Mrs. Thatcher when she was alive. Very fond."

"Terrible woman," the priest muttered under his breath.

"Who d'you mean Frank?" Mrs. O'Dredlin asked sharply.

"Both of them if he's any sense," the granny remarked as she ghosted her way out of the room again.

"Is Mr. O'Rourke on holiday like myself or on business?" Ryan asked for no good reason, other than the making of synthetic conversation.

"Family business so I understand," Mrs. O'Dredlin replied. "A matter of some land that his uncle left in his will. Ah, that'll be my aunt coming downstairs now. You must meet her while you're in."

Mrs. Quinn smelt the tea and propelled her sadly arthritic legs into the room as quickly as she could. Her face exuded a confidence and youth that seemed to be at odds with her bent frame and wispy grey hair. Her mouth appeared to be locked in a permanent smile.

"Will you have some tea with us Lilly?" Mrs. O'Dredlin asked in the loud manner frequently used to address those whom one presumes to be deaf but aren't.

"I will Mary thank you," the aunt said, seating herself painfully.

"This is Mr. Ryan from England. He'll be staying with us until his car is fixed."

"I used to live in England," said Lilly with the third variety of her strangely permanent smile that Ryan had noted so far, "near Warwick. Do you know Warwick Mr. Ryan?"

"Yes, I used to live in Warwick and still have an aunt there," Ryan lied for a reason he found impossible to fathom. He had always been good at lies and they seemed to trip more easily and naturally off his tongue than the truth, with all its unpredictable consequences and implications. He was startled when the granny, who had spirited herself back into the room without being noticed, tsk-tsked, as if she could read his mind.

"I thought as much," Lilly said in her harsh Belfast accent, "you have the look of a solid Conservative gentleman about you. Warwick is a very conservative place, very traditional."

Ryan smiled pleasantly at her, not liking to point out that on the mere two occasions when he had strained himself to vote he had opted for either Liberal or Labour candidates. He caught sight of the granny's strangely mocking expression in the mirror over the fireplace and shuddered a little. She said,

"He doesn't look much of a Conservative man to me. I knew a Paddy Ryan whose uncle was in the Easter Rising. If a grandson of Paddy had voted for the English Conservatives he'd have eaten the wood from his own coffin and rattled his bones so hard they'd have shot out the soil like knives. You're not a Conservative now are you Mr. Ryan?"

"Well, not exactly," Ryan said evasively.

"A sort of not quite English Conservative to match your sort of English Catholicism," the priest suggested with poisoned innocence.

"Now, now Frank," Mrs. O'Dredlin said reproachfully.

"I was in the Conservative and Unionist club in Warwick," Lilly continued, as if oblivious to the trench warfare that was developing around her. "We had a visit from Mrs. Thatcher, a wonderful woman, wonderful. When she shook my hand I felt as if I was in the presence of a higher being."

"Probably floating on her own hot air, that'd make her higher," Father Delaney muttered into his teacup.

"My heart sank when that poor, great woman was stabbed in the back," Lilly continued, her smile becoming positively beatific. "Eleven years work rejected in a week. How could they? She could have saved us all, Britain and Ireland in one."

Father Delaney nearly choked in the process of biting his teacup and from the expression on the granny's face she looked set to become the first pensioner in space.

"Look what the incompetent windbag of a woman did to you," the priest spluttered, "you crossed the water as a woman of reasonable means and came back flat broke. The only lasting talent the harridan had was for making her banker friends rich and everyone else bankrupt. It was all the English industrial jobs that she threw out the window that paved the way for the Brexit vote - and look what a mess that's made for everyone this side of the water. Good riddance to bad rubbish and thank God she wasn't born in Ireland."

"If she'd been born in Ireland there wouldn't still be an Ireland," a new voice that had seated itself quietly in the corner said.

"Hello Mr. O'Rourke," enthused Mrs. O'Dredlin, greatly

relieved to have the chance to stop the conversation from dancing on the gelignite of Mrs. Thatcher. "This is Mr. Ryan who'll be staying with us for a day or two. I was just telling him about your business with land."

O'Rourke gave Ryan a look that would have made a surgeon's knife look blunt. He said,

"What is it that you'd like to know about my business Mr. Ryan?"

"Oh, it was just social chit chat," Ryan said nervously.

"I see," O'Rourke said in a manner that suggested that he saw the kinds of things that could lead grown men to draw pistols at dawn. He kept scrutinising Ryan as if he was measuring him for a coffin. A cry of,

"I warned you, you little furry sod!" erupted from the garden next door, followed by a single shotgun blast. Something was heard to shatter into a thousand fragments.

"That'll be the Sergeant's greenhouse," Mrs. O'Dredlin said. "His aim is a perfect model of inaccuracy. Last week he tried to shoot Liam Maguire's cat for having stared repeatedly at him in a venomous manner and mortally wounded a bucket. It's a comforting thought to know that if ever he goes completely doollally with that gun I'll be perfectly safe as long as he's aiming at me."

"Sounds just the kind of man that should have taken Mrs. Thatcher on a rabbit hunt," O'Rourke said with a quietness that contained a menace as threatening as death itself. "The little creatures would have been perfectly safe and there'd have been one more divil back down in Hades."

"Mr. O'Rourke!" Mrs. O'Dredlin gasped, astounded. "I won't have such talk in my house, no matter how unpleasant the person in question might be said to be."

Lilly finally rose to the challenge. Pulling herself up with some difficulty she surveyed all present in a severe, schoolmarmly manner. She said,

"There's not a person here, including meself, who would have been fit to even stoop to tie the shoelaces of Margaret Thatcher when she was alive."

"I'd have tied them round her neck given half the chance," the granny muttered.

"That's right, turn all your hate into violence!" Lilly hissed. "It doesn't frighten me and it wouldn't have frightened her!"

"Another grand exit," the granny said to no-one in particular as Lilly limped out of the room. "I'm surprised it took so long to get her going today."

"You shouldn't wind her up like that mammy," Mrs. O'Dredlin said, more in sorrow than in anger at what was clearly a daily entertainment for the granny. As the aunt exited a strange, drawn looking man of thirty or so wandered in behind the kind of worried look that might be seen on the face of a soul that has stumbled upon its own grave.

"There's a bugler at large in this house and I'm looking straight at him!" he yelled sternly at Ryan.

"He gets his words all in a muddle when he gets excited," O'Rourke said with a smirk. "He thinks you're a burglar."

"That's what I said!" the accuser yelled. "Don't just sit there all of yous, do something. Grab the thieving rogue before he makes off with the silver!"

Mrs. O'Dredlin said,

"This is my other brother Mr. Ryan, you'll have to excuse him, it's one of his bad days when his imagination runs so fast it trips over itself. He can be quite peaceable and quiet when he sets his mind to it."

"Take him away and lock him up, all two of him!" the accuser roared.

"You should be taken away with the rest of this house," the granny mumbled.

Feeling himself to be in the middle of a play for which he was totally unrehearsed Ryan shifted uneasily in his chair. His accuser, meanwhile, was looking distinctly irritated at the complete absence of compliant helpers. He strode angrily out of the room muttering, "If you want a job doing then do it your bloody self," then re-entered almost immediately brandishing a set of Garda issue handcuffs. O'Rourke's smirk blossomed into a delighted leer as Ryan's wrists were forcibly seized by his accuser and the cuffs snapped onto them. Mrs. O'Dredlin and the priest rushed over and freed the shocked and terrified Englishman before matters could leap any further out of control. She said,

"Patrick, you've picked the sergeant's pocket again after I

expressly told you never to do it again – these are his cuffs and if he finds out you've taken them you'll be in the cells quicker than you can sneeze. I'll have to wait until it gets dark and throw them onto his garden path in the hope he'll think he must have dropped them."

"Right, that's it!" Patrick yelled, ignoring her complaint. "If I can't arrest the bugler, then it'll have to be Barabbas that's cuffed for aiding and abetting!"

He grabbed the handcuffs back off her and stalked determinedly out of the room.

"Will you stop givin' me poor dog such a sacrilegious corruption of a name!" Mrs. O'Dredlin almost shrieked. "I named him after Barnabas the saint not some blessed great murderous heathen! If you want to use the bible for your lunatic fantasies at least get things the right way round."

"Don't you dare touch Barabbas!" the granny yelled, rocketing out of her chair with an athleticism that belied her age.

"Don't worry," Father Delaney said, catching her arm, "Barnabas can look after himself."

No sooner had he spoken than a ferocious growling and snarling interspersed with third degree barking broke out, followed by the sound of buckets, plant pots and other unfortunate objects being knocked over in what was clearly a spectacular and high speed chase at the immediate rear of the house. The one-sided battle was soon over and the still shaking Ryan was relieved to see his clearly terrified accuser shoot past the open doorway and up the staircase with Barnabas/Barabbas, the less than friendly household Doberman, hot in pursuit. A bedroom door was heard to slam on the floor above followed by the frenzied barking of a frustrated hound denied its desert.

"He'll stay up there for the rest of the day," Mrs. O'Dredlin said quietly. "I'll make sure he doesn't bother you again. He's the black sheep of the family I'm afraid, poor man. He spent so much of his youth playing computer games he's lost all touch with reality. On top of that he's had the pick-pocketing of policemen problem since he was three, and as his elder sister I've had a lifetime of anonymously returning things to mystified guards through the post. He's always seen it as a great game instead of a crime and I've never been able to make him change his mind on the matter."

Ryan nodded numbly, too traumatised to take in much of what she was saying. Dragging himself shakily out of his chair he said,

"I think I'll go for a walk, stretch my legs."

"You do that now," said Mrs. O'Dredlin soothingly, "there's some lovely walks round here. If you're looking for some peace and quiet as well I recommend a leisurely stroll down by the river bank. If you go down as far as the Christian Brothers' Retirement House and then turn round you'll be back in time for an evening meal."

"Thank you," Ryan said, "I'll see you later."

Putting his feet outside the front door seemed like an escape from a prison of insanity. He looked hopefully at the two other guesthouses he passed on his way down to the river but both had no vacancies signs prominently displayed.

The walk itself was as pleasant and as peaceful as Mrs. O'Dredlin had led him to believe it would be, the sun bursting free from its grey chains and bouncing its light exquisitely off the gently rippling water and the lush greenery of the river bank. His mind floated off into a luxury of numb timelessness as he let all the disturbing events of the past few days recede into a temporary vacuum in his brain. The two or three people he met in passing all seemed as reassuringly normal as he could have wished and he began to conclude gradually that the Bogle and everything that had happened at Mrs. O'Dredlin's were just anomalies and that the world, or at least his experience of it, hadn't turned upside down at all. It was then that he heard the thrashing.

"One's a reminder!" - Thwack!

"Two's an outward sign of sin!" - Thwack!

"Three's a punishment!" - Thwack!

"Four's four more than you'd wanted!" - Thwack!

"Five's a bitter harvest!" - Thwack!

"And six is your salvation!" - Thwack!

Startled, Ryan looked over a nearby wall to see a red faced, bull-built man in his mid-sixties standing, strap in hand, in deep contemplation of a battered cushion bound and all but gagged to a tree trunk. In the near distance was a large, grey building with a sign informing those bold enough to read it that it was a Christian Brothers House. A voice from behind said,

“You’ll have to excuse Brother O’Flogga. He gets a bit carried away with enthusiasm for his old calling sometimes. Ever since the schools were all handed over to trusts or whatever and he retired he’s hankered after his old job.”

Ryan turned round to find an elderly Brother behind him.

“He’s reliving what it used to be like every September when he was in training for the start of the school year,” he explained, “knocking seven bells out of a cushion always helped him get his aim right. The aim is very important to a man who believes that a precisely placed wallop can be a first step for a sinner on the road to heaven.”

“Isn’t it a bit of a brutal method of saving a soul?” Ryan asked. “It’s like me going up to someone, punching them on the nose and then expecting them to be a good Christian.”

“It most certainly isn’t,” the Brother remarked. “A thwack on the behind is a missionary in disguise, whereas a punch on the nose is the divil’s work. A Christian Brother could never confuse the two. Here, I’ll show you... Brother O’Flogga! This gentleman has just clouted me one on the nose would you believe!”

O’Flogga strode grim-facedly over to the wall.

“A terrible thing, a terrible thing,” he said to Ryan, “did you not know you’ve just committed an act of which Lucifer would be proud?”

“He wants you to help him Brother. He tells me that when he was at school a good thwacking always used to cure him of such sinful acts. He wonders if you’d be so kind as to oblige.”

“My privilege!” O’Flogga beamed. “There’s nothing like a good traditional thrashing to save a soul and keep the old arm in practice.”

Before Ryan could utter a word he’d been hauled over the wall by his lapels and flung prone over a garden bench. The old Brother tried to explain to O’Flogga that he’d simply been demonstrating a point, but the latter was too intent on the task in hand to hear. Ryan was totally unable to wriggle free from his iron grip and had to take his punishment like a man.

“One for your thoughts!” - Thwack!

“Two for your acts!” - Thwack!

“Three for the Lucifer inside you!” - Thwack!

“Four for the Mephistopheles who’d like to join him!” -

Thwack!

"Five for the renouncing of your sins!" - Thwack!

"Six for salvation!" - Thwack!

Ryan's backside felt as if it had been flattened to envelope size and popped inside an electric toaster on full blast.

"And how d'you feel now," O'Flogga asked enthusiastically, "a renewed spirit freed from the iron grip of the divil?"

"I can feel me bum, me poor sodding bum!" was all the shell-shocked Ryan could murmur, wandering away from the two Brothers in a baffled daze, back in the direction from which he'd come. Earlier on, he'd thought the world outside Mrs. O'Dredlin's was decidedly safer than that within, but now he was beginning to wonder whether he'd got things the wrong way round. He stumbled back in through her front door in a trance. Hauling his weary frame upstairs he went into the bathroom, filled the sink with cold water, and plunged his bottom into it. It was then, as the fierce tingling that had been stabbing away like a forest of malicious needles began to subside, that he realised that he'd forgotten to drop his pants first.

Tea at the O'Dredlin house was a peculiar affair. Ryan found himself seated at a table with O'Rourke and a curious looking individual in a tweed jacket of about thirty or so. The meal itself was served by a pretty young woman who had chosen to deny nature's virtues by shaving her head almost down to the scalp.

"Sharon's seventeen and wants to be a pop singer," Mrs. O'Dredlin said by way of explanation for her daughter's strange appearance.

"I'm Dermot McGarrity," the tweed jacket said, "just arrived for the night. I come here as often as I can. Beautiful part of the country, beautiful."

"Dermot's a lecturer at Trinity Mr. Ryan," Mrs. O'Dredlin said, flitting in again in pursuit of her daughter, who, in a fit of ill humour, was banging people's plates down in front of them with a force that was teaching the food to fly.

"You know who I am," O'Rourke said with a grimace that could equally have been an ironic smile or a facial seizure.

"Are you a reading man Mr. Ryan?" Dermot asked.

"A little," Ryan replied.

"I love books," Dermot said. "Almost an unnatural love you

might think. I desire them, crave them in bed. I'd sell the last shirt from my back if it ever came down to the choice between books and clothes. A book to me is food for the soul. If I starve of books I die, it's as simple and terrible as that."

"We all die," said O'Rourke, "I'd want to be sacrificed for something more than a book."

"But there must be something that you've read that means at least as much as anything else in life," Dermot suggested.

"I like reading wills," O'Rourke said sourly.

"What about you Mr. Ryan," Dermot continued, "there must be something of special appeal to you?"

"Dickens I like," Ryan said unenthusiastically, hoping that so unoriginal a choice would kill the interest of the persistent enquirer.

"Lots of deaths in Dickens," said O'Rourke.

"Is it the deaths that fascinate you?" Dermot asked.

"Death is a fascinating subject," O'Rourke said with an unpleasant smile, "we should all think about death."

"Now with that I can agree," Dermot said, while chewing with some difficulty the strangeness that Sharon had just delivered wordlessly onto his plate. Noting its peculiar nature, Ryan wondered whether it had been designed for the cat but delivered to Dermot instead as a result of Sharon's displeasure at the world. He noticed also that Dermot's eyes riveted themselves to the contours of the young woman's anatomy every time she passed and that she returned a look that would have withered Attila the Hun, Genghis Khan and the entire Fifth Panzer Brigade.

"Death is something that has always puzzled me," Dermot continued, "the point of it and where we go if go we do and who it is we'll meet and all this business of sin, redemption, forgiveness and damnation. There's an entire night's conversation just in the preliminaries to the discussion of death, and even then it's doubtful that an assembled company would be much more enlightened at the end than they were at the beginning."

"I find embalming a fascinating subject," O'Rourke interjected. "I often think of people I'd like to embalm."

"But isn't that more of a concern with the theatre of death rather than the big questions that surround it?" Dermot enquired, oblivious to the look in O'Rourke's eye that suggested the person he'd most like to embalm was the one currently babbling.

O'Rourke smiled pleasantly. Checking to see that Mrs. O'Dredlin was nowhere in sight, he delicately lifted the raw egg that Sharon had inventively placed on the cake tray, slipped it into the top pocket of Dermot's jacket and patted him on the chest, squashing the yoke completely in the process.

"If you want some salt with it as well let me know," he whispered confidentially and then strode contentedly out of the room.

"Have you had enough Mr. O'Rourke?" Mrs. O'Dredlin asked him as she passed on her bustling way back into the room.

"Oh yes, I've had enough," he said.

Dermot was strangely silent for the rest of tea. Sharon, who had seen the terrible act with the egg through the serving hatch, brought another one and after placing it artistically in the middle of the cake tray, smiled with sweet meaningfulness at Ryan. Then, her eyes aglow, she delivered to the unfortunate Lilly something so peculiar that she let out a little half scream.

"My God! What's that child?"

"It's a Thatcher pie," Sharon smiled, "granny told me you'd like it."

Before anyone could properly cast their eyes over the strangeness that was causing all the upset Mrs. O'Dredlin had swept in and covered it in a cloth so large that it looked like a tarpaulin. In the same sweeping motion of her arm that unleashed the cloth she delivered a cracking smack to Sharon's face and frogmarched both her and the offending delicacy from the room.

"I'm too old for her to belt," the granny muttered subversively from the corner of the room where she and the shadows of the giggling sun were keeping mischievous company.

Having finished his tea, Ryan bade goodnight to the still silent Dermot and went up to his room to lie down and contemplate the assorted weirdnesses of the day. He had no sooner laid his weary frame to rest than the bed began to sob, a strange thing for a bed to do and a considerable surprise to Ryan. Finding no visible signs of tears on the pillows or anywhere else, he was just about to consign himself finally to the lunatic asylum when he spotted a decidedly female looking leg with an accompanying foot sticking out from under the side. Thrusting his head down in order to see if a complete anatomy was attached to the visible parts, he found underneath the bed a remarkable likeness of Sharon.

"I'm Sharon," the remarkable likeness announced.

"I know," Ryan replied, "I met your double downstairs."

"I always used to come here and hide under the bed when mammy belted me when I was little. There were hardly ever enough guests then to fill this room. I didn't know it was yours."

"Neither did I until I arrived," Ryan said with unhelpful logic. "Does your mother often hit you?"

"Hardly ever. Not for a year or more. Tonight was the last straw I think. Winding up Lilly was too much."

"And Dermot," Ryan added.

"Oh him," Sharon said dismissively, "I'd like to wind him up properly, like a little metal Mickey Mouse and send him marching, clickety bloody clack, straight into the river."

"He might go rusty," Ryan said, surprised at his own wit. Sharon giggled a little.

"I want to be a singer," she said, "but I can't bloody sing. I tried singing a U2 song to the trees this afternoon but all the sheep bolted up the hill."

"Could've been worse," Ryan said, "just think how you'd have felt if the trees had bolted up the hill as well." He was even more surprised than before at his good humour and put it down to the fact that for once he had encountered someone who found his jokes at least a little amusing.

"My boyfriend's said he's going to whack a chrissie brother tonight," she said in a matter of fact way.

"Why's that?" Ryan asked.

"Brother O'Flogga caught us with a condom in Gallagher's barn last night. He gave us both a lecture on the condoms of hell, how we'd both be strung up in a giant rubber above the hottest flames and be roasted for all eternity. Then he said he was going to tell both our dad's to give us a good pasting."

"Is that why your man wants to top him?"

"He always wants to top him. He loathes him."

"Do you think he will?"

"He's all talk and as weedy as a flea. O'Flogga would have him strung up by the balls before he got within a foot of him if he tried."

“Are you going to spend the rest of the evening under this bed or am I going to be able to hold a conversation without having to hang my head upside down until I get dizzy?” Ryan asked.

Sliding out from underneath with some difficulty Sharon pulled herself up to her full five feet four and said,

“Don’t tell the mammy about the rubber, it’ll be more than a clout I’ll get if she finds out. I’d better get out of here as well before she gets the wrong idea.”

She slipped out of the door before Ryan could reply. Just as he thought she’d gone for good she briefly popped her head back in and said,

“You’ve got odd socks on by the way, just thought you should know. They say it’s bad luck round here.”

“Odd socks?” Ryan asked, surprised and raising both feet in the air saw that the girl was right. As he said the words a cold breath of wind seemed to rush through the room. Looking up, he saw that Sharon had left the door open and presumed it was the draft from that. Quickly shutting it, he lay down on the bed again and promptly went to sleep.

When Ryan awoke it was a good four hours later. There was a commotion that thought it was two commotions in the street outside and even if he had wanted to ignore it, it would have made its business known just the same. Lifting his window and looking down into the half light below, he saw the same Sharon who he had found under his bed earlier, screaming in terror. Sergeant Throttler and Father Delaney as good as had her by the throat and Mrs. O’Dredlin looked as if she was about to tear her limb from limb.

“It was your idea wasn’t it, go on, admit it! That boy hasn’t got the wit to think up a half brained murderous idea like that for himself,” the policeman roared.

A cold shiver ran down Ryan’s back and he went downstairs into the hall. There was a little crowd gathered peering out of the front door.

“What’s happened?” he asked the granny.

“It’s her young man,” she said. “He surprised Brother O’Flogga when he was out for a walk in the woods and tried to give him a belt on the nut with a hurling stick. The brother pushed him away with the force of a demon and he fell in the river and drowned. They're saying it's Sharon's fault, that she put the idea in his head with all her contrary ways. It would never have happened had your friend been here at the time."

"What friend?" Ryan asked bewildered.

"The feller that's standing right behind us," she replied, "the one who's just moved into the room next door to you."

Looking round, Ryan nearly jumped out of his skin. There, as large as life and death combined, was the Bogle.

"She's right," it said solemnly, "had you had an ounce of tolerance and Christian forgiveness within your heart we would never have been parted and I would have been here to do something to stop that drunken fool of a boy before he took on the one man equivalent of the Roman army. As it is, he hit the water an hour before I arrived and I can do nothing. Resurrection after such an interval isn't among me permitted powers. The only reason I'm here at all is because you said 'odd socks' and I wrongly thought you were calling my name."

"Well, if you think you're so damned capable you can at least go and persuade that bunch of lunatics out there that that clot of a girl had not the slightest idea that her idiot boyfriend would actually do what he had threatened and it was all his daft idea, not hers," Ryan said, with rather more of a desire to harangue his unwelcome friend than any genuine sympathy for a damsel in distress.

"Can you do something as simple as that without making a mess of it?" he hissed. "I wonder. By the time you've worked out what to say they'll have throttled her and put her on the mortuary slab as well."

The Bogle appeared to have had a considerable infusion of competence since their parting, as, ignoring completely Ryan's jibe, it strode efficiently out into the centre of all the commotion, parting the little gaggle of gawping guests down the middle as if they were the red sea. Removing first Sergeant Throttler's clenched fist of a hand from the left lapel of Sharon's tattered denim jacket and then Father Delaney's from the right, the Bogle wrapped its arm protectively around the desperate girl and let her sob onto the comfort of its shoulder. It was then, just at the moment he was becoming impressed, that Ryan spotted the source of this super-confident handling of the situation - a flask of whiskey sticking out of its back pocket.

"I can assure you," the Bogle said with the conviction of Moses, "that this young lady had no intention of endangering her young feller's life whatsoever and that what he did was all his idea and nothing to do with her. She's twice as stricken by mortal grief as anyone can be - and three times as any of you. Now will you stop persecuting the child in search of a scapegoat and have the decency to offer her some consolation."

The whole assembled crowd was as taken aback as if John the Baptist had just come into their midst and told them of the Second Coming.

"Who in God's name are you?" Sergeant Throttler asked, recovering his normal fearsome composure somewhat.

"In God's name you might well ask," the Bogle replied and with a look that silenced any further intention to question it, led the young woman through the throng into the depths of the house. Alcohol-assisted its finest hour might have been, but even Ryan was by now impressed. The granny looked up at him accusingly. With the strange, seer's look that she had first greeted him, she said,

"Once more will you cast out your friend into the cold, and once more, death will follow. Once more a chance to pull your blackened soul back from the divil's grip will have been wasted."

"What do you mean?" Ryan asked. "How can you say these things?"

"I'm the seventh nun of a seventh nun," the granny replied and Ryan realised she'd been drinking as well.

With slow, heavy footsteps he climbed back up the stairs, dragged down by a dread of what the Bogle's return might foreshadow in the way of more disasters to dwarf no doubt all of those that had blighted his holiday so far. He had a deep suspicion that it and the granny were in some kind of a conspiracy to make him feel guilty for all the wrongs and woes of humanity for reasons he couldn't even begin to fathom. For that reason he decided he would try and avoid them both until his car was finally repaired and locking his door firmly for the night, resolved that he would take an early breakfast in the morning, before them both. He would then spend the day on a long walk to get as far away from them as possible and not return until they had hopefully finished their tea and wandered off, allowing him to have his in peace. The Bogle knocked quietly on his door at about half past eleven and asked if it could have a word, but Ryan feigned sleep and it went away.

At seven-thirty Ryan rose quickly and pausing only to check, squint eyed, on the brightness of the sun, slipped hurriedly downstairs to breakfast. Despite the fact that he had heard the Bogle snoring soundly through his bedroom wall as he left the room, he bolted his breakfast so quickly that he was in danger of choking. A deep feeling of dread came over him as the granny entered the breakfast room. He downed the remainder of his tea so fast half of it shot down the front of his shirt and then dragged himself hastily upright for an instant escape. She fixed him firmly with eyes that were as merciless as those of a hanging judge.

"I knew you would," she said.

"Knew I would what?" he asked.

"Leave your friend out in the cold," she replied.

"My friend, as you call him, has been left out cold by the whiskey, not by me," he said with an inventive dexterity that surprised him, given the time of the morning, "and I'm going out for a walk. We'll all be out granny, one way or another."

"Remember what I said last night," she said, "if there's no forgiveness or trust in your heart there will be terrible consequences for someone."

"If I don't get a decent walk today there'll be terrible consequences for my sanity," Ryan replied. With as much of a smile as he could muster, given that the granny was beginning to be about as welcome a presence as an Archbishop at an orgy, he slipped past her and out of the front door.

The morning was as fresh as an angel in a basket of clean linen. The sun drew shadows in the fields with the quiet skill of a master craftsman and the breeze played as gently with Ryan's hair as a curious kitten discovering for the first time a ball of wool. The further he went, the lighter his step became, until he believed himself almost to be walking on a cushion of blissful solitude. With his customary difficulty in considering sympathetically the fates of others he managed only the briefest of contemplations of how Sharon might be feeling after the trauma of the previous night. Then his mind automatically pressed the delete button and all thought of her was wiped from the hard disk between his ears for the rest of the day.

He followed tracks that seemed to be saved for one pair of human feet a week, leading him past abandoned cottages that hugged the secrets of their long dead owners quietly to their ruined walls and through fields of sheep that gave him less attention than the fleas that tickled their backs. He seemed to be entering a land where the mind and the near silence around him blended into a peaceful unity that previously he had only dreamt of.

It was a rude and cruel awakening, therefore, when he re-entered the little town at tea-time to find a battery of things he'd much rather had been the lot of someone else. The day, he was soon to feel, had been merely storing its disturbances for a single extravaganza, instead of liberally distributing them throughout itself as had been its preference during the past week.

The beginning of his troubles came when he realised that, in the distraction of the day's beauty, he'd still not worked out even half a solution to the problem of the Bogle and the granny, or the nature of their puzzling game. He'd arrived back earlier than intended and given the loud shouting inside his stomach for an urgent infusion of food and drink, wouldn't be able to avoid them at tea. He'd have to start working out a short term strategy as to how best to react to their joint strangeness extremely fast therefore.

As he approached the guest house, his feet suddenly started to feel as heavy as ships in mud and all the lightness of the day went from him. He saw a car pull up outside the house, from which the dour bulk of O'Rourke emerged. Beyond him, Lilly could be seen, determinedly struggling against the ravages of the arthritis that so clearly bit into her knees. As she reached the car she looked clearly annoyed by something.

"Mr. O'Rourke," Ryan heard her shout, "your boot isn't shut properly!"

Her tone, Ryan thought, was remarkably like that of the imperious Thatcher woman she so worshipped. An unclosed boot was an untidy boot and untidiness was not to be tolerated. She hit the lid feebly with her sadly gnarled hand, but in doing so, only caused it to fly open. She let out a scream that put to flight a previously idle cat and a good two gardenfuls of sparrows.

"Guns!" she shouted to the street, the sky and all the listening lamp-posts. "There's a murderer in our midst. This man has machine guns in his boot!"

O'Rourke, who had got as far as the front step of the O'Dredlin house before the outburst, looked remarkably like a man who'd just peered down below his waist having seen his trousers walking off in the opposite direction.

"You stay exactly where you are," she commanded, "I'm going to get Sergeant Throttler."

As she spoke the sergeant, home for his tea, had indeed wandered out to see what all the commotion was about. Unfortunately his attention was immediately grabbed by a little mound of earth on the tiny, pristine patch of land that counted as his front garden. He bounded back into the house instantly in search of his gun, issuing all kinds of curses, threats and insults in the general direction of small, furry tunnelling creatures.

"Sergeant!" Lilly shouted. "Come back, we've a murderer in the house. Come here at once!"

O'Rourke, who had been fingering something anxiously within his inside jacket pocket, clearly was getting close to the point of panic.

"One more word!" he yelled as he started to move hurriedly towards his car, the whole street now having come out to look. Lilly scuttled over to the driver's door before he could get to it, her knees nearly buckling under her with the effort.

"You're not going anywhere!" she informed him determinedly. "I have hold of the door handle and there's nothing you can do that will prise me off it."

"Get out of the way damn you, you stupid old woman!" O'Rourke hissed, pulling a pistol out of his pocket and sticking it in her chest.

"You won't frighten me with that," she said haughtily, "there's a whole street full of witnesses to anything you do."

"I'm telling you for the last time, get out of my way," he said desperately.

"Do as he says!" a neighbour shouted, before diving behind his hedge.

"I'll not budge!" Lilly yelled back determinedly. "Mr. Ryan, don't just stand there like a flag pole without a flag, go and find that useless policeman before this hooligan escapes."

Her words were followed instantly by a single gunshot and she crumpled like a raincoat that had fallen off its hanger. A startled mixture of screams and oohs and sighs went up from the street and Ryan stood inert and unmoving, possessed by a terror that was so great he couldn't take his eyes off the man with the gun. O'Rourke, mistaking his unshakeable gaze for a precursor to some uncharacteristically heroic act, pointed the gun straight at his head.

"Want yours as well do you, you gobshite Englishman?"

Another shot blasted through the air, followed by a cry of,

"I warned you, you horrible little furry git!"

To Ryan and everyone else's surprise, it was O'Rourke who lay dead on the tarmac, not him. True to Mrs. O'Dredlin's estimation of his aim, in trying to hit the elusive mole, Sergeant Throttler had shot the Dublin hit man clean through the heart. While Jimmy Murphy's (aka Seamus O'Rourke) original intention had been to lie low for a week or two in the middle of nowhere until a gangland feud had died down, he was now lying far lower than he had ever intended.

Within a minute of the second shot, the local GP and taxidermist, Dr. O'Donnell, had arrived and determined that Lilly had been wounded in the shoulder and might yet survive. As he stopped the bleeding and prepared her ready for the ambulance's arrival, Ryan, still in a state of shock, made his way through the crowd towards the guest house and determined to go upstairs and lie down. He had got no further than the gate when the granny collared him. She said,

"I warned you but you wouldn't listen. I can see these things you know."

"If you can see these things why didn't you warn Lilly?" Ryan snapped, stung out of his trance by the sharpness of her accusatory tone. "You didn't tell Lilly because you don't like her. That's right isn't it?"

"If your friend had been with you he'd have been able to stop it, you can't deny that."

"And where is 'my friend' that he wasn't able to stop it?" Ryan demanded.

"He's there," the granny said pointing over the dividing wall between the guest house and the next. Ryan peered over to see his strange ex-companion curled up like a baby in a flower bed, a bottle of empty unconsciousness beside him.

"That says it all doesn't it," Ryan laughed sarcastically, "O'Rourke's isn't the only corpse round here."

"He'd never have had the time to hit the bottle if he'd been with you," the granny insisted. "He was terrible offended when he saw you'd gone out without waiting even to have a word with him and spent the day getting drunk as a result."

"More like deeply grateful for the excuse rather than offended," Ryan replied. "That no good specimen is about as much use as a surgical truss made from spaghetti."

"There's not an ounce of compassion or mercy in your heart for the poor man," the granny said.

"Oh, I'd say that was something of an exaggeration," Ryan said, squeezing past her, "an ounce perhaps to balance the pound of contempt on the scales. I had enough of him and all his deranged magical ways some time ago. As far as I'm concerned he can go to hell."

As soon as he'd spoken the air around went strangely cold and a thick fog sprang up as if from out of the earth itself.

"Is that your last word on the subject?" the granny asked, her voice seeming to echo within the mist as if she were standing above some great, deep chasm.

"It is," Ryan replied curtly. "Now where the hell's the front door, I can't see a thing in this damn fog."

He had a sudden, strange feeling of being somewhere else and a definite impression that there was only himself, the unconscious Bogle and an unknown presence there. Of the granny there wasn't a sight or sound. As he flailed worriedly and blindly around with his outstretched hands, every hair on his head, his back and in places where previously he had never even suspected the presence of a follicle, stood on terrified end. There was the sound of slow, heavy, crunching footsteps, each one seeming to crush and crucify the very ground beneath it and a smell so vile that Ryan felt too bilious even to throw up. Whatever it was that he could hear passed very close to him, causing his body suddenly to feel painfully hot in the middle of the freezing chill of the mist. It walked a little beyond, paused as if to pick something up and then came back the same way, this time causing a cigar in Ryan's top pocket to catch light and start smoking itself with the heat as it passed. He stood completely still and terrified, hardly daring to release a single breath until the footsteps had faded into the distance.

Then, gradually, the mist began to clear and he could hear the sound of the crowd milling around the arriving ambulance. He was amazed to see a large hole in the wall over which he had recently bent to scrutinise the sleeping Bogle. Looking down, his blood turned almost to ice as he saw a series of claw prints burnt into the ground, one set going towards the wall and the other coming back from it. Peering over, he saw to his horror that the Bogle had been removed, the only evidence of its prior presence being its whiskey bottle, the label of which had been burnt so black it was unreadable.

"Yes, he's gone," a voice from behind said. Ryan turned round to face its owner, the granny.

"You were his last chance," she said, "and you rejected him. In showing him no forgiveness Mr. Ryan you condemned him to a life with the divil. Yes, you don't believe it, but your mercy would have been a lifeline for the poor unfortunate. When the good Lord came to make His final judgment on your friend's spiritual fate, he found that he had even spoilt his good deed for Sharon by thieving a half full bottle of whiskey out of Mrs. O'Dredlin's kitchen when she wasn't looking and drinking it like pop. So there was no-one who would say or pray a good word for him. Only you to say he should go to hell, so down he's gone, back with Old Nick for all eternity. God would have listened to even one plea for mercy... Forgiveness can be a wonderful, sparing thing Mr. Ryan, but it's in terrible short supply. I'm no perfect soul, but I know the state of the world."

Unsurprisingly, Ryan felt that his sanity had now completely gone. He could hardly take in the shootings of Lilly and O'Rourke, never mind the seizure of a delinquent ex-angel by the devil himself. Shaking his head in bewilderment, he started to walk unseeingly into the house, his mind as much a fog as the one in which he'd just been drowned. He'd gone no further than the hall when the granny shouted after him,

"I'm the only Bogle left on earth now - how are you going to treat me? Are you going to learn to forgive before there's no-one alive who'd want to forgive you?"

As he stopped dead in his tracks, he had a feeling that her words had just walked over his grave.

The night that followed was the most sleepless one he had ever experienced. At every turn of his restless body he heard an echo of the granny's words about forgiveness and the alleged burden of his guilt. On the one hand, he dismissed them as a nonsense devised by someone whose credibility had been shot to pieces already by her continual taunting of the dreadful Lilly and her admission that she was a Bogle. But on the other, images of all the people he'd chosen not to forgive in his life kept dancing through his mind like an ever recurring line of accusatory judges. Perhaps he was an intolerant man, perhaps he was even as selfish as the male Bogle had alleged, perhaps he was a completely different person to the one he'd always thought himself to be, somebody of such great unpleasantness that even he wouldn't want to meet his own person if he passed it in the street. Could he go on as he was, what on earth was it that he was? He had never thought about the nature of his own person in so much depth before and the experience was both unnerving and unwanted.

As his exhaustion grew, his thoughts switched to a limpet like focus on the fate of the male Bogle, seized from the middle of the helpless sleep he now so desperately desired for himself and dragged unconscious and un-warned down into the bowels of hell. Was it really his fault that such a thing had happened given all of the drunken and other excesses of the creature - and did it even happen? Was the whole episode simply an illusion, the result of some hideous insanity on his own part that gradually was eating away his mind? And what of the granny, how could she be a Bogle as she claimed if she had given birth to mere mortals and one apparently so God-fearing and sober as Mrs. O'Dredlin? And if she wasn't a Bogle how could he take the need for any of this soul searching so seriously?

The more questions he asked the more confused he became, until he reached a point where he shouted, "Will all these thoughts not leave me alone, what is it I have to do to get a good night's sleep?"

"Well, for a start, why not promise to turn over a new leaf and be a kinder and more considerate man from now on?" a little whispered voice said in his ear.

Startled, Ryan sat bolt upright, expecting to see heavens knows what in the bed beside him, but there was nothing. The only possible source of the whisper seemed to be the wall against which the bed sat and walls, as any sane individual well knows, are not in the habit of whispering. He assumed he must simply have imagined the little voice as a result of his desperately tired state and lay back down on the bed, his mind still a whirl of unstoppable, nagging thoughts. But then it happened again. The little voice whispered,

"Try it, just promise what I said and you'll find you can sleep like the proverbial log."

Ryan dragged himself back up to a sitting position, but could see nothing in the room that could account for the voice. Out of tired, half-demented desperation more than anything else and with no genuine sense of conviction he shouted,

"Alright! I will be these things!"

"Thank God for that," the wall replied, "I'm just about at me wits end with all these hours and hours of yer agonising."

Isolated phantom whispers were one thing, walls that engaged in intelligent conversation were entirely another.

"What's that?" Ryan said, pinching himself and finding, alarmingly, that the pain was very much that of the real and waking world.

"I'm exhausted," the wall went on, "your thoughts were so impossibly addled that the business of unscrambling them has fuddled me own brain."

"Who are you?" Ryan asked.

"I'm the wall of course," the wall replied, "are you losing even the ability to remember who it is you're speaking to in the middle of a conversation?"

"Walls do not normally reply to those who talk to them," Ryan pointed out firmly.

"Always the same, always the same," the wall replied, "when people talk to a wall and it doesn't reply they complain, when it does reply they complain. All a wall hears from morning to night is blasted complaints."

"I know that voice," Ryan said.

"Well that makes two of us as so do I," the wall replied.

"You're the bl..."

"That's right, the bloody Bogle!" the wall replied, instantly bursting out of itself and leaping into the centre of the room in a blaze of light and plaster dust. Transforming itself simultaneously from masonry back to the familiar alcohol bloated shape that Ryan had come so much to dread, it pulled a bottle from its back pocket, took a swig that was so disgusting in its accompanying sound effects that it would have made a pig blush and sat down on the bed edge.

"So all that stuff about you being carted off by the devil was just another party trick," Ryan said angrily.

"You could say that," the Bogle replied, "but as highly effective a trick as ever you'll see. After all, haven't you finally seen yer deepest faults and made up yer mind to do something about them? And doesn't that mean that me job with you is finally done? D'you know, you're me first success. A couple more punters like yerself and I'll be halfway back to heaven."

The Bogle took another self-congratulatory swig. Ryan, who by now had steam scorching out of both ears, grabbed the bottle from it and emptied the remaining dregs onto the potted geranium on the bedside table. Then, grabbing hold of the neck, he rolled back the bedclothes and raised himself to his full six feet. The Bogle looked decidedly concerned.

"Why are you looking at me like that?" it asked. "And what's the business with the bottle?"

"The look is to decide how many lumps I can fit onto the top of your head if you don't get out of me room and leave me alone forever," Ryan replied, "and the bottle is for putting each in its allotted place. I'd rather like to have an equal balance of bumps on each side of your bonce. For neatness' sake you understand."

"Now wait a minute," the Bogle said, "all me deceptions were very much for the best from both our points of view. Haven't I put you half way further down the road towards the saving of your soul than Father Delaney could dream of doing in a hundred years? And what about the promise you've just made to be a new and forgiving person?"

"I was lying through my teeth, I didn't mean it," Ryan replied, raising the bottle with determined intent and eyebrows so fiercely concentrated on the task in hand that they met in the middle and became as one. The Bogle edged its way down to the end of the bed, where it was within fleeing distance of the door.

"You know I could turn that bottle into useless powder in your hand if I wanted to?" it said.

"I'm sure you could," Ryan said, "but with the amount of drink you've downed from its innards I greatly doubt if you can remember how to do it."

"I'm warning you, don't provoke me," it said. By way of reply Ryan dealt it a smart blow on the crown.

"There, I've just provoked you," he replied, "and now I'm going to provoke you and provoke you and provoke you until you're so provoked you'll never dream of provoking me again!"

As each use of the provoking word 'provoke' was accompanied by an attempt to imprint a succession of bumps on the Bogle's head, the dodging of which made it even harder for it to concentrate on how to disintegrate the offending bottle, it decided the best course of action was to make a run for it before its brain ended up in its boots. The cumulative effect of Ryan's experiences had clearly left the man deranged. Screaming blue murder and several other colours of terminal violence besides, it shot down the staircase and out the front door, with a wildly roaring, bottle-flailing Ryan hot on its heels. Mrs. O'Dredlin, who had been sitting downstairs unable to sleep after the day's events, ran out after them to see what was going on.

"Mr. Ryan!" she yelled. "What are you doing? Hasn't there been enough violence in this street for one day?"

As she spoke, Sergeant Throttler stepped out into his front garden, gun in hand, to see what was going on.

"Is that yet another murderous swine you're putting up in your house?" he shouted by way of enquiry after Mrs. O'Dredlin. Before she could reply his eyes fixed manically on a small, furry head that had just popped out of a mound in the low glare of a streetlamp. With a vengeful fury he took immediate aim. Seeing the disaster about to happen, Mrs. O'Dredlin screamed at him,

"For God's sake Sergeant, please, no!"

Her words were followed by the crash of a single gunshot. Ryan crumpled to the ground, the bottle smashing hopelessly on the pavement beside him.

An awful silence ensued, which was succeeded by a quiet hubbub as people came out of their houses and stood staring with Mrs. O'Dredlin at the second corpse of the night. Dermot, his dressing gown the wrong way round in his hurry to get out, said,

"Now isn't that the very man dead I was discussing death with only yesterday, or the day before. How strange a thing is life."

"The life's gone from him you deranged example of verbosity gone mad," Father Delaney interjected, having run from the parochial house like a man with his arse on fire, as, considering the friction generated within his chastity belt, it most probably was.

As the priest administered quickly the last rites in the hope that Ryan's soul wasn't too far away already to hear them, Sergeant Throttler began taking a statement from himself on the nature of the killing.

"The strangest thing about death," Dermot went on, oblivious to the priest's hostility, "is that when you see it in its most common form, the body still intact in all its externals, it's impossible to believe in it. No matter how I look at this man's obvious decease, I can't for a minute believe that he's dead. It doesn't make sense, to be one minute and not be the next. It goes against the whole point of someone being created. Who would create simply to destroy? There's no point in sobbin' Mrs. O'Dredlin, Ryan's not dead. It's just that we can't find him in his body."

"It's because I can't find him in his body that I'm weeping you eejit!" she yelled, bringing matters back down to immediate practicalities.

The Bogle meanwhile, seeing her distraught tears that yet another death in the space of two days had occasioned, was feeling extremely uncomfortable. To make matters worse, it was certain that the mishap of Ryan's death, in the middle of a possibly mortal sin, was going to be a considerable setback in its quest to regain its angelic wings. God might well hold it at the very least jointly responsible with the incompetent policeman. At best, like the granny, the only other Bogle in existence, it could end up with a sentence of having to live seventy of its years as a human being, stripped of all its angelic powers other than second sight. Something most definitely was needed to save it from that. It was then a familiar voice said,

"Are you a Bogle or a mouse, can you not see that there's a drop of life in the feller while you stand there losing your mind with useless thoughts?"

Startled by the fierceness of the intervention, the Bogle found itself looking down into the eyes of the granny herself. She continued,

"If you intend getting your wings back you haven't a hope in hell – very literally – if you let this eejit die in a state of mortal sin. It's about time you pulled your finger out and started reviving him."

"You're right, of course you're right," it said, "if only I can remember the Angel's prayer for deliverance from death, that will do the trick."

"You'll only recover the memory of how to do it if you do penance first for your own state of darkness and sin," the granny said. "Believe me, I know these things."

"What – there isn't time, with all the bottles that I've been knocking back it would take six months in a hair shirt before I'd made up for even half of me sins. The man will be long in his grave by then."

"Stop your panicking and use your loaf," the granny instructed. "Do a quick penance now as a deposit and then make a firm promise to do all the rest after the poor feller here is pulled back from the jaws of death."

"Are you sure that will work?" the Bogle asked.

"Isn't the good Lord a merciful being?" the granny said. "Of course it will work, but God help you if you make the down payment and renege on the rest of the debt."

"But what can I do as a quickie penance, me mind's a blank?" the Bogle asked, still full of panic.

"Oh for heaven's sake, use your imagination," the granny said. "Look, here, I'll put me handbag on the ground – now, dance ten times round it waving your hands in the air and make a complete arse of yourself. That will do for now – the humiliation will be good for your soul and the words will come back between your ears and Bob's your uncle, your man should rise from the ground and save both your bacons."

She laid a handbag the size of six normal handbags on the ground and after a moment's dread and fearful anticipation the Bogle began to do as instructed. The onlookers gasped in surprise, amazement and fierce disapproval at such inappropriate behaviour on the occasion of an apparent decease and began hurling abuse and mockery at the manically dancing strangeness before them. Being naturally clumsy the Bogle managed no more than eight circuits of the bag before it managed to trip over the thing. Simultaneously the strain that the leaping around had caused to its already threadbare braces caused them to snap. Like a felled tree it toppled onto the granny and pinned her to the ground with its trousers round its ankles. Seeing the most unholy spectacle in front of him Father Delaney roared with anger,

"Sacrilege, profanity and irreverence in the presence of a soul deceased, all wrapped together and parcelled neatly in one man! It's a Delaney chastity belt for your heathen vitals whoever you are and I'm taking you for a fitting before your loins explode with the fire of your lusts!"

He grabbed the startled Bogle by the scruff of its neck and hauled it upright and it was at that moment that the words of the prayer came back to it. It shouted them to the heavens with its arms outstretched. Instantly there was a sudden and deep exhalation from Ryan as if spewing out water after a drowning and his eyes opened like lights in the dark depths of the ocean.

"In the name of all the saints it's a miracle!" an astonished Mrs. O'Dredlin declared. Dr. O'Donnell, whose leisure time hobby of taxidermy had been leading him to fanciful thoughts about stuffing and displaying as a curiosity the first man in history to be shot by a bullet aimed at a mole, gasped in harmony with her surprise. He said,

"The path of that bullet was so malign it would have killed any normal man within a minute or two of the hit, yet the exit hole in his back has healed so much you'd think he'd been no more than bitten by a flea. In all me years of curing, burying and stuffing things I've never seen anything like it!"

The granny tapped the baffled Father Delaney on the shoulder and said,

"I'll take charge of that man if you don't mind. It was his kind words that pulled Mr. Ryan's soul back from the edge of the abyss while you were too preoccupied with your misreading of the state of his trousers to do anything useful at all."

She unhooked the priest's hand from the Bogle's collar and removed her charge to a place of safety, sitting on Mrs. O'Dredlin's garden wall while she busily repaired the connection between the braces and his trouser waist. She said,

"We'll leave them be for a minute or two while they try and work out what on earth happened. For a useless delinquent of a half fallen angel you've finally made something of yourself that will do both of us a bit of good – me for galvanising you into action and you for saving an eejit from dying in a state of mortal sin and disgrace. Keep this type of behaviour up and you might actually get your full angel wings back - and I'll be well on the way to getting at least half of me own powers back as well, what you might call a win-win situation."

Ryan had pulled himself upright and was trying to take in the contradiction between the vast bloodstain on his shirt and the now almost complete lack of physical evidence of his ever being shot. Sergeant Throttler simultaneously was in a state of fury at the unanticipated need for him to completely rewrite his statement and the difficulty of reconciling his previous account of the mortally slain Ryan with the very much alive body of the allegedly deceased that now confronted him. Having reattached the Bogle's trousers to the remains of the braces so firmly that the waistband now sat just below the nipples, the granny pushed her way through the crowd to the bemused centre of its attention. She said,

"Now then Mr. Ryan, it's time that we had a little word. Make way everyone, make way, this gentleman has had a nasty fright and needs a good sit down and a nice cup of tea away from all your prying and curious eyes. I'm taking him back into the house. He'll speak to you all soon enough when he's had time to recover and work out what exactly it is that's happened. And as for you and that eejit deadliness that passes for a gun sergeant it would be better if you pointed it at that pigeon up on Mrs. O'Dredlin's chimney – the only thing you'd hit would be yourself and we'd all be a lot safer as a result."

With her usual mixture of brusqueness and adroitness the granny propelled the still shell shocked Ryan into Mrs.

O'Dredlin's pristine breakfast room and sat him firmly down in a chair. Seating herself so close her nose nearly met his tip to tip she said,

"It's time that you and me had a little talk, because if you don't listen to what I've got to tell you there'll be no second chances - the next time that eejit policeman or any number of possible diseases or other disasters comes along to catapult you from this world into the next that will be it. If you go out with a blot the size of a mountain on your copy book then you'll be looking to meet the feller down below and all his accumulated nightmare friends from Hitler to Vlad the Impaler – and you can imagine what fun that little lot would have at your expense, do you get me drift?"

Ryan nodded, suitably terrified, the bloodstained shirt all the while reminding him of how near he had come to a one to one with the Grim Reaper.

"So," the granny continued, "are we agreed that this mad, demented temper of yours is something you're going to bring under control, that your criminal disregard for the lives of others with all your madcap driving is something that will cease now and forever - and that you're going to start being a little less self-obsessed with all of your interests at the expense of everyone else's?"

Ryan thought hard on the matter for a full minute before replying, during which time the granny's eyebrows became raised more and more as each second passed, until they seemed in mortal danger of passing right over the top of her head and travelling down to the back of her neck. At length he said,

"I could give all sorts of vacuous promises while the memory of what's just happened is fresh in my mind. But the truth is that when I go back home, go back to work, I'd be the only one not thinking of myself and that would just make me prey for all the predators around me. The whole culture I work in and indeed of much of the country, as well as other countries around the world, whatever, is dog eat dog and if the cat's available the first one who can will scoff that as well. There's a surface courtesy and kindness that survives, but you've only got to drive down the brutality of a motorway to see how skin deep all of that is. That's why I drive the way I do, I'm simply playing by the rules of the game as everyone like me plays it. You can't come the meek and mild stuff if you want to hold on to your nads. So how am I supposed to change my ways when the result would be the same as lying down in front of a steam roller?"

"One word," the granny replied, "one word, a simple word as simple as meself changes everything and that word is courage – the courage to be different and the courage to be kind. Stand up to the Rottweiler's by all means, there's no need to be a dog's dinner, but you don't have to be *like* them. They're the ones on the slow escalator to the divil's kitchen and when they've finished trying to gobble up all of the weak he'll haul them on to his chopping board and gobble them in turn. I know these things, I've very nearly ended up on it meself for all me past and present failings. Look, I freely admit it, you're getting a lecture on the need to be saintly from someone who's far from being a saint, particularly in the way I lose my cool over that Lilly woman. I've even been demoted from the role of bog standard angel to bog standard human on account of me past deficiencies – and in giving you this advice I have to admit that the act of so doing will benefit me as much as you in the way of spiritual brownie points and things. But what I'm telling you is the truth and if you kick it aside as soon as you get back to work you might just as well stick your head in a vat of boiling custard and serve yourself up for tea – because that's what the divil will do if he gets his hands on you and no mistake."

Having promised to carefully think over what the granny had said Ryan escaped up the staircase. After changing his shirt he lay down on his bed to recover from all the strange shocks and surprises that had befallen him in the last few hours or so. He mulled over what she had told him, together with the bizarre accidental shooting and his apparently miraculous recovery and with a sad predictability, began to make an alternative reality out of these various events within the narrow confines of his self-centred mind.

The more he thought about it the more the granny was simply barking mad. Her manner was eccentric at the best of times and there was little reason for him to take anything that she said seriously. The most sensible thing to do was to put her out of his mind entirely and concentrate on the other events. Whatever the

Bogle might or mightn't be, it had certainly been a source of annoyance and frustration to him and he felt no guilt at all at having lost his temper with it. If he had been so wrong in his lashing out at its latest outrageous provocation, and if his adrenaline fuelled driving habits and his 'logical and natural' tendency to always put his own interests first were so wrong, then why had he been thought worth snatching from the jaws of death and repairing as good as new? Such a feat could only have been performed by powers far greater than the Bogle - and the granny's characteristically mad supposition that it had all been down to such a strange and lunatic creature was clearly as off the wall as everything else she came out with. No, some great force of destiny had decided that he was something *special*, a man worth preserving over all others and it was for that reason alone he had been brought back from the apparently dead. It was a vindication of everything about him and not, as the granny had suggested, a second chance for a man lost in the depths of some great sin. He had a mission and nothing of what he had seen, or felt or heard suggested that he was a man in need of any great reform. Such a man needed to get back to his normal life as soon as possible, given the importance of its every detail that his dramatic return from near death must surely show. He resolved to head for Dublin first thing in the morning and get the earliest ferry back to England that he could. He needed to get on with his existence as before, not change it, to wait for the dramatic moment when his great purpose in life – some kind of leadership role perhaps – would be revealed. This was something that would set him apart from all of his rivals in the office, the pack of wannabees that clawed at and competed with him on a daily basis to fight their ways up the greasy pole to the top. He was the chosen one, a man of destiny, a great role model for the ambitious everywhere, in every company and every country, whatever – maybe, even, he had been spared and set apart to become one of the great business *'thought leaders'* of the twenty-first century?

The morning was exceptionally damp, with banks of fog that came and went in a random and dangerous fashion. Having gobbled a quick breakfast and paid both Mrs. O'Dredlin's bill and that of her brother, the garage man, who, as promised, had the now fully repaired car ready for collection, he set off to Dublin.

He had to cut their curiosity and concern as to his well being brutally short in order to have a chance of making it to the boat on time. Having noted that he should just make the one ferry with car spaces left if he drove like the clappers, he shot off at a speed that would have turned the face of a ghost as white as the proverbial sheet.

He had been driving flat out for an hour, with his customary disregard for anyone else's life or limbs, when he came to a bend at the same time as a bank of thick fog slid over the road from the waterlogged banks of the nearby river. He slowed down a little, perhaps half as much as a wiser man would have done and ploughed on into the bend. Unfortunately, what he couldn't see within the fog was the shivering midwife wobbling along on her bike on the other side of the road. She in turn couldn't see or be seen by the battle tank of a pantechnicon lorry that was ploughing forwards with equally unwise determination behind her. At the very last minute the driver of the hurtling lorry spotted the cyclist's feeble rear lamp and swerved to avoid her. At precisely the same moment Ryan shot forwards from the opposite direction. He met the lorry head on, with the result that his newly reassembled car was instantly disassembled into so many different pieces and parts that the scattered mess looked more like a do it yourself vehicle assembly kit than anything else. Simultaneously, the recently resurrected Ryan was for a second time hurled without warning from this life towards the next. At the same moment precisely the granny sat bolt upright in the armchair in which previously she'd been slumbering. She let out a strangled cry and as she did Ryan's final breath left his lips. A single thought seized hold of her brain and sat between her ears with a grim and grievous certainty. His second chance had been and his second chance had gone.

"What an eejit," she sighed, "to drive like a criminal madman after everything I said and to succumb to the sin of pride, to have been given two chances and to have squandered both. And there's the divil's meeter and greeter, all confused, writing Ryan's name in his little book, then having to rub it out again, only to find he has to put it back all over again and claim his man. What a way to end one life and begin a new one, the wrong one, down in the dark and the depths of the land of despair."

Intermission 1

The end of Jimmy's story was greeted with tears, sighs and subdued laughter all mixed in and the reddest shirt on Mullahy's rock and its owner took a bow that blended grandeur, humility and self-mockery as if they were one. When the applause had died down he smiled and waved and then slipped deftly away, leaving the audience to chatter among themselves about the good and the bad points - and those in between - of his performance. Ben and Liam had each been taking notes, with Ben typing vigorously into his iPad while Liam, who preferred his own digits to all things digital, had used them to write furiously in a notebook of a more traditional kind. Sean, anxious not to be seen to be advantaging either one of them over the other, kept his own counsel, making purely mental notes on all that he'd seen and heard. While their bets would win one of them the land, his, he hoped, would win him enough to cover the cost of the two new tyres that would be shortly due for the van.

Ben turned to him and said,

"It's someone called Pattie Gleeson next – what do you know about her Uncle Sean? Are there things to look for in the way she performs that might make her stand out from the rest?"

"That there are," Sean replied, being careful to address Liam as well. "Pattie likes the big surprise and the sting in the tail of the tale, if you see what I mean. She's strong on the old human frailty, particularly the gullibility that allows crooks, charlatans and the dangerously mad to take control of things and wreck the lives of the innocent. Whether it's a more traditional style of tale or something entirely new she chooses it'll generally be one that has all of that at its core, one way or the other. What else can I say about her – well, she likes a tale with strong women and they can be the good, the bad, the sad or the mad. Like Jimmy, she has a fondness for the comic tale with a very dark edge – and even a bit of the old bawdiness here and there. She's a commanding presence as they say and she'll hold onto the audience's eyes and minds as if they belong to her. You'll see what I mean by that for yourselves – she's just come into the tent at the back there."

After a few quick words with Fierce Betty, Pattie walked up to the front of the stage and briefly surveyed the audience like a captain inspecting her crew. She was a handsome woman of forty, with the face of an adult in which the stage-struck child still shone through. Her eyes were knowing and her lips betrayed just the hint of a mischievous smile. At five feet six, her slim frame was hugged by denim, a deliberately anonymous choice of cloth to minimise any distraction from the tales she told. Her auburn hair was cut close to the shape of her head and gave her a slightly elfin look, a not unhelpful feature for a teller of tales. As the spotlight was switched on again, ready for her to begin, it brought out to full and startling effect the sea blue brilliance of her arresting gaze. While Fierce Betty introduced her she turned and stood with her head down and her back to the audience, as if she were a magic doll waiting to come to life. Then, the instant Betty said her last she spun round, snapped her head up and seized the attention of all with the sheer musical power of her voice. It was an instrument that, through some canny, intuitive means, powered her words in such a way that they spoke not to but directly within the minds of each. It was an effect that was both mesmerising and almost impossible to describe adequately and Ben and Liam understood instantly what Sean had meant when he'd said she was a 'commanding' presence. She said,

"Hello everyone old and young, it's good to see you here in this magical little space where dreams are conjured out of the air and the possible and impossible leap into life as if they'd always been here. I'm going to wave my wand and wish into existence a little town and all its folk and the tale of a very strange and disturbing thing that happened there, something so ridiculous that it was as comical as frightening and a warning to anyone who might be tempted by superstitions or cults, or anything that's a little too much away with the fairies. It's a warning also to all the ladies present to be as beware of powerful women as they are of commanding men – the temptations of hubris take no account of gender, race or age - and a warning also never to take too much notice of what a feller says when he whispers in your ear. If those ears are of a delicate nature then I should further warn you that one of the characters is much prone to crudities. If he in any ways causes offence you have only to ask and I will provide everyone here with personal earplugs and a warning whenever he is about to speak so that you can stick them in…

The title of the tale is *The Woman with a Man in Her Hat*, so fasten your seatbelts and get ready to be surprised, amused, appalled and fritted out of your wits as we go deep into the exotic world of Kenmullough, a little town that thinks it's a village, one that you won't have heard of before - and never will again…"

The Woman with a Man in Her Hat

Pattie Gleeson's Tale

"Like a drum or a thump or a bang or a clang, the one clog kicking is a sound to astound," the impressively sphinx-like Mairead pronounced enigmatically. Her tone was as prophetically weighty as one might expect from the seventh nun of a seventh son.

"You say the same thing every day at the same hour in the same place. But you never tell us what it means Mairead", said devout and devoted middle-aged Angela, who had had two bunions and a wart cured since she had started following the prophetess in her daily wanderings in the low mist of the hills above the pastel riot of the streets of Kenmullough.

"It means what it means and the meaning is hidden within the meaning. My words are a labyrinth and my soul the key to the way in – and the way out," Mairead replied.

"That it may be, but it's a bit of a bollix if the locks are both a combination kind of device is it not?" Padraig said innocently. "You'll need a code not a key if they are."

"Be quiet Padraig!" Christine, his thunderstorm of a woman

hissed.

Padraig, the doubting Thomas to the utter certainty of his fiercely all-believing spouse, had been dragged along compulsorily 'for his own good' on their day off. They ran a tea shop in the little town that hid prettily below the mist that soaked them. His irrepressible wit made him an extreme insurance liability in the eyes of all those who encountered the terminal sternness of his most holy of wives, and Dr. O'Brien, with whom he would share the occasional medicinal whiskey, knocked a further three months off his estimated life expectancy every time he heard him crack another irreverent joke within range of her pious ears. Indeed, on one memorable occasion, he'd actually started writing the death certificate for the poor man after the devout Christine had overheard a particularly unfortunate joke involving two fraud bishops and a horse's arse.

"Tell us Mairead, what is it you see in those long silences, those times you go off into a trance?" the all-trusting Angela asked.

"I see what I see, and what I've seen has never been seen by any seer but me. My thoughts are bathed in the deep mystery of revelation and my soul alone ..."

"Is the key - or the combination number perhaps?" Padraig volunteered.

"Yes," Mairead replied with a hiss, casting a glance that would have exploded the Blarney stone from fifty feet had she not as good as swallowed the whole damn thing already.

"So, if your soul is this key kind of a thing, you'll be able to unlock the whole shebang and tell us straight away precisely what it is that all these great mysteries of the universe are about," Padraig said.

Mairead had a sudden and prolonged coughing fit, during which conversation was impossible. Padraig had noticed earlier in this farcical afternoon how tricky questions could bring on such uncontrollable exhalations, but that their conclusion usually coincided miraculously with the provision of an answer. Often not a very sensible one, or an answer that made any sense at all. Sometimes he wished *he'd* been senseless at the moment she opened her prophetical mouth to murder the very idea of sense in the most senseless assortment of words. Sense, indeed, was becoming an obsession for him.

"My words can only be unlocked by other minds if the soul of their owner has fused with mine in the grand catastrophe of hidden vision," Mairead replied.

"I'm going to have a catastrophe in me pants if she doesn't stop talkin' such utter bollix," Padraig whispered into his shirt collar. The fierceness that was his other half gave him a swift clip over the ear that sent his little golden glasses so far down to the tip of his thin nose that it looked as if they were about to leap off and make an end of things.

With a sudden air of urgency Mairead said,

"Wait, the angel of enlightenment is coming down to me. Please, be silent. I need complete peace and quiet to hear his words."

"Is he comin' on the end of a parachute d'you think, or hitching a lift on a flyin' pig?" Padraig whispered, provoking a sharp kick in the shin from Christine as a reward for his curiosity.

A due hush fell upon the little group. Mairead suddenly cried out ecstatically,

"Oh, great one, welcome. Reveal to me what it is I need to hear."

"Thruuuuuuuuumph!"

Mischief and impatience with 'such nonsense' had led Padraig to cast upon the unprepared ears of the little throng a fart of such enormity that even a corpse six feet under would have needed ear plugs not to have heard it.

Everyone turned and bathed him in a collective glare so hotly fierce that he had to look down to make sure that his trousers weren't on fire. Christine grabbed the scruff of his neck, marched him over to a nearby tree as if he were a small boy, and told him to wait there and behave himself until it was all over.

Mairead continued,

"I see a tree... and a candle, I can feel the heat from a candle behind me..."

"No, not a candle in sight, it's just the hot air from talkin' out of your arse," Padraig muttered, a little too loudly for his own well-being.

"It is the tree of life," the prophetess said, "lit by the light of a Pentecostal flame. I can see before me all the threads of the universe, as if they were unravelling down from the hem of the holy mother of God herself."

"Can you hear anything Mairead?" Christine asked, excited.

For Padraig, this was all too much. If they wanted to hear something then hear something they would. Being of farming stock he could imitate with ease the mating call of a duck or the lament of a sheep bereft of a mate, or, indeed, any animal that an unwitting innocent might unwisely choose to name. Slipping quietly behind the tree he unleashed a startlingly believable reproduction of the coital growls and grunting of a randy gorilla with an uncontrollable flatulence problem. The precision and volume of his complex performance would have made it heard from the top of the hill to the bottom, had there been sufficient pairs of ears around to do the listening required.

Christine, recognising instantly a party trick that she had heard too many times ever to forget, turned with the ferocity of an underfed Rottweiler on a particularly bad hair day and stalked towards him, her prayer hands clenched into a boxer's fists. Deciding that a tactical withdrawal was his sole chance of survival he held up the car keys and said,

"I have me keys and I have me feet, and one will take the other over to me little rust heap where I shall wait until the visionary of Kenmullough has finished her soliloquy to the angels."

With that he fled. Christine stopped reluctantly in her tracks as her quarry made off over the fence and headed back towards the roadway. There would have been nothing quite like a good slap on the chops to knock the heathen out of her excuse for a man. Mairead, meanwhile, had fallen on her knees in a posture appropriate to that of an ecstatic visionary on a hotline to heaven.

"Oh glorious angel, what is the meaning of this great vision? Look he's beckoning me towards him, it's too much for my poor heart, I must go with him."

Heaving her great bulk upwards with an agility greatly impressive for the possessor of such a poor heart, Mairead trotted forwards in the wake of the invisible angel. Unfortunately, her ecstatic posture of arms stretched out and head raised upwards, as if she could see the heavenly being floating above, was not conducive to the spotting of such earthly inconveniences as the common cowpat. In no more than the twitching of an eye she flew arse over elbow and crashed face down into a collection of the things, which seemed strangely to have gathered together as if in need of companionship.

"Holy shit!" she muttered to herself, in an appropriate if un-prophet like commentary on her fate.

And that was how, on a mellow day in fair September, Padraig Maloney first encountered the passion that was to kill. From this most ridiculous of beginnings the cult of the prophet Mairead (an ex-nun defrocked officially on the grounds of heresy and unofficially on the grounds of idiocy) gained a few fatuous followers and seemed unlikely ever to progress beyond the small club of their collective naivety. But then the grand joker, fate in search of an eejit to lead a herd of the daft, stepped in with both of its enormous feet at once...

The local parish priest was a sane man of advancing years. After seeing the bizarre effect the little cult was having on some of its more gullible followers he decided reluctantly that he must denounce it from his Sunday pulpit and as good as ban it. Having obtained the approval of the bishop, he duly delivered a sermon on the foolishness of heresy. No sooner had his last word of measured condemnation been spoken, than the mad prophetess rose up out of her pew and stormed over to confront him at the foot of the pulpit. Spitting teeth like a machine gun, she called him the very son of the divil's own son and cursed his feet, his ears, the hairs on his bottom and the mole on the end of his nose. She ranted that he'd as good as threatened the personal representative on earth of the Virgin Mary with the bell, book and candle of excommunication and that if he ever tried it again she'd belt him with the book, shove the bell up his jumper and stick the candle very forcibly where the sun never shines. She screamed a command that he should be struck down dead on the spot for his nasturtiums, a word which those trying gamely to look for sanity in her outburst misheard as the rather more appropriate 'aspersions'. Having a weak heart and a nervous disposition, he duly obliged, as any sick man or woman confronted with such a fearsome ogre might. From that moment on, the prophetess was a woman of power in the eyes of the easily led, a transformation that left the doubting Padraig in a very tricky position.

It needed only one more miraculous event for her to be

declared a saint in the eyes of the most credulous of those around and such an event of course occurred. Driving home from his brother's on the other side of the bay one night, Padraig skidded on a patch of black ice and flew wildly off the road into a field full of goats. The whole event was seen by a young boy who was bicycling home on the other side of the road. Once his aunt, who had been following some way behind in her Jeep, had plied him with promises of enough food and other treats to sink seven battleships seven times and more, he seemed to have become aware of a lot more than originally had met his eye. It was a mere coincidence that the expander of his story, his aunt, was the good Mairead.

It appeared, in the enhanced version of events, that Padraig's car had flown too fast around the bend and had been coming straight for the boy when he cried out Mairead's name in a desperate cry for the help of a prophetess. As soon as he'd done so, a brilliant shaft of light appeared between himself and the car when it was no more than a yard away from the end of his nose. An angel stood at the heart of the beam, and with a single sweep of its hand, cast the car sideways into the field and stopped it from most certainly having killed him. No matter how many times he was asked about the story and by whom, the locum parish priest or the local guards, little Michael stuck to it religiously.

The temperature having risen a good five degrees during the early morning after the event, there was of course no sign of the black ice that Padraig so vehemently and correctly claimed had been the real cause of his near demise. Incredulously, he found himself being formally warned by the guards on the other side of the bay about the near lethal carelessness of his driving, and was, he felt, saved from prosecution only by the difficulty of getting an angel to give evidence in court. But, given the marked inability of the goats to provide testimony on Padraig's behalf, Michael's story was enough to convict him in the eyes of Mairead's expanding bunch of local followers. He was seen not only as an outsider in his rejection of her ludicrous claims as a prophet, but also to be morally derelict, as now was evidenced by his near slaughter of an innocent. Worst of all, from his point of view, his was the 'crime' that had been the occasion of the second demonstration of her divinely inspired powers. It was at this point, seeing the careful, opportunistic calculation involved in his fall from limited grace to none at all, that Padraig realised he was dealing with someone who was rather more compos mentis than he had first allowed.

There followed thereafter a series of claims of cures and miraculous visions associated with the prophetess, none of which would have stood up to any rigorous enquiry and which would most certainly have failed every test used at Lourdes. Given that Mairead wisely ensured that any enquiries that were made by the populist press or others in need of a sale or two were conducted on her terms alone, there was little danger of any such rigour being applied. Accordingly, some of those who lived in the hope of being witnesses to a miracle for this reason or that, both good and bad, holy or self-serving, and who had found disappointment at Knock or Lourdes, or in the long penitential traipse up Croagh Patrick, now switched their hope and their allegiance to the cult of the Prophetess. Given her mixing in with her heady brew of quasi religion a strong dose of politics that was so far to the right that it almost met the left at the other extreme, she was able to attract also a sufficient number of the bangers of heads to ensure that those who voiced their criticism of what she was doing always came to feel, in retrospect, that perhaps their words were not quite as wisely chosen as they might have been.

She included within her brew sufficient Christianity to allow her followers to feel that their feet at least remained on enough familiar ground for them to be safe, while blending in with it a variety of strange fantasies involving angels and personal messages from God. Many of these ultimately seemed to invite her followers to donate or 'loan' significant funds to facilitate the missionary work of Mairead the Blessed. Those who had done their sums with the devotion of an accountant might have concluded that Mairead must have intended to take her mission to the four corners of the earth while driving a Mercedes and quaffing crates of champagne, so great were the sums aspired to. But it is not the part of the teller of this tale to cast doubts upon the merits of her vocation by indulging in such speculative thoughts herself. And given that she is a notable coward anyway, she would hardly dare do so, just in case a head banger or two remains loyal to Mairead's cause still and is prepared to make something of it.

For Padraig all of this was not good news. With each new claim of a miracle the faith in the Prophetess of his verbal assassin of a wife doubled and his own complete lack of belief became more of a barrier between them. He found it wise to be as little around the house as possible, and when he could not avoid being at home, to ensure that he always had something to do in a room in which his good wife was not. All of this came to a head, however, after he had decided to take a bath, and had, in good faith, left all of his clothing in the bedroom, save the towel that he wrapped round his waist to protect his modesty from the baleful gaze of the cat. On returning to the bedroom cleansed and refreshed, he found that, in his absence, a plague of cloth eating locusts seemed to have been through every garment that did not have a female shape and a size three quarters of his own. He shouted, somewhat plaintively,

"Me trousers, where on earth have all me trousers gone?"

"They're in the bin."

"The what?"

"No, not the what, the bin."

"In the name of pity, why woman?"

"Because they're the rags of a profane and sacrilegious man."

"Who's sacrilegious?"

"Yourself, as well you know."

"When, when on earth have I ever been sacrilegious?"

"When have you not?"

"When have I not? You're suggesting sacrilege is some kind of twenty-four hour preoccupation of meself? I'm sacrilegious at me breakfast, I'm sacrilegious in the jacks, I'm sacrilegious even in the simple act of askin' for petrol - is that the kind of madness you think I'm about? And me shirts, where in God's name are me shirts?"

"There you go again."

"And me socks... and me knickers woman, what on earth have you done with me knickers?"

"In the bin. The lot. They're all in the bin. No, correction, they were in the bin."

"Were? What have you done with them since, shoved them in

the oven? Heavens knows, it smells often enough as though you're cooking me socks for tea."

"They're not anywhere here. The bins have been emptied. No more than ten minutes ago."

"Jaysis wept, have you gone stark raving mad?"

"There you go again with your constant stream of profanities, sacrilege on two legs."

"I am not being sacrilegious - I am a man without his trousers, his knickers, his shirt or his socks, and a man in such a predicament is in no position to take on the cat, never mind the Almighty. I can't even step outside me own front door in this un-garmented state, never mind pick a verbal punch up with the creator of the known universe."

"Oh, you can, you can."

"I can what?"

"Step outside me front door."

"Apart from the daftness of such a comment, how is it that the door has suddenly ceased to belong to me as well as yourself?"

"Because, Padraig, as a heathen, you're moving out."

"Oh really and when is it that this unilaterally decided departure of me presence is supposed to occur?"

Christine picked up a long skewering fork from out of the cutlery drawer and made her way up to the bedroom. Holding its fearsome prongs at precisely the height of Padraig's goose-pimpled behind she said, with chilling purposefulness,

"Now - and if you don't go as instructed you won't be able to sit on your over-fed rear end for a year."

"Have you gone the other ten per cent and turned completely stark raving mad woman?"

"I'm not having a sacrilegious and degenerate man to corrupt me within the house for a second more. The divil must be cast out into the street wherever he takes hold, and he should be as naked as the day he came into the world. As you've become the divil in all but name I'm casting you out. You can go under your own steam or on the end of me skewer. You've got 'til five to decide. One..."

"Christine, this is planet earth calling, come back to me darlin'."

"Two..."

"Look, for heaven's sake, can't you see this Mairead woman is as crazed as the day is long, if you keep swallowin' every loony word she says as if it were gospel they'll be puttin' the lot of you away and givin' the key to the budgie."

"Three..."

"Christine, let's be practical about this, you may have the skewer but a man is always stronger than a woman when it comes to a struggle, it could be you who ends up with the blessed thing up your bum, whether I intend it or not."

"Four..."

"Alright, come on just try it. See if I haven't warned you. It's going to be you out on that doorstep, a madwoman too dangerous to be let into her own house. It'll be a case of havin' to call the guards and..."

"Five!"

"Yeeeeeeeeeeeeeaaaaaaaaaaaaaaaaaaaaaaaaaarrrrrrrrrrrrrrrgh me bum woman! Ow! Yeeeeeeeeeoooooooooooooooooow! Arrrrrrgh! EEEEEEEOW! Alright, I'm goin', look, I'm on the stairs, you don't have to keep stickin' it in, I'm off, for God's sake woman, I'm not a piece of pork. No, no, I can find me own way, look, I'm in the hall, front door knob, look, I've got it, see, I'm steppin' out, look, aaaaaaaaaaaaaaarrrrrrrrrgh? What the hell? You've put tacks all over the step woman! What in heaven's name did you do that for on top of everything else?"

"To get rid of you! I don't even want you on me step, never mind me house, now go on, clear off and take your divilish ways elsewhere. I don't want to see you ever again!"

And so it was that Padraig found himself suddenly amongst the homeless. Apart, that is, from a brief homely spell in the cells while Sergeant Molloy established the veracity of his explanation for being found naked apart from an oak leaf in the shrubbery of a devout and easily shockable neighbour's garden. It was only after being clothed by the kindness of the St. Vincent de Paul's society that he was able to make his way in decency to his brother Anthony's farm. There he secured a room for the duration of his exile in return for night time duties within the piggery and the cowshed, the details of which his nose and his stomach would have preferred to remain ignorant of. Anthony was a man long known to prefer the company of sheep to that of humans, and who would sometimes remain all night in the fields with his flock. For much of the time Padraig therefore was restricted to his own company.

On one calm weekend afternoon, when both men were in almost silent occupation of the kitchen, an unfamiliar sound remarkably akin to a knock broke the spell of their dreaming.

"There's a man at the door," Anthony said.

"No, no, it'll just be herself in drag," Padraig replied. "If the he has a moustache, a beard and a face like a boil then it's definitely a she. The one and only Christine Maloney."

"That's a very sexist remark if I may say so," a most definitely male voice said from behind. Padraig turned round in surprise to greet its owner, the very modern curate who had taken over from the elderly parish priest after his catapulting from this world into the next by Mairead's famous outburst.

"Oh, afternoon Father, sorry, I didn't realise it was you. Whenever I think of me wife strange things come out of me mouth."

"It's her I need to speak to you about," the priest said. "The poor woman seems to have been completely programmed by this cult that's so all over the place here."

"You mean the Catholic Church Father? Don't worry, only joking."

"Say what you like Padraig - I've never been among the Church's programmers as you call them. I believe in a mind that makes up itself. That's what worries me about Christine - she seems to have lost the ability to think for herself."

"To be honest father, that could be a blessing in disguise. Whenever she's thought for herself in the past it's been about the best way to clobber the innocent, namely meself."

"You're not missing her then?"

"Not in the slightest - I give meself a clip over the ear and a strong verbal pasting over the breakfast table every morning and it feels just as if she's right beside me still."

"Padraig, you mustn't be so hard on the woman. She means well."

"Indeed she does Father. Once every leap year I think. But she makes up for it the rest of the time."

"You are her husband man. You have a responsibility to try

and do something to help her."

"Father, if you listen to the woman then I'm a heathen, a sacrilege on two legs, a gibbering joke of an eejit and the divil himself with hush puppies over his hooves. What can I do when she won't even let me over me own front step, never mind listen to me? As far as she and the rest of the crazy gang are concerned I'm the son of Sodom with a soul as black as me boots."

"I'm talking kidnap Padraig, do you not understand? She won't listen to any of us in her current brainwashed state. Well meant force, as gently applied as possible, is the only way of saving her."

"Could we not pop her into the bank Father? That would be an excellent way of saving her and I'd try never to make a withdrawal."

"Can you not be serious man? This is a woman's life and her soul at stake here."

"Now the stake bit I do appreciate Father. It's either that or a silver bullet at dawn. There's not a lot you can do with the undead once the sun's pushed its snout above ground level."

"Padraig, I need you to drive the van. That's all you need do. We'll run her up to the Convent of St. Cecilia of the Forest in Donegal and the sisters there will do the de-programming. They've made dealing with cult members their speciality."

"But the woman's programmed herself as much as been programmed," Padraig replied. "She'll probably programme the lot of them and they in turn will programme the bishop and all the clergy except yourself and you like me will end up as a lone sane voice in the face of a multitude of the daft. And then where would we be?"

"Don't be so defeatist man. If we can get just one of the core cult figures to recant all of this dangerous nonsense publicly then it could be crucial in causing the whole ludicrous business to unravel. And you would get your marriage back."

"What a terrifying thought," Padraig replied. "That clinches it - no way would a man in his right mind put his head back in the vice once he'd managed to release it."

"Padraig, you're a desperate man."

"True enough Father, any man or woman with a desperate spouse would themselves be desperate."

"Will you not even consider doing this one act of mercy for her?"

"Father, putting me within a hundred yards of the woman would be equivalent to throwing the Christians to the lions. I'd rather pole vault over the moon with a hedgehog shoved up me arse, if you'll pardon me French."

"So you'll agree to do what I ask Padraig?"

"If refusal amounts to consent then it would seem that you have my firm yes and no."

"I must confess Padraig, I took you for a more generous and compassionate man. You've left me sorely disappointed."

"That's true Father, I am a most disappointing man. I disappointed me mother who'd wanted a beautiful child instead of the backside of a cow she got from her labours, me father would have been even more disappointed, had he known who the hell I was, I disappointed me wife by virtue of the fact that I'd been born at all, and I've disappointed meself by failing to drive the witch out of the house with her own broom stick. Now you can't get any more disappointing than that."

"Indeed you can't Padraig. Good day to you."

As he disappeared out of the door the priest said with a notable determination,

"This will not be the last you hear from me on this matter."

Padraig shuddered as if his grave had just walked over someone. He said to Anthony,

"If there really is the heaven and hell that the church has always gone on about then me wife is as good a preparation for meetin' the divil as anyone could hope to get."

It was two days later, no more nor less, that Padraig quite unexpectedly managed to completely repair his image in the eyes of the parochial man. Having exceeded his normal alcoholic moderation of no more than a half or a pint a day by several times several, an act of wantonness brought on by an over-long contemplation of the sorry state to which his fate had lowered him, he set off back towards the farm and the irresistible call of the piggery. He was filled with a degree of Dutch courage that, if spread amongst thousands, would have been enough to persuade an entire retreating army to turn back on its heels and attempt to sweep all that pursued them into the sea. It so happened that the good Mairead was holding a meeting of all of her holy followers in the town on the same evening. As Padraig passed the building where the inspirational event was occurring, the sound of her lilting tones floated into his ears and caused him to go and stand with his head around the door to see if he could spot the threatening shadow cast by his other half. There indeed she was, seated adoringly at the right hand of the prophetess as she held forth unto the multitude. But it was what he heard that astounded him, not least because echoes of his own fate were so explicitly contained within her words. Mairead was saying, in an inventive re-working of the gospels from documents of peace and love to something more approximate to Terminator II,

"Those who are not with us are against us and those who are against us must be dealt with severely. If it is your husband or your wife that is the opposition then you must dispense with them before they contaminate you with their heathen doubts. If you can, throw them out of the house - by force if necessary, there can be little room for gentleness when everything that is good that we have built is threatened by everything that is bad. The sons and daughters of Satan, by virtue simply of their status as the divil's own servants, cannot be shown the luxury of non-violence when they will respond to no other means. Get rid of them, sell off all of their goods and give the proceeds to our sister Christine, who has already provided a shining example of how to act in such circumstances. Every penny we get will be used for the good of everyone here and the spreading ever wider of the message of peace, love and righteousness that has been entrusted to us. There can be no room amongst us for those who doubt, or those who would wish to try and lead even one of our number from the salvation and the happiness that is ours, providing that we keep strictly to the new gospel that I have been preaching to you under the divinely inspired instruction of angels sent by Christ himself."

Without warning, even to himself, Padraig shouted,

"And which Christ is this who's been sendin' all of these invisible angels into your presence you great hypocrite of a liar, Christ the boxer? Go forth and box the ears of all those who dare to say you're as had as a matter, are those the words of the feller? It's a dangerous business casting the slightest word of doubt on the lunacy that you spout, is it not, Mairead the spinner of fables and yarns? Whether he be god or a man you're as great a mockery of the true Christ as has ever walked the earth."

Mairead was stopped in her tracks. As one, the entire audience turned in shock to see who it was who dared to address a handmaiden of the angels of the Lord so. Seizing the moment he continued,

"Mairead, as a 'prophet' you're a dead loss. The feller you're claimin' as your personal chum was the complete opposite to being violent, even a heathen like meself accepts that. And neither was he a supporter of the kind of legalised theft you've been using to con the gullible out of their hard earned savings. You're a fraud of a woman in every sense of the word and the best thing any of this lot can do for themselves is get their heads examined for even beginning to listen to such poisonous drivel. Look, all of yous, I may be a little more drunk than I am sober, but even I can see me way to the truth of the matter. If yous wants to build a religion around some notion of 'God', then at least choose one that gives you something to look up to, something that is without faults. I mean, what in the name of Moses and all the tablets in his bottle is the use of puttin' your faith in someone who's as petty and weak as yerselves, someone who's only 'message' is intolerance, hate and violence? The next thing you know you'll all be signing up for dancing classes run by Mr. Hitler."

The relevance of the last point was slightly lost even upon Padraig himself, but he was fairly sure he'd got a firm grip on the earlier ones.

The wrath of Mairead scorned was a sight to behold but, for safety's sake, not to linger on. She roared,

"There, before you now, in this very place, at this very hour, is the divil's servant himself! A man so lost in the darkness of his soul that his entire being has become the mouthpiece of Satan! This is the scale of the threat that we face, this is why you have to use every means at your disposal to clear your homes and towns, and eventually this whole sacred land, of all such servants of Lucifer. This one man could cost anybody here their soul just through fooling them into accepting the seductive but entirely false logic of his arguments. This is a man you must destroy!"

As a couple of heavily built farmers at the back of the hall began to move towards him Padraig had the distinct feeling that some of the darker forces within human nature were about to be unleashed onto his intoxicated being. It was fortunate for him that Sergeant Molloy happened to have been in the vicinity during the delivery of his address to the mentally evacuated. The policeman now stepped forward to quell any expectations of a holy duffing up, grabbing Padraig by both arms and announcing that he was taking him away for questioning. As he propelled his charge down the street and out of harm's way, Padraig asked,

"Does the questioning bit mean I'm formally under arrest or something?"

"It means I'm going to ask you some questions," the sergeant replied.

"Such as?" Padraig asked, perplexed.

"Such as what colour is green cheese and why are policemen's boots always one size two small for the feet that live in them?" the sergeant replied. "Now," he said, stopping on the corner of the road that led away up to the farm, "you said exactly what I or half of the remaining sane people in the town would have said had we been drunk as skunks and completely unaware that we were addressing the spiritual equivalent of the Hole-in-the-Head gang."

"Don't you mean the Hole in the Wall gang?" Padraig enquired, thinking back to his youthful fascination with the cinema.

"No, where this demented lot is concerned, Hole-in-the-Head will do fine. Now unless you've got one too I'd recommend that you hotfoot it back up to the farm from whence your two feet carried you this morning and lie low for a couple of days until this latest lunacy has calmed down."

Hotfoot it is precisely what Padraig did.

It was a week later that the good sergeant and the priest were having a quiet drink in O'Driscoll's Bar. The priest was explaining how he had come to acquire a bandage on his head.

"There was a knock at the door and a knock on me head and that's the last I remember of anything. But I'd seen some of those women who hang out with the dreaded Mairead lurking on the corner opposite shortly before and they all had their eye on the parochial house – I'm sure it was them."

"You'll have to give me all the details you can remember in

the morning and I'll set me hand to trying to flush out the culprits. This is a shocking state of affairs, it's as if every tenth person in the town's gone mad. Who'd have thought a gaggle of such respectable women would have turned to violence?"

"It's in the heart of all of us Johnny," Father Martin said, "in every land, in every man and woman, the capacity for the darkest deeds lies waiting only for the corruption of our souls to turn a good thumpin' into a way of life."

"That's as may be father, but the way things are going I'll be having to jail enough women to fill half the parish hall in a cell the size of a crapper, if you'll pardon me French. That's assuming I'll ever be able to arrest them without meself being hand-bagged into a pulp."

"It's not only the women who're up to the violence, Johnny. There was Jimmy Murphy up at Finn's fish farm. He floored Sean McGuire with a frozen trout over the question of who had the rights to his wife, a sore and inflammatory debating point given the polygamous rules of some within this ludicrous cult. And Peter O'Malley dunked Kevin McNulty's head three times in the gents at Rose's Bar over his publicly calling the good Mairead a fraud and a liar. These are not isolated incidents among the men of the town - this is a problem that's getting out of the control of us all."

"There's nothing for it - I'll have to ask for reinforcements."

"And so will we both - I need the bishop himself and a posse of priests to work seven days a week for a fortnight at least if we're even to stem the rate of converts to this nonsense, never mind begin rolling it back."

"And what makes you think a dozen priests will be any more successful than the one on his own Father?"

"Ah, Padraig, I didn't see you there. I think strength in numbers would be the simplest answer to your question."

"But if you're all selling them the same product, if you see what I mean, why should twelve salesmen be any more successful than one? If your customers have all thrown away what you're selling as yesterday's hat, then why should they be expected to rummage around in their bins and put it on again just because there's a dozen men in black saying 'buy, buy, buy' instead of one."

"You mean we need something different to 'sell' them I suppose?"

"Righty tighty. You need somethin' different than the weekly repetition of the same old mass for all the kids that the Church is losing, and a less of a joy-killing line on the old contraception. But for the lot that you've lost to the loony Mairead it's somethin' different. They're all well into families, or middle age, or both and there's other reasons why they're turnin' to this stupidity. You'll have to discover the reasons before you can even begin to change their minds."

"The man's got a point," said Molloy. "This is only a police matter because the Church can't handle it. We know the half of them believe in the excuses that Mad Mairead passes for miracles, so half of your answer is to prove she's a fraud. That would be a useful job for your clerical friends before they did anything else. But then you need to find the other reasons people have left in favour of such a bucket of nonsense and ask how the Church could have lost the battle against an army led by a dimwit."

"Whatever else Mairead is, she is certainly not dim," Padraig observed.

"Indeed. The man has another good point," Father Martin said.

"A point but not a pint," Padraig added.

"On me," Molloy said, "a small price to pay for such valuable thoughts."

"While you're getting them in I'll pay a visit to the conveniences," Father Martin said, disappearing through the door that led into a dank little room so unimaginable in its nature that it is best not imagined at all.

At that point the door of the bar flew open, letting in a howling blast of a wind that bit everyone in the arse with the ice teeth of its merciless breath. Three of Mairead's fiercest looking followers strode in.

"I've come to throw out the divil from each of the heathen present," said Mary Kelly, a woman long renowned for being as terrifying as she was mad.

"No need, the fellow's already gone, he made a bolt for it the moment he saw your ugly mug comin' in," Padraig said, a little louder than he'd intended.

Mary switched her acid glare straight into his eyes and said,

"In your case there's no bolting to do seeing as the two of you are one and the same. The only casting out of the feller can be the casting of yerself out into the street and that's just what I intend to do."

Without pause or ceremony she grabbed the unfortunate Padraig by the scruff of his neck and the seat of his pants and propelled his person through the door as if he were the weight of an ant on a diet.

"Right, that's an assault," the Sergeant said, "I must formally caution you and..."

His next words were taken away by a combination of a large and unexpected sneeze and a ferocious stone that bounced off his skull as if it was a tennis ball. He crumpled instantly to the ground.

"By the holy stone of St. Clare of Anjou I hereby cast out the divil that is within into the world that is without and pronounce you a man..."

"It's the divil within yourself that you need to be doing the casting of," Padraig added before Mary could finish, having brushed off the mark on the seat of his pants where her boot had connected and propelled himself bravely back through the door.

"A man free of the divil and born again in the light of the Lord," she continued determinedly, pulling a brick out of her canvas shoulder bag and hurling it in the general direction of Padraig. Anticipating the event, he ducked at precisely the right moment, causing the projectile to fly over his head into the raised pan of a set of large ornamental scales at the end of the bar. Unfortunately for itself, the owner's bedraggled cat was slumbering peacefully astride the second pan, which naturally was forced upwards at high velocity by the impact of the sizeable missile on its counterpart. The little creature was in consequence flung a good three feet into the air and landed with a baffled squawk on the bald head of the bar owner, giving him the appearance of the man with the ultimate rug.

"Jaysis wept, if that great thing had hit me I'd be stone dead twice over," Padraig gasped.

"It was no more than a test to prove beyond all doubt that you and the divil were one and the same - a normal mortal could never have ducked in time," she replied. "The only way to save the souls of everyone here is to send you back into the flames of hell itself. I'll be back as soon as I've made the necessary arrangements with Mairead."

"You'll be making no arrangements that will be in any way credible," Padraig said vehemently, "anyone seeing what you've just done so crazily with stones and a brick that's the size of a planet would judge you instantly to be a madwoman and no one, no matter how gullible, will want to be led by a loony like Mairead who allows her even madder followers to go around felling men of the law."

Mary walked over and thrust her face directly into his. She said, with a smile like a knife,

"And who is there to tell what you in your misguided heathen ways would call the truth? The Sergeant is most unlikely to have much of a memory of where the blow came from given that he sneezed in the middle of his oration and didn't see the unleashing of the missile, and then there's only the word of you and a collection of bar drunks against that of meself and the irreproachable Anne and Maureen here. And given that half the town knows full well that you're the divil there's no one who will believe a word you say. You think I haven't thought these things out? There's only one likely culprit for such a heinous crime, when all the lies of your friends have been disproved, and that's the divil himself. And as you and he are proven as one, it's you who will pay the price. Goodbye Padraig."

As she exited with her acolytes Father Martin reappeared from out of the gents. Seeing the prostrate Sergeant on the floor he said,

"Not again Johnny, this is the third time in a month that I've seen you flattened by the drink. It's not the way for a man of the law to go on."

After an ambulance had whisked the good sergeant away for treatment, Padraig made his way back to the farm. The smell of the pigs in the yard almost persuaded him to about tail and go back to the bar, but his tired feet had a row with his nose, and given that in such a case there were two against one, he sided with the stronger party and followed them in through the door (the toes, of course, being in the lead as is the normal manner of things with the human anatomy). Being exhausted in mind and flattened in spirit, he retired to bed an hour earlier than normal, without even the consolation of a drop of whiskey before he attempted to set sail into the nightly dark seas of his sleep. His brain was so perturbed by all of the recent events that he found himself counting sheep that were in turn counting other sheep, without the slightest sign of success in his trying to float off into unconsciousness.

After he had been lying in this unhappy state for a good hour, he became aware of a faint hubbub in the distance which sounded remarkably like the chanting of some ancient mantra interspersed with a variety of out of tune hymns. As he listened with initial disinterest, the sound became gradually louder, until it was clear that it was progressing up the hillside towards the farm. Vaguely perplexed, he pulled his dressing gown over his shoulders and went to look out of the window. What greeted him was a puzzling sight. There seemed to be a quasi religious procession on the march, with blazing candles held high in the air illuminating a banner similar to that of the Legion of Mary, the kind of thing that one might expect at three o'clock in the town on a Sunday afternoon. However, given that it was midnight on a Saturday, the sight seemed more than a little strange. A cold chill began to sink into his bones as he realised that all of the marchers were wearing hoods, and that the bulky female figure at the head of the procession was carrying a flaming cross in front of her. It was undoubtedly the good Mairead and there was more than a slight possibility that she was coming to settle the score with himself.

Pulling his clothes on so quickly that he zipped one of his fingers inside of his fly, which promptly stuck and refused to release it, he began to feel that he should have taken the threats that mad Mary Kelly had made in O'Driscoll's bar a little more seriously. By the time he had managed to free his imprisoned digit the procession had surrounded the house and the only way out was through the chimney pot. He peered down at Mairead through a gap in his hastily redrawn bedroom curtains. In a manner fittingly bizarre, she was wearing her teapot of a hat on top of her hood. One or two others within the little procession were wearing their own hats in the same way. Seemingly familiar with the lay-out of the house, she shouted up to him,

"Satan whose name is Lucifer and Padraig the degenerate man

in equal part, I am here to cast you back down into the flames of hell so that this town might become pure and night become day, so that the rule of the angels shall prevail over all of the sinners of this county. Show yourself so that we may begin our cleansing and fire the fountain jets of our love through all the dark places that you have corrupted."

Concluding rapidly that his only chance of avoiding whatever mob lunacy that was to follow was to make the mad woman look even more ridiculous in front of her deluded followers than she was already, he grabbed the bucket by the side of his bed - the one that caught the rain whenever the heavens delivered anything more than a trickle - flung open his window, and hurled the stagnant water directly over her. The result was a scream so loud and terrible that all the caterwauling moggies in the neighbourhood stopped rigid and listened in terrified admiration. Unfortunately, however, not enough of the wetness fell on the flaming cross to extinguish it, and the good and drippingly soaked prophetess Mairead promptly pronounced the fire's survival to be another sign and affirmation of the rightness of her divinely ordained purpose. A rousing cheer of admiration for her clearly impressive powers promptly went up and Padraig's hopes of escape shot downwards in parallel. Concealment up the chimney seemed the only possible option and he scurried downstairs to see how this could best be effected. At the same time a relentless battering started on the locked outer door, and stones came crashing through two of the downstairs windows. Remembering the fate of Sergeant Molloy, the last thing he wanted to do was to re-enact the martyrdom of St. Stephen on the hard stone floor of the kitchen. After delicately testing the fire's still dying embers to make sure that the way was safe, he stepped into the hearth, and with his back firmly against one side of the wide lower chimney breast, raised first one leg and then the other, and then, with both feet planted firmly on the other side of the brickwork, wriggled and slithered his way upwards until his presence was completely invisible to all but himself.

No sooner had he concealed his person than the door burst open and the fearsome Mairead powered her way into the kitchen, with three equally burly farmers and a host of the righteous in tow.

“Fan out and hunt the divil down!” she shouted, her still dripping hair gleaming from under her hat, around the cherubic roundness of her now un-hooded face. Thirty assorted pairs of boots, trainers and farmyard wellies pounded up and down the stairs and through every part of the mouldering house, but with no sight or sound reported concerning their quarry. The only living thing that they found was the comfortable fatness of the old farm cat, which, being recently fed and considerably deaf, slumbered contentedly through the entire riotous proceedings.

At length, Mairead summoned her herd of assorted clompers to the kitchen, where the confined nature of the space meant their gathering took upon itself a most unholy proximity, with Mairead herself pushed back into the fire place. Tripping unavoidably on the high stone hearth she crashed downwards, upsetting the coal scuttle, on top of which the previously oblivious and contented cat had slumbered peacefully, and landed heavily on the unfortunate little creature’s tail as the backsides of both hit the hearth simultaneously. With a scream and a screech that would have twice raised a corpse and then caused it to drop dead again from the shock of its hearing, the desperate animal yanked itself free, ran three times round Mairead and the hearth in enraged pain and flew up the chimney to escape its attackers. It shot past the terrified Padraig, scrabbled desperately to get a hold in the brickwork three feet above his head, failed, and then, with outstretched claws, plunged back into his lap. The knife-like pain of the experience caused him to roar like a wounded lion. Recovering her composure in an instant, Mairead grabbed a candle from her nearest accomplice and stuck it and her head up the chimney to see where the divil was hiding. Unfortunately for the wounded Padraig the flame went straight up his bottom and caused his already faltering grip on the brickwork finally to fail. With a desperate cry from himself and another terrified squawk from the cat, the two of them hurtled down into the fireplace, cracking the inquisitive Mairead’s head onto the hearth and knocking her out stone cold.

“My God, he’s killed the saint,” a shocked follower gasped.

“No, no. She’s simply stunned I think,” the devout Angela said with relief while pulling the blessed one free of her attacker, and with the assistance of three burly farmers, laying her out on the stout and ancient wooden table.

"A degenerate and a black cat swooping down from on high and attacking the saint together - a definite sign of the divil," Mad Mary Kelly observed, pointing accusingly towards the cat and Padraig, who lay one on top of the other, a stunned and terrified twosome.

"We must get rid of that divil now before he does for the rest of us," an extremely short-sighted spectacle with a hat the size of a house said.

"What the hell are you on about you deranged bunch of eejits?" Padraig said. "I'm me, the cat is the cat and the divil is the divil and never the three shall meet."

"You see, almost as soon as he opens his mouth the words 'hell' and 'the divil' come tumbling out," Angela said, horrified.

"S'right, indeed 'tis," Mad Mary said, "and as the divil is known wherever he goes for lying, even when he's telling the truth, there's not a word of his denial that can be believed."

"Jaysis, Mary and Joseph," Padraig gasped, "by the sense of your logic a man is a woman, a horse is a duck and the Pope an atheist."

"Did you hear him?" Mad Mary said. "The Pope an atheist - taking the Holy Father's name in vain in a way only the divil would."

"It's all very well," the hat the size of a house said, "but if Mairead stays out for the count who's going to take the responsibility of dealing with the man? I'd like to drive him out of town right away with me boot up his arse - and his tail."

"What tail in God's name? Are you people on something or what?" Padraig spluttered.

"There he goes again, his every second word as sacrilegious as only the divil can be," the hat said. "It's out of the town with the man and no comin' back if he wants to pass from this world to the next in possession of his own backside."

"I'm for that, but let's give him a drubbing he'll never forget first and then throw him out," a burly farmer with boots the size of boats said. "That way he'll think twice before ever coming back."

"I'm for gettin' him out of the country, never mind the town. Let's put him in old Dan Finnegan's pea green boat and sail him out to sea with the owl and the pussycat," a fearsome woman said.

"And a price on his head if ever he shows his face back here again," the boots replied.

"It's what Mairead would have wanted had she been in possession of her senses. Yes, let's give him a damn good drubbin' and leave him half way between the quick and the dead at Cork - we can shovel him into a container and send him off to France for free," Mad Mary said.

"So we're all agreed on the drubbing?" the boots said.

"I'm not and neither is the cat," Padraig said, "and it hardly needs me to do any remindin' that a single laying of your hands on meself will be an offence in law in every sense."

"No problem me fine diabolical friend, there'll be no singularity at all. There'll be so many hands at work that the matter will be entirely without blame," Mad Mary said with a cackle of which a witch would have been proud.

"The cheek of the feller - wantin' a say in his own beating. He'll be telling us next he's goin' to do the job himself. A gentle slappin' about the ears with a wet fish and a firm crack over the head with a lump of jelly perhaps?" the hat said.

"Wait! I've changed me mind - Mairead said nothing about sending this divil anywhere but back down to the searing flames of hell. 'Tis hell he came from and hell he must go back to," Mad Mary said, flip flopping her view on matters in a way most uncharacteristic for a twice convicted woman of such deep conviction.

"And how precisely are we to achieve this?" Angela asked in bewilderment.

"By lighting the kitchen fire and sticking Padraig in the middle of the inferno - that way you'll send him back the way he came into the room to attack me, straight up the chimney, except this time as flames and ashes. When every trace of him has disappeared and the smoke has died down we will know for sure that the divil has gone back to his own."

Everyone looked in surprise at Mairead, the owner of these harsh and violent words, whose eyes still remained closed as she lay on the table being tended lovingly by the good Christine.

"How are we to explain his disappearance to Sergeant

Molloy?" Angela enquired.

"Ask the man in me hat," Mairead replied.

"What?" Angela said.

"The man in me hat. Ask him," Mairead replied, pointing to the hat that lay upturned at the side of her.

"I think poor Mairead needs some rest - best leave her alone for a while," Angela said.

"What d'you mean leave me alone?" Mairead said. "I'm as fit as a fiddle apart from me headache and back ache. I always ask the man in me hat when I need some advice."

"No Mairead dear, it's the Lord that talks to you, we all know that. It'll just be the bump on the head that's making you think such a thing," Angela replied.

"I've never claimed that the Good Lord talks to me, only his angels," Mairead replied. "Everything else comes via the man in me hat. You'd be an eejit if you didn't know that. It's the man in me hat that speaks to the Lord."

Thirty pairs of gullible eyes exchanged worried glances, realising for the first time, perhaps, that all might not be as they had assumed with their most holy of prophets.

"And where precisely in your hat is this little man Mairead - are you sure he hasn't gone home for his supper, because none of us can see him," Angela said delicately.

"Gone home for his supper?" Mairead replied. "Are you all mad? You think the man in me hat's gone home for his supper?"

A chorus of relieved sighs encircled the room as everyone concluded at once that all was well and that the good Mairead had simply been pulling their legs.

"We knew you were having us on Mairead, can you open your eyes now?" Angela said.

"Of course I can't, can you not see?" Mairead replied.

"See what Mairead dear," the good Christine asked.

"Him," the prophetess replied.

"Who?" Christine asked.

"The little man," Mairead replied.

"Where?" Christine asked, perplexed.

"Stretched out on the lids of me eyes, his head on one and his feet on the other," the prophetess replied.

"And his arse on the bridge of her nose," Padraig murmured to himself and the cat, "for sure I hope the little beggar doesn't fart."

"Mairead dear, please don't tease us, it's most unlike you and you'll make us worried," Christine said.

"Who's teasing? The poor soul got a nastier belt on the head than I did and fell onto me face - and he's still out for the count. Can you make him a little bandage d'you think Christine?" Mairead asked.

"Mairead," Christine said, bending down and looking straight at her serenely closed lids, "you are having us on aren't you?"

"Of course she's not you silly bitch!" a deep and thundering voice said. It was then that Christine saw what nobody but Mairead had seen before. There was indeed a little man stretched across the bridge of her nose, and one that was now very much awake. As she peered closer in disbelief his arm suddenly reached up towards her. It moved with the speed of a bullet, and as it did so, the hand telescoped up to the size of her own, grabbing her nose and twisting it three different ways in the space of a second until the blood ran so freely onto the white of her jumper that it seemed as if she had an open tap on the end of it. Everyone recoiled in gasping horror as Christine screamed so far up the scale that a glass of water on top of the mantelpiece exploded, drenching Padraig and the cat with its contents. The increasingly beleaguered little creature shot straight up the chimney with the same lack of success as before, crashing back down into the fire place within seconds, causing a large fall of soot to drop on it to complete its bafflement at the world and all of its doings.

"What in God's name's happening Mairead?" Angela asked.

"I'm happening!" the voice said. "It's me you've been following for these past several weeks and as Mairead has so unhelpfully let the cat out of the bag I'll have to give up all pretence that things are anything otherwise. In future you're dealing directly with me and you'll do as I say - no ifs or buts, desertions or second thoughts. Now you've signed up no-one signs off."

"I'm out of here," the boots, aka O'Leary the dairyman gasped and lunged forwards towards the door. The arm telescoped after him before one foot had had the chance to follow the other. It grabbed him round the neck, winding itself around his throat as if it were rubber, and squeezed and squeezed until he went as blue as the varicose veins in his legs. When the last desperate wheeze had passed from his lips it released him, letting his lifeless body crumple untidily onto the hard stone of the floor. The room suddenly was full of hysterical screams and sobbing.

"Silence or I'll throttle the lot of you!" the voice said. "From now on we'll jettison all of the niceties and the subtleties - you're my slaves or you're dead. It's a simple rule with a simple penalty. You, yes you with the face like a cow's arse, go and rip a joist or a rafter out of the barn and cut it to the size of a stake."

"The stake wouldn't happen to be intended for the burning of my innocent carcass?" Padraig asked, in quiet disbelief that he was addressing a man the size of Tom Thumb.

"It would," the voice replied in a careless monotone.

"And you want me dead because I'm one of the few half-wits who'll try and stop you in whatever it is you're trying to do?"

"Of course. And I want you dead because you're the divil," the voice replied.

"But if I'm the divil who on earth are you?" Padraig asked.

"I'm the divil that knows no mercy," the little man said in a whisper so low that only Padraig could hear it. "I'm the divil that waits for its moment and turns the most placid of souls into one of the baying chorus at the crucifixion."

"Well if you're the divil and I'm the divil then either one of us has been cloned or you're a liar," Padraig said.

"Words, words, words - it's convenient to my purpose to call you the divil so the Convenient Divil you are," the voice said. "Let's just say this whole town's not big enough to hold the two of us. I'm doing a little downsizing..."

"You'd be pushed to be any more downsized than you already are," Padraig muttered, deliberately pretending to misunderstand the diabolical midget's meaning.

"For that I will devise a particularly painful death for you," the little man said.

"I would expect no less from the divil himself," Padraig replied, "but even you must allow the condemned man the traditional favour of a last meal before the falling of the axe. Even the cat has had its supper and I've had nothing as yet."

Padraig had read the little divil's way of thinking perfectly. It said instantly in response,

"If the cat has dined then you shall eat as well as the cat. You there, open that can of Kitty Fish on the cabinet and give it to this iniquitous fool in the cat's own bowl. We'll all watch him lick it up like the depraved beast that he is."

'You there' obliged in an instant, not daring to even half arouse the wrath of so powerful an almost invisible being. He placed the bowl in front of Padraig.

"Now then," the midget growled, "let's see you start slobbering your fat chops round that little lot, just like the good obedient pussy cat that you are."

Padraig picked the bowl up and wafted its pungent odour two or three times under his nose with a look of disdain. The action of so doing was enough to attract into the farmhouse doorway the unkempt heap of fur that passed itself off as the local wild cat, a specialist thief that would have stolen its own grandmother's dinner at the drop of a hat. It approached to within three feet of Padraig and crouched down, lion-like, ready to pounce as soon as an opportunity presented itself. Satisfied that all was as he had planned, Padraig without warning threw the bowl's entire contents at the little man. His action had such force that it knocked the latter off his perch on Mairead's nose and sent him spinning down onto the floor. Almost all of the stinking fish dropped on top of him. The spectacle was too much for the waiting wild cat, which pounced so quickly that the divilish midget didn't even have time to threaten it. Seeing what it could only presume to be a struggling mouse in the midst of its dinner, it assumed that Christmas had truly arrived. It wolfed both the 'mouse' and the fish within seconds, holding down anything that moved with its claws until its teeth had had the time to do all of the necessary munching. Padraig and all of the assembled company watched with grim fascination as nothing but the little divil's shoes were left uneaten and intact.

No sooner had the macabre meal been completed, than the cat's head began to tremble, shake and spin with such velocity that it seemed that at any second it must explode, and a roar more terrifying than that of any lion erupted from deep within its tiny throat. The divil might have been surprised, but clearly he was not as yet in the slightest respect beaten.

Padraig, however, had anticipated such a possibility. He now unleashed the second wave of his attack, running out into the muddy yard and untying from its kennel ring the huge Alsatian that was supposed to guard the premises. Normally he was so frightened of the treacherous beast that he would not go within six feet of it, but desperate straits required desperate measures. Being as stupid as it was fierce, it was not in the slightest bit deterred by the roaring of the cat and bounded straight for it with its enormous jaws opened wide for the kill. Even the divil in the cat was caught off guard by such mindless determination and had to take rapid evasive action while thinking out a strategy for dealing with it. The cat and the unwanted guest in its head accordingly bolted out across the yard and into the large field beyond, with the salivating Alsatian in hot pursuit.

What the divil resident within the cat forgot, given the intensity of its concentration on matters other, was that the field was spectacularly finite. It ended in a sheer sixty feet drop down into an old disused gravel pit and it was into this that the cat plunged head first with the mad Alsatian cannoning down on top of it. The little creature passed instantly into the world of cats deceased upon impact and the divil suddenly found itself without any temporal form in the near vicinity within or on which to lodge itself, the cat's own tiny body having been crunched into a pulp by the mad beast crashing down on top of it. The two animals lay as dead as the proverbial door nail.

After a good three minutes had passed without the sound of any further disturbance within the yard or field, Padraig permitted himself a huge sigh of relief. The prophetess Mairead looked at a distinct loss. She was sitting bolt upright, with her now empty hat in her hand, trying to work out how she was going to go about her day-to-day business without the voice of the little divil in her ear to guide her in all her ways of holy wickedness. Surveying both her and the shell-shocked collection of followers that filled the kitchen around her Padraig said,

"Come on, all of yous, back to your beds. It's over. You've seen now the true nature of the diabolical lunacy that you've been following thinking you were treading in the footsteps of a saint – heavens knows what evil that little divil was going to draw you into had I not sent him packing. Now go and get yourselves fixated on some good and useful cause instead. Remember the famine for Chrissake - there's a whole world full of the starving still that needn't be starving - go and wrap your minds round that and see what you can do to help. But, once you've made her pay back all of the money she conned out of you for her personal gain, forget about this sad Faustian fool. Mairead sold her soul to a divil whose plan was to spread wickedness and barminess combined in the name of religion through her, with you lot as the side-show. Go home and get your lives back. Leave Mairead to Mairead and the divil to the divil and be grateful that only one of you died as a result of this idiocy."

"Not so fast, not so fast, everyone stay where they are," a commanding voice said. The little assembly turned to see the doorway blocked by the substantial bulk of the flattened Sergeant Molloy's temporary replacement, Sergeant Maureen Hanigan. Behind her were three guards of equally shed-like construction. She said,

"We've been called to a disturbance here and a more disturbing disturbance I have rarely seen. Because there appears to be a fatality in the room this is a potential murder scene from which no-one is to move – it seems to me that everyone here has a bucket load of questions to answer and answer is what you're all going to do."

"It was her sergeant," the hat like a house said, pointing at the discredited prophet. After a brief stunned pause another repeated his words, then another and another and another. Mairead's mouth opened and closed noiselessly like a fish as a hefty guard handcuffed her before she could even think of making a move.

As the questioning and taking of witness statements commenced Padraig looked at Anthony's ancient and bedraggled cat and the cat looked at him. He said,

"Well Fireside, this lot are going to have a job on their hands if they're to try and convince the good sergeant of some of the things that you and I have seen tonight – and as they'll all deny ever having had even the slightest intent to harm a single hair on me head there's not a lot of point in me hanging around to try and persuade the guards of what really happened. So, seeing as nobody's looking, why don't you and I sneak off upstairs and return to that from which we were both so rudely awakened – a good night's kip."

With that the man and the cat crept out of the kitchen and up the stairs. Each flopped exhaustedly onto the bed, the cat on one pillow and the man on the other and then, leaving the multitude below to tell their impossible tales, they fell fast asleep.

Intermission 2

There was a momentary silence following Pattie's ending of her tale as the audience got to grips with everything that had happened in the startling denouement. That was followed by applause that started slowly but grew into a thunder whose volume three times outnumbered the pairs of hands in the venue. It took the scale of the noise to wake her out of the spell that she had cast as much upon herself as those present and the little girl that years ago had dreamed of such a night shone out again through her smile as she bowed three times, blew a kiss, then ran hurriedly off the stage and out and away through the flap at the back of the tent.

Both Ben and Liam had been very scientifically noting the length of the applause, with Liam studying his trusted old analogue watch and Ben glued to a digital clock he had accessed via his iPad. Each had made voluminous notes as the tale progressed and Sean wondered how either of them could have kept enough of an ear on its finer detail when distracted by constant flurries of writing things down. For him, of the four of Pattie's performances that he had seen this was by far the strongest and the tale the best of all her previous offerings. Whether it would be good enough to beat Jimmy's and the rest of the field was yet to be seen, with some strong storytellers still to come. His thoughts were interrupted by Ben, who was studying something on his screen. He said,

"The final revisions to the programme have just been announced on the festival website. The feller who was due to be up next has been delayed by a puncture and will now be appearing later in the day. There's a Brendan Walsh that's been moved into his slot – do you have the old low down on him Uncle Sean?"

"Ah, well now, there's a character for you," Sean replied, again being careful to address both nephews. "Brendan was a journalist for years and worked his way up to being a crime correspondent on a couple of different papers before he retired. He made the quirky and the bizarre his own and his columns became noted for their strange revelations about incompetent crimes and most famously about two guards who accidentally arrested each other in thick fog. One of the guards was not amused and lay in wait to nab him on a drunk and disorderly when he staggered out of the pub on his way home from the office Christmas party. He's never forgiven this terrible act of revenge and every tenth tale he tells seems to centre on baffling encounters between disorganised crime and some of the least organised members of Ireland's finest. If I've got me sums right that's the kind of thing we should be in for tonight. Anyway, we'll find out soon enough, he's just come on to the stage ready to be announced."

Once Fierce Betty had cowed the audience into silence and done the necessary introduction Brendan took command of the stage in a gently shambling kind of a way. He was a small man in his mid sixties, a little rotund with surprised looking eyes. His riot of unruly white hair looked like it had had a fight with a comb and won. His lips seemed constantly in danger of smiling, until remembering that humorous tales are often best told with a serious face. He stared intently at his shoes for a moment or two as if trying to remember what on earth it was he was supposed to be talking about and then, in a hypnotically lilting voice, said,

"Before I start I should say a word or two of reassurance for those of a sensitive or delicate disposition – this is a tale with a death or two within it and one or two other things of an unsavoury nature. These are not kind times and indeed kindness has been at a premium for most of history, but whereas most violence is terrifying, sickening and all manner of appalling things, the stuff you get in my tales is of a more farcical nature. So if there's anyone thinking they'll need to dive under their seats there really is no need – and if you do you'll only flatten the invisible bunnies that live under them. And if there's anyone thinks I'm being fanciful in me knowledge of where the secret bunnies live then I have to tell them, in the strictest confidence of course, that my five year old granddaughter is my source and I've never had cause to doubt a single word she's said... Now, hold on to your hats, your seats, the cat if you've brought it and everything else – our little journey is about to begin. Ladies and the many gentlemen seated and wise, may I present, for your delectation and delight, the farcical tale of *The Day of the Deadly Daft*...

The Day of the Deadly Daft

Brendan Walsh's Tale

A voice said,

"At four o'clock this mornin' I shot meself, but I appear to have got the wrong feller."

Sergeant O'Neill turned round from his watering of the Garda station geraniums to find himself being addressed by words bereft of an owner.

"So rather than spend the rest of me life on the run I've come to turn meself in."

The words again came from nowhere. O'Neill took six cautious steps forwards to the mountainous lid of the station counter and looked left and right in search of the invisible desperado. Having detected nothing by virtue of such normal investigatory procedures, he tried the unconventional and looked up in search of a fallen angel and down in case he was dealing with a delinquent dwarf. Down it was that he found his man, flat on his back and content, his hands clasped and resting on his chest in the manner of a well laid out corpse.

"May I ask what you're doing stretched out on me nice clean

floor?" O'Neill asked.

"You can indeed," the unsuccessful self-murderer replied. There was a long pause.

"Am I not going to get any sort of an answer?" O'Neill enquired.

"An answer as well? I thought you just wanted permission for the question."

O'Neill, who until now had thought he might be dealing with a possible eejit, concluded that he was dealing with a definite member of the species.

"A man who stretches himself out on a Garda station floor is generally a man in danger of a drunk and incapable charge," he informed his horizontal visitor.

"In danger you say? The lack of the definite in your implied consequences of me flattened state gives a small hope of me escaping at least one of the litany of charges I was anticipatin'."

O'Neill, detecting the growth of an insurmountable hurdle of confusion, decided to cut right through to the core of things.

"You said you'd tried to murder someone, but I must have misheard you because you said it was yourself."

"No, you're not entirely wrong. Your ears were almost honest listeners and me words were the fullest summary of the truth. I shot meself but I appear to have got the wrong feller."

"I see," said the Sergeant, who saw only the danger of his own impending insanity, "so let's get this straight. Are you telling me that you were trying to shoot someone else, but were so incompetent as to get yourself instead, in which case your currently horizontal state explains itself - or were you trying to shoot yourself, but hit some other unfortunate as well. In short, if anything so terrible confusing can ever be less than long, is it a wounding or an attempted murder, a manslaughter, or even a full blown possible murder that we're looking at here?"

"Yes," the uncertain perpetrator of the even more uncertain offence replied.

"What d'you mean, 'yes'?" O'Neill hissed.

"I confess to everything you say," the self-accused replied.

O'Neill decided to approach the matter from another angle.

"How many fellers are we dealing with here besides yourself?"

"One, just the one."

"So you're trying to tell me that the unfortunate in question has been wounded, but is still alive despite being murdered, and has been killed by means of manslaughter as well? He must be the most remarkable of all the world's remarkable men."

"Well seein' that he's also a woman that would indeed be a remarkable case."

O'Neill leant forwards resignedly on the desk and put his head in his hands. Everyone else he'd started with in the guards twenty years ago as raw recruits now had a string of bank robbers, drug dealers, or notable fraudsters and even a corrupt local politician or two to their credit. All that graced his ever more desperate service record was a long list of eejits whose confusing tales usually won them unconditional discharges in the interests of judicial sanity. Now, half awake at six-thirty in the morning, he was faced with the daddy of them all. The Almighty clearly was trying to tell him something about the appropriateness of his chosen vocation. Perhaps it was time to exchange the cloth of the guards for the grey and become a monk.

"You're telling me now that the impossible has become the possible and that a man can be a woman and a woman a man and both at the same miraculous time?"

"Am I?" the eejit asked, astonished. "I thought I was simply informing you that one of the parties additional to meself was a feller and the other was me wife."

O'Neill blinked. A thin gap had suddenly opened in the familiar darkness of his confusion and a blinding stream of clarity shone through. Briefly.

"So may I enquire precisely why it was that you did the shooting and who precisely it is that's been shot and what precisely the condition of each of the affected parties is? It would be convenient to know all of these things in case we're in need of a doctor or two you understand."

"To your first question there is an easy answer, to the second there is an even easier one and to the third there is no answer at all. And yes you may indeed enquire."

"Thank you - and may I indeed have an answer or two?"

"You may."

After a patience stretching pause the sergeant said,

"Let me put it another way. If I don't get the answers I've

asked for, I'm going to come round to the other side of this counter, I'm going to take the very large spout of this watering can and I'm going to insert it..."

"No, no, say no more, I'm not a man who can stand the thought of violence, I'll confess everything. You wanted to know why I did it?"

"I did - and then I wanted to know precisely what it was that you did."

"But if I was to tell you what it was I did I would only incriminate meself. On the other hand, I'm quite prepared to tell you why I did it."

"Well then, let's start with the easy bit and work our way upwards to the point where I box the living daylights out of yous to get to the difficult part."

"Fair enough, but I'd like to have a legal man present when you beat the crap out of me, just for the formality of things."

"Indeed you can. I'll beat the crap out of both of you and then we can be as absolutely formal as you can get."

"That's settled then. It was a crime of passion."

"What was?"

"Ha! You're a bright spark Sergeant! You'll not trick the truth out of me that way."

"Precisely what kind of passion is it that we're talking about here?"

"The passion that dare not speak its name."

"Dare it not. But you're a brave looking lad, you can speak it. Go on, be a hero, tell me what this forbidden name is."

"Harold."

"What?"

"The name of the passion."

"That's the name of a feller not a passion."

"So it is. It was a passion for Harold the Englishman."

"Whose passion?"

"Hers."

"Her being your wife?"

"Was she? I should have guessed, what with all that business with the ring and things and the priest at the altar, d'you know it's been a revelation in itself me comin' here tonight."

"Apart from the fact that the night is the morning, and all

policemen are not thick as your presumption seems to think they are, I detect a slight hint of the Michael being taken in very large quantities here. How does the thought of an appearance before the beak for the offence of wastin' police time take your fancy?"

"That would be as humane as ever I thought the soul of a policeman could be and far more lenient than even an Archbishop with seven angels pleadin' his innocence could hope for, but unfortunately it would be completely the wrong thing to do. You see, there is the slight problem of the blood."

"What blood?"

"This blood," the eejit said, lifting the left side of his jacket to reveal what appeared to be a shoulder wound.

"Is that your blood?"

"No, 'tis not. It spontaneously appeared on me body in holy imitation of the wound of St. Ding Dong of Dungarry after he accidentally impaled himself on the horn of a unicorn – it's a mark of me spiritual purity and a regular cause of pilgrimages from all five corners of the earth."

"Ding Dong my arse!" O'Neill hissed.

"No, thanks for the invitation, but I prefer to get me musical delights in more conventional ways if you don't mind," the eejit replied.

"Right, that's it. It's the cuffs and the cells for you. I've wasted enough of me time trying to make sense out of nonsense while you busy yourself making nonsense out of sense. You're either a drunk or a wastrel or both and I'll not have either such specimen cluttering up the polished neatness of me floor."

"Lay unfriendly hands on me and I'll not say another word," the eejit said. "And then you'll be the one with the explainin' to do. What's your boss going to say when a man with a bullet in his shoulder is hauled up before the beak and you haven't the slightest inkling of a clue as to the crime which has so obviously been committed? No, you'll have to leave me where I am and wait for me to tell you in me own good time. Do anything else and you'll end up banished to some godforsaken Tipperary backwater of a station with nothin' but geraniums to be watered all day."

With steam coming out of both of his ears at once O'Neill said,

"If you take the mick one more time I'll swear I'll..."

"Swear you might, and stamp your feet in a dance of rage," the eejit replied, "but you still haven't had the courtesy to ask if the blood that is so artistically decorating the armpit of me jacket is puttin' me in any danger of departin' from this life into whatever might pass for the next. Is that a Christian way of thinking for an officer of the law? What if I was to die on your floor when someone had seen me staggerin' in half an hour ago and you hadn't even bothered to call for a doctor? Would it be criminal negligence they'd have you on d'you think, or manslaughter perhaps, or, if it was indeed decided that I'd done the original damage to meself, accessory to an act of self-murder?"

"Right, I'm calling the doctor. And if the blood's tomato ketchup, or not your own, or is indeed a fake miraculous manifestation in imitation of the wounds of some long ago martyred saint, then you go straight in me cells and we'll take it all from there."

O'Neill picked up the station phone and started dialling furiously the number of the local medic.

"But it's the doctor I've shot," the eejit said.

O'Neill paused in mid-frenzy. He said,

"You've shot the doctor?"

"Of course. Why else d'you think I'm lyin' here mortally injured without a soul to even tie a bandage round the end of me nose."

"So you're tellin' me, in the middle of all your misplaced pedantry, that you're a murderer?" O'Neill said.

"Am I? How can I be a murderer when the incompetence of me aim caused me to do no more than wound the man in the foot," the eejit replied.

"So he's not in fact dead then?" O'Neill said.

"He's not? Praise be, another miracle," the eejit said. "And there was me thinkin' the next time I saw him he'd be six feet under."

"I would have thought you'd have needed x-ray eyes if you were to see him that far beneath the ground," O'Neill hissed in some exasperation at the ever more circular direction that the interrogation was taking.

"Now who's being the pedantic one?" the eejit asked.

“Tell me,” O’Neill roared, “is the man dead or is he alive, because by the name of all that’s sacred if you don’t clear the matter up soon you’ll be the first corpse of the day on the Tipperary murder list.”

“That’s a terrible alarmin’ thing for a man of the law to say. I’m not a medical man, but I’d say that an absence of breathin’ and the presence of rigor mortis were reasonable grounds for assuming the absence of life, wouldn’t you think?”

“So if you only wounded him in his foot how did he die?”

“Of fright I think.”

“Right. So your pointing the gun at him caused him to have a massive heart attack, he died of fright and it’s a charge of manslaughter we’re dealin’ with here? That’s one part of the jigsaw solved at least.”

“Well if it is you’ve got a couple of the pieces in the wrong place.”

“What d’you mean?”

“It was me wife chargin’ into the room wieldin’ a cast iron fryin’ pan that did the job.”

“She was headin’ for him?”

“No, but he thought she was and that would have been enough to put the fear of God into any man.”

“So the thought that she was going to belt him when her real intention was to belt you was what you’re tellin’ me killed him?”

“Indeed.”

“And what happened to her?”

“As dead as a rock.”

“And how, dare I ask it, did that happen.”

“I fired a shot.”

“And it hit her, or did she die of fright at the sound of the bang?”

“Not at first.”

“She didn’t die of fright immediately,” O’Neill said incredulously, “she had a think about it then decided that if die she must, that would be the way to go?”

“No. I meant the bullet didn’t hit her at first,” the eejit said.

“Oh. It went out for an early morning stroll perhaps and then came back in to finish the job after it had had its toast and marmalade?” O’Neill said.

"I'm telling you that I fired over the mad woman's head to frighten her off and that the bullet ricocheted off the wall behind her, shot thought the budgie's cage, singeing the poor little divil's feathers, and passed straight through her heart at the precise moment that she'd raised the pan above me head to pummel me senseless."

"And then the fairies came in from the garden with bows and arrows and twelve foot clubs and it was the sight of them that fritted her to death rather than the bullet that you'd never intended to fire at anything more than the budgie's tail?" O'Neill said.

"You still haven't had the kindness to ask how it is that I've been wounded, or to express more than a passing concern about me health," the eejit replied. "For all you know I could be about to expire."

"You'll forgive me for saying this," O'Neill replied, "but it has occurred to me that there is a slight discrepancy between the leisurely manner of your account of all of this and the presence of an implied medical emergency on me nice clean floor, and it is that fact more than any other that has led me to conclude that, whatever state you're in, there are little if any grounds for believing that it is one of any immediate danger. But please, you've had half of me day already with the tellin' of your fantastical stories, by all means have the other half and enlighten me as to how your armpit came to be stained with what may or may not be blood."

"T'ank you for your resoundin' vote of no confidence," the eejit said. "I shall tell you me own piece of the jigsaw for the sake of neatness and completeness and me public duty as a citizen."

"Please feel free to talk out of whichever end of your anatomy you think is the most appropriate," the Sergeant said ungraciously.

"Ignoring such undeserved insults, I shall now make me own statement, followed by me last will and testament, so you'd better have a pen and paper ready," the eejit said.

"I'm all ears," O'Neill replied.

"Oh I wouldn't say that," the eejit replied, "there's the four eyes and the nose like a hook to be accounted for as well."

"Get on with it," O'Neill hissed.

"Well, the said mayhem having occurred in precisely the

manner that I have told you, I was of course distraught and decided at once to kill meself."

"You have not at any stage looked a distraught man to meself," O'Neill observed.

"No, well appearances can be deceptive and you have all the perceptive powers of a horse's arse, if you'll pardon me French," the eejit replied. "Anyway, distraught I was, so I turned me gun on meself, aimed for me heart and missed."

"That hardly surprises me, given, no doubt, that you were standing a good twenty yards from yourself when you took aim," O'Neill said sarcastically.

"Well, such untoward frivolities aside, the fact is that the gun is a heavy one, I wasn't holding it properly, and it slipped in me hand at the last minute. So instead of killing meself I wounded meself, and the trajectory of the bullet took it straight through me into the doctor's heart, making it look as if I'd killed him when in fact he was already dead."

"Oh I see," O'Neill said, "now everything really is beginning to fit together. So having shot the doctor dead, together with your wife, you inflicted a minor wound on yourself to provide an alibi that you'd hope an eejit of a Garda officer would fall for."

"That, if I might say so, is a very ungenerous interpretation of the truth," the eejit replied. "The Pope himself would be regarded as a mass murderer by a man with a mind as suspicious as your own."

"So the only thing we're short of now is the motive for all of this alleged carnage and details of where I'll find the scene of the crime."

"Oh the motive's the simplest bit of all in the midst of what is a rather complicated matter. You see, the doctor and I were the best of chums, right up until the moment I found he was also having his way with me wife. So, having caught them at it, I aimed for his knee and shot him in the foot as a warning to them both and it was then, when me furious wife ran off to get the frying pan, that things began to spin out of control and to lead to the moment when you found me flat on me back on your nice clean floor."

"A fascinating tale," O'Neill said disbelievingly. "And speaking of me nice clean floor, I'm going to get you off it and into a cell. Then we'll get some medics to check you over, and if, indeed, shot it is you are, then we'll whisk you off to hospital, and then when you're all fit and well, we'll zip you back to a cell and some very large gentlemen far less understanding than meself will discuss the real truth of these matters with you - and then we'll recommend that a judge locks you up, in a prison or an asylum, depending upon whichever seems to be the most appropriate. How does all that sound as a happy day's plan for a fine, wholesome picnic? We'll even give you a little hamper to take with you."

"You! Yes you with the face like an arse, put your hands above your head and keep your big mouth shut!" a heavily accented voice yelled. O'Neill looked up to find himself confronted with two men in hoods brandishing pistols. He did as instructed.

"I've got to admire you O'Hennesey," the larger of the two huge unexpected visitors said, "we'd never have thought of looking for you in a cop shop."

"If you'd never have thought it Ivan you'd never be here," the eejit pointed out.

"Always the clever arse, but not clever enough this time. You left a trail of bloody drips," the largest of the men with a hood for a head said.

"And lo and behold, a couple of bloody drips followed it, and here we all are," the eejit aka O'Hennesey replied. "You were lousy shots the first time, d'you fellers think you can finish the job off from close range, or should I join in and have a go meself?"

"One more time or you're a dead man," the smaller of the two said, "tell us where the money is or you'll be the ugliest looking corpse I've ever seen. We don't want to waste the knowledge on Mr. Policeman, so here's a pen and paper you can write it on."

"Now wait a minute," O'Neill said to the eejit as was, "are yous telling me you've spent half me morning tellin' me some cock and bull story while these maniacs were on the loose waitin' to follow you into me nice clean station and threaten to pepper me freshly painted walls with bullet holes?"

"Don't worry about it Sherlock," the eejit said, "it's been wondrous enjoyable for me to pull your leg and buy a bit of time in the safest place I could think of to hide me bullet-riddled corpse. What better place than a police station run by an eejit who couldn't even arrest himself? And anyway, why shouldn't a condemned man die with a twinkle in his eye? You see, I accidentally separated a Russian gentleman from a rather large sum of money without realising that the dispossessed was a terrifying Mr. Big of a crime lord no less. Now he wants his money back and meself dead I think. Only, given that his main men are all tied up on some big deal he's sent two crewmen off one of his boats after me, a couple of eejits so dense that it's a miracle they managed to leave their ship on the landward side instead of falling into the sea. I'd hoped that while I was safely concealed here they'd think I'd legged it elsewhere and set off in hot pursuit of me ghost. Only me wound was rather more weakenin' than I'd thought and I was in no position to escape from either them or you. So here I am, a wondrous murder waitin' to happen right on your doorstep. What more could a policeman in need of a promotion ask for?"

"Do you two think you're some kind of double act - one more word from you Mr. Uniform and I'll shoot you in the arse and blow your brains out," the larger of the hooded unpleasantnesses said. "Now, O'Hennesey, we want the name of your partner and precisely where it is that he's stashed his half of the money, and we want to know where you've hidden yours."

"Boys, boys, there is no name. The man is dead. When you missed me the second time you got him by accident. He was hiding behind a tree, which is the only way that you managed to hit him, if you see what I mean."

"We've killed him?"

"No, but the effect's exactly the same where death's concerned."

"Well, that just leaves you then doesn't it? I'm going to count to ten and if you haven't given me the details by then I'm going to shoot your big toe, and that's just the beginning of your troubles Irish."

"Gentlemen, gentlemen, by some sheer fluke you've already shot me in me right shoulder and surprising though it may seem, that's made me a less than happy bunny. I couldn't even allow the eejit of a sergeant here to get me a doctor to dress me wound in case he gave me somethin' that knocked me out and left no chance of an escape at all. So with the wearying pain from that I've had enough of as many enoughs as you could imagine. One more shot into any part of me anatomy and that's it. I'll tell you nothing whatsoever, even if you kill me. In fact, kill me and I swear I won't even give you the time of day. Then what's Ivan Ferocious going to say when you return without a bean for all your efforts?"

"Right, that's it. You've heard of a golden hello - well this is a golden goodbye to your big toe Mr. Funny Man."

The largest of the hoodies pulled the trigger and emptied six empty barrels into O'Hennesey's terrified toe. The toe's owner looked up at him incredulously. He said,

"Do you fellers not think you'd better call it a day? You missed me with nearly all the other bullets before and now you've excelled your previous best by tryin' to shoot me with an empty gun. Thick as the Sergeant may be, it's never a brilliant idea to attack a man in a police station."

The hooded incompetent hurriedly loaded six fresh bullets into the gun. He said,

"I may have an arse for a brain and be completely useless at half the things I try and do, but not even I can miss from six inches. You're a clever man with words, but all your Irish mockery can't save you now."

With that he pulled the trigger once more, then twice, then thrice, but each time the gun jammed due to an over-hasty loading of the ammunition into a delicately precise and sensitive chamber. He hurled it at the wall in enraged frustration, whereupon the violent impact set the unwilling weapon off to spectacular effect. A bullet thumped into the formidable bulk of the second hit man, causing him to drop dead the instant before he could squeeze the trigger on his own weapon and finish the toe job that his companion had been so unable to start. The first hoody was in such a state of shocked confusion as a result that O'Neill was able to leap over the station counter and sweep up the dead man's weapon before his companion was able to register what had happened.

"Right, I'm in charge now," O'Neill said. "Put your head above your hands!"

Snapping out of his temporary trance the hooded desperado made a lunge for his own unreliable weapon. O'Neill, who was never much of a shot in unpressured circumstances, never mind the high drama that had unfolded before him that morning, fired three times in quick succession to try and stop him. The first shot sliced through the window and caused the startled station cat to leap for its life from its perch on the outside ledge, straight into Flynn the window cleaner's bucket as he walked by. Having assumed the bang to be no more than a backfiring car he was greatly puzzled to find that his bucket had suddenly acquired a sizeable extra weight and the mystery of a flailing tale. The second just clipped the desperado's left ear causing him to shoot head first into the station wall and knock himself unconscious. The third seemed to go on a complete mystery tour, refusing at first to leave the faintest clue for anyone as to where it might have chosen to abscond to.

As O'Neill handcuffed the fortunate unfortunate, the incompetent toe assassin who he had himself failed to assassinate, the voice from the floor, aka O'Hennesey, aka the eejit, said,

"It could only happen to me."

"I've no doubt," O'Neill said, "and whatever it is that has happened you most certainly deserve it, unless it's an act of human kindness, or a random stroke of good luck."

"No, neither of those," the voice said. "If there was to be a competition to try and find the most useless policeman and the most hopeless hit men, then the three of yous alive and dead within this room would have hit the jackpot. It's the supreme irony of me life and death that those whose ultimate purpose was undoubtedly to kill me could only kill one of their own, while the eejit whose job it is to protect me on behalf of all the sons and daughters of Irish justice is the one banana that succeeds in turning out me lights."

"What do you mean?" O'Neill asked guardedly.

"I mean your third bullet found a target," the voice said, "and it feels remarkably like it's meself."

O'Neill turned to contemplate the source of the complaint and noticed that there did indeed seem to be a new and growing patch of deep crimson on the front of O'Henessey's shirt.

"No, nothing to do with me," he said. "If anything hit you at all it was the ricochet from the first shot that was fired and that was most certainly not by meself."

"Jaysis wept," the voice said faintly, "I'm about to pass from this world into the next and the best the eejit can do is blame me death on a bullet that had claimed a corpse before the shot that killed me was even fired. I'm surprised you don't suggest it was the deceased himself who rose briefly from the dead and whacked me. I could at least then die with the satisfaction that, according to your take on the world, I would have finally achieved a place in history, the first man alive to be snuffed by a stiff."

"No, no, no, let me explain. The first bullet from me own gun is accounted for, as me cat will testify," O'Neill said, pointing to the drenched and disgruntled station moggy that had escaped from Flynn's bucket and come inside to get warm and dried out. "Look, you can see where the bullet skimmed right across her fur causing apoplexy and flight in equal proportions. The second nailed your man on the floor there, a piece of shooting that Wyatt Earp would have been proud of. As for the third, I didn't get quite the aim I should've due to the heat of the moment and hit the wall instead. You'll find the bullet embedded somewhere in the brickwork over there."

"Will I bollix," O'Hennesey spluttered, "unless I and the wall suddenly traded places at the moment when you misfired that excuse for a weapon. I distinctly heard the metallic zing of the bullet as it hit the middle metal bar in the window, and in less than the time that it takes for half of one half of the blinking of an eye, it had bounced back and thumped into me chest like a hammer. I'll be dead and buried by the time an ambulance arrives, even should it occur to the lump of lard between your ears that it might be an idea to call one."

"You've cried wolf once and you'll not catch me out on a second attempt," O'Neill said. "If you're so convinced that my bullet bounced off that metal bar then I'll prove to you that it couldn't have hit you even if I had hit the bar – it's as clear as daylight that the angle is all wrong and the bullet would have gone nowhere near you. Watch and learn - I'm going to shoot directly at the bar from exactly where I fired the gun before."

"You were not standing there yous eejit of a policeman," O'Hennesey rasped, "yous were a good two feet to the right and if you stand where you are now and actually manage to hit the thing you're aiming at there'll be two of us for the undertaker's slab before lunch and that's no fantastical lie, believe you me. The bullet will fly straight back and nail you between the eyes."

"I was standin' here and that's an end of it," O'Neill replied determinedly. "The world looks a very different place when you're flat on your arse and flat you have been for a good hour at least. Take my word, I know where me own feet have trod, it's as if I were standing in the prints of me very own boots. It's a tracker's instincts, call it what you like."

"A crapper's instincts more like," O'Hennesey muttered

"Right," O'Neill said, ignoring his derision, "we'll settle this once and for all and then get you an ambulance to test this latest allegation of your state of near decease. You can stop your moanin' and groanin', this'll take a second or two and no more."

As the sergeant took aim at the guilty bar O'Hennesey muttered,

"With an aim like yours the only way you'll hit anythin' you're shootin' at is to try and get somethin' on entirely the opposite side of the room."

For once in his life, however, O'Neill put paid to the doubts of his critics. He hit the bar with a precision that surprised even him. Luckily O'Hennesey's words of warning had not been entirely in vain. They persuaded the would-be sharpshooter to take the precaution of ducking as soon as he fired, causing the rebounding bullet that otherwise would have belted him right between the eyes to whizz straight over his head. Unfortunately it then rebounded off a thick steel pillar that was providing a temporary support until the sagging floor of the storeroom above had been strengthened. With a diabolical determination it headed straight for his backside, causing him to yelp in surprise and topple heavily onto the floor. After a full five minutes in which no breath or other living sound could be heard from his prone and unmoving personage O'Henessey rightly concluded that the unfortunate sergeant had been the victim of an undiagnosed weakness of the heart and had expired in shock. Whether the bullet or surprise at the startling degree of his own incompetence had been the greater cause of O'Neill's shock was a question that was too complex to fathom for a man whose own proximity to judgment day was increasing by the second. He had just enough time to shake his head slowly in despair before himself breathing his last.

It was four hours later before O'Neill's emergency replacement arrived to take charge of the station. Sergeant McMuster, who marched in like Fortinbras at the end of a particularly bungled and downmarket version of Hamlet, was accompanied by two detectives whose job it was to try and sort out the sorry mess of a massacre that O'Neill had bequeathed as his legacy. The immediate assumption was that the deceased policeman had died in a heroic gun battle with the two other corpses and had even managed to wound and handcuff a third member of the invading criminal gang, before himself succumbing to a bullet. It was only when, two days later, forensics revealed the baffling fact that the heroic sergeant appeared to have shot himself with the very gun that was found in his hand, that McMuster began to suspect that he was looking at a classic case of the incompetent O'Neill of old. As the evidence mounted to support this second point of view, the two visiting detectives began to write a report that would overnight transform 'this most heroic officer', as he had just been described in the Irish Times, back into the bumbling no-hoper that all his colleagues had known and loved. McMuster, a man of humanity beneath the Garda cloth, persuaded them that a kinder account, from the point of view of his distraught widow, might involve the losing of the bullet that had indirectly killed him and the report that had shown it to be his. He said,

"Gentlemen, let us remember that there is no evidence that, with the exception of himself, O'Neill occasioned the death of anyone who had not, by their own actions, placed themselves at direct risk of such a fate. The only true victim of the incompetence for which he was renowned seems, therefore, to have been himself. We can surely afford a special charity towards a man so considerate of the well-being of his fellow men that he never endangered anyone innocent other than his own person. At least for the sake of his widow, wouldn't you say? Had he to our knowledge occasioned the death of any other innocent than himself, then the story would have to be a different one, with the full apparatus of an official enquiry and everything that goes with it in place. But in this case, for the sake of poor Mary O'Neill, I t'ink the eejit should remain a hero."

With this judgment of Solomon the bullet became suddenly lost and the forensic man forgot ever having had such a thing placed before his eyes, or having written a report about it. Mary O'Neill in her turn was able to become the proud widow of a hero, and in honour of the memory of the man that she had loved, never revealed to anyone her belief that there was no way on earth that poor, hopeless Sean could ever have fired more than one shot from a gun without putting himself more at risk than anyone he was trying to aim at. She was, in truth, simply relieved that he had been found holding the deadly thing the right way round.

Through such small but generous means the dignity and heroism of flawed humanity is preserved as an example to future generations. And so, to the greater glory of an understanding God do we here commend the soul of Sergeant O'Neill, a stranger to perfection in his every word and deed except for two, his devotion to duty and his love for Mary, his woman. Amen.

Intermission 3

To say that Brendan had the entire audience on the edge of their seats by the end of his tale was to talk of two meanings, for while many were fervent fans of his work, all were hungry enough to eat the legs of their chairs or even their own legs by the time things drew to a close. The fact that the two preceding tales had been so long had pushed the first half of the day's competition well into lunchtime. There was a brief burst of loud applause - and then a mad dash for the exit so as not to be last in the queue for what now undoubtedly would be lukewarm offerings in the food marquee. As Sean and his charges joined the rushing throng Sean said,

"Now this is going to be a really difficult one to judge. Had he been in a later slot Brendan may even have got a standing ovation instead of a race from a standing start. Running so far over into lunch has meant instead a running away and we have no means of knowing how long people would have clapped in an earlier or afternoon slot. That means both we and the judges are going to have to go more on our own judgments of the tale than in the case of its earlier rivals, where we could easily see how the audience reacted in all its detail."

What was left of the time for lunch went quickly, with Sean

chatting happily with a member of the organising committee he knew well from previous visits, while Ben and Liam sat at the opposite ends of a great long bench, shovelling down chips while pondering their notes on Brendan's meandering tale. They'd hardly had chance to finish when the post horn sounded again and a Tannoy announced that the next story would begin in ten minutes. Ben was tempted to grab a pint from the bar to take with him, but then decided against in case it clouded his judgment for the next tale.

As they resumed their seats in the venue a woman in a long green dress took to the stage. She looked like a collision between a new age hippy and a traditional folk singer. Her swirling snake of a scarf was wound twice round her neck and swung here and there whenever she moved, a multicoloured marvellous weave of sunbeams catching and reflecting the spotlight. Her dress, by contrast, would have looked at home at an old time country fair. Her long blonde hair made her resemble an angel and Liam was instantly smitten. He had to make a mental note not to be distracted by his reaction to her appearance. He said,

"That's a very fine lady Uncle Sean, can you say a bit about her."

"Well, yes, I can," he replied. "She was in real estate prior to the crash and then had a bit of a conversion on the road to Damascus and turned herself into a full time storyteller. I've seen her three times - her nickname is Mystic Meg on account of the kind of tales she tells, but underlying all of that is first hand knowledge of what the harsh realities of the real world are all about. That means you get an interesting mixture of the fanciful and hard reality. Her real name is Valerie O'Dowd from Donegal. She writes most of her own stories and mixes echoes of folk tales and fairy tales and the current state of the world to make a powerful concoction. She has a sharp wit and an ear for dialogue that rewards close listening, but she's more sparing in her use of the funnies than some of the others we've seen so far. She can start with the most prosaic everyday conversation in a bar, or whatever, and then confound you completely by hurtling into the darkest of fairy lands. It can be quite a roller coaster when she gets going on a good day. She's much sharper and much, much less dreamy than you'd first expect – she'll do the dreamy act to the point you think she's nuts then hit you with the hard or the everyday stuff. Her versatility is at times astounding. You'll get your money's worth out of her and most probably an ending that you didn't expect, but as with everyone else, you'll have to make your own judgment as to how high up the table her tall tale sits."

Fierce Betty's terrifying gaze brought his summary to an instant end. After the usual introduction she handed the stage over to 'the Story Queen of Donegal', to use her own phrase. The Queen startled everyone by singing - a single high pitched note that started quietly and then rose rapidly to a crescendo that caused all those who'd brought glasses with them into the tent to fear they would explode. She raised her right hand upwards in line with the rising volume and cast her head back, following the air splitting note with her gaze. Then she stopped as suddenly as she had begun and dropped her head into her bosom, before slowly lifting it again and staring, it seemed, straight at Liam. She moved forwards across the stage, in a slightly crouching gait, arms outstretched, almost as if she was about to dive into a deep pool for a swim. She cast her gaze around the audience as she advanced, prompting an exclamation of "Jaysis, Mary and Joseph," and some giggles from somewhere near the back of the tent. Then, in a low and hypnotic voice, she said,

"This is a tale of something immortal, something unknown - something that comes in the clothes of a beggar, but which has the power of an angel or devil, something that at first seems weak, but then so strong that it could break you in two. This is a tale that starts with an eejit, but only an eejit thinks that it's there it will end. Wrap up well and watch out behind you, where we're going is deadly and cold. Follow me now into Connemara, into a little village at noon. Come with me, deep, deep, deep and down, into the land of *The Eejit's Tale*."

She put on her glasses in a comically theatrical way and then, looking over the tops of them at the audience, switched into yet another mode entirely and began speaking in the voice of the first character...

The Eejit's Tale

Valerie O'Dowd's Tale

"I had in me own personal garden a plaster cast of the divil himself," the man said.

"Did you indeed," O'Brady said flatly.

"'Twas the strangest thing. One leg was up and the other was down, as if he were riding a bicycle. Can you imagine the thought of it, Lucifer on a bicycle?"

O'Brady's fingers drummed the table impatiently as he sat in the dark cafe's depths, his desire to escape from the uninvited lunatic who had seated himself opposite outweighed marginally by the desperate wish of his stomach for food. The waitress arrived, a young, nervous English girl, smiling uncertainly at her notepad.

"I'll have steak pie and chips with a sprinkle of peas. And two doses of coffee, one large, one in a bucket. The bucket's for pouring over the head of this eejit," he confided quietly. The girl giggled without looking up from her pad and went back to the kitchen. The eejit turned out to have good hearing.

"I threw a bucket over the plasterful cast I did - of water that is. It was dark you see and it looked just like a drunk lying on me grass. I understood fully the posture, because I'm often the same meself. So when nothin' moved I brought me torch, and then I saw the horns, the tail and the cloven hooves. I shouted to me wife and she did the only sane thing. She bolted the door - with me on the wrong side of it. 'It's him you're wanting and good luck to you!' she shouted to the strangeness. Always a one to know where me best interests lay she was. It was then, finding meself unmolested or dragged off to hell, that I saw it for what it was, just a cast of the old plaster with hollow insides - but could I persuade her of that and get her to let me back in? No sir, I couldn't and there I was and here I am, a man made homeless and condemned forever to a life as a gentleman of the road. You wouldn't by any chance have the price of a coffee now would you sir, me throat's getting a bit dry with telling me story."

"No I wouldn't," said O'Brady irritably. Being a man who tried every Sunday to evade the SVP poverty box when coming away from the charade of his visit to mass, and every time being outmanoeuvred by a skilful octogenarian collector who regarded the catching of him as equivalent to a game of tag, he was in no mood for further charity.

"No matter, no matter," the keeper of the devil's plaster cast said under his breath. "Given yer Dublin accent I can count meself lucky I've still got the shirt on me back, never mind hoping you'd pass a portion of yer thieving gains on to a poor and deprived man like me."

"What's that?" O'Brady asked darkly.

"Oh nothing, just saying me midday prayers. It's an old Galway custom you see sir. Always remember your midday prayers wherever you are. And whoever you're with. Now a man who's been as close to the divil as finding in his personal garden a cast made from Lucifer's own diabolical body, now that's a man who makes sure he says his prayers."

O'Brady eyed him and the inconsistency of his dishevelled and tattered state with the fluidity of his verbal abilities with massive disinterest. The garage had said his car would be ready by two. That should be just enough time to finish his meal before making his get-away from this lunatic village. He never enjoyed his trips to the fierce rock lands of Connemara. He was fed up with the rain, the mist and the fanciful madmen who seemed to hunt him out whenever he went there. But some of his company's deals were too sensitive to negotiate in the commercial goldfish bowls of Dublin or New York. Sometimes it was necessary to set up a meet in the wilds of Ireland's west coast, where the only prying eyes would be those of the birds and the sheep. But at least he'd got today's business over. The people he'd met had left by helicopter and soon would be on a flight back to the US. He'd brokered the right deal at the right price as far as his company was concerned. The fact that it was entirely the wrong price for the farmers in Africa who would run the risk of being poisoned by the banned pesticides at the heart of the contract was not a thought that troubled him, or even entered his mind. All he wanted now was to be back in Dublin, in the safety of his warm office, in the right place to protect his back should one of his rivals want to stick a proverbial knife in it. The pie and chips arrived.

"Now for sure that's a terrible kind of pie," the eejit remarked. "I've seen three people of as fine a constitution as yerself fall ill and one of them die after eating only a bit of the same thing - and that's this week alone. In fact that pie looks the same as all the others, only a bit smaller perhaps."

O'Brady flashed across a look that growled and quartered the pie ready for a quick despatch to the starving depths of his stomach.

"That's what it is!" his culinary adviser said. "That's why it's smaller! It's the same pie that's been tidied up and re-served after the fatality. It'll be fascinatin' to see if I'm right - if you survive as far as the third mouthful that is."

O'Brady thrust the first quarter of deadly pastry between teeth that looked ready to leap hot and snapping out of his mouth and bite without warning into the source of his annoyance. Munching contentedly, he decided that a policy of staring at the sauce bottles with an affectation of deafness might be a sounder way of neutralising the persistent botherer than the apparently ineffectual gesture of a threatening glare. The eejit continued,

"I've been thinking, how unfair it would be for a fine Dublin man to croak his last on a rebellious piece of pastry so far away from home. And I must tell you sir, I can't, for your own best interests, allow you to take a chance with a pie that might be after your blood. You must let me be your official taster sir, a humble, God fearing friend of a servant. Let me taste the pie and then we'll know whether things are as me deeper instincts suspect. If I survive the eating of the thing, you'll know it's as safe as the proverbial houses."

O'Brady continued with his consumption of the pie as if he were alone and unbothered. He started to reconstruct in his mind the symphony he had been listening to on his car radio when the fatal breakdown had occurred. He tried to imagine that the rambling of the eejit was the turgid and unstructured meandering of a first violinist stumbling late onto the stage after an extra hard night on the booze, and that sooner or later, the playing of everyone else would drown him out.

"Of course, the pie's only half of the problem," the violinist continued. "The cook that shaped the ugly face it turns towards a beauty lovin' world cannot confine his misanthropy to pastry. And the saddest testimony to the truth of that is the fate of the owner's cat - a great spud lover if ever there was one. The last plateful of chips he stuck his delicate whiskers into was the instrument of his decease. No sooner had the first chip slipped through his tiny lips than he up-ended with a pathetic, desperate croak and a tail so rigid that the adding of a wick and a lighted match would have made it indistinguishable from a candle. So stiff and inflexible was the furry little rod that the tiny coffin had to be shaped around it and an explanatory note to the Good Lord slipped inside. That was the kiddies' idea you understand. No sir, a plateful of deceitful, vicious chips is an undignified means of effecting one's translation from this world into the next. Far better to let a man with nothing left to lose sample them for you - just to check that the murphys that were the parents to the chips themselves were of a purity that would please a saint. Only a man himself with a potato for a brain would fail to see the wisdom of all of that."

O'Brady looked up threateningly and growled,

"You're saying I've got a potato for a brain?"

"A spud, heavens, no. Just a figure of speech sir. If there was indeed a potato between your ears it would have an IQ so large it'd break the scales - the most intelligent spud that a thinking man could dream of. No, the only potato thoughts I had were on your plate, dancing a worried way round the poison of your chips. For your family's sake sir and your own good sake, you must allow me to taste the foul, disgusting things before your next breath becomes your last. It might be a worthy act to lay down your life for a friend, but hardly for a chip. In the name of all that's good and holy, pass across your plate and let a humble, uncelebrated man take your fate upon his strong and weary shoulders. If any man is to die this afternoon sir, let it be me not you."

O'Brady stared across at the eejit's mischievous, laughing eyes and said,

"If you want some bloody chips you'll have to buy them yourself."

"Oh no sir, no," the eejit replied, "I'll not flirt with death except in the cause of another's soul. If you don't want the free benefit of me concern I'll simply leave you to your fate. I'm not a man to stand in the way of a heroic stalwart who dices so courageously with the slow knife of a poison potato death. May God go with you - and may the stomach pump revive you. Amen."

O'Brady nearly choked. Stomach pumps were the last thing he wanted to think of in the middle of a desperately needed meal. He looked across at the eejit's persistent face for a second or two, then grabbed him firmly by the chin and hauled his head to within an inch of his own.

"I'm a hungry man," he said, "and a hungry man is a ruthless man. If I hear one more word from your banal excuse for a mouth I'll fill it so full of this bottle of sauce that the only way to get it out will be to knock it further in. Do you get me drift now?"

"I do, I do indeed sir," the eejit said.

O'Brady continued staring into his eyes, a thousand mental bullets shooting across the inch or two that separated one from the other.

"Good," he said at length, "then that's understood then." Simultaneously he thrust the eejit back onto his seat.

"I think I'll go outside and compare the air without to that within," the eejit said, "you never know when the balance is going to fall out of sorts."

"You do that," O'Brady said. "And take your time, as many

years as you like."

The eejit grunted and shuffled out of his chair, down the long, dark cafe aisle and out into the light.

O'Brady munched his way rapidly through the remaining chips. Paying his bill with an ear that was deaf to the friendly exhortations to a conversation proffered by the cafe proprietor, he grabbed his mac and briefcase and strode out determinedly into the dull rain. To his relief there was no sign of the bothersome eejit. Walking sightless down the street, as if it had never existed, he sailed like a proud galleon into the garage and collected his repentant Range Rover. As soon as his foot touched the accelerator he felt re-born, a man about to escape back to civilisation. He roared down the high street and out into the wild Connemara countryside as if speed limits were only for the dead and the dreary.

He'd gone no further than a mile into the barren shadow lands of the brooding hills, when a primal mist as thick as doom descended all around him and forced even his speed-desiring instincts into something resembling caution. As he peered blindly out into the swirling, foggy path cut by his searing lights a voice said,

"You'll never find your way through this sir, not even with a map from heaven and an angel with binoculars riding on the roof."

O'Brady jumped so far out of his seat that he nearly hit his head on the roof.

"Who the hell are you?" he asked the strange vision that had suddenly appeared in his rear view mirror.

"Just me, only me," the eejit replied. "I got into your car on account of it being a warm place and likely to stay in the garage for at least a night. A marvellous place for a kip sir, a grand spot to lay a weary head. I'd no idea it was yours or that it'd be out on the road so soon."

"And out on the road is what you'll be my farcical friend," O'Brady rasped, pulling into the pebble strewn side of the invisible road. "Go on," he thundered, "get your idle fat arse out of me car."

"I would, I would," the eejit replied, "if only I could. But me poor arm slipped down the join of the sumptuous leather of the seat while I was sleeping - and I can't get the blessed thing back."

"Oh, can't you indeed," said O'Brady. "Then let me give you a friendly little hand of help."

Turning round, he grabbed the eejit's shoulders and pulled him forwards so violently that the consequent force normally would have freed ten trapped limbs at once. The eejit's arm stayed fast.

"You've grabbed the metal frame behind the seat haven't you?" O'Brady shouted angrily. Pulling even more violently he said,

"Come on, let go! If you don't I'll rip your arm out of its socket and throw the flea infested thing to the sheep."

"It's no use, no use at all," the eejit shouted, "me arm is stuck and that's that. It'll need a garage man to free it."

O'Brady continued yanking and pulling for a good four minutes but could make no headway. Finally, sweating profusely with the unaccustomed physical effort, he gave in.

"Alright," he said, "very clever. You've got yourself a free ride for the moment. But as soon as we see a guard I'm going to hand you over on a charge of breaking and entering me vehicle."

"Now that's a terrible thing to say and a far worse one to do," the eejit replied. "You're a man without a scrap of mercy in your heart. If I were you and you were me, you'd now have a full stomach of kindly shared chips and an ear so full of sympathy for the appalling fate of me arm that it'd be unable to accept a single other sound. You're a hard man O'Brady, hard as a soul bent on hell."

"How do you know my name?" the hell bound soul enquired. "You're not the kind of man I introduce meself to."

O'Brady grabbed the eejit so firmly by the throat that the poor man's eyes almost popped out. Unable to think of a threat worse than any he had already uttered, he thrust his unwanted guest back onto the seat and re-started the engine. He said,

"You wait until we get to a garage my smart-arsed country friend. If necessary I'll have your arm sawn off to get your foul smelling person out of me car."

"There'll be no garages where you're going," the eejit muttered.

"What's that?" O'Brady hissed.

"Nothing you'll understand until it happens," the eejit replied.

O'Brady growled and edged the car back onto the road. The fog, if anything, had grown even worse, and he could hardly see beyond the end of his bumper. Completely without knowing, he slipped off the main road and onto a side track that cut a slow, majestic route between peat and peaks, before ending at a point whose grim and desolate appearance precluded the possibility of a beginning. The further he went down the track, the further the fog closed in on O'Brady, until he was sure it had let itself in by the side door and was sitting, ice-fleshed, in the passenger seat beside him.

"You're nearly there, nearly there," the eejit muttered.

"What d'you mean you mumbling fool, nearly where?" O'Brady asked.

"Where you're going," the eejit replied.

"And where is where I'm going when it's at home, for all I can see I could be going straight up me own backside."

"Indeed," said the eejit, "you are a perceptive man. That's precisely where you're going."

O'Brady growled again and dreamed of ripping the entire back seat out of the car and dumping both it and the attached eejit in the nearest bog. As he did so an echoing, unearthly howl filled the air around and rose up in a crescendo to the top of the invisible surrounding peaks.

"What the hell was that?" O'Brady yelled.

"Was what?" the eejit asked innocently.

"Didn't you hear - the banshee scream that jumped on the car and all around as if it was after me soul?"

"No, no. Can't say I did," the eejit lied. "Are you often hearing these banshee things? Bells as well perhaps? Or a hidden voice that speaks only to you from the inside of your shoe?"

O'Brady muttered a curse beneath his breath and put his foot down on the accelerator. As he did so a piercing, hyena-like laugh burst out of the seat beside him where fancy had imagined the fog to be. He was shaken so much and so violently that only his seatbelt stopped him from falling sideways out of the car. One hand on the door handle, his best foot on the brake and his terrified head simultaneously trying to hide within and behind itself, he stared, dripping fear, at the vacuum that filled the vacant seat.

"Is there anything the matter down there?" the eejit asked, peering over and down at the crumpled mass of humanity that looked likely at any moment to bite a chunk out of the steering wheel and scream for its mother.

"D'you mean you didn't hear?" O'Brady stammered.

"Hear what?" the eejit asked. "Not your banshee friends again, doing a bit of a song and dance on the bonnet were they? Tell me Mr. O'Brady, you're not a drinking man are you? You look to have a slight case of the DTs if you don't mind me saying. Or perhaps it was the pie d'you think? D'you remember, the one you were too mean to let a poor man have a chunk of? Perhaps it really was the poisoned offering I predicted."

O'Brady hauled himself slowly back into an upright position. Looking first at the mocking face of the eejit, then at the impenetrable bank of mist around, he began to wish devoutly that he'd begun the day by getting straight back into the bed he'd so foolishly got out of. Still in the grip of a cold, terrified and uncomprehending sweat, he tried to regain his humiliatingly drowned composure. He edged the car once more forwards, this time trying nothing dramatic with the accelerator.

After several minutes of intense concentration and slow progress, he was distracted by the sound of an enormous sneeze in the back of the car. Glancing momentarily in his mirror, he was startled to see no sign of the eejit. Slamming on the brake, he turned round and peered over the back of his seat. To his total consternation, he realised that the sneeze had been either a strange and wondrous event unattached to any human host, or the cause of the eejit's disappearance into thin air. Had God intended sneezes to be inwardly occurring things, then he might simply have presumed that its dramatic viciousness had caused the sneezer to inhale himself. But the externality of the air thrust offered no such consoling possibility. The eejit had disappeared from the car without opening any of the doors and therefore without any immediately visible cause or explanation. An electronic alert would have told him if any door had been opened even an inch. O'Brady was on his own.

After several frozen moments of terrified immobility, he slowly slipped his large, chubby hands back round the steering wheel and prodded the accelerator gently. All that happened was that the car went forward a distance no greater than its own length and thereafter started rapidly to go down. At first O'Brady couldn't take in at all what was happening - the slow, hungry, squelchy, gurgling noise, and the fact that the ground appeared to be creeping up the side of the vehicle instead of running along underneath in the normal accepted fashion. Gradually, as the drowning engine began to cut out, the awful truth of his impending marriage with a bog began to dawn on him.

At first feebly, then, as terror took over from confusion, ferociously, he began to try and force open first the driver's and then the passenger door. Finding both too far submerged to yield to anything short of an explosion, he desperately opened his window and tried to force his moderately overfed frame through it. All went reasonably well until the contours of his 'big end' met those of the window frame, which had been reduced in size by the window motor cutting out due to the encroaching bog, leaving him with a much reduced escape hatch. His backside and the frame became apparently inseparable companions. No matter how hard he pulled and heaved and grunted, he was stuck fast. Just as he was concluding that he was drawing finally the last breaths of a less than benevolent and considerate life, a voice said from inside the car,

"A man who's filled an already over-fat gut with one pie and chips too many is a man in need of special help, and I'm indeed a specialist in the kind of help you need."

Baffled to the point of verbal incoherence, O'Brady was able to do little more than mumble incomprehensibly as his mind tried to grapple with the apparent presence in the car of a man who clearly wasn't there.

"Now," the eejit said, "let's see if we can't give you the place of honour as Ireland's first man in space."

Bending his struggling frame round far enough to peer inside the vehicle O'Brady saw indeed that the eejit once more was within. What was much more disconcerting was what was within his hand, for there seemed little doubt that it was a blow torch. No sooner had O'Brady had the worst fear but one that a man can have than anticipation turned to experience. With a swift, single sweep of his arm the eejit singed the immovable bulk that confronted him and gave its owner the enviable power of flight.

When O'Brady had unscrewed his eyelids far enough and removed his front teeth from their unnatural union with his bottom lip, he realised that in an instant he had been catapulted a full six feet and was completely free from the still sinking car.

Trying as hard as he could to ignore the various pains arising from his flight and subsequently violent descent, he found himself so deeply swallowed by the fog that he could see no further than the end of his nose. Of the magnificent car of which he had been so proud an owner, there was no sight, only sound. Lying in desperate, ear-straining hopelessness, he heard a final, suffocating glug and a hiss so low it might have been a sigh, and then no more. Whether the eejit had got out in the same way that miraculously he had got back in he had no idea, for from him also there was no further sound.

O'Brady lay dazed for a good half hour, stiff and plagued by pains that seemed to be on the march to every part of his body, his round, mid-thirtyish face gradually coming to match the colour of his thick overcoat as it became caked in the mud in which he'd landed. His neatly groomed and greased dark brown hair became so saturated with droplets from the thick mist that a sudden switch from fog to sunlight would have given him the unlikely sparkle of a saint.

The more his mind cleared as the effects of the singeing, flight and fall wore off, the more it clouded up again with the bizarre returning memory of all that had happened. Finally, managing to drag himself up into a sitting position, he tried to guess the direction from which he'd come from within the tight, binding mist that wrapped itself all around him. He decided to walk for twenty paces in four different directions, starting each time from the same spot, until he found the track that had so treacherously tipped him into a bog. No sooner had he gone five steps forwards than he realised that he was being followed. His heart beating as loud as a mallet, he stopped, only to find the squat, squelching echo that had been behind him stopped too.

"Who's there?" he demanded through the still, foggy silence, his voice as loud and as steady as he could make it.

The only reply was a single enigmatic squelch, and then all was as silent as before. Deciding that perhaps he was imagining his pursuer, he started off once more, only to hear again the footsteps of one unseen. Turning round in the blindness of the fog, and hearing again the silence of another's unmoving feet, he said,

"I know you're there. It's you isn't it, the eejit who sizzled me haunches with a blow torch. Come on, show yourself or I'll not be answerable for what follows."

Half way up the hillside, which stood invisible beside him, something or someone blew its nose, a loud, unearthly, echoing snort that was followed by a sniffle and a third noise beyond his past familiarity and experience. Simultaneously, an ear stabbing shriek of high pitched laughter sliced the air around, causing him to start so violently that the top row of his teeth nearly changed places with the bottom. Faced with the eerie silence behind and the echoing remnants of something unknown and awful above, he didn't know which way to turn. Instinct deciding the matter for him, he started to run, only to discover that his own fleeing footsteps were matched by the almost simultaneous squelches of another pair of feet. Trying desperately to run faster, he found the squelches behind him keeping almost perfectly in step. What was worse was that a second set of running footsteps started some few yards to the side of him, then another, followed by another and another and another, until the whole invisible valley was filled with the sound of rapidly squelching feet, each pair more or less in synchronisation with his own.

Torn between an increasing desperation and disbelief, he drew suddenly to a halt. Sure enough, all the other feet stopped simultaneously. Feeling now a sense of surreal farce as much as fear, he attempted a brief tap dance on the flat rock on which he stood. Instantly the refrain of dancing feet filled the valley, a strange, almost comical mix of taps and squelches determined by the distribution of rocks and mud.

"Alright! Alright!" he yelled. "Just what the hell's going on? Whose are all the feet that think it such a grand joke to take the Michael out of me own? Come on, show yourselves, who the hell are you?"

Almost as soon as his angry outburst had finished, his momentary, unthinking courage returned to cold fear as he heard his words repeated round and round the valley, sometimes at the volume he had shouted them and seemingly quite close, sometimes in a low whisper, coming apparently from several directions at once, and sometimes in a strange, monkly chant, echoing as if from within the cloisters of some concealed hillside monastery. Finally, once more there was silence. O'Brady felt like a little boy, lost without his mother and about to burst into tears. Then, to his horror, the sound of the assembled feet started up again, this time independent of any movement of his own. Sweat started to pour down his now colour-drained face as he realised that they had all fallen into line and were marching determinedly towards him.

He stood, transfixed, as all around the sound of what now seemed like legions of feet squelched to within a few yards of him, then, as one, stopped.

Suddenly, without warning, the piercing hyena-like laughter that he had heard before cut through the air and seemed to boomerang back and to around his head, inexplicably merging with a throaty roar of echoing mirth that grew and grew in volume until it filled the whole valley. Then, as suddenly as it had all started, it ceased and for a full thirty seconds there was silence. O'Brady pulled his hands down from in front of his terrified face and peered around him, still unable to see anything but the grey wall of the fog. As he did so, he heard the slow thud of heavy footsteps start up in the distance and start coming methodically towards him. Whoever the feet belonged to, he or she was both substantially built and knew the ground well enough to step each time on rock rather than mud.

The footsteps kept on coming for a full ten minutes. Unsure as to whether there would actually be anything physical to see when the owner of the advancing feet reached his person, O'Brady was shocked suddenly to find a towering figure emerge out of the mist and stop directly in front of him. The creature, thirty feet tall at least, with a Viking helmet and horns and a wildly exuberant beard of un-Nordic blackness, seemed rather more than human. Dressed in a fur three quarter length brown garment, with huge hairy legs visible from the knees downwards and a pair of what appeared to be early twentieth century army boots laced firmly around its feet, it looked simultaneously odd and threatening.

"Who are you?" O'Brady asked, terrified, without any great expectation that so strange a creature would be prepared to pass the time in small talk with the relatively insignificant likes of himself. The creature roared a laugh so loud that both of O'Brady's ear drums popped. The roar was taken up by all in the assembled invisible multitude, filling the valley like an enormous motorbike revving in the hands of a novice. Suddenly the partial Viking imitation stopped and everyone else fell silent simultaneously. He pulled a large, dirty handkerchief out of his pocket and blew his nose, an event itself so thunderous that the surrounding mountains shook.

"You'll have to excuse me," he said, "even giants catch colds."

Stuffing the rag back into the depths of his huge coat the creature said,

"I am the lord and spirit of laughter. I fill the valley and the ears of all who pass through it with the sound of hilarity. You are a guest and a prisoner in my kingdom."

Then, turning to the invisible hordes around them, he shouted,

"Tie him up, hand, foot and nose."

"And nose?" O'Brady asked bewildered.

"It's for your own good," the giant boomed, "none of my followers ever take a bath. The smell of their company would be well nigh unbearable if we didn't tie the sides of your nostrils together."

"But why seize me in the first place?" O'Brady enquired. "If you're the spirit of laughter you're not doing a lot to amuse me."

"He didn't tell you what kind of laughter he's the lord and spirit of did he?" a second voice said from out of the mist. Its owner stepped forward to show himself and O'Brady was face to face once more with the eejit.

"Just who the hell are you?" O'Brady demanded.

"Oh, just a simple eejit. That's what you thought back in the cafe now wasn't it? Just an eejit, someone you could treat like dirt. And so, to you, that's what I'll remain."

"You work for him don't you?" O'Brady asked.

"I don't work for anyone with feet or a soul on this earth," the eejit replied.

"Stop playing games," O'Brady demanded, "and what did you mean about him not saying what type of laughter he's the lord of?"

The giant had been watching O'Brady with quiet fascination.

"What a hilarious little feller," he said, "he appears to enjoy talking to himself as much as anyone else. Come on, let's have him bound! And don't forget to take his shoes and socks off first. We don't want anyone choking on leather or shoelaces like the last time - and a pair of ripe socks really spoils the flavour."

O'Brady's face went nearly as white as the dainty feet about to be exposed.

"Me shoes and socks? What is it you're thinking of doing to me?" he spluttered.

"We're going to grease you from head to foot and roast you over a spit," the giant replied. "We haven't had a really good roast for months!"

His laughter erupted again, emulated immediately by that of his followers, and the whole valley shook to the throbbing, unearthly sound for a full four minutes. By the time it ceased, O'Brady was as trussed as a chicken ready for the oven, and yet he hadn't seen a single one of the hands that had so roughly performed their efficient work.

"This murderous buffoon can't see you can he?" he said to the eejit. "No man who could would accuse me of speaking to meself."

"That's true indeed," the eejit said, "just as sure as I can't smell him, thank God. Just see and hear him - and that's bad enough."

His teeth chattering violently as his goose-pimpled, naked feet shuddered against the freezing mud, O'Brady said,

"You still haven't explained your remark about the type of laughter that this lunatic claims to be the master of."

"Oh, now that's a simple thing," the eejit replied. "He's the master of sadistic laughter of course, a fact which I'd have thought was made obvious enough by the state of yerself."

"Still talking, still babbling on to his own self, as if he were the listener as well as the speaker!" the giant roared, his laughter booming back and forth across the valley. "Right me boys, let's be having him greased and a fire set up."

Once more O'Brady found himself being pummelled by invisible hands, the violently applied grease at least serving to make him marginally warmer against the dire cold. What worried him was the much greater warmth that he could see being prepared in the form of a gigantic, sizzling bonfire no more than twenty yards away. As he stared goggle eyed at it, it seemed to burn its way right through the dense fog into the back of his terrified eyes.

"What have I done to deserve this?" he demanded of the eejit. "Why should a man who wouldn't know a sadistic laugh if he heard one be delivered into the hands of a demon?"

"Who wouldn't know a sadistic laugh if he heard one?" the eejit echoed mockingly. "O'Brady, O'Brady, half yer life has been filled with sadistic laughs. D'you not remember them, the 'witty', sick jokes at the expense of anyone weaker than yerself, the bullying jibes you aimed at anyone who seemed unable to hit you back in the school playground. All in the service of buildin' yer reputation as the cock of the yard. The number of times in recent years you've laughed at the expense of the helpless poor for example, the ignorant parasites as you called them. Do you want me to list them? Shall I write it all down in the mud? No, Patrick O'Brady, you are not a nice man. So you see, it's quite fitting you should be here, you're in the company of like minded people. Only they take your everyday sadistic glee to its logical conclusion. They're the product of lots of little remarks like yours, added to hundreds of little remarks of others, all combinin' together to inspire a single, terrible act, the burning of you for fun and food. Such a large and terrifying end, you see, can be traced back to very small beginnings. And it is entirely fitting that as a part of the beginning, you should also be part of the end. There's plenty of healthy flesh on your hams - I think they're looking for a grand and juicy feast."

"You're saying those lunatics are the product of people like me?" O'Brady spluttered. "You're as mad as they are only twice as much. I refuse to accept this, any of this. I will not die as a dinner. Not even the lowest rat would be given such a fate. If you've the power to be invisible to all but me, and the power to get in and out of me car without the opening of the door, then you've the power to get me out of this."

"Have I indeed?" the eejit asked. "Now that might be the case, and then again it might not."

"What d'you mean it might not?" O'Brady screamed desperately as a long pole was thrown on top of him and his bound limbs in turn bound to it.

"Right," the lord of sadistic laughter boomed, "shove the bacon over the fire and let's get it roasted in time for tea!"

No sooner had he spoken than O'Brady's terrified, grease encrusted body was jerked into the air and marched off to the fire by a squad of invisible bearers.

"For God's sake help me!" he yelled to the eejit, his head hanging so low it several times hit the ground before the fire was reached.

"To help a man is a wonderful thing," the eejit said while bending down unconcernedly to scrape some mud off his boots. "I've always admired the helpers in life, the doctors and nurses, the Mother Teresas. Would you like me to tell you a story about one nurse I knew? Very heart-warming I find it - it might help to cheer you up."

O'Brady could feel the grease already starting to melt as the long pole was slotted into a stout wooden framework and a makeshift handle fitted.

"Come on, hurry up, start turning him!" the giant commanded. "It'll be no fun for anyone if he's burnt to a cinder on one side and under-cooked on the other."

O'Brady screamed in desperation, the fierce redness of the flames below burning into his eyes, while his back started to feel as if a thousand needles had been rammed into it. As he was pulled slowly round, the eejit leaned over him, seemingly unaffected by the heat.

"Well, they've started to stoke the old fire up good and proper now," he said.

O'Brady, sweat and grease pouring off his face, could only whimper.

"Now," the eejit said with calm disinterest, "about this business of getting you out of this little mess, it seems on reflection I might be able to do a thing or two."

"Might? What do you mean might?" O'Brady croaked from amidst the smoke. "I need more than 'might' to save me burnin' bacon!"

"It'll require the answering of a question or two," the eejit said.

"Questions? I'll answer every question in the world if it'll get me out of this," O'Brady replied.

No sooner had he spoken than a crack of thunder echoed from end to end of the valley and back again. It was followed instantly by a torrent of night-black rainfall, so heavy that it seemed like a whole river of darkness was being poured out of the sky. The scorching pain of the fire was doused in a second and the giant and all of his followers went scurrying for cover, seeming to find the strange water as terrifying as O'Brady found the flames. The eejit cut the ropes and the cancelled lunch dropped heavily on to the sodden ashes, the remaining grease sucking them onto his scorched trousers like a malevolent vacuum cleaner.

"Now then," the eejit said, "let's see how good you are at answering me questions. If you pass the test then you're off the menu. If you don't play ball then your hungry friends will be back and you'll still be their dish of the day."

"What test?" O'Brady mumbled, still dazed from all of the strangeness that had happened.

"Oh just a few simple questions that you need to answer," the eejit replied. "First, if the moon, a sausage and a frilly nightie were all placed one on top of the other what would be the height of the little pile from top to bottom in centimetres?"

"What? You're taking the mick," O'Brady complained.

"I'll take that as a don't know," the eejit said. "Question two, if you crossed a hedgehog with a giraffe and an elephant what would you get?"

"I can tell you what you're going to get if you keep on taking the piss," O'Brady rumbled.

"We'll take that as another don't know. Still not to worry, those were just the warm ups to put you at ease. Now here's the serious question, so put your thinking cap on and see if you can solve the conundrum I'm going to put to you. What, for you, is the ultimate question?"

"What do you mean, ultimate question?" O'Brady asked. "What kind of sense does that make?"

"Perfect sense," the eejit replied. "This one's the serious bit, so I'd give it some thought if I were you."

"The only ultimate question I can think of is the universe and everything, where did it come from and all that stuff," O'Brady said grudgingly.

"Not the right answer, but yet not entirely the wrong one. That leaves you out of the fire, but not yet out of the frying pan."

"And what on earth does that mean?" O'Brady asked. "Am I free to go or aren't I?"

"In theory you are, but in practice you're not," the eejit said.

"What in God's name do you mean by that?" O'Brady thundered, unwisely forgetting the change in his status from dominant heavy to dependent supplicant.

"Well," the eejit said, "you're free to go as far as I'm concerned, but I think there might well be others who have a different perspective on the matter. From my point of view, you half passed the test, but from theirs you half failed it, which effectively means more preparation and then a re-sit."

"What do you mean 'preparation'?" O'Brady grumbled.

"Well, in their eyes 'preparation' translates as a trial by ordeal."

"Which means?" O'Brady said.

"Well, you've just had a bit of it as preparation for the first test – the near roasting of your behind and all of that. So, it's more of that kind of stuff really, but with a bit of a variety in terms of whoever it is that puts the shits up you."

As he said this the rain ceased and the fog suddenly returned, blocking out once more the rocky, green, steep sided valley that enclosed them. In the distance, the ghostly, echoing sound of monastic chant started up.

"What on earth's happening now?" O'Brady demanded, only to find that the eejit had vanished again. Trying to haul himself upright so that he could begin to scramble frantically back in the direction of the track which had led him into this mess, he found that his body had become paralysed from head to toe. He was able only to flop back helplessly into the mud. Incapable even of moving his lips, he lay in terrified anticipation as the ghostly plainsong grew nearer and nearer. The closer it came, the more a cloud seemed to fill his mind, until he had only the faintest awareness of anything around him and began dimly to conclude that he was at the point of death.

What followed seemed completely unreal. Suddenly, as if from nowhere, ten monastic cowls peered down at him from out of the mist. Their depths were filled with shadow and nothing else.

Simultaneously O'Brady found his numb body lifted by hands he couldn't see or feel and heard faintly the slow slap of sandals as he was carried off up the valley side. All he could make out, as his head hung helplessly backwards, was the all pervasive fog and the grey robes of the monkish figure that brought up the rear.

After what seemed like an eternity of a journey upwards into what might well have been the sky itself, he heard suddenly the creaking of a huge and ancient oaken door. Within seconds he was inside the dark, cavernous grandeur of an abbey that was a larger and more finely carved building than any he'd seen before. His mind finally seemed to be clearing and some degree of sensation was returning to his body. As he was carried down the seemingly endless main aisle he could see dark cloisters on one side of the echoing church and a huge, vaulted ceiling far above. All around, what little light there was was coloured with the distant brilliance of stained glass windows that, even from afar, looked so delicate that they could have been painted only by an angel. Finally, a sudden jolting alerted him to the fact that he was being carried up the altar steps. Before he could begin to imagine why this could be, he was swung through the air as if he were a sparrow's weight and dropped none too gently onto the bare altar. The cold marble of the slab wakened instantly the remaining suspended sensitivities of his flesh and he gasped, like a man falling through ice into water. To his total confusion he found his hands and feet being stretched out and bound to four short brass corner posts. Still unable to speak, he lay totally helpless as the strange, faceless monks started to light a myriad of candles around the altar. Looking up, he could see a huge pentagonal tower lined with stained glass of such brilliance that it seemed to spin wildly in front of his eyes. The one thing that was clear was an enormous and decidedly unusual gold leaf painting on the domed ceiling. Even in the wake of all the other strange happenings of the afternoon, such a fierce depiction of St. Michael being cast down into hell by the devil stood out as the oddest sight yet, especially given its commanding position at the centre of a house of God. Then the chanting started again, and this time O'Brady realised with a slow, cold, terror, that he had got things quite the wrong way round, as indeed had the monks. Now that he could hear every word in the perfect acoustics of the abbey, he realised that he was listening not to traditional monkly prayers, but the Lord's Prayer in reverse. That explained also the absence of crucifixes and the quite probably lethal service of which he was to be the central part. Straining futilely at his bonds, he tried without success to scream as his shirt was ripped open and his chest liberally anointed by a cowled, satanic master of ceremonies with particularly cold hands.

Finally, finishing the ritualistic preparations, the monk beckoned another of the assembled ghouls with a large dagger to come to the altar. The underling then raised the knife high above the hapless sacrifice and held it there while another round of this time excited, almost wild, chanting began. O'Brady's insides felt as if they'd been wrapped three times round themselves as he gasped, open-mouthed, at his impending death. The chanting got louder and ever more excited, until it seemed like a huge, echoing roar filling the whole building. Then, just at the point where he had resigned himself hopelessly to oblivion and closed his eyes before they were closed forever for him, a voice said,

"Do you want to get out of this or don't you?"

Looking with startled eyes in the direction from which the voice had come, he realised that the cowl above him actually had a face hidden deep within it. Finding at last miraculously his voice he said,

"I do! For pity's sake I do!"

"Then you'll do anything I ask?"

"Not you again!" O'Brady gasped, recognising once more the voice of the eejit.

"Who I am or what I am is of no consequence," the eejit replied, only just being able to make himself heard over the chanting. "In a time so short there's hardly a watch to measure it these lunatics are going to come up here and each place their hands over mine. Then, as one, they'll plunge the dagger deep into your fat belly and you'll be just another corpse. If I release you from all of this you'll do absolutely anything I demand of you, good or bad? You'll rob from a widow and take the last crumb from the mouth of a starving man even?"

"I will! I will! For pity's sake just get me free!" O'Brady screamed. Then, after noting the eejit's failure to respond, it dawned on him rapidly that his characteristically unprincipled answer might be in danger of causing him to fail the very test necessary to set him free. He quickly changed tack,

"I mean, I would if I were a man with a hole where his conscience should be. Being a man more inclined to kindness than cruelty, I could not go to the extremes that you suggest."

"Right second answer in terms of the sentiment claimed," the eejit replied, "giving you another half pass. Unfortunately the fact that you didn't mean a word of what you said, as your first answer made clear, means that you have also half failed, which is good news and bad news as they say."

"The good and bad news being?" O'Brady asked, his terrified eyes fixed unswervingly on the dagger about to catapult him from this life into heaven or hell knows where.

"Well, you get to live but you'll have to take another re-sit," the eejit replied. "Tell me, was this the story of your life when you were at school now?"

No sooner had he spoken than high up in the domed tower deep bells started to chime. With each note the peal grew faster, until gradually the whole building started to shake. The cowled would-be butcherers stood transfixed, as if each had been hypnotised by the din from above. The shaking turned rapidly into a crumbling and dust and masonry began to cascade down all around the altar. Suddenly, with an enormous, thunderous roar, the entire building imploded in a spectacular shower of stones as if its very foundations had been dynamited.

As the choking fog of dust gradually began to clear O'Brady found that the altar and himself were the only things, apart from the eejit, that had been untouched by debris. The cowled maniacs were completely buried, involuntary sacrifices at their own high rite. Pulling the dust covered cowl down from his head, the eejit cut the captive free and handed him a document and a pen.

"What's this?" O'Brady asked.

"If you don't want this lot to start crawling miraculously from under the stones just sign your name in the place indicated," the eejit replied.

"But the whole blasted thing is in a language I don't understand," O'Brady spluttered, "I could be signing away the rights to the shirt off me back."

"Given the state of it you wouldn't be losing anything," the eejit said drily. "If I tell you that the signing of this will bring no ill to you personally will you do as you're told?"

"You're sure now?" O'Brady asked uncertainly.

"On me word of honour you'll be no worse off than before you met me, although it could mean a death or two for some other unfortunates."

"Very well," the liberated ex-sacrifice replied, "given the threatened alternative I'll sign and have to trust you at your word."

As he signed the eejit said,

"Oh dear, oh dear, I thought I'd give you a little extra chance just to check that your second answer to me test was as insincere as I assumed it to be and you've just confirmed how right I was. You didn't even query the bit about the deaths of others – your only concern was saving your own skin. The powers that be won't like that. It's an ill wind that brings the next ordeal."

No sooner had the eejit said this than he vanished. Simultaneously an enormous swirling tornado exploded from nowhere, no more than ten or twenty feet from O'Brady, blasting dust into his eyes and pelting his vulnerable, over-fed body with chunks of debris as if he were the star attraction at an Old Testament stoning. He threw himself onto the ground with his hands clasped protectively over the back of his head. Suddenly, from somewhere deep within the enraged, roaring vortex, an enormous suction force started to pull him back down the rubble strewn remnants of the aisle, along which he'd first been carried, and out into the violently battered greenness that looked down on the dank valley below. In an instant his body was lifted high above the hillside and then dropped by the now concentrated power of the wind, which blew madly all around him. At a dizzying and ever-increasing rate of knots he fell back down towards the scene of the failed feast, encased by a tunnel of insane, howling air. His ears felt as if they were being pummelled by a particularly vicious prize fighter as the roaring wind quarrelled with itself all around him.

Then, with a bump that was far less than comfortable, but much less violent than he'd expected, he hit the unyielding solidity of plain mother earth. At exactly the moment of impact the wind stopped and the sky cleared to reveal a startlingly bright late afternoon sun. To his total confusion, birds started singing in non-existent trees. Dragging himself up painfully into a sitting position, he found that his heavily mud-stained but nevertheless salvaged and usable car stood nearby and empty, its engine inexplicably ticking over as if he'd just got out of it. Too baffled and traumatised by all that had gone before, O'Brady didn't waste any time asking questions he had no expectation of being able to answer. He stumbled over to the vehicle and sank into the driver's seat. With no inclination of any sort, other than the simple will to survive, he started to head back towards the main road.

From now on, everything proceeded like clockwork, in fact too much so. O'Brady had the uncomfortable feeling, which he didn't care to test, that had he jumped out of his car it would have travelled back to his house on its own and parked itself with a perfection he'd never managed to achieve amidst the clutter of golf clubs and executive toys that filled his garage.

Arriving at his expensive and rambling executive house in an even more rambling Dublin suburb, he went exhaustedly inside and collapsed onto the sofa, pausing only to switch on the lights. Almost immediately he drifted off into a sleep as deep as death.

It wasn't until the early hours of the following morning that he awoke. Delicately prising his eyes open, he found the place to be in a mess that suggested the aftermath of a party he clearly hadn't had. Empty beer cans and wine bottles were everywhere, half eaten sandwiches were randomly distributed throughout the room, and an un-enticingly carcinogenic pall of stale cigarette smoke hung over everything like death in waiting. Hauling himself upright, O'Brady made slow and puzzled progress into the kitchen. The scene there would have caused even an electric dishwasher to pack its bags and sneak quietly out of the back door while no-one was looking. Amongst assorted objects floating serenely in the washing up bowl was a shoe, a lavatory brush and the plastic duck that his ex-fiancée had bequeathed at high velocity to his left ear when storming out of his life forever. A large, expensive glass vase on the window ledge had been filled with a mixture of mud from the garden, porridge and a long deceased sausage with a condom stretched delicately over its tip. The goldfish bowl had been clouded with an unappetising blend of Guinness and Alka-Seltzer, and a small bust of the Pope, the origin of which was mysterious, had been inserted somewhat incongruously in place of the missing fish. The electric toaster offered the strange sight of two scorched inner soles from his fishing wellies protruding from its innards, while the attractive winter snow scene that surrounded the kettle suggested that someone had been boiling soap flakes. Presumably their absence was explained by the fact that they'd also drunk the resulting beverage and were now laid out deceased in the back garden. He had a look through the beer stained curtains but could see no-one. Plucking up courage he went upstairs to the bathroom. There he found the fish, swimming contentedly in the avant-garde see-through cistern. In the bath there was a hungry cat, its tail tied to the taps with a piece of string. The latter was just long enough to let it repeatedly scramble and slide its way far enough up the slippery porcelain sides to get sight of its breakfast in the cistern - but no further. The fact that he couldn't remember ever having seen the little creature before seemed almost irrelevant in the present circumstances. He untied it and shooed it away downstairs.

Wandering through the disorder of the bedrooms, O'Brady found only mysteriously stained sheets, crumpled pillows and several discarded pairs of his own underpants. A large pair of female lips had been drawn on his dressing table mirror with some of the make-up his ex-fiancée had left behind, but the artist hadn't left any signature.

Becoming more baffled by the minute, he returned downstairs to inspect the lounge more closely. On his retro record deck he found not the expected black vinyl, but a large apple pie spinning round and round with the stylus presumably long blunted by the solidity of the pastry. The CD player was full of spaghetti. The culprit clearly had been saved from electrocution by the fact that it was plugged in only to the potted geranium on the nearby sideboard. A packet of tacks had been emptied over the seat of his favourite armchair and above it hung a largely empty plate of curry, nailed to the wall in place of the missing mirror. In wondering where the curry that hadn't dripped onto the floor had gone, he remembered the strange appearance of the cat's fur. His prized ship in a bottle had been violently liberated and set afloat in a lemonade filled waste paper bin. The pendulum on his most beloved heirloom, an early nineteenth century grandfather clock, now wore a bow tie and shoe, while two big eyes and a smile had been drawn on the clock face in permanent ink.

As he stood completely bemused by all of this, half lost in a dream-state paralysis, suddenly and without warning, the disorganised mess within the house began to come alive. With a slow, mechanical, clomping step, shoes and slippers appeared from under the settee, out of the hall cupboard, the front porch and the kitchen pantry and started to march heavily, one by one, up and down the stairs in a procession that seemed almost a rehearsal for perpetual motion. Outside, the beer bottles that had been strewn around the garden started to dance a tight, chirpy, but almost tediously efficient clinking Charleston, their hollow bottle echo ringing around the brickwork of the patio. In the kitchen, pans could be heard delicately pirouetting on their handles, while empty coffee cups chased each other playfully around the sink.

With a heavy, thumping, castor-less bounce, the cooker attempted to corner and seduce the washer, only to find a row of snapping scissors and the variously assorted contents of a threatening toolbox forming a defensive ring around its prey. In the dining room, fractious dining chairs started kicking each other, while the unfortunate and soon very bruised table tried hopping from left to right in a vain attempt to avoid their wildly inaccurate lunges. On the shelves and overcrowded display unit, books started reading each other out loud, while the carpet began to munch contentedly the generously scattered crumbs that sat helplessly on its pile. Little cries could be heard as each crumb in turn was despatched unwillingly to its ultimate maker. A long forgotten violin on top of an upstairs wardrobe started playing itself, rather badly, and several pairs of socks strewn randomly around the house began to jig. The record deck began to spin wildly, hurling deadly portions of rock-hard apple pie at everything in sight. Upstairs, two pairs of gloves started a boxing match, while a golfing shoe ran amok in a bedroom wardrobe, kicking merry hell out of the seats of as many pants as it could find. The contents of a tissue box leapt out, blew several invisible noses, and then threw themselves tidily into a waste paper basket. The microwave began to ping, to indicate that a sock that had been shoved mysteriously inside was now adequately cooked, while the iron started ill-smelling work on a slab of cheese that the fridge playfully had ejected. In the garden, a loud scream came from the fashionable nude sculpture in the fishpond as the gnome from next door expressed unwanted physical affection. Upstairs, a hurling stick started beating a violent protest upon the wardrobe, from on top of which the violin was playing its appallingly discordant jig. Unabashed, the tone deaf legions of socks continued dancing within and all around the over-crowded linen basket. In the bathroom, in a moment of whimsy, the cistern flushed itself. In an instant the unfortunate goldfish found themselves riding turbulent rapids deep down into the lavatory bowl, only narrowly avoiding a terminal descent beyond the S bend.

O'Brady could take no more. Clasping his head with both hands in the fashion of one demented he screamed out,

"Stop it! Stop it! For God's sake, all of you, stop it! What the hell's going on here? My bloody house is full of poltergeists!"

As one, everything stopped, but then turned slowly in his direction. The cooker lumbered leadenly over to the kitchen door to view the giver of such an unprecedented and disrespectful command, followed by the coffee cups, the iron and everything else imaginable. Socks crept stealthily down the staircase and shoes moved together - for defensive or aggressive purposes it wasn't clear - into a group. Upstairs, eerily and ominously, the violin began to play a horribly out-of-tune death march. As one, the contents of the house began to march in step to the unpredictable, dark drone of the tune of doom. They encircled O'Brady, leaving no safe exit for any creature without powers of flight or instant invisibility. Then, standing no more than two yards away from him, they prepared themselves for merciless attack. A knife and fork that had travelled across in the back of a mortally wounded pumpkin began to sharpen each other on a half brick that had uprooted itself from the patio and smashed its way in through the kitchen window. Several pairs of gloves, some old, some young, partook in throat throttling simulations, or threw well aimed punches at the thin air around them. A large potato pan carefully sized up the measurements of O'Brady's head, in order to decide whether it or one of its larger companions would be most suited to wedging itself over his skull. The contents of his toolbox engaged in a long debate as to who should have responsibility for which part of his anatomy, with a bitter dispute erupting between the pliers and a monkey wrench as to which of them should have the privilege of twisting his nose.

O'Brady stood in appalled and helpless contemplation of the pandemonium around him and began to wonder whether he might just have drunk all the empty whiskey bottles that lay strewn around the floor himself. Losing all confidence in his remaining ability to discriminate between the real and the unreal, the sane and the insane, he began to laugh quietly to himself. Taking some relief from the liberating release of tension that this engendered, he raised the volume of his nervous mirth as high as his voice could manage, in the hope that the relaxing effect it produced would increase in proportion. At the point where his laughter turned into a roar, several empty Guinness bottles smashed themselves on the floor in a spontaneous and enraged response. This sudden and unexpected act of mass suicide caused every source of noise in the room, O'Brady included, to fall silent.

Then, after only a few seconds of soundless outrage, the cooker began to lumber forwards. As one the others followed, the assorted boots and shoes starting to kick at his legs from knee to ankle, while the gloves leapt up and began to box his ears. Chairs kicked him in the backside, while the pliers beat the monkey wrench to his nose and started to pull and twist it with dedication and delight. Through the hell of it all, O'Brady could see the cooker waiting for him to collapse so that it could jump crushingly up and down on his chest, while several sharpened kitchen knives were readying themselves for the final, fatal blows that would separate him from life forever.

Just at the point where he felt he was about to go down he heard the not entirely unexpected voice of the eejit.

"In trouble again?" his timely visitor asked.

"You said if I signed your wretched piece of paper no ill would come to me," O'Brady complained, "and yet all I get is another variety of infernal terror. What is all of this, have I died? Am I in hell, with you as my personal torturing demon?"

He was unable to continue as a gardening glove delivered a slap straight under his chin, snapping his mouth shut as if it was a mouse trap.

"D'you not want to be released from all of this turmoil?" the eejit shouted above the din of frantic cutlery and flailing boots.

"Released for what?" O'Brady asked, sagging helplessly at the knees. "For an even worse nightmare? Why don't you just let me get killed and see if things get better for me after that."

As he finished the sentence O'Brady finally collapsed, sweating, bruised, battered and completely exhausted. As he did so, the cooker started to jump up and down with anticipatory vigour, managing to get higher on each occasion, to the point where it was nearly ready to thud onto his chest. The eejit leaned over him, smiling benignly as the kitchen chairs kicked the stricken unfortunate's heels.

"Now come on O'Brady, you're not telling me you're going to submit to such a ridiculous death? This is hardly the way for a man of substance like yerself to be despatched into eternity. Why don't you just let me get you out of this and quell this rebellious house once and for all?"

The cooker clearly was getting to the point where the final, fatal jump onto its helpless prey was becoming imminent. A pair of old golf gloves gripped the poor man so firmly round the throat that he felt that his eyes were about to pop. Deciding finally, through the dim light of his fading consciousness, that this was indeed hardly a dignified or credible means of departing from existence, he croaked hoarsely,

"Alright, go on, get me out of it then."

The eejit bent down amidst the turmoil, himself remaining miraculously untouched by any of it, and thrust a pen and paper into O'Brady's flailing hands.

"You don't need me to tell you the drill now do you," he said, "just sign and you'll be released."

Feebly, O'Brady duly signed and at once all the lethal activity around him ceased. Socks and gloves fell limply to the floor, the cooker crashed down into permanent stillness, and knives, forks and coffee cups clattered and clunked on top of each other in so lifeless a manner that it was impossible to conceive of them ever having been capable of movement.

"What now?" O'Brady asked exhaustedly. "What have I signed up to this time?"

"Oh, it's not so bad," the eejit replied. "You've just agreed to undergo another little test starting more or less now. So, if you're ready, here's the first question. How many legs has an eight legged pork pie?"

"Oh not again," O'Brady said, "you're taking the mick for the sake of it and I'm in no state to cope with such a thing."

"No, I'm deadly serious. If you don't answer the questions your house will come back to life and you'll be dead. It's a simple choice – a man with the brain of a mouse would know which way to decide."

"Oh for God's sake, I don't know, it's a ridiculous and farcical question, so perhaps you should ask a man with the brain of a mouse for the answer. If the thing has eight legs then eight legs it has."

"Now there you're wrong," the eejit said. "A proper thinking of the question through would have made it obvious that a pork pie can't have any legs, given that the only matter within it that was once connected to legs is both deceased and encased within a thick pastry. Never in the history of the universe has pastry or anything deceased been known to grow legs. You'll need to think a good deal harder on the second question if you're not to make a mess of the test. Are you ready now?"

O'Brady groaned in desperation.

"I'll take that as a 'yes I'm raring to go'," the eejit said. "So, get your thinking cap on for the next question, which is, how long would it take a man to travel from the North to the South Pole using only a unicycle and a pickled egg for transport?"

O'Brady rolled his eyes at the bizarre nature of the question. He thought for a minute and then said,

"The journey would take as long as the eejit on the bike took to reach the sea, because once there he would drown given the inability of a unicycle to float and the complete irrelevance of the pickled egg to the whole affair."

"Well done! You're finally getting the hang of things," the eejit said. "Your answer is one hundred per cent right. These little light hearted puzzles have a serious purpose in training your mind to think out of the box, you know, because while you're in the box you're never going to get the answers to the really serious stuff, which is next. So, brace yourself for a thunderclap of inspiration between your ears, because that's what you'll need to solve this little conundrum and free yourself from further ordeals. Here we go, this is the second occasion of asking, so you've had plenty of time to think of an answer. And don't forget what I said about thinking outside of the box of your usual thoughts. What, for you, is the ultimate question?"

O'Brady looked as blank as he did when he'd first been asked the same thing. After several minutes of increasingly desperate thought he said,

"I can't think of anything different to what I said before. For me, the ultimate question is how did the universe and everything begin, how did life begin. What could be more ultimate than that?"

There was a pause, during which the eejit stared enigmatically at O'Brady, who in turn stared anxiously back. Then the questioner gave his verdict.

"Well, time waits for no man or his ferret, as they say in Donegal. I was hoping you might rethink your answer in the time available, but as you haven't done so I have to tell you that you've failed again. Tick tock, what's o'clock, time for another white knuckle adventure I'm afraid."

O'Brady groaned in despair and put his head in his hands. The eejit said,

"Now, now, that's not the kind of cowardly defeatism I'd expect from a man who was so fierce in defence of his pie and chips just a day or two ago. You should look on the bright side. Let's see if the latest ordeal helps you find the concentration and reflection necessary for a correct response to me little question next time I ask you for it, now wouldn't that be a blessing? That's what all these terrifying little challenges are supposed to be about you see, giving you an incentive to think long and hard enough about your miserable life to solve the conundrum I keep setting you – if you can finally get the answer then you may well escape from all of these nightmare experiences for now and forever. The forever bit depends on how you conduct yourself after you've found the answer. But if you can't get it right, then sooner or later it could be goodbye to Mr. Chips, or Mr. Pie and Chips in your case. If the doom and gloom of that deadly prospect can't focus your mind then nothing can."

Then, his attention grabbed suddenly by the chime of

O'Brady's grandfather clock, he said,

"By the Holy Sock of Saint Sollom is that the time, I must be off and off is what I am."

No sooner had he finished speaking than he disappeared into thin air again, leaving a traumatised O'Brady trying to imagine what might next be in store for a man who already had experienced ten times more trials and ordeals than he could stand. He dragged himself up and grabbed a much needed swig from a half empty whiskey bottle. However, no sooner had he done so than the room started to spin, at first slowly, then like a washer on medium speed rinse, then with the frantic, sickening whizz of a Catherine wheel. He began to wonder whether the drink had been spiked. At the point where speed seemed to be about to destroy consciousness, he was sucked suddenly and violently into and up the chimney and then fired out the top as if by a cannon.

For what seemed like a good half hour, he flew like a human rocket, high above the early morning dew-soaked greenery glistening in the golden sun below. The wind rushed breath-freezingly past his numb cheeks and his hair flew and flapped around his forehead like a tussle of frantically writhing snakes. So unreal did everything seem that his mind was unable to do anything other than process the cool calm of the glowing green land below as he soared endlessly, effortlessly over it.

At length, just as he had begun to believe that his entire future would be spent as a projectile, he started to lose height. Looming below, he saw the sparkling blue waters of Connemara, smiling up like a welcoming aunt. Then, going down in a graceful curve, he started to lose speed as well as height, plunging finally into a lake whose name he knew not and which was unlikely to tell him. The freezing water restored the full immediacy of his senses. He swam hurriedly to the surface and then desperately to the shore, where he lay, draped over rocks and pebbles, like an exhausted and shivering rat. Unexpectedly, the benignly glowing sun developed suddenly an out of season warmth which soon dried him out and he fell into an easy, deep sleep, from which no sound or subconscious urge could raise him for over twelve hours.

When O'Brady finally awoke, it was to the sound of a young woman's gentle humming. Scraping the mud and dirt of the lakeside from his eyes, he peered half blindly around and then spotted the nymph occasioning all the gentle commotion about twenty feet away. She was wearing a pure white silk dress, which seemed somehow to belong to an earlier century, and a set of beads that glowed with every colour of the rainbow around the long, sun gold hair that trickled gently down the back and sides of her slender neck. She appeared to be collecting firewood. Seeing him looking across at her she said,

"Hello, who are you?"

"I'm O'Brady. I fell out of the sky," he replied, deciding that reality had so far distanced itself from his being that he need no longer worry about whether his answer sounded sensible or not.

"Oh," the nymph said, "I hope it wasn't too heavy a fall. I'm Three Things. I only fell out of a womb."

"Why Three Things?" O'Brady asked, dragging himself and his mud stained clothes upright.

"Because for every three things good that I do, I do three things bad," she replied. "I'm a very balanced person."

She paused while arranging the firewood neatly in her basket to make sure none of it would fall out. She continued,

"You're in luck. I've just done three wicked things, one so wicked that even the sun turned its face and the foxes and squirrels put their paws over their eyes in horror. So it's time to be good again. I'm very kind when it's my duty to be. Would you like somewhere warm to spend the night?"

The words were like serene kisses to O'Brady's now severely tormented mind and he nodded his head vigorously, quite unable to believe his luck.

Then for tonight you shall come into my bosom," she replied, smiling with a sweetness that was so concentrated it would have caused a whole mouthful of teeth to rot had it been eaten. O'Brady felt a sudden surge of anticipation, mingled simultaneously with doubt, a contrary state occasioned by his uncertainty as to whether the sensuous young lady was speaking literally or figuratively.

"Come," she said, "follow behind and I'll show you where I live."

The less salubrious side of O'Brady's already less than salubrious mind decided that hers was one behind he'd follow anywhere. Forgetting completely his exhausted and battered disposition, he sprung after her like a man uncoiled, quite oblivious to the sharp brambles that kept stabbing at his knees and hands.

At length, having travelled half way up the nearest valley side, the nymph stopped in front of a small dwelling that appeared to be woven out of a strange, glistening and enchanting patchwork of evergreens and spiders webs. The structure was suspended from convenient and stockily firm tree branches and inside a seductively glowing fire crackled and spat away without any sign of the unpleasantness of smoke. Entering through a narrow gap she beckoned him to follow, and together they drew up their knees by the fire's warmth as the late afternoon sun set slowly in the now cold distance. She smiled with apparent innocence at his wandering eyes, seeming not to notice their preoccupation with the alluring softness of her thighs.

"What else can I do for you?" she asked brightly. "There's another two good deeds to go yet."

"Oh, I think I can suggest something," O'Brady stammered, his heart beating in contemplation of imminent heaven on earth.

"Oh, now it's a shame I know, but rules are rules," she said. "I'm the only one allowed to think of the kind deeds that I do for others. The thing must always come from my own head or it doesn't exist or worse. And believe me, what is worse is not to be contemplated."

O'Brady's mouth sagged, saying by its single action more than any words could. He couldn't think of any kind deed he wanted other than the one he couldn't ask for.

"You look tired and ill all of a sudden," she said. "I've given you somewhere to sleep, but you should eat first. That's my second kindness - a feast. Close your eyes."

She leaned over and gently pushed O'Brady's lids shut. His mind was focused only on the fact that two of his kindnesses had now been decreed and he seemed no nearer the one his whole being was on fire with lust for.

"Right, you can open them now," the nymph said after a couple of minutes. He did so to find the earthen floor in front and around him covered with all the edible and drinkable delicacies he might ever have dreamed of, all laid out in the seductive manner of a wedding feast. Laughing gently at his amazement, the nymph dipped an oyster in three different strange and exotic looking sauces and then placed it slowly and mischievously onto his tongue. Her eyes now no longer seemed those of an innocent. Holding it quite still for a moment in his mouth, as the sweet odour of the juices swirled gently around his palate, he began to suck the oyster like a sweet, his eyes all the time locked on hers in rapt anticipation. She placed another oyster and then a small, mouth-drowningly beautiful sliver of unknown, deep water sea creature onto his tongue, before washing both smoothly down with a glass of wine that belonged only to the gods. Taking the glass back from his moist lips, she kissed it all the way round the rim before refilling it and placing it into his trembling hand, her fingers catching and softly stroking his in the process.

"Feast my hungry one!" she commanded silkily, pointing at the giant spread that lay before him. Acting almost as if this was some preliminary test before an even bigger treat - the one he most desired - O'Brady lurched forward on all fours and began devouring everything in sight. Soon the juices of a hundred delicacies ran like rivers down his chin, whole chicken legs vanishing between his hungry dog teeth in an instant and bottles of wine being drained as if they were water. All the time the nymph clapped and urged him on, his eyes continually searching hers for approval as if he were a faithful collie pup learning its first tricks.

Finally, the entire floor being covered in bones, pips, crusts and empty glasses, the desperate feaster broke wind in a most unceremonious and unintended manner and drew to a halt. The nymph gave him a prolonged round of applause and a little cheer.

"Well done!" she said. "You're the most vigorous eater of a man I've ever set eyes on. You deserve a special prize - my third and final act of kindness. To you, O'Brady the Great, King of all the lechers and gluttons, I offer my sweet body for the night. You shall be my lord and mighty conqueror for an entire evening!"

It was here! Now! The moment he'd been waiting for. Without even a moment's thought O'Brady ripped open the remnants of his shirt and tore off his trousers and Y fronts simultaneously. Then, standing like Godzilla with two hairy arms outstretched ready to clasp round her, he collapsed face first onto the one remaining cream cake and began instantly to snore and snuffle like an amplified hedgehog. The nymph looked sweetly down at him and said,

"What a sad and terrible shame, a man so willing yet so unable to take up my kind offer. Now, my three good things being done, I have only unpleasantness to offer. Sweet dreams my poor darling, sleep peacefully while you can."

In the lukewarm light of the partially clouded mid-morning sun, O'Brady finally awoke. Looking up from within the lead weighted, skull-squeezing agony of his hangover, he found himself gazing once more into the depths of the nymph's all-seeing eyes. She smiled.

"Tell me," he said slowly and deliberately, trying hard to remember all that had passed the night before, "have I had me three things good?"

"As far as it was possible," she replied, still smiling.

"Then what happens now... is the three things bad?" he asked haltingly, a little man with a drum running round and round inside his head as he spoke.

"Indeed," she replied, still smiling. Looking desperately round for his clothes, O'Brady decided it was definitely time to be off. Unfortunately, he couldn't see even a shirt button.

"Here, take these," the nymph offered, handing him a pair of trunks that were modest enough for a monk. Hoping desperately that the proffering of other garments was to follow, O'Brady slipped them on as quickly as his thumping head would allow. No sooner had the band snapped around his waist than something terrible happened. Looking down in horror, he found the trunks had turned instantly to concrete and gripped his skin so firmly that it was impossible to remove them without removing also all that he held most dear.

"What, w…what in God's name's happened?" he stammered.

"The first thing bad," the nymph replied serenely, "something to guarantee a young woman's safety in the face of your most obvious virility."

"You can't, you can't leave a man like this. What are you going to do?"

"Something even worse," she replied. "Now close your eyes and you'll get a surprise."

His eyes snapped shut instantly and involuntarily. Helpless and lost in his temporary darkness, he felt suddenly her hands, moist and luxurious, start to massage him gently and thoroughly from head to toe. The fact that the concrete stayed intact was considerable testimony to its indestructibility. At length, at the point where he felt himself to be so far lost within paradise that he could never find his way back again, she stopped and reopened his eyes.

"That was supposed to be the second thing bad?" he asked from the puzzled heights of his ecstasy.

"Indeed it was," she smiled. "Look, your whole body is glistening."

Following her eyes he saw that every inch of his visible flesh was indeed as moist as the early morning dew.

"What have you covered me in?" he asked nervously, half expecting that at any moment he would start to dissolve.

"Oh, a special treat," she replied.

"For me?" he asked sceptically.

"No, for my hungry little friends," she said fondly, a haunting cacophony of wolf-like howls erupting further up the valley side as she spoke. "It's their favourite scent. Go on, get running, you mustn't deny them the fun of the hunt."

"Run? Run! With me essentials wrapped in half a ton of concrete? I can hardly stand upright never mind run."

"And there was I thinking you were such a manly man," she said, pushing him so hard in the chest that he fell over and started to roll, barrel like, all the way back down the valley side.

Poor O'Brady bounced and whirled and swirled, the world spinning wildly past his terrified eyes, and all the time the heavy concrete girdle that encased his hopes and fortunes refused to crack. The one thing his rapidly numbed senses hung onto, amongst all the pain and the thudding of his dull head against hard earth, was the sound of the pursuing hounds, wolves, or whatever it was Three Things had sent after him. With an awful, final thump, he crashed into a large, all too solid log on the lakeside and came to a halt. Dragging himself slowly up, his concrete chastity belt weighing him down so heavily it felt as if his knees were glued to the earth, he started to stumble towards the lake, the water being the only medium in which he felt he could outstrip his rapidly approaching furry nemesis. With a loud splosh he leaped into the deep depths that were already waist high at their nearest point to the shore and threw himself forwards onto his chest. He tried to slip away to safety with the lightning swimming skills that he imagined to have been his trademark at school. Not only was the excess flab of his over indulgent belly against his ambitions however, but the concrete underwear around his midriff served simply to pull him firmly beneath the icy cold surface of the water. Reaching desperately down with his feet in an attempt to find the reassuring solidity of the bottom, all he discovered was that the lake sheered so steeply away from the bank that he might just as well hunt for a golf ball on the bed of the Atlantic. The momentum that he had gained after throwing himself forward in his failed attempt to swim had carried him already beyond any point where he could touch the bottom without becoming fully submerged. Pushed downwards by the weight of his concrete underpants, he sank rapidly a full twelve inches beneath the surface. His lungs bursting for air, he flailed around helplessly trying to make his way back towards dry land. Finally, at the point where his last seconds of consciousness were about to depart forever, firm, ungentle hands grabbed his sagging thighs and propelled him back upwards towards the surface. Half choked, he gulped in more air in a single second than most men would in ten, coughing and gasping in bizarre accompaniment to the angry hounds' barking and growling around the shore. His invisible saviour continued to push him along until he was back to a point where he could rest his feet once more on the bottom. A labourer's strong hand started to slap him vigorously on the back to help expel the unsavoury water that he'd swallowed. A familiar voice said,

"Well, if ever there was a moment I'd thought you'd had it that was surely it. Mind you, with the hungry thirst for your blood of those angry little fellers on the bank it could be curtains for you yet."

O'Brady gulped and gasped almost simultaneously.

"Well, well," he said with understandable hoarseness, "fancy meeting the likes of you here."

He continued to gasp desperately as the eejit's hand pummelled his heaving back. With great difficulty he said,

"I suppose you've brought me another piece of paper and

another sodding test for me to fail before being catapulted into yet another sodding nightmare?"

"And aren't you the one that should have been a mind reader," the eejit said, stopping finally the vigorous thumping that had threatened to become as much of a life taking as a life saving exercise. "I have here indeed in me pocket - a little wet you'll understand, or certainly you'd be a strange man if you didn't - just the same piece of paper your remarkable foresight expected. Now shall we see how much further yet your truly magical powers can go? Can you tell me what I'm about to ask?"

Looking darkly across at the starving hounds licking their slavering teeth in desperate lust, yet so strangely afraid of the water, O'Brady said,

"Just give me the pen and paper."

"Have you lost all interest in what it is you're putting your name to these several times?" the eejit asked.

O'Brady said, shivering,

"All you'll tell me is that the putting down of me name will do me no harm, but I'm beginning to wonder you'll understand. It's becoming a long time since I can remember coming to any good."

"Is that all you can remember?" the eejit enquired. "The stuff that relates solely to yourself?"

"Standing chest deep in balls-freezing water, with half the world's unfed hounds reading a menu with my name on it, that's more than any sane man could be asked to remember."

"Is it indeed?" the eejit remarked. "There's nothing there then at the back of your head - about what the fullest implications of the desperate signing of your signature might possibly be? You remember the little difficulty we had earlier when you were unconcerned about the possibility of a death or two resulting from your signing of another of my little pieces of my paper – and if you think back further into the shadier areas of your past, you'll come across previous examples of similar unconcern. In light of all that, how shall we put it, history of callous selfishness, are you not in the slightest bit ashamed of yourself? Have you no concern about the possible consequences for those other than your precious self if you sign up now to heavens knows what? Have you no interest at all in checking if such consequences apply and what they might be before scrawling your signature on whatever I stick in front of you?"

"How can I be concerned about anything when I'm bounced from one terrifying and ludicrous predicament to another without any of it making the slightest sense?" O'Brady asked. "All I know is what you tell me, and all you tell me is that you can offer me an aspirin which will kill the pain for a very short while. And then, when things get even worse than before, you return with another aspirin - and another, and another. I don't care any more, about anything. Just give me the piece of paper, set me another test which I'll undoubtedly fail and let's get it over with. You can start the next ordeal then and we'll meet all over again - probably for ever as far as I can see."

"Indeed?" the eejit said. "Has it never occurred to you that that's a matter over which you have some control?"

"What d'you mean?" O'Brady asked, shivering twice as much as before, but by now quite acclimatised to such unpleasantness.

"What I say, no more and no less," the eejit replied. "Perhaps you ought to think a little more closely about our meetings. I've kept asking you the same question, the question that's the key to your freedom from all of this and on each occasion you've failed to even begin the soul searching that might enable you to find the right answer. Perhaps that's because there are some thoughts you've decided not to think. Now that could be a problem for a man."

"And that's how it's going to stay if you insist on puzzling me with riddles I haven't a chance of solving," O'Brady replied.

"Some riddles are made only in the minds of the listener and have nothing to do with the speaker," the eejit replied, creating another riddle.

"What on earth are you on about now?" O'Brady shouted in frustrated desperation, quite unnoticing that the hounds had disappeared and that he was once more clothed and on dry land. "I've had enough of your games. The one thing I need to know more than anything else is how the hell to get out of this nightmare and back to normality. I want to know when you're going to stop playing with me."

"With me, with me, with me," the eejit replied mockingly, "I hear an awful lot of me's but little enough of anyone else. D'you remember now, when you nearly throttled what you thought was the likes of me in the cafe? Or when you tried to manhandle me poor tired self out of yer car? There were a lot of 'you's' in your mind then and none of the 'me's' that referred to me or anyone else. And it's still the same, a head full of yerself and damn the rest. Ah well, no matter. Every man to his own skull and the particular strangeness of its contents."

"Just tell me what new little slice of hell you have lined up for me next and let's get on with it," O'Brady said acidly.

"I think the time has come for us to go on a very special little journey," the eejit said, "but before we do I'll give you one more chance to answer that familiar little question and liberate yourself from me and all of this forever more. Forget signing the paper and everything else – just give every bit of your mind, memory and soul to thinking this through. Take your time, all the time in the world if you need it. So here we go – what, for you, and notice how I stress the 'for you' bit, what for you is the ultimate question? If it's any help I've given you so many clues in the last minute or so that only a man with the brain of a flea could miss them."

"So if I get this wrong again you're telling me I'm a flea brain," O'Brady said. "What a complimentary and kind feller you are."

"Just fix your mind on the question and see if you can get it right this time," the eejit replied. O'Brady sat down and stared into infinity for ten minutes or more, a look of profound disgruntlement sitting heavily on his face, causing his eyebrows to furrow so deeply that they were in danger of meeting below his nose and turning into a moustache. Finally he sighed and without looking at the eejit said,

"You kept going on about me only referring to me, so the clue I guess was that and that I should refer to people other than meself."

"Go on, go on, you're getting warm," the eejit said.

"So the ultimate question for me would be the ultimate question for more people than me - and the only question I can think of that might be called 'ultimate' for so many is where are we all going, where will we all end up when we've run out of life and lie in line in front of the door of the crem."

"Well, that's an important question no doubt, but for you, it is not the ultimate question unfortunately," the eejit said.

"What a surprise," O'Brady said sourly. "So it's off again on another adventure I presume, this 'special' little journey you referred to. I've been on several of the things so far, all with the most terrifying results, so what's different about this one? What particular humiliation have you planned for me that will stand so head and shoulders above the rest?"

"Oh this will be a voyage of discovery," the eejit replied.

"Of what?" O'Brady asked.

"That's right. Of what, yourself and everything else besides," the eejit said, "including the answer to the question that you've proved so incapable of supplying."

"Wonderful," O'Brady said sarcastically. "And when do you intend that I should go?"

"When? Right now of course," the eejit said with a smile, hurling his inquisitor headlong into the lake. Within no more than a few seconds O'Brady found himself plunging helplessly down what seemed to be a deep underwater passage. His lungs bursting with the pain of hot irons thrust deep within his chest, he travelled so far down into the cold, silent blackness that he felt, to the extent that it was possible to feel anything in the middle of his agony and panic, that this time death really would claim him as its own. Finally, at the point where he could hold his breath no longer, his mind evaporated into a blank mist of unconsciousness.

The first thing O'Brady noticed on awakening was the multi-layered echo of a single, heavy drip of invisible water falling from some unseen, gloom-bound height onto the cold stone floor on which his cruciform body was stretched. Lying exhausted and still on his goose pimpled back, he flickered open his tired eyes several times, to see only semi-darkness and the reflections of shadows. His mouth sagged as if lead weights were pulling his chin down onto his chest, and his mind, battered by so many unspeakable and incomprehensible events, motored quietly and resignedly in neutral. Gradually, he became aware of his own breath echoing repeatedly around and above him and of a cacophony of whispers that contained his name somewhere deep within them. It seemed that they were telling him something, that he was in a cave, the cave of echoes. He could only muster the vaguest of interest in this un-startling information, having already concluded as much himself.

Suddenly he became aware that the sound of dripping water had turned into that of a definite trickle. The matter was of no discernible initial interest, his jaw remaining as deeply dropped as before. The contact of the ice cold liquid with his anatomy changed everything in an instant, however, and he shot upright with the agility of a man who has just had a round of buckshot fired into his backside.

He was shocked to find himself staring into the cold reptile eyes of a man with a viper's tongue. He could see no more than the creature's head: greenish, snake-skin in texture and reflective of the fraction of light that bounced in unison with the whispers around the vast chamber that surrounded them. The head beckoned him forwards, unthreateningly, because its own awfulness was threat enough. O'Brady followed, stepping gingerly across a sharp-stoned, freezing floor, lost in mist he could only half see.

"Hell's teeth," he said to himself, "I can't even see me own feet."

The creature led him through a narrow neck in the cave, within which the whispers concentrated and collectively became as loud as shouts, and then out, into a passageway lit only by the echoes of a light that had been long since extinguished. On either side he sensed there was something solid and reaching out with both hands he indeed found it, row upon row of metal beds with steel-barred ends. The further they walked, the more he smelt blood and suffering, although only the occasional failing whimper conveyed the presence of anything human within the hidden depths. Then, in a swirling gesture of a silence louder than noise, the creature cast its eyes back across all the deep-shadowed beds, unleashing simultaneously a fire-red, searing light that bathed everything around in a harrowing, flare-like brilliance. In every bed, broken, cruciform, mangled or retching, crumpled figures lay in hopeless, eyeless desperation and decay. O'Brady recoiled with horror, every direction in which he turned revealing something more horrific than before. The images that burned themselves into his mind became even worse when he tried briefly to close his eyes.

"Who, what, what is this, who's done this?" he mumbled, as

much to his confused self as to the bizarre creature whose eyes had turned into spitting furnaces. The thing swung round at him, its bodiless head rearing up in front of his face as if it were on an invisible pole.

"You!" it roared in a voice that simultaneously and impossibly managed to be a whisper. "You!"

"No, not me!" O'Brady declared limply.

In a reply as terrifying as anything that could be imagined, the heads of all the rapidly expiring human shadows turned towards him, and from deep within them, an ethereal, deathly chorus rose,

"Yes O'Brady, you. We're dying because of you and the contracts you delivered. You acted as the go-between for the pesticide company that off-loaded all of its stocks of chemicals banned in the west onto poor African farmers, the people who knew nothing of the poisons that were being sold to them to line fat pockets in the west. You were the man who enabled it to all happen, you are the killer of the innocent poor. You are a killer as sure as you fired a gun at us."

"But I didn't know all of this would result – how could I?" O'Brady pleaded.

"The only reason you didn't know was because you couldn't be bothered to think it through, you just focussed on the money, on getting the deal done!" the creature with the viper's tongue roared.

"But there's hundreds of people who've done far worse than I have," O'Brady wailed at the snake head. "Why pick on me instead of them – or this horror instead of all the other horrors that occur every week in every part of the world?"

The creature said,

"Because you were capable of so much better - and yet you have caused all this. You were born carrying the hopes of the angels, yet chose to sell your soul to the devil and become the sour monster that you are now. Yours is a fall from grace that laughs in the face of all the good you should have brought to the world. It's time you paid your debts O'Brady, time to hold you to account."

The accused had had enough. The snake man had become a conductor of the prosecution choir, each blink of his fire red eyes raising the volume of the deathly voices further, until the very floor seemed to rumble and vibrate with the resonance of the horrific sound. O'Brady turned and ran, the voices following him still and growing ever louder. The passage and the grisly death ward seemed to go on for ever. He began to feel that this was his own personal hell and that he would spend the rest of eternity running to escape a curse from which in reality there was no remission. Just at the point where he felt his lungs, heart and mind were about to explode simultaneously, he burst out into the daylight. He collapsed exhausted onto the warm ground. Suddenly he became aware that the sun was partially blotted out. Looking up, he saw a familiar figure silhouetted against the fierce blue sky. The eejit said,

"So now you know the answer – for you, the ultimate question was how could you help those less fortunate than yourself instead of damaging and even killing them? How could you make up for what you've done and start anew? Your various ordeals forced you to focus all of your thoughts on the little conundrum that was set you and yet at no stage could you reflect on your past and even begin to work out the answer. Even when it was given to you on a plate at the end you refused to accept it and ran away like a coward. So, now there's a new question, the final question, O'Brady, and that's what to do with you next."

"You could just leave me alone," O'Brady moaned.

"We could, but we won't," the eejit replied.

"Who are 'we'?" O'Brady asked.

"Well I could say the fates or even the furies, forces that had been unleashed in response to your crimes, but if I told you who we really are you wouldn't believe me - and knowing would be irrelevant anyway," the eejit replied.

"Why?" O'Brady asked.

"Because we've decided to send you back to the egg, if you get my gist and eggs can understand nothing at all," the eejit replied.

"What egg?" O'Brady asked woodenly, while hauling himself to his feet.

"Well, it's all a case of potential gone badly wrong, as our friend with the snake head said. You were expected to be such a good feller and instead you've made such a mess of your own and other people's lives - and been such a generally unpleasant piece of work to boot - that we've decided to make you pay your debts and save as many lives as you've cost. We're sending you back to the moment you were born O'Brady and this time you're going to do everything right – you're going to use that potential in the way you were supposed to. We'll be watching you, every step you take, every day you live and you're going to repay every debt you owe. Then, when you've sweated and toiled for the good of everyone but yourself, then we'll take a second and final look at what to do with you. In short, you're going to have to live your life again. You may think of it as another ordeal, but it is instead a privilege, one rarely if at all given and only then in circumstances that are far more special than you. But again, there's no point in telling you what they are, because your memories of now are about to end."

"Are they indeed – and you want to send me back to the moment I was born you say? Nobody sane or lunatic would think of doing such a thing – it's unnatural in every sense," O'Brady replied.

As he spoke he noticed two things that were disconcerting. The first was that he seemed to be losing height – and quickly. The second was that his deep, bass voice was going rapidly up the scale. His clothes soon were twice the size of him, then three times and more. Possessed by panic and a fear so deep and fierce that it as good as burned a hole right through him he shrieked,

"What's happening, why am I shrinking?"

His voice was now that of a seven year old and his emotional discomfort was translating as that of a small child instead of an adult. As the seconds ticked by even that level of comprehension faded and his grasp of the world around him declined first to that of a toddler, then to an infant's, then to nothing at all.

He had become once more a fertilized egg, alone and waiting to grow into a foetus and be born in a womb as yet unknown. The eejit, consciousness and everything had gone.

Once his clothes had been found by the guards O'Brady was one more puzzling entry on the missing persons list.

Next time around, he would have a different name. In that sense, the end was the beginning.

The eejit, meanwhile, sat in another café, in another land, waiting for his next assignment to arrive and order a meal…

Intermission 4

The twist at the end of Valerie O'Dowd's tale was unexpected enough, but what followed was even more so. With a flourish that upstaged even her introduction, eight theatrical 'fog' devices went off in a little circle around her, obscuring her entirely from view and creating the desired impression that she'd gone up in smoke. When the fog cleared a pair of empty shoes and her spectacles stood where she had been, with no sign of O'Dowd herself, causing a ripple of laughter and applause from the audience that lasted a full two minutes.

Sean said,

"Now there's the second great complication of the tales so far, how do we work out how much of the applause was for the party trick at the end and how much was for the tale itself? As with Brendan, you're going to have to rely largely on your own judgments about her story, with little or no account taken of the audience reaction. You're not going to have much time to get your thoughts together either, the next act is already on the stage. Oh, no - on second thoughts there'll be no such hurry. It's the feller who was due in Brendan's slot but got delayed, he gets delayed in everything he does. They call him the professor."

"Why the professor?" Ben asked.

"Well, in his earlier life he was an academic in Wales and that's part of the story," Sean replied, "but the other is all about how he looks – if ever there was a man you'd think was a professor then Chris Costello is he. Everyone here likes language or they'd be somewhere else, but for him it's an obsession. He prides himself as a craftsman, with words as things to be carved and shaped and glued into place. He fine tunes the way he uses them to just the right bits in his tale. For a miserable looking feller he has a real way with the funnies and he can switch the tone of his tales from the poetic to the tragic to pure slapstick with elegant ease. He can go from the real world to a dream world and back again and make you believe in both – and his sympathy for the plight of his characters is as strong and tangible as if they were really alive. In short, he's a constant surprise on two legs. He's terrible fussy though where venues are concerned - he needs all kinds of things to be just right before he starts and he'll be provoking Fierce Betty to become fiercer still by all the demands he'll be making about three of this and five of the other. Look, you can see the steam starting to hiss out of her ears while he's over there talking to her now. He won't speak without a microphone and he still won't speak if the blessed thing's not precisely the right height – look, he's got his tape measure out and he's measuring it now. Then there'll be the spotlight, if that's not right he'll sit on his hands until it's just as he wants. Then there'll be this and that of a totally random nature that nobody in their right mind would even think of. We'll be a good fifteen minutes or more before it's all settled – oh, no, I eat my words, Betty's on the case. She's pushed the microphone down to the level he's demanding and confiscated his tape. I've not seen that happen before. That's all he's getting and he doesn't look pleased. She's giving him the right old rounds of the kitchen – and by heavens they're off! She's going to announce the start come hell or high water."

Betty once again commanded that silence rule and rule it did. Her introduction to the professor was briefer than any before and her irritation with him cut through her every word like a razor that threatened to slice him into a Sunday roast should he unwisely dare to whinge again. Just to rub the point more deeply into his brain she gave him a time by which he must be finished so that the remaining acts could have their place in the sun as well.

With an expression as dark as a full eclipse Costello

approached the mike and surveyed the audience. At five feet eight and always late, he was in a weak position should he wish to challenge Betty anymore, given that she was three inches taller than him and well capable of boxing both his ears in the time it took for him to sneeze. Having weighed her up and found his prospects wanting, he was clearly going to speak rather than lose the chance of winning. But he was not happy and his mood was carved into the air around him in capital gloom. His voluminous white hair was the only bright spot on his face and he stared into the audience like a mourner at a funeral. But then something clicked at the back of his brain and his expression changed, a small smile flickering at the side of his mouth. He'd somehow risen high above all his trials and tribulations and the one thing now at the centre of his mind, like the light from a cinema projector, was his tale. It was a living thing, his child ready to be shown to the world and from the man at the funeral his face had changed magically to the proud father at the christening party. He was ready to pop open the bottles and deliver his speech. Liam whispered to Sean that he'd never seen anything like it in terms of the sudden transformation of a man. The professor said, in a lyrical, lilting voice with a curious and harmonious blend of Welsh and Irish accents,

"This has not been the best of starts, with a puncture to test the patience of a saint on my way out of Dublin and a less than warm greeting from one or two on the organising side of things here, but all that is ducks off a water's back as the long lost Wrong Way Round tribe used to say, before they fell off a cliff they thought was upside down. I've a head full of people that want to get out and who am I to stand in their way. Before you meet them I should give you a warning or two. The first is beware – beware of thinking what follows is going to be either kind or brutal, because it is both of these things. Beware of thinking that it is either funny or serious because it is both of these as well and sometimes all at once. But most of all, beware of the feller in black, him with a scythe and a skeleton's grin – if he escapes from the tale and starts heading for you it's time for an exit stage left and no mistake. And if that's not a giveaway then nothing is – let's leave all our worries and wisdom and wits and everything we might regard as sane far behind and follow the shadow of *The*

Grim Reaper's Apprentice."

He raised his right hand as if he were about to give the blessing at mass and said in a priest like tone,

"The tale starts thus…"

The Grim Reaper's Apprentice

Chris Costello's Tale

In the beginning was the end.

We start in Dublin, between the hills and the sea. In a bar with the soul of a ship, awash with sailors. The tide ripples up and down to the height of the marble topped counter and slops over the knees of the old port pilot at the top end. All in the head of course, but then so is everything said Macridis, the philosopher who drank like a fish and looked like a fish, while seated every mid-evening in his captain's chair, staring at lost horizons and guzzling oysters to remind himself of the dangers of swallowing the deep. In the dark corners and shady recesses of the admiral's cabin, thirty or forty salt hardened faces surveyed each other, and everyone who came and went, while discussing, at a variety of volume levels, the affairs of the day. The smell of seaweed and shellfish hung over the door like a weave of old fish nets. In this, the oldest bar of three within Seamus McDoolahay's, the pub with an invented name, time hangs heavily in the air.

We move next, much earlier in the day, to a dark, poorly furnished room in a small Georgian terraced house in Dun Laoghaire. We find here an engaging incompetent who has just fallen out of his sleep into the pressing drabness of another working day. We encounter him at a difficult moment. Three pairs of shoes and one man is a conundrum that can be beyond the best and the brightest on the worst of days. Danny Kearns was having just such a day. His alarm had had a longer lie-in than he, his last pint the night before had been two more than his head was equipped to deal with and his shaving foam had resolutely refused to leave its container (by virtue of the fact that he had used the last drop the day before). And now, on the point of departing for work, he was confronted with a puzzle that would have baffled Sophocles. Three pairs of his shoes had become mixed together on the floor and he was in no fit state and too much of a hurry adequately to determine which belonged with which. His left foot stuffed itself into the right shoe of his best brogues, while his right foot went one better and one worse by inserting itself into the right shoe of the sad rejects he had bought for a song and used only for gardening matters round at his mother's (and trampling through the unmentionable contents of her compost heap). Realising instantly that all was not quite as it should be, he removed his left foot from the right brogue and inserted it hastily into a third shoe that matched neither of the other two. Seeing still that he was confronted with chalk and cheese he wrenched his right foot free of the gardening reject - which he threw in anger across the room, accidentally divorcing his late great aunt's vase from its perch and transforming it instantly from one object to two hundred and forty-six - and inserted it into the right hand brogue that would have matched perfectly the left, had he not removed it some several seconds before. Such fine details being now beyond both memory and care he tramped resignedly out of the house sporting one highly polished black shoe with a square toe and a dark brown one of equal brilliance - with a round toe. This was not a promising start to the day of a man who had enjoyed few promising days in his kind, short and lonely life.

From chez Danny we move to a neat Dublin suburb. It's lined in military style by a parade of 1930s semis, each with their own proud little gardens and well polished cars. Here, in the back bedroom of number twenty-eight, we find Mary O'Virgin. Her mischievous nickname, coined by the young women of her own still youthful acquaintance, resulted from the very public nature of her rejection of the best of itself that local manhood could throw at her. But this well advertised restraint was due less to a fixation on the importance of celibacy outside the married state than a determined saving of her grace and favours for Six Pack Man. He was the perfect physical and intellectual being that she was confident would surge through the mediocre hordes of her admirers to carry her off to marital bliss and a middle class life of beautiful people, with beautiful children, in a beautiful house, with two beautiful cars, in the very long drive – one fine day. In the meantime, mentally, she arranged in military formation the details of when she wanted children, how many to have (2.4 seemed to be the statistical ideal, but this was causing her problems in the translation of the theoretical figure into practical human form…), which very posh schools and universities they should go to, which refined part of Dublin they should all live in, where their second home in the country should be and so on and so on and so on. Hidden deep below this very shallow surface was a hint of kind humanity, struggling to get out.

Now in the final months of a Master's degree, she was getting ready for a spot of fieldwork. She was going to spend the first of several nights working in McDoolahay's for the purpose of 'anonymised observational research', observing and recording the various habits and foibles of the local drinking population. By way of preparation she was trying to select a skirt and blouse that would be smart enough for an employer with a concern for such things, yet unrevealing enough hopefully to preserve her from the wanderings of inebriated and over-heated hands. She found, in a prudish grey little number, precisely what she had been looking for, a skirt and blouse that looked as though they had been starched in a freezer. The sleeves of the blouse gave the impression that each on their own was capable of boxing the ears of anyone who developed an unwanted interest in Mary, without any instructions from her being necessary. All she needed now was her most school-marmish pair of specs and her suit of armour was complete.

From there we go to the flat of Jenny O'Riley, twenty one and twenty one times flummoxed by the mysteries of the universe. In bed, alone, in the still dark early minutes of pregnant dawn, Jenny's head was spinning out of control. She had been doing the unpardonable in the age of ever-on smart phones and constant distraction, and thinking about life. Not about diets or 'lifestyles' life, or Calvin Klein 'life', or online 'life', or even the latest soap, but about the real thing. The thing that would exist without all of these add-ons should she be left naked and bereft of anything in a desert where the words 'shopping', 'TV' and 'the internet/Facebook/Instagram/Snapchat' had never been dreamt of. She was trying to get to grips with the notion of where she had come from for the umpteenth time in her short life - of how something could always have existed from which she in turn had sprung, whether it be as complex and unfathomable as the notion of 'God', or simply the basic matter from which all things ultimately evolved, when all her instincts told her that *everything* must have a beginning.

She was the brightest of people, born into a family of modest means, well educated, familiar with the core rudiments of all the latest scientific theories about the origins of life and the universe, and yet this fundamental question still bit away at her ankles like a worrying terrier. How could anything have existed forever without creation, for, she felt sure, nothing whatsoever could have come from nothing, and nothing could have existed without having first come from something. The whole idea of forever was to her impossible, and yet if it was impossible, so was she. How could she exist, how could anything exist? Her mind spun and spun with the burden of the conundrum, until she felt physically sick, until she had to block the inconvenience of her thoughts out of her brain and focus again on Calvin Klein, on smart phones, soaps, her boyfriend and the internet. But she knew very well what she was doing. She understood very precisely the nature of her self-deception and how these same thoughts would not go away. How they would simply go underground for a while and then keep on popping up repeatedly throughout her life. How some day, at the moment of death perhaps, they would hammer at the door of her head and demand full admittance to the heart of her being.

We travel later in the same day to a green, and on this occasion, unpleasant land. Father O'Hanlon, a hunched but otherwise sprightly man of sixty-six, lay dazed in the grass of Phoenix Park. Blood ran gently down the side of his grey stubbled cheek onto a large, white toadstool that stood like a sentry beside his felled body.

"Where's your Jaysis to help you now you feckin' eejit?" a fourteen-going-on-two thousand year old voice yelled in derision. The little mob triumphant picked up the brick that they had thrown at him for the purposes of future recycling when they next stumbled upon an elderly, defenceless priest, or anyone who looked vaguely different, foreign or helpless, and ran off. Father O'Hanlon, too shocked to speak, but otherwise fully in control of his senses, thanked the much derided Christ that they had not put the boot in, or gone to work with a knife for good measure. Pulling his handkerchief out of his pocket, he held it to the side of his head to try and prevent any more blood from dripping down onto his clothes, and pulled himself slowly to his feet. He had got used to the fact that the various scandals of the minority of clerical perverts, the spreading decline of traditional deference and the growing mismatch between the image of the Church and the aspirations of many of the city's youth, had meant that respect for the cloth was not what it had been. But he had not been in the slightest bit prepared for this. As he staggered unsteadily back down the footpath up which he had come, he saw an expensively groomed young couple approaching and determined that he would ask their assistance. They must surely carry mobile phones. His own had been stolen by his assailants, who had attacked him as he stood distracted, answering a call from a parishioner. He stopped to ask if they could ring for a taxi to meet him at the nearest exit and take him to the hospital, but found that the shock had dislocated his powers of speech. Not only did his words not come out right, but they were slurred.

"Will you look at that," the 'daughter' of Armani said to the 'son' of Versace, "it's not even midday and there's a priest that's been hittin' the bottle as if it was Christmas."

"Just ignore him," the 'son' of Versace replied, "he's yesterday's people. There's no place for the old witch doctors now. He's probably realised it the old fool, or maybe he's one of them preverts tryin' to drown his preversions in drink."

Father O'Hanlon, the son of Oxfam, at least as far as his new jacket was concerned, stood rooted to the spot as if he had been hit by a second, far heavier brick. In his head he cursed every priest and bishop or lay zealot that had ever brought the Irish church into disrepute, while simultaneously wishing no harm upon any of them. For Father O'Hanlon was something of a dying breed. A man who, despite, on occasion, being known for a blunt and honestly abrasive tongue, in truth loved everyone unconditionally in poor exchange for the heavily qualified love of the few. In that sense, he mused, the son of Versace was probably right. He was yesterday's people.

Back in McDoolahay's the fiddlers were rehearsing upstairs for the night ahead. Wednesdays and Sundays had always been the traditional music nights and this was the biggest Wednesday of them all. It was the day of St. Paddy. The usual crowd would be swelled by tourists lured in by the sound of the fiddles and the thumping of feet that made all three bars of McDoolahay's the heart of everything that mythical Ireland was supposed to be about. Fergal O'Leggetty, the owner of owners and inventor of even his own name, had come down to view the preparations at this jewel in the crown of his empire of bars and clubs. Deep in the darkness and desolation of his wallet sat a letter from the lawyers of McGinty and Hoskins, property developers. He had been offered a cracking deal if he would sell the pub and its land for redevelopment. The fact that the location was right in the heart of one of Dublin's prime business areas guaranteed a fantastical price for the premises given the expected 'Brexit exit' of some finance operations from London to Dublin. However, O'Legetty, not normally a man to pause in the face of a fortune, was inclined to caution in consideration of the fierce outcry that would arise should he sell this cornerstone of Irish and mock-Irish culture into the hands of the demolishers. Such a thing could damage enormously his chances of getting a government contract of greater value in the north of the city, and one had most certainly to be balanced against the other.

O'Legetty had dropped by in order to be seen as the true guardian of the night of the saint, having made certain that the press would photograph him at the helm within his flagship of bars on the day the shamrock danced. He had made a simple decision that if the consequent publicity reached a high enough level then he would keep the three bars open for another year at least. Should it not do so, then they would be axed, fiddlers, shamrock, craic-on-tap and all. O'Legetty was a man who counted sheep in terms of their market value when trying to get to sleep.

And now, with all of this spread out on the table, the hands of the clock moved forwards until the stage was set for the night of the saint. In the social room upstairs, with its dark wooden panels and cream ceiling, a room the colour of stout, the three fiddlers bow-sawed their strings with the divil's own frenzy, while the lord of percussion thumped and pummelled like a man possessed. The air vibrated to the driving rhythm of the souls that danced in the hearts of the fiddles. As one jig blended seamlessly with the next, the feet of the players gradually took up the beat of each on the hard polished floor, first with a gentle tapping echo, then gradually becoming louder and louder, until the crash of boot upon wood became like the hammering of nails into a row of coffins, or into the crippled wrists of the crucified Christ. There was a frenzy to the dances that moved from the cheerful to the chilling, as if, somewhere, between one bar and another, the fiddlers had changed their minds and chosen to summon up the spirit of a divil rather than that of the saint. That struck even the shallowness of Mary O'Virgin, as she stood outside at ten to six, smoothing the creases out of her skirt while listening to the pandemonium that roared and howled like a beast on heat from the open window of the social room above. She knew then that this was not going to be any ordinary night.

In a pizza palace but five minutes short walk away, Jenny O'Riley, as pale as death yet as beautiful as a lily in the sun, sat smiling quietly as her man of the moment told her the tale of his day. He was a wag and a wit of a feller, with the smile of a rogue and the eyes of an angel, and his soft deep voice played in her ears like the bass line of a cello. They touched hands as he spoke and she felt a gentle ripple of electricity run up and down her spine, unleashing invisible lips that kissed tenderly her delicacy and left it sweetly moist. As the last dregs of their coffees drained they decided to spend their evening in McDoolahay's, before going who knows where into the space between dreams and silence. They walked, arm in arm, down the gold paved streets of the slowly setting sun, she with her long slim legs and figure hugging skirt, he in his Italian white shirt and trousers with creases like razors. To all the casually glancing folk who registered each for a second as they passed through them, like two soft-gliding yachts through a sea of souls, they seemed just like any other fashion slaves out for a night on the town and a bit of the divil's fancy.

Jenny O'Riley was no ordinary young woman of the city, however. Her mind tonight was wandering between dreams of her lover's touch, to imaginary meetings between herself and all of her ancestors, going back indeed to the time when flesh first sat on the rocks of Ireland and warmed itself in the rising summer sun. She wondered how they too had felt when courting for the first time someone who aroused their deepest hopes and passions and how their relationships had developed or died under the harsh, searing pressures of the realities of life. She was a woman who felt, when kissing, the softness of her great grandmother's lips within hers, and heard the echo of the words of great, great grandfathers and long beyond within some of her own words. Almost uniquely among her peers, she felt at one with the living and the dead, as if both lived simultaneously within her single being and she within them. It may be the case that intellectually she couldn't understand how, at the moment of creation, something came from nothing and how she in turn could exist, but her deepest instincts allowed no doubts about the connections between herself and her ancestors. She knew, as soon as she heard the music jigging wildly in the air around McDoolahay's, that these were tunes that spoke down the centuries and carried within them still the souls of those that had shaped and re-shaped them in the image of their own passions and desires. As she walked in through the door, across to the dark, bustling cabin of the old sailors' bar, the fiddlers, still playing, emerged from the upper room and descended slowly down the stairs, causing all eyes to turn on them as they spun through the air a jig that would have given the lame the power to dance and caused even the buried dead to tap their bones against the cold, rotting wood of their coffins. One had the red beard of a Viking and the eyes of an elf, another a face like a moon and the smile of wisdom's child, while the third, a man as tall as the others were short, had eyes that cried tearlessly with a sadness whose secret only his soul could know. The percussionist, with jet black, curly hair, and a beard on loan from Lucifer, looked to be a man in as much turmoil as his music, and every thump and thud upon his drum seemed poised on the brink of a madness that, if unleashed, would hit everything and everyone around like a storm in a crockery shop.

As the music descended down amongst the gathering crowd, Jenny felt suddenly that within it she could hear a battle for the soul of everyone present, between the saint himself and the very divil who danced invisibly between the skins of the percussionist's bodhran. Feeling her own spirit running like a wild thing into the very heart of the jig, she took her man by the hand, and pulling him into a rapidly clearing space in the adjoining bar, began to dance without any prior word or warning, other than an ancient kiss delivered in a single glance from her eyes into his. Finding the power of her sudden will too much to resist, he joined in almost without thought and the two of them began a jig that neither had learnt from any living being, but which ran like a rushing stream into their bodies from the dark soul of the music itself. The musicians moved into the middle of the room behind them. As they did so they speeded up the jig, until the dancers were thrown into a frenzy that was so fast and fierce that every hand put down its glass and began to clap in time to the thumps of the drum and the screams of the fiddles as the shoes clomped round on the hard oak floor.

When the dance and the music finally finished and the exhausted dancers sank into chairs or each other, the compere said,

"And the next act is a bit of a surprise, a man pretending to be St. Patrick's Aunty Hilda's eccentric great, great, great, great, great nephew Seamus would like to do an impersonation of himself, Seamus, talking to himself – work that out if you can... Hens and cock-a-doodle dos, may I present to you, St. Patrick's Aunty's far distant nephew doing a gig on the saint's very own night!"

The Seamus impersonator stumbled onto the stage, and sticking his head between his knees, began to ask a question. His words were largely drowned out by the clinking of glasses and the general hubbub of conversation, which still was centred on the excitement of the dance.

"Who's he talking to, is it a mobile phone he's pretendin' to be using?" one curious onlooker asked of another.

"No, he's talking to his arse," his companion replied.

"Talking through his arse you say - the man's a politician."

"No, to. The man is talking to his arse."

"Holy shit, he'd get a bollix of a surprise if it talked back to him."

"It just did."

"It what?"

"It just did. If you'd listen to what was goin' on instead of yattering all the time you'd have heard it."

Flynn did as suggested and filled his mouth with a bun the size of a mountain. As he did so, the backside did indeed begin to speak.

"Seamus," it said, "from my point of view, it seems the whole world is upside down. I mean we're all destined for the bone yard or the oven, yet there's hardly a soul here tonight that won't continue to behave as if it'll live forever."

The general din of the crowd was so loud that, despite the microphone being full on, the words could hardly be heard by even Seamus himself. Having had more drinks than were wise before he came on and being a comic prone to depression on the best of days, he felt instantly that this was one of those times and places where his act had bombed before it had even started. Such was the flood of despondency that rushed into his brain, drowning all before it, that there seemed precious little point in continuing a moment more. With more resignation than indignation he decided to see if anyone had noticed even a word of what had been said so far.

"Did you hear that?" he asked a man, who asked another man, who asked another man who turned out to be a woman.

"We did Seamus," they all replied, almost in unison.

"And what did you hear precisely?" the Seamus impersonator asked. "What exactly was it that was said?"

"Aw now, that's a complicated one," two said in harmony while the third nodded and the fourth was preoccupied with successfully preventing an escape attempt from her rebellious bra.

"You must remember a word or two at least," Seamus said.

"A word, maybe one, 'oven' was it now, there's so many words in the world Seamus, with all this television, smarty pants phones and stuff, why listen, isn't that just mine goin' off now as I speak. It'll be me brother Michael ringing to ask if I'm in the pub, and I'll have to tell him that I am, then he'll want to tell me something that he wouldn't even dream of bothering to discuss if he didn't have one of these wonderful bejaysuses in his hot little hand and nothing to do other than play with the thing, and we'll have a conversation about absolutely nothing at all but feel we've done the business."

"Can any one of yous remember anything more than a single word that was said?" the desperate Seamus impersonator asked, "The man in the shirt that shouts at the back there, you look as though you do sir."

"Aye Seamus, I heard you ventriloquising through your arse – a clever little act for a minute or two, but boring as watching the cat sleep beyond that. I've seen enough for now - go and get yourself a drink and let your hair down boy!"

"That proves me point," Seamus confided to his backside, "even if I do something as dramatic as talking through you instead of me gob, there's nobody capable of taking a moment's notice of what's being said: so many conversations without meaning going on all over the place, so much figurative talking through arses. You'd think if I took the dominant fashion to its logical conclusion that I might have at least a small chance of being listened to. What chance has a comic got in a place like this?"

"I listened," a gentle voice said as he made his gloomy way towards the bar. He turned round to see the chalk white, beautiful face of Jenny O'Riley.

"And what did you hear?" he asked.

"I heard what I think," she said, "but when I tell anyone they presume I'm talking out of my behind as well. I know how you feel."

"And where do you suppose all of this thinking is going to be leading you?" Seamus asked as the babbling, drinking crowd jostled and waffled all around them.

"Come away from that lunatic," Bernard, her man, shouted over the din, handing her the drink he'd crossed the equivalent of three rivers and half of the New Mexico desert to secure, "there's so many to choose from here tonight that you'll find another to be kind to soon enough. And anyway, it was 'thinking' that planted a feather and waited for a hen to grow. Come on now, it's me that wants to do the talking to you for a while."

Seamus the pretender smiled at her sadly. He turned back to make his own slow progress to the bar for one more drink than the too many he'd had already.

"Why did you have to be rude to him?" Jenny asked. "He looked so sad, I only wanted to cheer him up."

"Rude, I could hardly be as rude as a man who talks to his backside in public and then pretends he's the saint's distant relative on his very own night. The eejit had no reason to be hoggin' me girl when I'd gone to so much trouble to get her a drink."

"There's no one hoggin' me and if that's how you've taken to thinking as soon as I have an innocent conversation with another man I want us to leave. Let's go for a walk or something, get some fresh air and see if it'll blow the daftness out of your head."

Mary O'Virgin meanwhile was trying to cope with ten requests a minute for drinks and mixes that in many cases she'd never heard of, while simultaneously keeping a tally in her head of precisely how much the current round was costing. Her brain unsurprisingly was fizzing and popping to the point of boiling over with the strain. For this night at least, she'd had to give up all hope of doing her 'undercover' project work, given that she had no brain cells left available to cope with the overload that it would produce. That being said, her current customer was beginning to cause her a little concern. He'd looked in a bad way when he'd come in and welded himself irremovably to a bar stool, and was now on his third double whiskey and looking decidedly disconnected from the world. She was tempted to replace half of his upcoming double with water, but was aware continuously of the all seeing eyes of Fergal O'Leggety, that seemed to have been fixed on her like a limpet from the moment he'd seated himself on his personal stool at the far end of the counter. With heavy misgivings she placed the undiluted double in front of Father O'Hanlon and gently prised the last of his money from the half clenched palm that he almost unknowingly held out to her. She felt instinctively that he was a man seeking comfort in drink for the simple reason that there was no one else strong enough, caring enough or simply interested enough to listen to whatever it was that was so obviously troubling him. The sadness in his weathered face did something extraordinary and activated the latent kindness that normally hid so deep within her being that even an emotional potholer would have been hard pressed to find it. She would have liked at least to have offered him a smile long enough for his vacant eyes to refocus and realise that it was being given, but insistent calls for service were being hurled at her from five directions at once and she was conscious of the ever more watchful gaze of the owner of owners.

Watching her from further away, a good five yards and increasing as he lost his ground to the milling hordes all around, was Danny who, having ceased to care about the radical mismatch between his right and left shoes, had decided he'd have a drink or two at McDoolahay's on his way back from work. Bravely he had decided to see if he could do any better than usual in his increasingly disastrous attempts to find a girl-friend. The last bright night's hope that he'd briefly picked up on the Friday before had turned out to be a transvestite builder on a daytrip from Liverpool and the experience had been a little traumatic for both of them. For the moment, he was transfixed by the eyes of Mary O'Virgin. Despite all her best attempts to make her appearance asexual and anonymous, Danny had seen something within her smile for the priest that moved him, and her primmest of off-putting skirts could not be seen from where he stood, given the height of the bar counter. Unbeknown to her, Mary had occasioned that often most painful and unwise of emotions, love at first sight.

However fate intervened when suddenly Danny was propelled out of the door by a surging mob that had decided to head off for pastures new. It looked for a while as if the jury would have to remain out as to whether he would yet have the competence or good fortune to get a second sight of his newly beloved, never mind cross the not inconsiderable barrier of trying to find a way to ask her out that would not cause her to run the proverbial mile. But second chance he got, as, having being carried out on the crest of one wave, he rolled back in on another made up of a group of giggly office workers, who charged into the bar and carved a channel through the chattering throng straight up to the counter, just as Mary was slipping away for her ten minute break. Danny found himself deposited like a beached dolphin directly in front of her as she lifted the counter lid to make a temporary escape into the fresh air that beckoned from outside. Almost without thinking, in a desperate, shy panic, he said,

"I think you're a lovely woman. Your smile I mean. I watched your smile. I'm in love with your smile. I wonder, I know I'm not Mr. Universe to look at, but I wonder if you might consider a drink and a chat with me when you finish tonight – or any night really. Or perhaps you'd prefer a meal – I'd love to buy you dinner. If you'd like it, that is."

Mary's rarely released kinder, gentler self had by now tunnelled back down into the deep vault within which normally it hid from the world. She acted as if she hadn't heard a word or even seen the desperate soul that had addressed her so deeply from his jumping heart. She tried without success to push her way through the throng that blocked all exits from the bar as if it were a human form of the Great Barrier Reef. Danny, thinking perhaps she hadn't heard him due to the pandemonium all around, followed her in the few steps that she had managed to make towards the door and said,

"Hello. My name's Danny. I was wondering if you might be prepared to have a drink and a chat with me later. Even just a brief one, I'd love that if you could spare the time."

Mary, visibly irritated, turned her undoubtedly pretty head towards him, smiled and said,

"You can wonder all you like me fine feller but I'll not be drinking with the likes of you. And if you keep on botherin' me I'll ask one of the large gentlemen employed to deal with the drunks and pesterers in this establishment if he'll kindly throw you out."

To add insult to injury, she stepped back to permit the passage to the bar of a young woman in a dress so tight that a trout forced in at the back would have been forever mistaken for a plaice thereafter and accidentally trod on both of Danny's toes in so doing. The little dance of pain that this provoked from him caused considerable mirth in those around, and Mary did not trouble herself with an apology to a man so apparently unfitting of her interest. After joining in the general laughter she returned her attention to the pressing matter of trying to fight her way through to the door and the fresh air that her lungs kept gasping for. Danny had registered on her consciousness as no more than a nerdy looking oddity who was so far short of her vision of the perfect man that it was an impertinence for him even to think of asking her for her company, never mind persisting in the matter when she had so unambiguously ignored him. Suddenly, the great wall of people in front of her wisely parted to let a very large gentleman with a skinhead haircut, bull-neck and a ring in his nose pass, and she took advantage of the moment to slip through and out into the warm but fresh night air and away from the inconsequential spotty character that had briefly disrupted the calm determination of her intent.

Danny stood rooted to the spot. He had only a little alcohol within him and was very soberly aware that he'd done the best he felt he ever could in telling someone on a first acquaintance his feelings about them. He couldn't understand his complete failure to make even the smallest positive impression with Mary. It wasn't that he was unused to failure, he'd had plenty of that with women, but his puzzlement resulted more from the fact that he couldn't reconcile the look of kindness and concern that the woman had reserved for the drunk at the bar and the complete contempt that he seemed to have provoked by contrast. It seemed, in his current dispirited frame of mind, to be the ultimate statement of his inability to appeal to women. He tried to ignore the mocking looks and mickey taking comments that his embarrassment had provoked from some of those who'd witnessed the little scene and placed his glass heavily back on the counter without waiting to finish his drink. It seemed that night that he was a man who was never going to find the joy and consolation of a decent woman and that he might as well reconcile himself to a miserable life filled only with his own company.

It was with a heart so heavy that it hung down into his boots, therefore, that Danny Kearns left McDoolahay's to return to his solitary flat. He kept asking himself over and over how he had deserved to be rejected in quite so humiliating a fashion by someone who on the surface had appeared likely to be so kind. He felt so diminished that, should the pub cat have had to choose between himself and the resident mouse, he might well have been selected as the less troublesome target. As he slumped miserably and resignedly out of the door, he was elbowed forwards and then out of the way by the entourage of the owner of owners, who had decided simultaneously that now was the time for his exit, the press and all other anticipated interested parties apparently having departed.

What he had not allowed for was the presence of unanticipated interested parties. As he stepped out onto the street two motorcycles zoomed out of the shadows and mounted the pavement on either side of his party, their pillion passengers opening fire instantly with automatic pistols powerful enough to decimate a regiment. O'Legetty didn't even have time to curse as the bullets ripped his every vital organ to shreds within less than four seconds. The motorcyclists sped off into the distance, after having scattered a bagful of syringes and tablets over their victim, designed to suggest, rightly or wrongly, that the now deceased owner of owners had been involved with, or even a closet leader of, a drug gang. Danny Kearns, who previously had encountered syringes for no purpose other than his childhood vaccination jabs, was sadly among the casualties, having been, as always, in the wrong place at precisely the wrong time. A stray bullet had pierced his chest in a serious way and instead of going home he found himself bundled into the back of an ambulance and hospital bound instead.

Father O'Hanlon was oblivious to all the mayhem at McDoolahay's by virtue of the fact that he had left for home four minutes before it began. His journey back to his modest parochial house took the form of a mystery tour, devised for himself by himself, without any knowledge of his having devised anything at all. He progressed in a manner that suggested he was trying to dribble a football in slow motion through the world's trickiest defence, in which clearly there were at least six hundred full-backs to evade. As he weaved and wound his way along and between the endless procession of streetlamps that he came gradually to regard as equivalent to a ball of unravelled metal string (which, he presumed, must ultimately lead back to his own front door), he became suddenly aware of a second pair of echoing footsteps following directly behind his own. However, each time he stopped to confront his apparent pursuer he found no-one there. Not a hint, not a trace, not even the faintest odour of anything alive or solid. It was only on the fourth occasion of his abrupt halting that he noticed something distinctly odd. While he could still see his own shadow standing as hunched and familiar as ever, it was accompanied by something for which he had no explanation, a second shadow of considerable proportions, suggesting a well-built, hooded man of around six feet or more in height. Even in his inebriated state he could see that it was of someone who appeared to be directly facing him, yet all there was in front of his eyes was thin air and a wisp of hair that was undoubtedly a wayward and undisciplined piece of his own. Baffled, he turned back towards the direction that he had been heading in, without any certain knowledge of where in fact that might be, and continued the same unsteady progress as before. This time, he listened not only for accompanying footsteps, but kept checking continually for any indication that he might be accompanied by two shadows instead of the normally expected one. What he saw, through the corner of his inebriated eye, caused his heart to jump and his belly to suck itself so far inwards and upwards that it was in danger of popping out through both nostrils simultaneously. Each step that he took was being matched not only by his own shadow, but by that of his otherwise invisible companion.

He did as best as he could in the terrifying circumstances. Approaching the nearest of the apparent infinity of streetlamps, he began to circle it and re-circle it, first going one way and then the next, in the hope that if he did so on a sufficient number of occasions he would ultimately wrong-foot the extra shadow, or even cause it to become dizzy and fall over. After the sixth circling and re-circling, it became painfully obvious that he would have no such luck. Indeed, on the seventh attempted circuit of the lamppost, it was the priest that lost his balance and collapsed in an undignified heap and not the accompanying shadow. As he lay on the pavement trying to collect both his thoughts and his person into one coherent whole that might, without undue effort, pull itself to its feet, he decided that he was, as well as a mind so deeply intoxicated could tell, hallucinating. This was not greatly unexpected in light of his substantial intake of whiskey. That being said, there could be no second shadow to see except in the fantasy eye of his mind and nothing therefore to be afraid of. (Being a man who subjected every apparently supernatural experience to the deepest intellectual rigour, even when three times drunk and once over the horse's tail, Father O'Hanlon was never one to be fooled by such delusions for long.) Battling fiercely against his head's strong preference to go fast asleep on the pavement where he lay, he pulled himself up into a sitting position. He had the ambition from there to restore his person to an upright posture and then, taking care to acknowledge only his own shadow, to resume his determined, if geographically dubious, attempt to return to his parochial house. As he sat preparing himself mentally and physically for the task ahead a voice from behind said,

"No, I'd rest for a minute or two before you try to stand up if I was you. Lean your back against the lamppost, a little to the side of where Mrs. O'Leary's dog has just raised its leg. There's nothing worse than a wet jacket to add to the woes of a night too much on the drink."

Father O'Hanlon turned in surprise, only to find no-one there. The voice said,

"Well what did you expect, you don't believe in me shadow any more so you'd hardly believe in me if I showed me face. You'd just say I was a man half in control of me brain or drunker than yerself and go on your way in the firm conviction that you'd been lucky to escape from an eejit without verbal or physical assaults. Far better if I remain disembodied, then you've at least got to try and work out where me voice is coming from."

"It comes from the drink," the priest said without hesitation.

"Of course it does," the shadow said.

"Well that's cleared that up then," the priest said to himself, "I'll just pull meself up and be on me way."

"If you're sure you're up to it, here, let me give you a hand," the voice said.

"Thank you," the priest said, as firm hands gripped both of his arms and helped him to stagger upright without disaster. He'd no sooner done so than a shudder rippled down and up his body with the speed and force of a roller coaster. As before, there was no-one at all to be seen, yet he'd been helped to rise with a facility that would have been totally impossible on his own, even without a drop of alcohol within his body. He shouted out into the semi darkness that retreated away all around the glare of the streetlamp,

"Who are you, what's going on? Come on, show yourself, you can't fool a man of the cloth with some kind of cheap conjurer's trick."

"But I thought I was just a delusion brought on by drink Father Joseph," the voice said, using a first name that only the closest family or fellow clergy knew and would use.

"How d'you know my name?" the priest asked.

"I know everything about you Joseph," the voice said, "even down to the size of your socks."

"Well I'm very sorry for you," Joseph said. "A man who has a fascination with another man's socks is someone in need of a psychiatrist."

"It was a bad day in the park Joseph," the voice said.

"How did you know about that?" the priest asked. "Did you see everything and just stand by without stepping in to help?"

"There are things I can help with and things I can't," the voice said. "It's not up to me."

"Really?" the priest said. "So if you see someone having the living daylights knocked out of them you wait for instructions before deciding whether to give them a hand?"

"If what you're driving at is whether or not I leave some people to suffer the answer is yes. But then that's just what your eternal boss does and I don't hear you standing up in your pulpit and railing against him as if he were the very divil."

"That's different. I don't pretend to know the mind of God."

"But you do pretend to know the mind of meself. D'you not t'ink that's a bit of an assumption to make when you've never met me before in your life?"

"I know what I expect of a decent man. There's one set of rules for God and those are his affair. There's another for the likes of you and me and they start with an obligation to help anyone in need, unless you're a heathen kind of a feller, which maybe you are."

"So you'd condemn me for leaving you to your fate?"

"I condemn no one, it's my job to stop them from being

condemned, though few seem to care or worry about such things nowadays."

"That's reassuring to know. Listen, I've just had another call come through and I'm going to have to leave you to your own devices for a little while - just as I had to at the moment when the brick was going to be flung at your unfortunate bonce. Take one lamppost at a time and don't try any more circuitous races around the things. I mightn't be on hand to pick you up a second time and frankly Joseph, a street in this part of town is not the place to spend the night flat on your back in the land of nod. See you later."

The priest felt a soft whoosh of air across his cheeks and then, upon looking down, noticed that his shadow was now alone. Telling himself once more that the whiskey was playing more tricks than any sane mind could even half begin to deal with, he let go of the lamppost that he had been holding onto to steady himself and began again to try and pick his way through the confusing maze of streets that seemed almost like a foreign land in his presently inebriated state. This time, things began to appear more promising after twenty minutes or so. Having stumbled inadvertently over a cat that had unwisely approached to rub itself against his slowly shuffling legs, he recognised the fleeing creature as the walking hearthrug that lived at Mrs. O'Malley's, only six doors down from the parochial house. Leaning against the nearest gatepost at an angle approaching that of the Tower of Pisa, he took his bearings through half shut eyes. He saw indeed the small crumbling edifice that passed for his parochial house glaring reproachfully out of the half streetlit gloom, as if in full and certain knowledge of his abandonment of all restraint and sobriety in his desperate couple of hours in McDoolahay's bar. Taking a deep intake of breath, he used the extra oxygen to lurch forwards. Like a marathon runner at the Olympics he gasped the last few yards up to his front door and collapsed in a disorganised heap on the step. The force of his back slumping against the door dislodged the old brass knocker that had been gradually divorcing itself from the wood for the past eight months. It dropped heavily onto his head, producing a dull thud and a loud and angry ouch, followed by a metallic crash as it hit the hard stone of the step beside him. A light immediately went on in the bedroom window of Mrs. O'Toole next door. Oblivious to this ominous development, he pulled his keys out of his pocket. He fingered each until he was able to tell by shape which was the correct one for the front door, any visual identification being impossible due to the nearest streetlamp's dull gleam not reaching as far as his little house. Stretching his hands out across the step to try and push himself upright enough to insert the key in the lock and enter the damp, unwelcoming gloom of his hallway, he dislodged an empty meths bottle that a visiting alcoholic had earlier left behind, having failed to get an answer and the price of the proverbial cup of tea. It rolled down the short path and stopped at the feet of Mr. O'Toole, who, alerted by the earlier debacle with the door knocker, now stood ready with a billiard cue in anticipation of an attempted break-in at the parochial house. He watched silently as the shambolic wino that he could see in the dark shadow of the portico hauled himself up against the front door and began to try and work the lock, unaware that anyone was watching him. Good Catholic or no good Catholic, Mr. O'Toole no longer took any chances, or prisoners, in this less than salubrious drug-infested neighbourhood. Creeping up stealthily on his struggling quarry, he unleashed without warning three thwacks that would have flattened a regiment. With a low, desperate moan, Father O'Hanlon sank like a stone onto his own step. Without bothering to get a torch to look at the desperado's gloom-hidden face, Mr. O'Toole bound his hands behind his back with his dressing gown cord and marched off in triumph to call the guards.

The story of the priest's arrest is an inglorious one that should be whispered only in the ears of the soundly sleeping or written in white ink on the cleanest and purest of passing clouds. The Garda crew that picked him up were about to go off shift and removed him instantly and with total absence of ceremony from the step of the parochial house into the back of their van, without any checks, beyond the assurance of Mr. O'Toole that he was a desperate rogue who had been caught trying to force his way into the house. Had the heroic vigilante bothered himself to take one half of half a glance at the apprehended felon's brick and cue-bruised bonce, he might have amended his testimony in a somewhat radical fashion.

No more than ten minutes later, the priest was deposited in a less than half recovered state in front of a desk sergeant whom he had once baptised and twice confirmed, once by design and once by accident. Sergeant O'Flannery listened to the proposed charge and the account of the arrest, while looking the accused up and down in bemused awe. Having noted simply that the apprehended felon had removed his dog collar at some earlier time of the day, presumably as a result of it having become blood stained from one of the two large lumps now visible on his head, he said,

"Upon which eejit's authority is me parish priest whacked on the bonce, accused of breaking into his own house and then brought here like the prisoner of Alcatraz?"

The arresting officers suddenly felt in imminent danger of themselves being arrested. The sergeant had two brothers that were priests and a cousin who was so holy a nun that she was rumoured to have had personal visitations at least twice from Bernadette of Lourdes, and to have the power to bring comfort to the most distressed of souls by merely touching them on the forehead. He was not known to take kindly to those who cast doubt on the sanctity of men and women of the cloth, having such a prevalence of it amongst his own.

"We brought him in on the strength of the neighbour's evidence," the largest and most quick-witted of the pair announced.

"Without first having asked the eejit in question to cast his eyes upon the man he'd brained upon the bonce I presume?" the sergeant asked. "Father Joseph is a man so devoid of guile that he couldn't even break into his own confessional, despite its absence of lock or key, never mind into something as complicated as a building. And why, in the good Lord's name, might he want to break into his own house might I ask? Did you check, by any small chance, on the implement that this strange desperado used to facilitate the heinous crime of breaking and entering his own property? Was it a jemmy, an oxy-acetylene torch perhaps, a small explosive charge even? You presumably recovered the item in question from the scene of the crime?"

"We did," the largest of the duo said, so quietly even a church mouse would have been pushed to hit a more inaudible note.

"You did, good, excellent, and might I ask what the nature of this apprehended facilitating toolery of unimaginable crime precisely is?"

"We found a key in his hand," the chattier of the two inaudibles mumbled.

"A what?"

"A key."

"A what?"

"A key."

"A what?"

"A key."

"A what?"

"A key."

"A key? A key! And was this vile item of criminal intent by any chance the good Father's own key might I ask?"

"I t'ink it may be so."

"You t'ink it may be so. You t'ink it may be so! You blathering eejits! On the evidence of a man with no brain you've arrested a priest, yes, you heard me right, a PRIEST, for trying to 'break' into his own parochial house using his own front door key! Is there any reason you can give me now for not arrestin' the eejit that brained him and flingin' him and the two of yous head first into me cells instead of the good father here?"

"There is," the quieter of the two replied after a pause, his chattier colleague obviously having been struck dumb.

"Good God, a double miracle," the sergeant gasped, "the dumb speak and the talkative are struck dumb. Tell me, my miraculous friend, what strange, undreamt of cause is there for sticking the good father here behind bars instead of the two of yous?"

"He's pissed as a fart," the underling delicately replied.

"Now wait a minute," the sergeant said, "let me just try and get me mind wrapped around this most momentous use of terminology here. No, no, sorry, I have to confess, try how I might, I've never heard of, nor can dream of hearin' of, any type of a fart that a reasonable man might describe as pissed. Nor do I think it would be capable of tellin' anyone, or indeed, betrayin' even the slightest clue, of its predicament, were it to persuade a barman to stoke it up with the moonshine necessary to send it off its head, should it have a head that is, God forbid."

The priest, who had been until now more concerned with resting his aching head on the station counter than anything else, looked up at the sergeant in bewilderment.

"Sorry father," the policeman said, "I sometimes get a little carried away on account of all the eejits I have to deal with."

"I'm an innocent man," the priest said to no-one in particular, his grip on reality having long since begun to loosen to the point of being comparable only to an outsize pair of trousers without a belt.

"I know, I know," the Sergeant said comfortingly, "it's the guilty that I have in front of me and I'm about to deal with them now."

Patting the priest on the head as if he were a beloved hound, he said,

"Now, as for yous two masters of incompetence, may I ask what went out on all the day's bulletins concerning a certain matter in Phoenix Park?"

"An attack," the more sophisticated of the pair replied.

"Good, yes," the sergeant said, "and who was it an attack upon?"

Seeing an imminent danger of his less bright companion replying, 'The victim', the chattier guard said confidently,

"A priest."

"Yes, excellent," the sergeant said, "at last, a man who listens to the day's updates with one ear open, even if the other might be full of mud. Now all we need is to try and remember the name of the priest."

"Father O'Hanlon," the chatty guard said confidently.

"And what is the name of the priest we have here?"

The chatty one had again suddenly been struck dumb.

"Unable to recall?" the sergeant asked mockingly. "Despite the fact that his church and parochial house are at the centre of your allotted patch? And do yous two towering intellectual giants not think it to a large degree understandable that a man who had been brained in Phoenix and left for dead might be tempted to drink several times more than normal for one exceptional night in order to try and calm his shattered nerves?"

"Drink is never the solution," the quieter of the two officers said.

"Indeed, 'tis always half at least of the problem," the other replied.

"The other half I assume being down to eejits like yourselves," the sergeant said. "Had the two of yous staggered in here as drunk as you are already daft, then this whole matter might seem a little more comprehensible. But as you are both completely sober and at least twenty per cent sane, there can be no excuse for what is the greatest act of incompetence that I have seen in what feels like me hundred and fifty years in the force!"

"Aaaaaaaaaaaaaaaaaaaaaah..." the priest sighed, then crumpled heavily onto the floor.

"What the hell was that? Good God, it's Father O'Hanlon," the sergeant said. "Don't just stand there like a couple of loaves waiting to rise, get the man a chair."

"He's cold as a trout in ice," the chatty officer said, checking his forehead, "and deeply unconscious."

"What kind of a clout did that lunatic of a neighbour give him?" the sergeant said, while frantically phoning for an ambulance. The identical question was at the very same moment occurring to the good Mr. O'Toole, as he tried to glue the two halves of his fractured billiard cue back together before returning to the ice pit that passed for his conjugal bed.

"We're losing him," the neurosurgeon battling with the battered remnants of the priest's brain said, more to himself than any of those assisting him, an hour and forty minutes later. Father O'Hanlon lay like a plucked chicken beneath the struggling mercy of the surgeon's knife, his head shaved and opened, ready at any moment for his soul to float out and up into the unknown ethers of eternity.

"The next five minutes are going to be crucial," the consultant continued, "there's no more magic that I can work beyond that and our man will either begin to stabilise or start the slide into his coffin. It's with the Holy Mother and her litany of Mercies now, God help him."

"If the poor sod doesn't drown in a sea of your pious verbiage first," his irreverent sidekick remarked to a kidney dish as he dropped a soiled scalpel into it. His long suspicion that the will of the Good Lord had several times been used as a convenient mask for slips of his master's knife had made him a less than awestruck servant.

For Father O'Hanlon, all such matters were purely academic, being as far unconscious as it is possible to get without passing from one world into the next. It was then that he was rudely awakened.

"If I was looking for a walking disaster area on two legs then I'd have to say that you were it," a voice said.

The priest's eyelids shot open and his startled gaze fixed on a face whose familiarity was quite remarkable, given that he'd never seen it before in his life.

"How d'you do," the voice said, "we met earlier tonight, in the vicinity of a lamppost that you thought was a roundabout, as you may recall."

"You're the shadow?" the priest asked.

"No, once removed. I'm the feller who owns the shadow, in the sense that it'd have no liberty or anywhere to go at all without meself around to lead it."

"You look quite normal for a drunken delusion," the priest said, without any intent to be ungracious.

"Oh dear, oh dear," the stranger said, "the intellectual mind turns even the saintliest of men into the proverbial doubting Thomases."

"And what is it precisely that I'm supposed to be doubting?" the priest asked. "You're most certainly not going to try and tell me that you're anything more than a dream in the mind of a man with a battered brain?"

"But I can't be both a drunken delusion and a fantasy generated by a twice clobbered brain," the stranger said. "I may be one or both, or neither, but my chances of being two of these assorted possibilities are statistically very small."

"Are they indeed?" the priest said. "I fail to see the point of such frivolous deliberations of logic and meaning when me body is so apparently on the brink of death. I would much rather spend me time in prayer and preparation if you don't mind."

"And what better preparation could there be than meself?"

"What on earth do you mean?"

"Well, as the Grim Reaper's personal Apprentice, I'm one of the best informed of anyone you'll find on the subject of death."

"What fantastical nonsense are you on about, you know very well there's no such thing as the Grim Reaper. You can't spend your time talking superstitious rubbish to a priest, most especially when he's on the point of death. Now please, I don't wish to be rude, but I would be very grateful if you would leave me alone with meself and me prayers."

"Now then Father Joseph, you're not telling me there's no such thing as the Angel of Death - sure, the feller's already dotted the i's and crossed the t's on your name in the good book of imminent departures."

"Well, given that there are no i's or t's in me name for anyone to cross or dot that would make your fantastical angel a bit of a clot wouldn't it now?" Father O'Hanlon replied.

"Now who's being pedantic?" the alleged Apprentice asked. "And as just a small point, d'you not think it rather strange that we're able to have this conversation while floating around only a foot or so from the ceiling of this desperate carvery that's passing itself off as a hospital?"

Looking down for the first time the priest gasped. There, a good ten feet or so below was his poor, suffering near-corpse of a body being cut and stitched by a consultant worryingly nicknamed 'Hit and Miss' by the theatre nurses who had worked with him the longest.

After a second or two, Joseph looked back up at the strange but not unbenevolent face that was now observing his bafflement with gentle amusement and noticed for the first time that he could see only the top half of the creature that owned it, with no sign of the rest whatever. Following his gaze the Apprentice said,

"Puzzling isn't it? I've often found that a party trick or two is helpful in persuading doubters of the fullness of me powers. So, go on, who d'you think it is that's keeping your soul floating up around here so that we can have a half decent chat without all the gory medical distractions the while? D'you see anyone else than me?"

"This is all a dream, as I said just now," the priest said, recovering his composure. "I've heard too often before of the brain's ability to generate all kinds of fantasies and other near death experiences for me unconscious mind not to be able to conjure them up with the greatest of ease without any assistance from the likes of you, even if you did exist."

"Really?" the Apprentice said. "Then if I'm just part of a dream and you're the same, there can be no harm whatsoever in us having a little chat now can there?"

The priest looked distinctly vexed but chose to say nothing.

"You see," the Apprentice said, "I'm aware that you've been a little less than happy with the way life has treated you of late."

The priest still said nothing.

"You'd had all that pain and loneliness," the Apprentice continued, regardless of the unpromising silence, "when your mother died just before Christmas and when even the brightest days seemed like twilight gloom to you for months afterwards. Saying mass every day felt like little more than working on a production line and you came to believe that all notion of God, or good, or anything beyond the daily grind had left you forever. And then, with a little time, things began gradually to get better, until you had the confidence to feel that life could return almost to normal when, wham! You find yourself flattened by a brick for no reason while out for a walk in the park to cheer yourself up. Then, just when you thought that matters could get no worse, you get an even heavier beating on your own front door step from an eejit who thinks he's a vigilante hero felling the servant of the very divil himself. And yet, despite all of this unasked for suffering, you are, as we up here would be the first to admit, a man almost without the blame of any known sin or vice, beyond an occasional tetchiness - as the present moment well proves, dare I say it. Even though you are a soul unpossessed by the sin of pride, you understand well all of this, and that is why you feel such great unease. You feel completely baffled as to what real point there can be to all of the pain in the world, most particularly now that you have experienced directly so much of it yourself without seeming in any way to have deserved it."

The priest remained impassive.

Undeterred, the Apprentice said, "Am I not right now?"

"As right as a dream can be," the priest muttered, "but I'm not a man who holds any faith in the ramblings of the unconscious mind."

“No, of course,” the Apprentice said, “I shall stop rambling and be as brief as I can. You are indeed going to die tonight as you suspect. You will know instantly when it happens, without any unhelpful suspicions that your mind is pulling your leg.”

“It takes no genius to guess that someone who has been repeatedly hit over the head with the force of a steam hammer is likely to die,” the priest said impatiently.

“Indeed,” the Apprentice said. “So let us return to matters that might be of more interest before the moment itself comes.”

“To what purpose?” the priest asked.

“So you can die without bitterness inside you,” the Apprentice said. “That’s always very important in the long sweep of eternity, as you well know without any prompting from me.”

“Please do whatever you will,” the priest said, “I can do nothing to stop you. But, if you think you can put a bandage over me bitterness you may well be mistaken. Like yourself, I can give all the homilies in the world on the mysteries and merits of suffering to the poor and afflicted that I encounter on my day to day rounds of duty. But how am I really to persuade that most critical of listeners, the man that is meself, that my own suffering makes sense? I could take it all as far as the lamp-post, but the battering I got on me own front door step at the hands of an eejit was a bridge too far.”

“Well, it all comes down to how you look at it,” the Apprentice said, while keeping half an eye on the incompetent clod of a surgeon who was about to make the final, cack handed mistake of his ill chosen career. “If you look at the strangeness of what has happened to you through the blurred and inadequate lens that is the human brain you would be doing so in a very different way from an almighty deity who is able to see the bigger picture. You’re assuming that humanity, which took over two million years just to evolve something as simple and basic as the flushable convenience, can deal with God on the same level in terms of intellect and reasoning, presuming that such mundane means of trying to grapple with the essence of existence are of any relevance to such an unimaginable entity anyway. Without in any way wishing to sound patronising to one necessarily still bound by the limitations of flesh, do you not think that that’s a bit like a retarded hedgehog trying to first guess Einstein in a game of chess? Tell me Father Joseph, how is it that a species that's only just managed to put its big feet on soil hardly beyond spitting distance of its own planet can all of the time be so arrogant in its assumptions about the rights and wrongs of the natural order? Do you not think that just a little bit of humility and trust might occasionally be appropriate?"

The priest said nothing and avoided entirely the gaze of his questioner, who was sounding more than a little angry.

"I can see I might just as well be talking to the backside of an elephant for all the response I'm getting," the Reaper's man said. "Very well. For you, given that things are now so near their end, I will reveal two things that normally you would remain unaware of until after death. The first concerns the attack in the park. You see, the expensively groomed young man saw it happen from a distance while his girlfriend had stopped to answer a call on her mobile phone. But he didn't bother to tell her, or anyone, or do even the slightest thing other than watch with detachment and disinterest. So when she later thought that you were drunk when you tried to ask for help, he was being twice callous and once deceitful in pretending to agree with her and leaving you bleeding and without even the small kindness of phoning for a taxi to take you to the hospital. To him that seemed an unimportant and irrelevant event in a day where his only concern at every stage had been himself. But it was much more than that, human imposed though your suffering may have been. It was an opportunity for him to do something to rescue his own soul and even his basic humanity, which, as on previous occasions, he threw away without a thought. Your misfortune, you see, became one more of his tests, his final test in fact given that he is on me collection list for tomorrow – he's due to be run over by a speeding pizza delivery man if me memory serves me correctly. And I will tell you one more thing. Your final suffering, that which, thankfully, due to the invention of anaesthetics, you can no longer feel, is about to become the means by which this eejit of an incompetent horse butcher is finally put out of business before he sends any more innocents to an early grave. Look, can you see below the fracas that's going on, his assistant and the theatre nurse have both just seen him cut the remnants of your brain in precisely the wrong place. They've finally caught the pig ignorant clod red handed! Will you look at that for a haemorrhage? It's like a fire hose spattering the lot of them, poor eejits. Come on, it's time to go. You'll not be returning to your body now. You've done your last bit of good in a lifetime of many little goods - and some big ones too. It's time to meet the Reaper, although it'd be a lot easier for all of us if you could let go of this doubting Thomas routine. Come on now, don't look so reluctant, you'll like the feller, he's only an accountant type of an angel. Your books are almost in order as far as I can see, so there's nothing to fear. Come on, it's time we left those below to sort out the eejit that finally did for you. For heaven's sake man don't look so worried, think of your eternity like a large bottle of whiskey without the liver rot or the hangover."

"Now it's me intelligence that's being insulted, to match the battering that's been given already to me bonce," the priest said, as the theatre and all above and around dissolved before his eyes.

We move on two days and find Mary O'Virgin striding out on her way to buy a loaf of bread. There is a voice behind her,

"Mary, Mary, quite contrary. Will you play the virginal for me, oh so virginally?"

Mary turned to see behind her the leering face of Eamon the Sprout, so called because of the hairs sprouting from a less than delightful mole on the side of his nose, and a degree of sensitivity towards his fellow human beings that was often compared to that of such an unremarkable vegetable.

"Whatever you want the answer is no," she said abruptly and resumed her walk in the general direction of the corner shop.

"T'ank heavens for that and other small mercies," he said, "for what I wanted to ask you is would you like me to go away and not to give you a big friendly kiss on the old chops. Now that you've denied any such desire I can proceed in me ambitions with a full heart and the clearest of convictions."

"It'll be a conviction you get if you try any such thing," Mary replied, "go away and do something useful, like boiling your head."

"Oh Mary, Mary, quite contrary, such kind and tender words - how can a weak willed man such as meself resist the irresistible?" the persistent rogue said. "Me desires are ablaze within me heart and every part of me body is bristling with anticipation of the kiss that you're about to give me."

"A kiss you think you're getting," she said, while walking ever more quickly in an attempt to shake the eejit from her tail, "have you not slightly misheard your own thoughts? A kiss is only two alphabetical letters out from a kick, so it's an easy mistake to make for a man who clearly listens to himself as little as to anyone else."

"From you Mary, a kick would seem as heavenly as a kiss," he said, while simultaneously breaking into a half trot to keep up with her. "And besides, I know such an act would merely be the teasing temptation of a woman playing hard to get."

"You're the strangest of men Eamon Heaney and I don't have anything to do with strange men," she replied, while simultaneously breaking almost into a run.

"Mary, the kissing of you will be the making of me," Eamon shouted. "I've wagered half a week's wages with Tony Hennessey that I'll manage it tonight."

"Is that so?" Mary replied, getting slightly breathless. "Then you're going to be a man half bankrupt when all the clocks in Dublin knock twelve bells out of midnight. I'd sooner be thrown to the sharks than let anything resembling yourself come within a mile of my lips."

"Oh Mary, your every word is twice the come on of the one before. I need the warm touch of your skin against me like I need air to breathe."

"You'll be feeling the touch of me skin if you keep on pursuing me," Mary said. "Only it'll be the thud of me fist in your kisser."

As she rounded the next corner she saw that vandals had forced open the feeble wooden side door to the half derelict remains of O'Brien's Garage. Having a good ten yards advantage on Eamon as a result of a sudden, breathless sprint, she decided to slip inside. She pulled the battered door to behind her and managed to secure it silently from within by means of an old latch and a piece of wire that lay fortuitously to hand. Trying to keep her panting breath as quiet as she could, she retreated into the shadows in the hope that her odd pursuer would be baffled enough by her disappearance to give up and return to whatever slab of stone he had popped out from under. But within less than ten seconds of her having secured the door she heard it being rattled violently by the puzzled sprout. Fortunately, her crude locking device held and it sounded for a minute or two as if he had moved on. She was just about to try cautiously releasing the door and checking to see if her escape route was clear when she heard another door being rattled. It seemed at first that it too would hold, but then there was the sound of repeated kicking and the splintering of rotten wood. A feeble creak announced the door's surrender and Mary retreated back, deep into the darkness of the crumbling building and crouched down low behind what touch suggested were the remnants of a sales counter of some description. She held her breath and listened intently. After a second or two the scrunching sound of an old can being accidentally trodden on confirmed that the dreaded eejit was in the building. Whereas before she had felt merely pestered and annoyed she now felt threatened for reasons that she couldn't quite discern. The Sprout's oddness seemed suddenly to have taken on a more sinister dimension. The way in which he was creeping around the battered old ruin of a building did not seem to blend well even with the eccentricities of his usual behaviour. She crouched down even further, trying to compress herself into a form so small that even a hedgehog might have mistaken her for one of its own. There was the sound of a couple of light switches being repeatedly flicked by a man without the gumption to realise that a building half derelict was unlikely to remain connected to the power supply. After a brief pause, there was the sound of rummaging through an overfull pocket, followed by the scraping of a match on the wall. Suddenly there was a small, flickering light dancing in the centre of the crumbling building. It was just bright enough to reveal a rusty old oil lamp that had escaped the vandals' attention on a buckled metal shelf high up on a wall. The Sprout stretched up and pulled it down, giving it a shake to confirm the presence of fuel within it. Satisfied, he placed it on the rubble strewn floor and struck another match to light it. By so doing he filled the whole of the one-time reception area and front service bay with a light that, while dim, nevertheless left no hiding place for Mary beyond the desk behind which she hid. The intruder suspended the lamp from a rusty ceiling hook and she then heard the slow crunch-crunch of his boots as he advanced towards her across the debris-littered floor. As he drew up almost level with the desk she decided that she had better make a run for it. She attempted to jump up and bolt towards the door through which her troublesome pursuer had entered. The position in which she had been crouching had left her with severe pins and needles, however, and she found that her progress was disastrously slow as a result. She had managed to limp and stumble little more than a couple of yards when a firm hand gripped her arm and pulled her to an abrupt halt. She tried but failed to yank herself free and succeeded only in falling over, grazing both knees and cursing silently to herself as the soft skin of her cheek made ungentle contact with the grimy concrete floor. A rough hand grabbed her left arm and pulled her back up to her feet as if she were no more than a child in weight. Slightly dazed she took a second or two to focus on Eamon's curious face, only to find that what confronted her was a set of ugly features that she had never before seen. She recoiled and shivered with fear simultaneously, but the stranger's hand kept a firm grip of her arm.

"Who are you?" she asked. "What do you want? Let me go or I'll scream."

The stranger's eyes fixed on hers in a cold embrace of a gaze. His lips parted and stretched slowly into a charmless smile. Without warning he spun her round and forced her face downwards onto the sales counter which previously she had hidden behind and bound her hands behind her back with several strands of car electrical wiring that lay abandoned on the floor. He then turned her around again and forced her down into a sitting position with her back against the counter. Finding some more cable he bound her feet tightly also. She decided that her only chance of rescue from whatever the unknown maniac intended was to scream with all of the considerable power of her larynx, but found that he was one step ahead of her thoughts. Before she even had time to open her lips he had stuffed a dirty cloth from the floor into her mouth and precluded the chance of any sound whatsoever escaping from her vocal chords to the world outside. Taking the handbag that she had dropped in her fall he proceeded to rifle through it, but, curiously, instead of stealing all of her cash and cards, proceeded to remove only a handkerchief, with which he very loudly blew his nose. Throwing the bag onto the floor he turned back to face her and smiled again, even less pleasantly than before. She tried to avoid showing her fear and gave him the nearest that she could manage to a look of contempt. Her efforts seemed merely to amuse him. He pulled a packet out of his pocket and removed a couple of mints from it, which he flicked into his mouth with slightly surreal precision. He seemed to lose interest in her almost as soon as he had done so and meandered over to the other side of the garage. A slim but clearly strong man, he began tearing down the old wooden shelving that lined one of the walls and hurled it onto the floor in the centre of the room until he had a little pile, almost as if he were trying to lay the foundations for a bonfire. He scrabbled around for more junk, throwing each piece that he found onto the mound of splintered debris until it stood almost four feet tall. Then, after giving her a look that would have spooked a ghost, he suddenly grabbed the flickering paraffin lamp and hurled it onto the pile. A brilliant flame seared upwards and across the rotting timber and other detritus, until it seized and started hungrily to devour everything before it. She drew her feet as closely as possible to her backside, through fear of the heat from the conflagration singeing her toes. Her strange jailer began first to laugh and mutter to himself, then to dance slowly and whimsically round and round the pyre, with the grace of a deranged ballet dancer. Gradually the dance seemed to get faster and faster, his hands whirling and flailing about in time with what sounded like an incomprehensible madhouse rant. As it did so he moved closer to the fire, until the tails of his bizarre undertaker's coat started to smoulder and the welded souls of his shoes parted from their uppers, and to Mary's complete horror, his very eyebrows started to smoke. With a sudden and seamless series of dramatic gestures he stopped abruptly, bowed with enormous grace, smoke visibly rising from the seats of his pants as he did so and then, with an ear splitting, echoing cross between a laugh and a scream, fell back right into the heart of the fire. The flames roared up all around him, as if being fanned from the very furnace of hell itself and he sank in a stinking, melting mess, into the pyre.

Momentarily paralysed by horror, Mary was shaken out of her

trance when suddenly the burnt carcass of the figure that seconds earlier seemingly had thrown itself to its doom reared up in boiling, flesh-dripping awfulness. It roared and screamed so loud and terribly that she wet herself. She could feel the searing heat scorching her skin as it advanced slowly and painfully towards her. It opened the roasted bone of its jaw and gasped,

"Now it's time for you to join me, it's your special treat - for being so lacking in compassion and kindness."

His words were followed by a rasping laugh that cut through deep into her bones. Instinctively she curled up into the smallest ball that she could manage, while burying her face between her knees as the macabre ghoul breathed its hellish oven breath all over her, causing the plastic cable around her wrists and ankles to melt and drip into small puddles. Miraculously, however, her skin remained unburned. Gradually, the searing heat and the cacophony of terrifying sounds subsided. Peering up, she saw that the fiend had vanished and that the fire had diminished back to a level where she could have toasted a teacake or warmed her toes from a distance without any fear of anything other than a rosy glow to her countenance. She heard the disconcertingly ordinary sound of a loud sneeze. She turned to see an odd looking woman with a hat the size of a hill blowing her nose. She jumped twice out of her own skin and once at least out of that of a large black cat that had climbed in through a hole in one of the back windows and now sat warming itself in front of the unholy fire. Managing finally to spit the filthy cloth out of her mouth she said,

"Who on earth are you?"

"I'm the feller in the fire," the woman replied.

Mary's already confused brain did a back-flip between her ears.

"You look surprised," the woman said. "Don't worry, I'm only dressed as a woman for three days a week. I'm a man for all the rest."

"How can you be," Mary said, "the man in the fire I mean?"

"Oh that," the woman who claimed to be a man said, "that's just a party trick. We use it on people who disappear up themselves to help bring their feet back down on firm ground. You should see what I can do after a plateful of oysters and a couple of pints of the old holy water."

"But I saw him burned to bone," Mary said.

"All an illusion," the woman replied, "I was being arty farty, symbolic or bollixy, according to your point of view."

"Symbolic of what?" Mary asked, without any confidence that a sensible answer would be forthcoming.

"Of the fate that awaits the likes of you," the oddity said, "given your almost complete lack of concern for anyone but yourself. Of course, given that you're still half in the world of the living I'm not allowed to reveal too much of things on the other side of the fence, but where circumstances permit, I can let a small part of the cat out of the bag. Which, in your case, is to give you a flavour of the viciousness of the company you'd keep if you were consigned to the dark zone outside those proverbial pearly gates, the place you guys know as hell. The real nature of hell is the people you get to live with – forever. You can't know how bad that's going to be until you find out for yourself, so my little stage show gave you a taste of the fear you'd feel if left forever with people with a serious kindness deficit."

"What do you mean, my lack of concern for anyone but me?" Mary said, ignoring all of the additional detail.

"Well, as but one recent example, you remember poor Danny I presume, the perfectly personable young man you dismissed from your presence in McDoolahay's with a disdain that would have crushed a pride of lions, never mind someone so downcast and disastrously unlucky in love as his unfortunate self?"

"What about him?"

"What about him indeed. He's a man who very nearly died less than two minutes after you gave him the big heave ho. You didn't even give him half a look, or at the very least a kind and courteous refusal, because he didn't fit with your square jawed fantasy of perfect-in-every-detail Six Pack Man. All you're interested in is the guy that would give you your dream of a perfectly manicured, middle class, American-style life with two point four children - with a silver Merc to boot no doubt. Yet poor old Danny, the man who got shot for no more than taking the trouble to live, for all his dreaminess and faults, is worth more than any Superman look alike and you couldn't even let him finish a sentence without kicking him into touch. If he didn't take your fancy you could at least have been gentle in your dismissal.

There's kindness and a complete freedom from hypocrisy in the man, and he's someone who was serious in his misguided feelings of love for you. Being able to look into people's hearts is a privilege of me job, so I can vouch for the boy. It's just a pity that young bucks like yourself haven't learned how to look under the surface of a body - you'd be surprised at what you can find if you take the trouble to dig deep enough."

"The feller was a loser - you could tell it just by looking at him – and he had none of the looks I'd want to see in my children, when I have them that is. He seemed just like a guy who was too lacking in oomph to get anywhere in life and couldn't find himself a woman if they gave them away free with packets of spuds, so why should I waste my time with the likes of him?"

"You see, you've just confirmed my point. You can't see your way to being even half concerned about the man and the effect you had on him. After the merciless flattening you gave him and the bullet that he took on top of it, he's so far down in the deep that he'll never resurface without a hand the size of an elephant to pull him up. There is one and only one way of rescuing him and that's down to you."

"How so?" Mary asked, with a hint of dread in her voice.

"Well, a hospital visit to the poor sod and a few kind words wouldn't go amiss and the effort would hardly kill you, which is a very different situation to that of a young man who has been nearly killed. Would that be too much to ask?"

"It depends entirely on what other things you're asking," Mary replied.

"I'm asking as little from you as apologising to him for being so brusque and harsh on your last occasion of meeting and even if you could never dream of an evening out with the feller, of thinking up some words, encouragement, whatever, to help him feel that his is not a hopeless case with the women of this world - and that even if you and he are not meant to be, there will be someone else for him, as sure as there will be for you. Does all of that sound an impossible task for one so bright as yourself?"

"Ok, if that will get you off my case I can do that," Mary said, "but why all of the concern for this one unfortunate when there's a world full of them out there – and who are you that you think such things are your business anyway?"

“As an underwhelming vote of sympathy for the poor man that is an effort that will take some beating,” the oddity replied. “I think you’ll need to make a bit more of an effort to be genuine in what you say – you were considerate enough to that old priest who was worse for wear in McDoolahay’s, so there’s clearly a glimmer of kindness buried within that harsh exterior. Let’s see if we can find it for Danny. It was that little glimmer that got you this second chance in the first place.”

“What second chance, what do you mean by that?” Mary asked.

“Oh, didn’t I tell you?” the oddity replied. “You caught a stray bullet as well as Danny and you’re out for the count in a coma at the moment. It’s touch and go in the view of the docs, but my bosses have decided to give you a second crack at the whip, so you’ll wake up soon and after a week you’ll be back on your feet. It’s then that you can make your little trip to Danny’s ward and begin digging deep to find the nicer you that’s waiting to get out.”

“So this is all a dream?” Mary asked.

“No, not quite, let’s just say it’s a conversation that it would be difficult for us to have were you awake, but the fact that you’re offline changes everything. This is your one big chance to get a health check on your personality and decide to improve it when you’re fully back among the living.”

“You still haven’t answered my questions – why all the concern for him and who are you to be on his case – and mine as well for that matter?” Mary asked, again ignoring the bits of her strange companion’s comments that she didn’t find of interest or concern.

“Very well, to answer your first question,” the oddity said, “Danny was supposed to be carted off by the reaper until it was realised that there was something that he and only he could do that, in its apparently small way, would set in motion a chain of other small things that cumulatively would be to the greater good of humanity. Those of a literary disposition in the reaper’s office refer to it as the Middlemarch effect. That made the continued existence of Danny suddenly of the greatest importance and it was decided that he should live the normal course of a life and be taken off the exit list. As to why me, when obituaries are cancelled it’s my job to sort things out - it’s the social work side of reaping, although you'd never hear a word spoken of it in the normal way of things. In Danny's case all of that translates as me giving him back enough belief in himself to be actually able to do the things that he's been spared to do. As you're part of the key to all of that – and it's been decided to give you a second chance at life - I have to get you to make your own very necessary contribution, which is what I'm doing now, God help me and all the saints as well by the difficult look of things. My job was to rattle you from top to bottom until your soul acquired the necessary degree of kindness and charity, but it looks like I may have to do some more rattling yet," she said, while bending down to pick up the scythe that had been lying unnoticed on the floor. Thinking that she was about to be hacked in two by this strange, obviously unstable paranormal oddity, Mary screamed and started to pull feverishly at the wire that she had used to secure the outer door.

"Dear oh dear," the woman who wasn't a woman said, "there's no need for such a to-do. It's only the tool of me trade. Still, if more rattling of your complacent mind was needed, then that should have done the trick. Here, let me open the door for you."

Mary stood to one side trembling and watched amazed while the woman brought the scythe swishing down and severed the battered old wire that was holding the door with one stroke.

"See, I always knew it would be useful for something," the oddity said. "Now, time for me to be off - another appointment you know, all part of me job."

"What exactly is your job, your title or whatever, you still haven't really told me?" Mary said, still trembling.

"Me? I'm the Grim Reaper's Apprentice," the oddity said, disappearing simultaneously in a large puff of smoke - and with that Mary woke up, startled and blinded by the light a doctor was shining down into her eyes, looking for signs of consciousness…

We go back now three days in time, to the other side of Dublin. There we find a flattened soul in sorrow. The feet that had flown with the spirit of the dance now hung like rocks from the side of the armchair across which the shocked Jenny O'Riley lay strewn. She had seen it all, the slaughter of the owner of owners and the near death of the innocent of innocents in the helpless shape of the hapless Danny. She felt like the whole world had been sucked down a sewer and drowned in an ocean of pain. For a while.

But Jenny was a woman in touch with the past and the future as a continuous whole. As she lay, her head held back so far that her hair draped the floor, her mind slowly spinning still from the drink that had tipped slightly the balance of her normal thoughts, her place in the natural order of things came back like a briefly forgotten dream. She felt again the weight of the past and the screams of the future, and saw through all of it a thin spiral of love that burnt with the force of a laser through the darkness around. She could feel the presence of a thousand Danny's, all in the wrong place at precisely the wrong time, some of whom survived and lived successfully afterwards as this or that, some who were maimed forever and lived sad and crippled lives in the stink of the gutter, and some who died from their wounds and became early food for the blood licking worms. She knew suddenly that she had been witness to no more than the continuous flaw in the nature of humans that had stabbed like a knife into the back of millions in the past and would slash and slaughter still for as long as the living had the gift of free will. Life had to go on, no matter what. Or so she thought…

Her musings were interrupted by a ring on the doorbell of her flat. She dragged herself up and went to see who it was. The sight that greeted her was more than a little surprising. Her visitor was dressed from head to foot in black, with a hood over his head. He had a long, viciously sharp looking scythe in his right hand. Assuming at first that it must be a friend in fancy dress, she thought only of how whoever it was had managed to pick precisely the wrong moment for such a prank, given the events that she had so recently witnessed. She peered into the hood to see if she could recognise who it was but found only a small pair of cat like eyes staring inquisitively back at her.

"Well, bugger me," the figure said, "you're as alive and well as the day you were born Jenny O'Riley. There must be some kind of a mix up here, let me just check me diary..."

Momentarily shocked by the sight of the inhuman eyes, she gasped, fearing that she had a variation on the theme of a mad axe murderer on her doorstep and tried to slam the door. Her effort failed due to the fact that simultaneously the strangeness that was her visitor leaned his scythe against the door frame, causing the door to thud ineffectually against the metal blade. She grabbed the potential weapon with one hand and tried to slam the door again with the other, this time squashing a thick black diary that had slipped through her visitor's long thin fingers onto the floor as he had yanked it over-zealously out of the innards of his cloak.

"Aren't I the butterfingers now," the strangeness said, while bending down to pick it up. Having failed to shut the door twice now, Jenny decided that she was taking no chances and attempted to slip past the hooded weirdness while it was preoccupied with the diary. She intended to run down the stairs to the caretaker's lodge and ask for the guards to be called. Unfortunately, as the oddity bent down its left leg splayed out. The long pointed shoe that slithered sideward as a result went unseen by the desperate escapee. She immediately tripped over it and went flying head first onto the floor of the corridor. As she lay motionless, the figure looked down at her and said,

"No, I appear to have the right day after all."

As he began to leaf through his diary to confirm the date, Jenny stirred. Unnoticing, he found finally the correct page and said to himself,

"Right day, wrong month. Now isn't that a sod."

"Who on earth are you?" Jenny asked, too disoriented to manage a scream. She checked her bruised temple delicately to see that there was no bleeding. Startled by her sudden revival, he said,

"Me, oh wrong address I'm afraid, somebody booked me as a Reaper-gram, you know, fancy dress and all that stuff, and I've made a bit of a bollix of it. Must be off..."

He'd got no further than the next door along when Jenny shouted,

"I don't believe you."

He stopped dead in his tracks. He'd hoped to get away with his mistake, but knew that if the cat had got out of the bag concerning a coming fatality then it was his job to put it back again until the proper day for the victim's decease - or face a stiff interview with the chief reaper. He said,

"What d'you mean, you don't believe me?"

"There's something wrong, your story doesn't match your

shifty tone. I'm going to scream and warn the caretaker that we have a lunatic in the building unless you give me the truth in thirty seconds flat."

Jenny had recovered her senses far more quickly than he'd anticipated and was a much pluckier soul than her gentle appearance might have suggested. He decided that a bit of the old 'party tricks' magic necessarily was in order. With a sudden sweep of his right hand he cast off the cloak and hood to reveal a clean shaven young man of stunning good looks in a suit that was sharp enough to cut the corridor carpet into shreds. Walking briskly towards her with his right arm outstretched in business handshake mode he said,

"Patrick O'Connor at your service, private detective..."

"No you're not," she said before he could go any further.

For the second time in less than a minute he stopped dead.

"What d'you mean no I'm not?" he asked, perplexed.

"You're too young," she replied, "nobody your age would be trusted with the kind of work private detectives do. Now I warned you, unless I get the truth I'm going to scream."

"Jaysis, Mary and Joseph, you're as bright as three light bulbs welded together," he replied. "Well, me name at least is right, I am indeed the one and only Patrick O'Connor of Roscrea."

"No you're not," she replied quietly but firmly.

"Why not?" he asked, now doubly perplexed.

"Because you've got your accents jumbled, there's more Scottish than Irish in everything you've said so far and whatever else they speak in Roscrea, it's not Scottish."

"Now who's the private dick?" he asked.

"So who are you really?" she enquired, with the same quiet firmness.

"If I told you now I don't think even I'd believe meself, you've so shattered me confidence," he said, this time with a distinctive Galway lilt in his voice.

"Try me," she said, gradually losing all remaining fear of the helpless case that now confronted her.

"I knew it'd be a woman that'd finally do for me," he said, as if to himself. "I've failed in every possible respect on this assignment and that'll put paid to me chances of promotion for at least another couple of millennia, not that time matters in quite the same way in such a context as eternity..."

"You're some kind of mischievous spirit aren't you?" she said, fixing him with a critical gaze. "Only not a very competent one or I'd still be scared to death of you. Those eyes inside the hood weren't human - you can shape shift can't you?"

"All right, all right, I'm a bit of a flop. But you'll never believe who I am or what it is I do, so there's no point in me even beginning to tell you."

"You'll not go until you have done," Jenny said firmly.

He looked into her determined eyes for a few seconds and concluded that it was pointless trying to flannel his way past such a fearless soul.

"All right, all right, I know when I'm beat by a ferocious woman. I'm the Grim Reaper's Apprentice's Apprentice," he replied mournfully. "I was a full apprentice but I've botched up so many of me missions that I was demoted by St. Peter himself. They had to invent a new job for me because I was so bad at me old one and bring in a replacement to do nearly everything that I used to do. They just trust me with the simple stuff – and even then trust is a bit of a strong word."

"So I'm categorised as a bit of 'simple stuff' am I?" Jenny asked gently, now completely unafraid of her strange visitor.

"What, no, I mean, look, please don't ask me questions like that, I'm not supposed to tell porky pies and I've already told one lot tonight. If they find out about that they could force me to hand in me scythe."

"I heard you when you were thumbing through your diary," Jenny said. "You've come a month too early. I'm supposed to kick the bucket at the same time next month, isn't that right?"

The apprentice's apprentice shuffled his feet and looked twice as embarrassed as a man three times embarrassed could be.

"You're right," he said, "I can shape shift. Would you like a quick demonstration? Look, from a man in a suit to..."

He screwed up his eyes and drew in his cheeks so far that one threatened to exchange places with the other and said,

"...a small piece of cheese!"

No sooner had he said this than a huge gust of wind swept down the corridor, which was followed instantly by a blinding flash of light and a crack like a thunderbolt. As the pall of smoke that filled the spot where previously he had stood cleared, Jenny could indeed see that a minute piece of camembert cheese had appeared on the carpet. No sooner had she got over the shock of what had happened than a mouse appeared out of a hole in the rotting skirting board, gobbled up the cheese in a flash and then darted back into its tiny lair. As it did so she heard a low, distinctly depressed groan from inside its little stomach, followed by a cry of, "Oh bugger!"

For the next minute or two she heard the sound of a desperate scrabbling coming from behind the skirting board as some kind of struggle occurred between the baffled mouse and the unexpectedly imprisoned contents of its stomach. Then, without any warning or ceremony the cheese that was a man, that previously had been a reaper, burst through the wall in the form of a dragon that was twice three times as startled as the woman who nearly had enough of a litter of kittens on the spot to eat the mouse six times over in the space of a minute.

"Holy shit!" it roared on seeing its reflection in the solitary corridor mirror. "I'm even buggering up me transformations. I was supposed to come back to you as the most handsome man in the world and I've ended up as a gargoyle with wings. Can I not get even a thing right d'you think?"

Recovering from her shock and no matter how hard she tried, quite unable to feel any fear at the sight of a dragon that was sporting a mini skirt that did nothing at all to flatter its absurdly chunky, knobbly-kneed hind legs, she said,

"Apparently not. Are you absolutely sure now that you're in the right job?"

The dragon that was a man and occasionally a cheese looked mournfully at its long-clawed toes and said,

"Most definitely not. But I'm completely useless at everything else St. Peter could have offered me, but marginally less useless at this than the best of the rest, so this is what I'm stuck with."

"My poor little dragon," she said with her characteristic and unsoppy kindness, "we must find something that you're good at. I have a feeling that telling the truth is one of those things. In fact, it must be, for God bless us and all the saints – should they exist, you're so terrible at telling lies, great or small, or in between."

"Now that's a fact," the dragon replied. "I couldn't lie for more than a minute at a time and even then so badly that even I'd hardly believe a word of anything I said. So the construction of any great fiction about me life would have to be done in so many separate instalments that me listeners would grow so confused and bored that they'd probably long have stopped listening before I got to the climax of the great lie itself - and then I'd have to start all over again. Then I'd get bored and fall asleep meself, and when I'd wake up I and all me listeners would have forgotten completely what the point of the fiction itself was supposed to be, leaving aside entirely, of course, the fact that, in truth, it would have been about no such thing."

"Yes, I know what you mean," Jenny said, as the easiest way of dispensing in an instant with the uncomfortable reality that she hadn't understood a word of what had just been said. The fact that this was itself a fib was a problem that she decided was a complication too far, even for the most honest of women, as she herself indeed was, and so decided to think no more on the matter.

"So," she continued, "if telling the truth is the only thing that you're really good at, then the truth is what you should tell above all else."

"Well, yes, I suppose," the dragon said, sensing that it was about to be led where it would not necessarily want to go.

"Then you can tell me very precisely what you meant when you said you had come a month too early. And there's no point in trying to skip the matter again, bearing in mind the series of disasters that have befallen you since the last time you tried such a trick."

"No, that is a point," said the dragon, surveying its decidedly ugly fizzog that was looking back at it disdainfully from a decorative mirror on the hallway wall.

"So?" Jenny said.

"Knit," the dragon replied. "D'you know, I could play these word association games for a lifetime."

"If you don't tell me what I want to know I'll tell every friend I have of your strange visitation and of your intent to come back for me in a month. Then they'll all be waiting for you with every means at their disposal to fight you off. You'll have such a struggle trying to cart my soul away, should I have such a thing, that you'd wish ten times in every second that you'd told me the truth of the matter when I'd asked."

"I'd be invisible to them, they wouldn't see me," it said.

"You're too incompetent to be invisible, you'd probably accidentally arrive with flashing lights on your head," she replied.

"This is very unfair, nobody's ever tried to blackmail a Reaper's Apprentice before," the mini-skirted dragon wailed.

"There's a first time for everything," Jenny said calmly. "Now come on, spill the beans..."

"All right, all right," the dragon replied, "you've guessed it already so I don't know what else it is that you want me to say. You're down to kick the bucket on this same day next month and I cocked it up and came too early. Now don't blame me for the unpleasantness of the news or ask me to do anything to change it because I can't. Your name has a big black asterisk against it which means that bringing you in is high priority. St. Peter himself has decided that you're needed in eternity on precisely that day and that nobody else can do whatever it is that he's chosen you for. Your curiosity about the meaning of death and life and everything has impressed him no end, so I'm told and he's got a vacancy that needs filling and yours is precisely the right CV. You should be pleased, being picked for an important job by Mr. Big himself."

"But if it's so important why has me reeling in been left to someone who normally only deals with the simple 'collections'?"

"I know, it's daft isn't it – I think it's a typing error in the reaper's admin department. He won't be best pleased when he finds that it's me on the job."

"And what about me fine feller of a boyfriend and all me other nearest and dearest, how are they supposed to feel about me suddenly being carted off and roasted like a giant fish finger down at the crem?" Jenny asked in a manner that was as near to anger as anyone of such a gentle disposition was likely to get.

"That you'll have to ask St. Peter," the dragon said, "in all such matters he's the zoo keeper and I'm just the performing seal, figuratively speaking of course."

Jenny tried momentarily to deal with the image of a dragon that was simultaneously a seal and decided rapidly that that way madness lay. She said,

"You keep talking about St. Peter as though I should automatically accept that everything in the New Testament is an indisputable fact, that he really is some kind of Mr. Big in the afterlife as all the doddery bishops claim and that all the stuff that you've told me about what he's 'decided' is gospel truth - but you've shown yourself to be a serial fibber, so all of that could be simply a fantasy, or a pack of lies. I've always struggled with the idea that there could be something that had lived forever, without a beginning, the whole idea of God. To drag me off now when I've found no answer to all me fears and doubts about the reality of a creator, life after death and everything is very cruel – I'll be terrified and it'll be all your doing. The only things I've got any proof of are that you exist, that people die and that you are telling me my goose is cooked. So, if you're right, how am I supposed to cope with my last month alive? What should I get done that I will never be able to do again, how should I prepare people for the surprise of my coming demise, and how do I deal with the fear of the unknown that lies ahead? I mean, your assurances about my being picked out for some kind of special job in 'heaven' are all very well, but given your strange and fiery form and the inhuman little eyes that I first saw within your hood, you could just as well be a divil come to cart me off kicking and screaming to some version of 'hell', should it exist."

The dragon ruffled its mini skirt in frustration and said,

"Jenny O'Riley, look at the blameless selflessness of your life and your endless searching after the meaning of existence and ask yourself if it would be likely that the divil would be the one hot clogging it to your door to carry off your immortal soul. Believe you me, he'd get a swift boxing around both ears from the chief reaper if he even dreamt of such a thing."

"Very well, if you're truly not a divil then you can prove it by giving me some good and credible advice as to what it is that a dead woman walking should do with her last days on earth."

"That's a most uncharitably impossible task for a person who finds it difficult enough even to blow the correct nose whenever he sneezes. No, don't look at me so sceptically, I'm not in the habit of exaggerating. I was at a funeral only yesterday where I atishooed with the force of a small explosion, yet became convinced that it was the officiating cleric that had performed the offending sneeze and blew his nose for him so hard that his glasses flew off the end of his nose. It was only when I sneezed a second and third time in rapid succession that I realised that the detonations in question were me own."

"If you weren't a divil you wouldn't play so fast and loose with me emotions, nor evade in so inappropriately mischievous a fashion questions that ask for advice that any God-fearing spirit would give with wisdom and pleasure," Jenny said in a quietly reprimanding tone.

"Not guilty on all counts," the dragon replied. "I'm simply too useless to answer such useful questions. In any case, the choice in such matters must inevitably be yours - that's the whole nature of free will. I know you don't find it easy to believe in the Almighty and the whole creation thing, but having met him on several occasions I can assure you that the feller exists as much as you or I, or McDoolahay's bar. I can't tell you how He came about, only that He 'is'. What I can also tell you is that He is hardly likely to criticise you for any decisions that you make that you feel genuinely to be good for all of those you'll leave behind."

Jenny eyed the dragon shrewdly for a minute, doing her best to ignore its sudden sneeze and its immediate and uninvited blowing of her nose. Pushing its claw away with mild irritation she said,

"If we put aside for the minute all me philosophical problems with the idea of the Almighty, then at least what you said is hardly a divil's answer. It's even half sensible, despite the fact that the gratuitous idiocy of your assault on me nostrils might lead any reasonable soul to suspect baser motives. On a good day, with the wind in the right direction and all me queries about creation and the nature of existence put on hold, I might even begin to suspect that all of this apparent lunacy is in fact a smokescreen, a ploy to try and conceal a level of wisdom that you're not permitted to reveal to those still alive."

"Would you indeed now?" the dragon said concernedly, beginning to worry that the intelligent percipience of its doomed companion was about to lead it into yet more trouble with the chief reaper. "Whether such a supposition was fact or fiction would make no difference to the simple advice that the best guidance you could seek would be that of the Almighty himself. You will accept that such simple thoughts can be offered equally well by the witless or the wise, given their minimal strain upon the brain will you not?"

"And if I should?" Jenny said, sensing immediately some kind of implied deal.

"Then I'll do me best to put in a request to St. Peter himself that you get the very best advice – if you'll take me word for the fact that he exists, that is."

"As a small penance for all your attempts to conceal your cock ups at my expense?" she asked pointedly. "There seems to have been a great deal of effort going on here to cover your own backside and all too little trouble taken to think of how you might cushion the blow to meself of the terrible news of me coming demise."

The dragon shifted uneasily from foot to foot, sensing yet another coming bollocking from the chief reaper once all of this was over.

"I'll do me very best, I promise," it said shame facedly, "and I won't come to collect you next month until the very last minute of the day in question, so that you get the most time possible to put all of your affairs in order."

"How kind," Jenny said with a sudden sadness, realising that everything she loved on earth would soon have to be left behind.

"Well, I'd better be off then," the dragon replied.

"Like that?" Jenny asked perplexed. "Don't you think a dragon in a mini skirt might cause a bit of a stir, whether it be O'Connell Street or heaven itself that it's padding through?"

Looking at itself in the corridor mirror the dragon nodded its agreement. "You're right," it said, "time for a change back to something a little more conservative I think."

It started weaving an out of tune incantatory spell in the air around it and doing a stumbling, lop-sided dance for which it seemed unable to remember every fifth step. It then pounded up and down upon the ground six times with both feet simultaneously as if its life depended on it. There was a sudden flash of light, followed by what sounded remarkably like the blowing of a large raspberry. As the smoke cleared Jenny saw that the apprentice's apprentice had returned once more to a human form, taking the shape of the sharp suited alleged private detective that had preceded the problematical metamorphoses into a piece of cheese and then a dragon. There was only one snag. While the suit remained precisely as before, a slim fitting garment that was exactly the right size for a man who was around six foot one inches tall, the apprentice to end all apprentices had come back with only three quarters of the height that he had previously possessed. The sleeves hung limp from his much shortened arms and the trousers concertinaed onto the floor around his shoes like two grey jellies that had collapsed into themselves. Jenny stared in disbelief at the sight that confronted her and shook her head. Seeing her look, the apprentice blushed visibly and tried hastily to pull its sleeves up above its wrists. Having achieved this dubious solution to half of its problem it pulled its trouser legs up until they rose above floor level. Trying desperately to hold everything up in place, it started to shuffle embarrassedly off down the corridor. "Bye for now," it muttered in a low voice, as if hoping not to attract too much attention. Jenny shouted after it,

"Why don't you try another incantation to shrink your suit to the right size?"

However, she knew the answer to her own question without the unfortunate apprentice's apprentice needing to embarrass himself further by answering it - to try one more cack-handed transformation would be too high risk a strategy for a spirit with such a level of incompetence. As she walked wearily and confusedly back into her flat, a sudden blinding flash of inspiration struck her. She sat down once more in her bedraggled but comfortable old armchair and pondered on whether what she had in mind would be an act of terrible unfairness or, in light of the apprentice's obviously long record of surviving disastrously bungled cock-ups, no more than a proverbial pebble in the ocean as far as the Almighty would be concerned, should he of course exist. At length, having thought the matter through with characteristic thoroughness, she decided that the latter would be the most likely outcome. Picking up the telephone directory, she made note of a couple of numbers and determined to ring them first thing in the morning.

The next month passed quickly. Had the apprentice's apprentice been organised enough to keep his eye on matters, he might have been a little puzzled as to why Jenny chose to give her man and all her friends only the most indirect of hints that very shortly all might not be well. However, given that most of his time was spent trying to get himself out of one mess after another, he wasn't in much of a position to take any close note of what she was up to at all. When the appointed day finally came he did at least manage to get it right at the second attempt and arrived at her front door, as promised, at precisely one minute to midnight. Checking his little black book for the fourth time in less than half an hour to reassure himself, he rang on the front door bell, purely out of courtesy rather than need, given his ability to walk through walls to collect the souls within them. There was a shuffling of feet from somewhere deep within the flat, followed by the flop, flop, flop of old slippers on the polished wooden floor. The apprentice's apprentice braced himself for what was never an easy task and held his scythe firmly to attention, being determined to give a more efficient account of himself on this occasion. The door creaked slowly open and a pair of seventy year old eyes greeted his strange appearance with obvious puzzlement.

"If you've come to take Miss O'Riley to a fancy dress party you've got the wrong address young man. She moved out this morning. I'm the new tenant."

"Moved? Moved where?" the appalled apprentice wailed. "You must tell me, and it has to be close because there's hardly any time left."

From within the flat the sound of an old mechanical clock striking midnight chimed out remorselessly. The apprentice's face dropped into his boots. He muttered,

"Oh bugger. She's outwitted me. The Grim Reaper's going to do his nut three times over. I'll be the first apprentice's apprentice to be demoted to the role of apprentice to the apprentice's apprentice. I'll be spending the rest of eternity washing shrouds and polishing scythes."

At the same moment, in her new flat on the other side of Dublin, Jenny O'Riley heaved a huge sigh of relief. Midnight had struck and the appointed day had passed. She was certain that St. Peter, should he indeed exist, would not be mean enough to act like a taxman and demand that she be immediately collected as an arrear. And as for the apprentices' apprentice, well she didn't share any of his panic or fear for his well being. His incompetence was of such an obviously longstanding and monumental nature that had the Chief Grim Reaper intended to seriously nail him for it he would have done so long before. Clearly, grim though much of its work might be, the Reaper's Office must have some kind of a sense of humour to have kept the hapless apprentice on its books, despite his confessed long list of cock-ups, of which her escape from the jaws of death was but the latest. She anticipated another firm ticking off, but was very sure that he would not be fired.

We end where we began, in the bar with the soul of a ship and those of all the sailors that had drunk in it. It is several hours away from being open once more to the living, but gathered within are four keepers of the dead. At a low table in the far corner a hooded figure is stooped over a Guinness as dark as his mood, all foreboding and awaiting of doom. In the doorway stand three more, two similarly dressed in black, scythes in hand and another clothed in white with the radiance of a saint. The Grim Reaper's apprentice is handing over to his boss and St. Peter the file on Father O'Hanlon so that the saint can open up the pearly gate to let him in when his brief spell in purgatory is finished. Then they look at their man and at each other and shake their heads in disbelief. They walk slowly over and seat themselves, one reaper either side of the apprentice's apprentice, with the saint in the middle. The beleaguered unfortunate looks in terror and dread, first at the Chief Reaper and then at St. Peter, who taps the table lightly with his finger and says,

"Now I know this is a daft question every time I ask it of you Artemus, but could you explain, from the beginning and without too much in the way of confusing digressions, what exactly went wrong this time…?"

Intermission 5

With the fate of the unfortunate Artemus hanging in mid-air the audience greeted the end of the professor's story with appreciative chuckles and then a long burst of clapping and cheers and even shouts of "More!" as the teller of the tale took several bows before disappearing through the flap at the back of the tent. Sean said,

"Well gentlemen, that's a difficult one in the judging. Several tales in one with some better than others and the best of the lot very clearly at or near the top of the audience's list. You'll need fine wisdom between you to judge how such a complex concoction weighs against the best received of the earlier ones – and that's not to forget, of course, the complications with the applause that we saw in the case of Brendan and Valerie's tales."

"It's a difficult job but I think I'm doing ok," Ben replied. "If all goes well - and I'm as right as I think - the land will be mine by tomorrow morning."

"And if you're not the land will be mine instead," Liam replied, giving Ben a look as grim as death. Sensing the growth in tension as the magic hour of the judges' verdict grew nearer Sean decided a change of subject was needed urgently. He said,

"The next on the list should be less of a strain on the old brain. He's the man with the longest name but the shortest stories in any festival he goes to. Believe it or not - and not would be a justifiable but incorrect response - he calls himself Declan Pagan O'Rendezvous Saint."

"Why on earth does the eejit use such a long and ridiculous name?" Ben asked.

"Well, when he's been asked in the past he's always given even more ridiculous answers," Sean replied. "On one occasion he said he'd chosen it after his brain fell out of his head and there was nothing between his ears to make a sound judgment. On another he said he'd plumped for it because he was the Pagan Saint of story telling. And that's half the problem with the man – he irritates some – like your good self - no end, while for others he's the best slice of cake on the table."

"Presuming it's fruitcake," Liam said dourly.

"Indeed," Sean said. "He's a terrible affection for shaggy dog stories and there's little doubt he'll hurl another at us tonight. They're usually set mostly in bars and can drive you half way round the bend in search of a point until you discover there is no point – but every now and then, just when you've twigged there isn't, the bugger goes and sticks one in at the end. He rarely wins anything and probably won't today, but since half of the audience always loves him half of the committee of every festival always invites him back. Speak of the divil, there's the man himself."

The divil, or pagan, or whoever he might be was dressed as much for a snooker game as for a festival of stories. He was neat and dapper with a smile in his eye and a sly grin. He was as tall as Fierce Betty and irritated her immensely by introducing her to his imaginary friend. When she remarked, in cold puzzlement, that she couldn't see anyone, he annoyed her even more by saying that was because his friend was as small as a ladder is short. Betty didn't do humour and gave him a scowl like a growl, which he affected not to see. She stalked over to the microphone and introduced him with as much enthusiasm as if she were announcing a disease. Very deliberately, she missed out all of the parts of his invented name that she found imbecilic and referred to him simply as Declan Saint. He found her obvious distaste highly amusing and made a point of thanking her profusely for the 'warmth and generosity' of her introduction and by so doing annoyed her to such a degree that she looked in severe danger of spontaneously combusting. He then said,

"The only thing wee Betty got wrong was the fact that me name is the reverse way round – if she'd have said Saint Declan then she'd have hit the nail on the head. Now, such frivolities aside, I have a little tale – a very little tale, so small it's only just learned to walk and throw its toys at the granny and I'd like to let it loose among you all. Are you ready for it Mullahy's Rock? What, no reply - has the rock no ears or a tongue to talk? Then I'll speak for it and say it's raring for the off and off indeed I will go with a witty little tale called *The Day O'Flanagan Died.* But before I do I should say a word or two by way of explanation of things. The first is that the tale is set in a bar, the second is that it is set in a bar full of inebriates and the third is that it is set in a bar full of inebriates, a dog and several more fearsome nuns than are good for it. In the middle of all that repetitious repetition is a clue that I'd like you to hunt for and hold onto when you try and understand what on earth it is I'm on about. And beware of confusing your bullies and Billies and the living and the dead – enough said. Now, to begin, I'm going to break with tradition and start in the middle or, to be more precise in a very precise way of being extremely precise, in the middle of a sentence, which is…"

The Day O'Flanagan Died

Declan with the very long name's tale

"...and the river rose up and threw itself back through the bridge like a rocket, fish flyin' everywhere, like they thought they were salmon... It was then that I knew somethin' big had happened. It was as if the roar of the wave, that huge, crested tidal messenger of doom, was formin' itself into the very words I was to hear as soon as me first foot preceded me second over the pub threshold – 'O'Flanagan is dead.'"

"If I might venture a small query concerning your feet in this matter Patrick," a diminutive, fish-eyed wastrel with a beer gut as large as a barrel said, "is there any precise way that you can tell which is the first and which the second, are they marked as such perhaps, with a large 'one' painted on one of your big toes and a 'two' on the other?"

"Me feet are an irrelevance as well you know Sean O'Connor," the man with irrelevant feet replied.

"Indeed they are Patrick. Are there any other parts of your anatomy that should be described in the same way d'you think?"

"Leave the poor man alone Sean," Vincent Malone said. "His brain's extended enough trying to think straight on one matter without you coming along and adding another. Carry on Patrick, we're only half confused as matters stand. Let's see if you can complete the circle and turn the half into a whole."

"That the bugger will and then we'll all fall down it, you see if we don't," Sean replied.

"Gentlemen please, let the unfortunate speak," the po-faced barman said.

"T'ank you Jimmy, it's a relief to know there's still one man left in the world who knows the meaning of politeness," Patrick said.

"Not one but two. I do as well," Vincent said.

"And me. That's three," an excuse for a man in a pullover made for six interjected. "And I know the meanings of lots of other things as well. Go on, ask me a word and I'll guarantee I can give you its meaning."

"Will yous mick-takers not shut up?"

"No, sorry Patrick, that's seven words at least," the pullover replied, "I only do one at a time."

"The story man, tell us the story," Jimmy the barman said.

"I would if I could. Every time I open me mouth to speak the air's filled with someone else's rabbitin' voice. There's no space left to put a single word of me own."

"You have our guarantee of near silence," Vincent said.

"That's right Paddy, not another word," Sean confirmed.

"Maybe a sentence or two," Vincent added.

"But definitely not a word - on its own that is," Sean said.

"Perhaps a grunt. Or a sigh," Vincent said.

"Or an explosion of coughing, a hiccup, or any of a range of other familiar noises a body might be inclined to emit unbidden," Sean added by way of elaboration.

"But definitely not 'a word'," Vincent said.

"Jaysis wept! There's no point in tryin' to speak in the presence of two fellas whose only purpose in life is takin' the mick."

"Don't let them put you off Pat," a man with a voice as deep as the ocean said.

"Hello Billy! Will you see who it is lads, Big Billy Flynn. What can I get you Bill?" Jimmy asked.

"I'll have those two rock pies that look like they fell off a mountain," Billy said.

"Pies it is Billy, anything to please a man who's twice as big as a house," Jimmy said.

"Thank you Jimmy, but I'm in a generous mood today. I can't eat the things meself when I see the eyes of two hungry bird-like creatures feastin' themselves on the sight of me grub like it was the last supper. Open your mouth now Sean McMahon."

"No, Billy, honest, I wouldn't want to deny you the pleasure of your pies."

"Oh, it's no problem Sean, I'm not a man to let another less fortunate than himself go without. That's it now, open wide, yes, what a lovely set of teeth, in we go, no don't try and close your mouth, it'll go all over your trousers like a babby, there we go, hasn't he done well lads, a whole giant pork pie in his gob at one go."

"Now, let's see if you're as clever Vincent Malone," Billy said.

"No, honestly Billy, I'm definitely not a pie man."

"Nonsense, what would herself say if she heard you sayin' such a thing, and her famous for every type of pie known to man, so long as it's apple or beef? Never have I seen a man and a pie so suited to one another. It's almost as if you were destined to meet. Now, open your mouth, there's a good boy, in we go, oh, yes! Did you see that everyone, twice as big as his mouth and it went in as one piece. Are you all right there now Vincent, you seem to have the look of a vaguely choking man about you. Now then Patrick, let's hear what it is you were trying to tell everyone when I came in. Sean and Vince seem to have lost their voices so you should be able to say what you want without any problems."

"T'ank you Billy, t'ank you. There are angels and saints in heaven yet and..."

"That there may Patrick, but they will all have their say when they choose. Now it's your turn. Go on, tell us what it was that you wanted our ears to hear."

"Very well Billy, whatever you say. You're a generous man and that you are..."

"Patrick..."

"Yes Billy. I was relatin' the manner of O'Flanagan's death. You remember Fingers O'Flanagan, a man like you, built like a mountain, but lackin' your heart of gold?"

“I do remember him Patrick.”

“Well there’s more theories about his dyin’ than there are cats in Mary O’Malley’s kitchen.”

“I thought it was the other way round Paddy,” a suddenly pie free Sean said, “with more Mary O’Malleys than cats. Sure, the woman breeds like a cross between a rabbit and a spider plant, self replicatin’ herself all over the neighbourhood, and no Billy, no, please, I’ve a mind to shut up, no I...”

“There we go Sean, waste not want not, eh? Just because a slab of pork pie leaps out of your mouth onto the shite of the floor is no reason not to put it back right where it belongs. Does it taste good now, with the added flavour of the god knows what and the dust from under your boot? That’s right, nod away, let me give you a helpin’ hand - nod, nod, nod. There, you see, a happy man and a silent man. Now, Patrick, pray continue.”

“Are you sure the poor man’s not chokin’ Billy?” Patrick asked. “The pie looks as big as a brick when you see the bulging in his cheeks.”

“No, no, Patrick, just wind, the man’s no idea about digestion. Now, please, say what you have to say.”

“Well, I was telling you about O’Flanagan and all the theories and guesses and lies about how he died and why he died and who put paid to such a man who everyone had thought had all the powers of the immortal. And the point of me bringing the whole thing up was that I know the one true story. I was told, detail by detail, blow by blow, exactly how the whole thing happened. I’m the man who knows.”

“I have to say, Patrick, that you’re the third ‘man who knows’ that I’ve met in six months, and each has a totally different version of the truth. What makes you so different from all the rest of them?”

“What makes me different Billy is that I got the truth from a man who was there. I got the bartender’s story.”

“I see. We’ll come back to that, if only because one of the fellers who tells the tale says that O’Flanagan was nowhere near a pub at the time of his demise. Tell us what you’ve heard.”

“Well, Fingers O’Flanagan was a man heavily into everything the divil might want him to be, he was running a brothel full of all the ladies of the night, each so spectacularly endowed that just looking at them was enough to make you explode as sure as if some swine had shoved a bomb up your behind..."

"Delicately put Patrick, delicately put," Billy said. "We know you t'ink the man was the divil's son in everything he did. We know all of that. But how did he really die - and why? Now if you've got a convincing story to tell on any of that, then I'm the man with the ears, as I'm sure we all are, is that not right Sean, and Vince? There seems to be a bit of food wedged in their gobs Patrick, but I know they'd agree if they could. Just nod your heads lads, that's right. Now you tell us something that we've not already heard and there's a drink on all of us for you. Go on man, let rip with this astoundin' tale that you have to tell."

"I will Billy, that I will. It all began when O'Flanagan was six..."

"The man was never six. He was born at seven and died at thirty seven. He was the seventh son of a seventh son and would have nothing to do with sixes from the day he was baptised to the day they buried him. It was rumoured it was all because he had 666 stamped on his backside and he wanted to distract everyone from the truth by puttin' all of his life into sevens. He had seven pallbearers and was laid to rest at seven o'clock on the seventh day of the seventh month."

"And who the hell are you that comes in from nowhere talkin fluent bollix as if he'd been born to it?" Billy asked.

"Me? I'm no-one," the newcomer replied, "me mother was so disinterested in the look of me when I was born that she couldn't be bothered to give me a name. I've spent me whole life being referred to as 'you' and 'him'. I was even christened and confirmed as such by the orphanage I was dumped on, 'You' being me baptismal name and 'Him' me confirmation title. I'm You Him Molloy if you want the nearest to a name that I can get, but it's hardly a title in the conventional sense."

"You were in a convent then?" Billy asked.

"Only for ten minutes, the nuns caught me almost as soon as I'd got over the wall and I was sent back for a hidin' before you could say McKelligan."

"I couldn't say Mcwhatsiname. I've always had a problem with big words," a flatulent drunk at the end of the bar muttered in between Krakatauan detonations of the most unasked for kind.

"Are there any more pies left Jimmy?"

"A dozen at least Billy. You want another large one?"

"That's right Jimmy, the hardest and most disgustin' that you've got if you please. T'ank you. Now, Mr. Molloy, you look to me a hungry man and I can't stand to see any man starve in front of me eyes. Open wide, there now, all in at one go. I'll take it that the look of shock on your face is at the amazin' level of me generosity, so think nothing of it. Enjoy your meal as they say in all the best establishments. Now Patrick, please continue."

"T'ank you Billy, that I will. You see O'Flanagan was a man who had made one big enemy, a man that nobody with the slightest drop of wisdom would ever have dreamed of upsetting to even the smallest degree..."

"Absolute bollix! O'Flanagan never made an enemy that was over three and a half feet tall - he'd have nothing to do with 'big enemies' as you call them. The smaller the man the higher he'd have to jump to have even half a chance of landing a punch on Fingers' chops."

"And who in the name of all the merciful angels are you?" Billy asked a pike faced oddity that had swum in under the door without previous detection.

"What? Well if you don't know I'm not tellin'. I've no time for ignorance. And ignorant is what you are. O'Flanagan's enemy was no taller than a teapot as sure as I'm a Catholic."

"Then why are you carryin' an Orangeman's hat?"

"What? The hat? An act of pure courtesy. I'd carry the hat of anyone who looked in need of the favour."

"Then where's the Orangeman to go with it?"

"What? The man? Good God, I've lost him along the way. Can you believe that? I've been talkin' to a hat for the last few minutes without any sign of the man, and me not knowin' it. Would you credit that? I wouldn't. Still, life's full of surprises."

"Like O'Flanagan's enemy being as tall or small as a teapot?" Billy asked.

"What? Who told you that?"

"You did."

"Right. Well, it must be true then. I never lie."

"If O'Flanagan went to war with a man the size of a teapot then I'm the Queen of England," Jimmy the barman said.

"Well, the Queen you may be, but your five o'clock shadow will make a rare picture when they stick your fizzog on the front of an English banknote," the strangeness that was the stranger said.

"Jimmy, do you have another of those pies going spare?" Billy asked innocently.

"For you Billy, I've as many as you need."

"Good, pass me the largest and stalest that you have if you please. T'ank you. Now, if I might address meself to the man with no name. I'm right in supposin' that you've nothing in the way of evidence to back up these claims?"

"Evidence? Is me word not evidence enough? If I say O'Flanagan's foe was a teapot in height then that's all the evidence a trusting man would need."

"A man with no evidence indeed - and a man with no evidence is a man in need of a pie. Open wide now..."

"Open what wide? The door perhaps, me eyes, or even me mind? There's very little I can do with so imprecise an instruction as me clue."

"Oh there's precision here all right, a precise pushin' of the pie into your over-active apology for a mouth."

"Yeeeeeeearrrrrrrrrrgh!"

"Oh, sorry, was that your toe I accidentally stamped on?" Billy said. "Well I never, look, it appears to be on some kind of rope and pulley connection to yer jaw – it's made it open wide enough to swallow an elephant. There we go, that's right, all in... will yous look at the way he's grippin' the crust between his teeth lads, with his jaw bone weighted right down onto the bar counter - just like a pig's head on a platter. Now then Patrick, where were we?"

"Gnnn, nnneargh glueeeeeeeedup megroob."

"Sorry Patrick," Billy said, "I think our nameless friend's trying to tell me that he's havin' a problem or two with the swallowing of his pie. Maybe his belly is bigger than his gob d'you t'ink? What a terrible shame, he can't speak at all. Still Mr. Anonymous, you'll get over the problem soon enough, perhaps we could teach you sign language? Or maybe go all heritage over the thing - how would you fancy learnin' a bit of semaphore? Pray Patrick, continue with your enlightenin' of our minds."

"T'ank you Billy, t'ank you. Now I'd got to the point where I was tellin' you about Mad Mattie Milligan, the enemy of all enemies, a man that no sane mortal would cross unless he was short of a normal means of suicide..."

"Has anyone seen three hot cross nuns?" a desperate man shouted as he burst desperately into the desperate bar.

"No, that's not the kind of a pastry that we make round here. We're entirely a pie establishment," Jimmy replied, while delicately slicing a stale pickled onion from the soul of his boot with a razor.

"What? I said nothin' about pastry."

"You asked after me buns."

"Buns? No, nuns you eejit."

"Just watch who you're calling an eejit."

"I am watchin' him and it's not a pretty sight I can tell you. I'll ask again, has anyone seen three nuns with faces like thunder?"

"Not in here friend, this is not a place for your godly kind of a woman," Billy replied sternly.

"There's nothin' godly about these three. I'm tellin' you lads, these are the nuns from hell. I'm the only survivor."

"Survivor of what?" Patrick asked.

"A retreat. Can you believe it, I'm retreatin' from a retreat."

"What kind of retreat?" Patrick enquired.

"The divil's own, I can tell you, the very worst. A husbands' and wives' week-end special. No booze, no telly, no pool, no music, no chat, nothin' that in the normal way of things resembles food, and a three hour sermon by a canon talkin' nothin but balls. I tell you fellers, it was drivin' me wild."

"So yous escaped?" Billy asked.

"Me and three others. We were sprung by a friendly priest in return for the promise of a bottle of whiskey in the post."

"So where's the others?" Patrick asked.

"All betrayed or recaptured. You've never seen anythin' like it. Our holy Mary's, our wives from the very depths of purgatory itself, they set the nuns on us. No normal nuns mark you. No, these three are the heavy mob in its heaviest form. Built like tanks with the noses of sniffer dogs. They can hunt down an escapin' husband like a tracker follows a trail."

"If they're so clever how come they haven't nailed you?

You're a prominent enough kind of an eejit, I'd have thought even a monkey with a hangover would have caught you by now," Jimmy said.

"Are yous lookin' for a fight?"

Before a single fist could fly the bar door crashed open and three enormous figures in black strode in from the glare of the midday sun, their shadows falling long and hard across the shiny wooden floor. An awed silence descended all around as they surveyed the entire population of the bar. Their rosaries swung threateningly at their hips, as if ready to down every man in the room with a volley of deadly Hail Marys. The largest and most terrifying looking of the three strode over to within an inch of Billy Flynn's nose, stared him straight in the eye and said,

"We've come for McNally. He was seen coming in here. We've come to take him back. The sooner you give him to us, the sooner we're gone."

Billy stared her straight back, his gaze unflinching. He scooped up a peanut from out of the jar on the bar without taking his eyes off her, cracked it between his teeth, and then, turning his head for a single tense second, spat half of it out. He said,

"There's no McNally here. All the McNally's were banned from drinkin' here because of their women. Nothin' but trouble sister. Their women were nothin' but trouble."

The other two nuns strode forwards, rosaries raised, and Flynn found himself hemmed in against the bar on all sides.

"We've got ourselves a wise guy," the mother superior said. "I remember you Billy Flynn when you were still in short trousers. Do you remember me?"

Flynn stared hard and mockingly. She pulled back her habit and the look of mockery changed in an instant to one of terror.

"Mother Michael!"

"The one!"

"Mother of God I thought they'd sent you back to run a house for the drunk and the violent in Dublin."

"They did. But the violence was kid's play Flynn. There wasn't a rogue in that place when I left who'd have dared raise a hand to a flea in me presence. So now I'm here to deal with the likes of you, and you don't terrify me at all. Now, I'm askin' you one more time, where's McNally?"

“I told you,” Flynn said, sweating profusely, “there’s no McNally here.”

“Do you remember,” Mother Michael said, thrusting her nose right against his, “what I used to do when you lied at the orphanage?”

Flynn shivered and trembled so much at the thought that his glass slipped out of his hand and smashed all over the floor. Without warning or ceremony the nun grabbed his left ear and twisted it so hard that he yelped like a dog, and then, yanking it downwards, forced him onto his knees. The assembled multitude of drinkers gasped in amazement and fear. McNally, meanwhile, after hiding himself successfully behind the fattest man in the bar, had managed to slip quietly around behind the counter and was lying face down under the beer pumps. Mother Michael said,

“I’m giving you one last chance Flynn, where’s McNally?”

“I told you,” Flynn replied, gasping with pain, “McNally’s not here.”

The nun tweaked his ear so hard he yelled out in agony, delivered a swift clip across his cheek and threw him face down onto the hard wooden floor. Standing with her heel pressed hard into his back she said,

“I’ve never seen such a spineless collection of drink sodden reprobates. What a bunch of moral weaklings, what a challenge! Now gentlemen, you’ve all seen what happens when someone tries to play the tough guy with Mother Michael. Who’s next for the medicine, or are you all going to act like good little boys and tell me where it is this pathetic wastrel of a truanting husband is? You, yes you with the face as fat as a football, you know where he is, I can see it in your eyes. Come on spill the beans if you know what’s good for you.”

Sean, whose mouth was so full of pie still that he could neither spit nor swallow, made a desperate attempt at a compliant reply. He said,

“Heeesshbehinnnnnnnshhhhhhhhhhhhderbarrrrrsishtta.”

“What’s that?” she asked. “Is this man just an eejit or is there something wrong with his speech? You, yes you with the swollen left cheek, answer me before I give you a right one to match it.”

Vince, whose slab of pie was now more firmly ensconced in his mouth than his dentures, could only attempt an equally incomprehensible reply.

"Heeeeeeeestelllllinkdertroooooooofsishtagulpheesbehiveder barrrrrrr."

"Another wise guy huh? I'll deal with you in a minute. You, yes you next to him, you've got ten seconds before my patience snaps. I want it now. The truth."

The anonymous man protested,

"Icaaaaarntspeeeeeeeeeekyooosillleeeeeecowshhh!"

Mother Michael shot over to the group of the assorted terrified and delivered a swift and painful clip across the ear to each of thc pie-filled unfortunates.

"Right," she said, sending a tray full of empty glasses smashing onto the floor with one swift sweep of her boxer's paw, "I've had just about enough of this. I've come to take a spiritual desert back to the holy water of God's own well before it's too late, and there's none of you excuses for the daft and the damned going to stand in my way. Either I start getting some sensible answers or there's going to be blood on the carpet."

"There isn't a carpet you silly cow," a disembodied voice said.

"What? Who was that?" Mother Michael screamed.

"I'm the Archangel Gabriel and you're the very divil," the voice replied.

Scanning the terrified assembly with a gaze that would have fried an egg she said,

"I can see all the dummies but where's the ventriloquist?"

"Behind," the voice replied.

She spun round like a whippet on skates. She said,

"I can't see anything behind!"

"That's because he's up your behind!" the barman shouted.

"Who said that, that was definitely one of yous at the bar! Come on, don't try and play the innocents with me. Sisters, did you see which one of the renegades spoke?"

"It was the one with the big conk sister," the shortest of the attendant nuns almost screamed in a high pitched little voice.

"Right, we'll give you a good sortin' for a start feller," the mother of all battles roared, so fiercely that, had it been present, the most fearless of lions would have burst into tears.

As she stormed towards the unfortunate Jimmy like a tornado on legs the disembodied voice said,

“Will yous look at yourself? The Alice Capone of the convent world! What in the name of anything have you to do with God? I mean, he’s the feller who’s supposed to be all about love and compassion and being a helping hand to a bunch of saddos like this lot, not a one woman hit squad.”

“It’s coming from over there!” the hit squad said with a satisfied ‘gotcha’ kind of a growl, and surged off at high velocity in entirely the opposite direction to where the invisible owner of the voice lay concealed.

“If I were God,” the voice continued, “I’d consider your every action and your every word as a slander on me name. I’d be shakin’ me head and wonderin’ why on earth I’d ever let the idea of free will loose upon the blighted curse that is the earth. If I’d seen you in the Garden of Eden cavortin’ about bollock naked with the snake, I swear I wouldn’t have been able to tell one from the other or the other from one. You’re the most poisonous excuse for a woman it’s ever been me displeasure to set eyes upon, not a patch on those lovely saintly nuns that tended me own dear mother at her last. They were what a nun should be. Now If I were you, a most unsavoury thought for an Archangel such as meself, I’d leave the innocent alone, turn me ugly tail arse about face and go straight back to the convent for a good long dose of penance and contrition for me rotten, persecutin’ life.”

Unbeknown to the voice, nemesis was about to strike. Mother Michael, having found the speakers from which its words were booming, was following one of the leads back to its source. The invisible commentator continued,

“If I were the divil himself and saw you, at the end of your reign of terror among the innocent and the free, laid out four square on the mortuary slab, well I’d barricade the gates of hell and do a deal with the Almighty to send you somewhere else, anywhere but...yeeeeeeeeeeearrrrrgggggghhhhhhhh!”

“Gotcha you slippery little heathen swine!”

Mother Michael had finally followed the cable to its source. McNally, both ankles suddenly seized and locked firm within her vice-like grip, dropped the barman’s ‘quiz night’ microphone in shock. He was dragged mercilessly face-down through all the slops on the bar floor and out into the harsh brilliance of the midday sun where, with what seemed like a mere flick of her muscle-bound wrist, he was hauled up and over her shoulder as if he weighed little more than a leg of mutton. As he hung limp and defeated in mid-air, his tongue wistfully licking the assorted alcoholic detritus that had been smeared across his lips in the journey to the door, she turned back to the awe-struck drinkers in triumph and said,

"Don't t'ink yous seen the last of me, especially you Billy Flynn. I'll be back for more of you when the time is ripe. There's not a man who crosses Mother Michael and expects to get away with it for long. Especially you with the big conk. You're thc top of me list after that sacrilegious crack. Get prayin' me fine fellers - there's no hidin' place for the divil's own!"

"My God," Flynn gasped from his still prostrate position on the floor, "what an ugly face! How could I have forgotten it! I'm done for lads, that divil will be the death of me."

"Now then Billy," Jimmy said consolingly as Mother Michael and her acolytes disappeared from view, "we've all had a nasty shock, but that's the beginnin' and the end of it. Next time she comes we'll know what to expect and we'll all be ready for her. She'll not floor big Billy Flynn twice in a row now will she?"

"You don't know the woman," Billy gasped, "you can't imagine..."

His voice trailed off into silence.

"Patrick," Jimmy rasped commandingly, "get back to the tellin' of that godforsaken tale of yours so that Billy can get his bearings back again. A sentence or two of your gibberish and it'll wipe Mother Michael from his mind as surely as if she'd dropped down a manhole. God knows, you wipe my mind as clean as a slate whenever you start your ramblings, so come on man, babble on and earn yourself a pint if you can."

"Seein' as you put things in such a flatterin' way," Patrick said in a manner so full of sorrowful hurt that each word seemed in need of a handkerchief, "then I'll begin where I left off for the sake of Billy but none other, includin' yourself. A lesser man would have taken his custom elsewhere long ago for even half of the insults that have dropped on me head in this place tonight."

"If you don't get on with it there'll be more than insults droppin' on your head," a now pie-free Sean barked menacingly from the bar. "I want to see if Big Billy is capable of a resurrection. If he's not, then you'll not leave this hole of all the holiest waters and wells without a pie shoved up or down your every orifice. I've a taste for a reckonin' with you Patrick O'Doyle."

"When I raise Big Billy like Lazarus from the tomb it'll not be a reckonin' you'll be gettin' a taste for," Patrick replied.

"Get on with it man," Jimmy growled. "If you don't hurry up we'll never get Billy back among the livin', and then who will there be to keep a rough house like this in order?"

"Very well," Patrick replied. "I'll start with the bit where O'Flanagan arrives at Kelly's Bar with a pretty young woman on each arm and a rose between his teeth. Are you right then fellers? Good, well, he'd no sooner sat himself down than he decided he needed to go to the jacks. It's always the same with the beer in that place, I'm sure the barman washes his socks in the barrels..."

"For God's sake get on with it man!" Jimmy barked.

"Alright, alright," Patrick replied, "keep what's left of your hair on. What I was going to tell you was that it all happened in the gents. No sooner had O'Flanagan gone in than three men who'd been lyin' in wait disguised as women followed him in with the intention of bumping him off..."

"Hold on, hold on, hold on!" Jimmy bellowed. "Why would three men dressed as women go into a male convenience?"

"Indeed," Patrick replied, "I must confess to a slight error in me recollection on the matter. It was three women dressed as gents, that was the way of it, and they all piled into the ladies with the intention of introducing Fingers to his maker..."

"But you've just said that he went into the gents," Jimmy said incredulously. "How could they have tried to get him if they'd gone into the ladies?

"Indeed," Patrick said, "and that's what makes me revelations so shatterin' of all the normal rules of crime and criminals. O'Flanagan was himself dressed as a woman in order to make himself invisible and safe from the enemy of all enemies whenever he went out for a pint. So he naturally went into the ladies so that no-one would suspect that he was in disguise, but they did and that's why they followed him in, despite being dressed as men. Their male disguise was the result of their incorrect initial presumption that at some point he would go into the gents, being, of course, a gent himself. So what I'd meant to say was that he went into the ladies but kicked the bucket in the gents."

"So you're tellin' me now that three women dressed as men followed one man disguised as a woman into the ladies and then topped him in the gents despite the fact that they and him were all next door?"

"Yes, that is almost if not quite the case, but impossible as it might sound, there's a perfectly rational explanation for all of this. You see the walls in that bar arc only paper thin. When O'Flanagan saw them follow him into the ladies he made a bolt for the open window, but slipped on a bar of soap – he skidded so fast and out of control that his huge frame shot straight through the plasterboard into the gents. It was there that he died of shock, mistaking his own reflection in the wall mirror as his terrifying twin, his ultimate nemesis, hurtling straight at him. Angels and saints, who's that with his hand on me bum?"

"It's no hand Patrick O'Doyle," Sean said guffawing loudly, "it's the snout of a wildebeest."

"Are you sure it's not a wolf with no dress sense disguised as a dog, or even a dog with no sense of reality tryin' feebly to disguise itself as a wolf?" Vince asked.

"Who let that excuse for a hound in me pub?" Jimmy shouted, springing up from his vigil at the still shell-shocked Billy's side to hurl a half pint of cold beer at the unfortunate animal. "That's the largest and shaggiest dog that I've ever seen in me life!"

The shock of the freezing baptism caused a chain reaction by which the only thing its instincts permitted was for the unfortunate creature to bite the nearest and juiciest backside in blind anger. Unfortunately for Patrick, the backside that fitted the bill was his. The surprise of the pain in turn caused him to topple onto the ample back of the overfed hound which, being the unhappy recipient of a second dousing of icy beer, shot out of the door as if it had been launched from a cannon. With Patrick hanging onto its ears like grim death, it raced like a mad thing down the street and up onto the bridge that McNally simultaneously was crossing as a captive of the three hot cross nuns. With blind disregard for anything in its path, it cannoned straight into Mother Michael, causing her to loosen her grip on the astounded prisoner and topple unstoppably over the side of the rails head first down into the dark muddy waters. With Patrick and the hound disappearing fast into the distance and the two remaining nuns jumping fully clad into the fizzling stream to try and rescue the struggling bulk of the unsinkable fisher of men, McNally deftly hopped onto a passing bus and disappeared in grateful joy in the opposite direction to the prison which had so nearly been his fate.

The insanity had been watched from afar by the astounded inmates of the bar.

"Well," Jimmy said, "that appears to be that. You see Billy, the woman's no more than the rest of us, a mere mortal as vulnerable as you or me or anyone else to the unpredictability of life. I mean, who'd have thought the harridan would be takin' a surprise bath with the help of a hound that believes it's a horse, runnin' hell for leather in all directions with an eejit that t'inks he's a jockey glued to its back?"

"That woman's no mere mortal," Billy whispered hoarsely, "there's no river or fire or flood that will hold her down for more than a day. She's me nemesis and that's no mistake. She'll be back, three times fiercer and with my name on her lips."

"Nonsense man," Jimmy replied. "Come on, every man back to the bar, the next round is on me!"

In the general excitement of the clamour for drinks the horror of no more than ten minutes previously was completely forgotten. Pint after pint was pulled by the barman with the speed of a reloading howitzer, one glass after another being fired into the anxious hands of the assembled inebriates. Only one man remained initially silent and inert. Billy Flynn sat alone at the end of the bar, his face that of a man waiting for the bogeyman to come in and claim him. Seeing his state, Jimmy the conk fed him three very large whiskeys in quick succession, knowing that the principle upon which Billy worked was the reviving of spirits through the imbibing of spirits. Given that Jimmy relied on him to throw out any toughs and troublemakers, he didn't want the potential brutal ferocity of his spirit to remain forever repressed by the thought of the bat-faced, enormous nun. By the end of the third liver-rotting glass his dour demeanour had visibly lightened and he looked as if his unaccountable fear of Mother Michael had been the product merely of the lack of a sufficient intake of the demon drink. No sooner had this miraculous transformation occurred, however, than the general sounds of merriment were brought to an abrupt halt. The pub door opened and a long shadow was cast once more across the floor. With a slow, heavy, deliberate series of squelches its owner strode over to the long mahogany altar of alcoholic intemperance, leaving a small trail of puddles in her wake. Billy Flynn had gone so white that a letter could have been typed onto his face without any problem other than the fitting of the end product into an envelope.

"I've come for you Billy Flynn," the owner of the shadow said.

"And what if I decide not to go?" Flynn replied hoarsely.

"You can decide what you like. What'll actually happen is another matter."

"I'll not leave this place until I choose and I'll go nowhere that I don't want to."

"But of course. And pixies will dance with policemen and the Pope take tea with the divil. Get your fat backside up off that seat Billy Flynn, you and me have unfinished business."

"Such as?"

"You can't guess?"

"Whatever it is it'll be far worse than any sane man could imagine."

"Indeed?" the dark figure said, calmly walking right through the solid wood of the bar counter so as to better address him from the other side. The recently dispensed vessels full of brimming beer simultaneously shot out of their disbelieving owners' hands onto the floor, the smashing of the glasses sounding like a ten pint salute for a man about to be buried.

"Yes, that's right," the shadowy figure said, eyeing the terrified and sweating crowd in front of her, "I drowned before the sisters could get me out of the drink. Me purgatory is to be spent in a manner appropriate to me demise, being a Grim Reaper for all those who suffer death by water, even that which the divil has made 40 per cent proof. A more miserable punishment for me sins would be impossible to contemplate. You've had all your chances Billy Flynn and that whiskey you've been drinkin' like tea for as many years as your neglected and penniless wife can remember has finally got the best of your liver. I've come for your soul."

"Don't talk bollix woman," Flynn replied, "I know an alcoholic mirage when I see one, and you're the most unpleasant kind of delusion that a poor drunk could hope to see. I know none of this will be anything more than a trick of the whiskey. You can do whatever you like, but I'm off home for me dinner."

As he strode over to the door he felt strangely light headed, his feet hardly seeming to touch the ground.

"Haven't you forgotten something?" the shadowy figure asked. He turned round to give as good a reply as three large whiskeys taken on an empty stomach might permit, and froze in his tracks. Forgotten something he most definitely had, the problem being that it appeared to be himself. He stared in disbelief at his lifeless body slumped across the bar, with several of the attendant drinkers trying feebly to resuscitate it. The figure, which now was clearly invisible to all except for himself, came and took him none too gently by the arm. It said,

"Welcome to hell Billy Flynn. I was lyin' about the purgatory bit. They sent me straight down here for a lifetime of using me holy office to scare the shit out of anyone that took me fancy. Bringing 'Him upstairs' into disrepute they call it. And as for you - all those bruises your wife told the guards were the result of her havin' a problem with her balance, all your playin' the big man while drinkin' the money away and leavin' her and the snapper with nothin' when it was already ill from the damp of yer apology for a house, that and all the rest of your miserable, selfish, bullying existence, it's all won you a prize to die for, if you'll pardon the pun. As one bully to another, I'm delighted to tell you that you've been condemned to spend eternity in the company of meself. Now aren't you the lucky man... a marriage made in heaven and endured in hell."

Intermission 6

The shocking surprise at the end of Declan's tale caught off guard even those who found his obsession with leading audiences on a merry dance irritating. There were a few gasps, followed by a short pause while people took in the enormity of the terrible fate of Big Billy Flynn and then a reasonably generous burst of applause. Declan bowed twice, turned on one heel and then did two cartwheels as he ran towards the exit, waving mischievously at the startled Fierce Betty as he went.

Sean laughed appreciatively at the cheek of the man and said,

"Well, I was absolutely right, he did everything I predicted, but today he succeeded in winning grudging applause even from those who he annoyed with his circumlocutions. I leave the two of you to judge for yourselves entirely where his entry stands in the overall scheme of things, but at the very least it's the best of the several tales I've heard from him over the years."

"He wound Betty the Fierce up something rotten," Ben said with a half smile on his face.

"Only a brave man would dare do that," Sean said. "He did well to skedaddle as quickly as he did, a few seconds more delay and she'd have given him a verbal lashing that would have floored an elephant."

A loud burst of what the virtuous might well describe as dirty laughter suddenly exploded at the back of the stage. Sean said,

"And there's the finale, the fabled Maggie Quinn, a woman with the face of a sinner but the soul of a saint, or so she once said with her fingers crossed about the second bit. The sins she's said on more occasions than one are reflections of those of others as much as her own. She's referring most to her father, a man who fell the wrong side of drink and swallowed so much it killed him. But not before he'd regularly clobbered her or her mother, or both, for no good reason other than bile. He was a terrible man by all accounts, a Big Billy Flynn times two – she'll have enjoyed the end of Declan's tale, with such a monster of a man getting his come-uppance. She's tried to come to terms with it all in recent years by spending time huddled away in corners of bars, watching out for people like him and fellers of every kind of temperament and hue who like a drink too many. She's made a study of them and uses it as raw material for stories. That's what we're most likely to get today I'd guess, although I've no idea what the likely plot might be or anything like that – she's very varied and inventive if the previous times I've heard her stuff are anything to go by. Like most of those we've seen today she has a darkly comic wit and that we'll get as well to one extent or another. And despite her love of a good dirty laugh - as we heard before - there's always a virtuous thread and a moral that runs through her tales besides all the mischief. On her best days she can be a winner, but she can be just short of the mark as well, so I'd make no predictions even if I was in a position to do so, which I'm not because of the rival state of play between the two of you."

"That's fair enough Uncle Sean and no more or less than I'd expect," Liam said in his usual dour way. "It looks like she's about to start."

Maggie was indeed now at the front of the stage, blowing a kiss to a smiling man sat at the back, who laughed and blew one back. She was about forty, with knowing, mischievous eyes and a lived in kind of a face that looked as if it had seen most of what life has to throw at the world. Her hair was inch short and dyed peroxide white, standing out in stark contrast to her black jacket and trousers, a visual metaphor for her saint versus sinner jokey persona. She looked as though she was having the greatest of difficulty keeping a straight face as Fierce Betty approached to do the introductions. They exchanged brief greetings and it was obvious Betty could read between the lines. She introduced the final performer in her own inimitable enthusiasm-free way and then handed things over to her. Maggie said,

"Hello everyone, nice to see you. I've often thought the dead get a dud deal, with a brief funeral, a wake if they're lucky and then an ever decreasing number of mentions as the years roll by. How nice it would be to give one or another of them the chance to tell their own story, to hang around a bit with the crowd and have the chance to make one last big mark on the world before they turn to dust. So that's what I'm going to do tonight – I'm going to raise the dead in a manner of speaking and see what happens. So, one and all, the living and the dead, sit back in your seats and get ready to be amazed by - *The Dance of the Living Corpse!*"

The Dance of the Living Corpse

Maggie Quinn's Tale

The corpse said,

"Life is a journey you make on a bicycle with no wheels."

"If I was going on a journey the length of a life I'd rather take a bus than a bicycle," Sean replied, "all that pedalling uphill and cycling through rain, wind and hailstones."

"You're assuming the journey is a long one," the corpse replied. "Mine was so short I had hardly the time to put the clips on me trouser bottoms."

"Ah, bottoms," Sean mused, "now there's a thought. A bottom of the right sex and quality on a saddle can be an inspiring sight. If ever evidence was needed of the Almighty's artistic talents then a good bum and an awesome sunset more than fit the bill."

The corpse smiled in a forbidden way. It said,

"Such thoughts are not for those beyond the grave. Tell me, the way you're holding your nose - have I begun to smell already?"

Sean tried to be polite,

"No more or less than any other of the deceased - a little bit, but not oppressively so."

The corpse sighed,

"They'll not be letting me sit here for much longer in that case. Yours will be the last pint I ever see."

Sean un-pinched his nose to allow himself to drink the beer without disaster. The corpse watched wistfully as the dark liquid flowed easily through his parched lips.

"Do people like you come here often?" Sean asked.

The corpse seemed to frown in annoyancc - even though such a thing clearly was impossible for one deceased - its chalk white forehead furrowing deeply within the dark shadows of the dimly lit Tipperary bar.

"That's a fatuous type of a question," it said, its sprawled legs twitching beneath the circular, dirt black table as if about to spring back into life. "Why should the dead come here when they're not even allowed to drink?"

"Then why are you here?" Sean asked.

"I'm here because this is where I ceased to be and where I have to remain until a decision is made by those responsible for such matters. It wasn't my choice. A corpse isn't usually asked for its opinion. In fact it isn't asked any questions at all. Even about something as basic as the story of its life. It's always someone else who tells it."

"Then perhaps you should tell yours to me," Sean said consolingly, not altogether sure of the wisdom of his offer.

The corpse contemplated on the matter for some minutes. Just at the point where Sean concluded that its last words - beyond its original last words - finally had been spoken, it said,

"Very well, if you insist. You will be made a privileged man in the telling. There are precious few who can claim to have been told a tale by a living corpse."

"I thought, by definition, that all corpses were dead and that it is your spirit alone that is addressing me from beyond the grave," Sean said.

"A body is a living corpse as long as its soul remains within it. Mine refuses to leave, or isn't allowed to go, one or the other. It's too fine a point for me to determine. Me body is dead, but me corpse is alive, in a manner of speaking. Do you see what I mean?"

Sean nodded and shook his head at once to be sure of pleasing his questioner. In truth, he understood less about the animate or inanimate nature of the corpse than before he had raised the troublesome question of how best to define his companion's state of existence. He decided to seek further clarification on the matter, saying,

"Whenever you speak I can't see your lips move at all. If, as you say, your corpse is alive in some funny kind of a sense, how can your mouth stay shut whenever you say something? If I could see a ventriloquist in the room I'd think he was projecting his voice to make it sound as if it was coming from you."

"Let's just say a living corpse doesn't need lips to speak and leave it at that," the corpse replied. "The technicalities are extremely complex and are beyond either of our understandings, so we might just as well accept them as given."

"If you say so," Sean replied, "but if I do spot a ventriloquist the game is up."

The corpse laughed quietly to itself and said,

"There's no ventriloquist to be found, I'm me own man as I always was when me body was alive."

There was a short pause in which neither spoke. Then the deceased sighed, its expressionless face shadowed in the half darkness of the bar. Seeming to look up into the dim light above the corner table at which they sat - even though neither its face nor its frozen eyes in reality moved at all - it said,

"It's the light you remember the most. Burnt red and gold at dusk and all the magic strokes the sun's fine brush cast across the people and places that fired you. Even where there were shadows, I still see the sun lurking, ready to burst free from the gloom."

"People you say, they must include women. Tell me about the women," Sean said.

The corpse laughed, a dry, throaty rasp of a laugh.

"There are things someone in my position is permitted to tell and things they're not. And anyway, it's all very well for you to start with such a personal question, but you've told me nothing of yourself. If you want to hear the story of my life you must first at least tell me a little of yours. I don't even know who you are. You could be a completely unreliable man, someone who'd sell me every indiscretion to me worst enemy for a pittance."

"But you know who I am," Sean protested. "The first thing you said to me was me name and then you asked if me mother had recovered from her boil. A man who knew nothing of me would not have asked about the boil."

"All that was just to put you at your ease," the corpse replied. "It took no special power or knowledge to glean such details. I overheard your conversation with the barman when you first arrived. You have my word of honour - I know nothing else about you. But I do need to know morc. I can only divulge me deepest confidences to a man who I know to be totally trustworthy."

Sean thought for a moment and then said,

"Then you will have to be as silent as a corpse is supposed to be, for I know far too little about meself to be able to guarantee total trustworthiness to any man, let alone one that's deceased."

The corpse sounded annoyed. It said,

"How can a person who knows himself by virtue of being himself seriously claim he has no knowledge of his own morality?"

"Now that's a strange and difficult conundrum with an easy answer, or an easy conundrum with a strange and difficult answer. I'm not sure which way these things are round in me present state of unconsciousness."

The baffling and forcibly spoken interjection had come from a previously unnoticed woman seated at the table opposite, an irascible regular of indeterminate vintage, colloquially known as Mary Contrary.

"Who invited you to join in?" the corpse rasped irritably.

"Why no-one," replied the elderly word boxer. "I am always invited to do this and that by No-One. I find him a most companionable and hospitable feller."

The corpse muttered something which would have best been described as under its breath, had it still been breathing, which of course it wasn't. The woman continued,

"As the old saying goes, he who thinks he knows the mystery of life knows nothing, and he who thinks he knows nothing knows all there is to be known by mortal man. And what greater mystery of life can there be than our own good selves?"

"Most certainly, most certainly that is the case," said a second philosopher, who until now had been completely invisible due to his having slipped from his seat and under the table.

"I've been on this earth fifty four and a quarter years and know less about meself now than when I was twenty."

"That's because you've been a drunken old sod for so long that you can't remember what you were like when you were sober," a grizzled pugilist of a man shouted from the bar.

"That's a lie and a fabrication! I've been sober every fifth day out of four as a matter of habit and principle for all me married life!"

"And God knows that's a miracle considering he's always been single," Mary Contrary said with an accompanying bellow of laughter that so startled the target of his mockery that he lost his dwindling grip on his seat and once more slid ingloriously under the table.

"None of this is getting us any closer to the story of your life," the corpse complained to Sean. "If I'd known this place was so full of eejits and half wits I'd have chosen somewhere else to do me dying. Now will you please forget all about this business of trustworthiness and what you do and don't know about yourself and just tell me your life story?"

For reasons known only to himself, Sean was not in the slightest bit anxious that the details of his life should become the knowledge of others, a fact that influenced greatly the nature of his reply.

"Is it a day by day account you want?" he asked. "Because if that's the case we could be here for months. I've been alive for thirty eight years and that's an awful lot of days to deal with."

"And that's the truth!" Mary Contrary exclaimed. "Three hundred and sixty five by thirty eight is nine thous, no, wait, twelve thous..., is an extremely complicated sum to compute and there'd be several more corpses to join you by the end of such a lengthy tale."

The corpse hissed an expletive that would do it no good at all in its entrance exam for the pearly gates. Looking somewhat shocked by what he had just heard, Sean wiped the back of his hand across his beer wet mouth and said,

"So it's a shortened version you'll be wanting. Very well, most of what I am or what I've done would not be considered significant by many. In fact my whole existence could probably be summarised quite adequately on the back of an envelope and then posted without loss into oblivion. You see, fundamentally, if the truth is told, I'm a boring man."

"Now that's something not even the seventh son of a seventh son would have known on a day of the most special inspiration," Mary said, while yawning in so obvious a fashion that two lovelorn flies in pursuit of a third disappeared into the back of her throat and out again without her being aware of their presence.

"A boring man is what I've always been and proud of it," the second philosopher rumbled from under the table. The man who resembled a pugilist smiled down beatifically at him and poured a little of his beer over his head. The corpse looked distinctly bored with all the talk of boredom. It said,

"Just tell me what you believe, where you came from, what you do and where you're going. I'm not asking the impossible."

Sean smiled, with more than a touch of mischief in his eyes.

"No, surely you're not. It is a very reasonable request and I shall take matters entirely in the order you've set out."

"Good," the corpse muttered with some relief, obviously sorry that it had ever begun such a conversation with so difficult a man.

"I believe in the Second Coming, although I'm not so sure about the first," Sean said. "I've always been a religious man, although at times I've been more an atheist than anything else. As to where I came from, now that's a mystery. My mother's womb would be the easy answer, but that only begs the question as to where I left in order to enter her belly. And that's a matter I've never been able to resolve. With regard to the things I do, then all of them have already been done, so there's nothing that I'm doing now other than speaking to you. The things that are left to be done will be done in five minutes, or five years, depending on their nature. But I can't say they're things I do until I'm actually doing them, as the slightest intervention of a malicious fate could bring an end to all me doings and make me every statement and description seem at best a presumption, or, at worst, a deceit. As to where I'm going, then plainly the answer is nowhere by virtue of me presence in this none too comfortable of chairs. Where I will be going is perhaps the marginally more interesting of possible questions. But marginally is the word, given that me only immediate likely voyage is to the jacks, should the need arise, as past experience suggests it will. I'm not sure any of this has been of a truly great help. Do you think the questions were a little flawed perhaps?"

The corpse drew deeply the breath it couldn't draw. It said,

"Of all the eejits I have met during me short stay on this lunatic earth, you are the most literal and pedantic. I'm not sure I could come up with any form of a question that would produce the answer I want from you."

"Perhaps matters might be more to your liking if I told you my story instead," the second philosopher said.

"Your story's in your hand," the corpse said, referring to the empty pint glass that hugged his sweaty palm. The philosopher looked highly offended without quite being able to recall what it was he should have been offended about.

"I am a very precise man," Sean said. "Ask me a question that is as precise as I am and you will get the answer you want."

The corpse sighed and thought on the matter for a minute or two. Deciding at length to make a final attempt to get some sense from his ultra precise companion he said,

"Tell me as many of the important things that have happened in your life and what they have taught you that you can fit into half an hour."

Sean smiled.

"Now that's a precise request indeed. That I can deal with. Or rather I could. The only problem is I haven't got half an hour to spare."

"Then how long have you got?" the corpse asked frustratedly.

Sean looked at his watch.

"Twenty nine and a half minutes exactly. Then it's back home to me wife or she'll be using the frying pan to play tennis, with me head as the ball."

"Then tell me as much as you can fit into twenty nine and a half minutes you imbecile!" roared the corpse, quite losing control of itself.

"Now I would, I would indeed," said Sean calmly, "but while we've been talking we've lost another minute and there's only twenty eight and a half left. So it's quite impossible for me to tell you all the things you want to know in twenty nine and a half minutes because me chair will be empty with a minute undealt with - and one in your position can hardly follow me down the street to hear the conclusion of the tale."

"Tell me, just tell me," the corpse hissed menacingly, "I don't care how long it takes, just keep talking until it's time for you to go."

"Well, most certainly I would," Sean replied, "but if I'm to do this in return for you telling me your life story, I'm not going to be able to hear a blind word of it if you simply tell it to an empty chair. How can I be sure that you'll still be here tomorrow night to fulfil your side of the bargain? You said yourself that you're starting to smell. The way things are going the landlord might have you six foot under in quicklime before the ringing of last orders. He's not going to want his pub to get a reputation as a mortuary for sure."

The corpse regained some of its patience and composure and pondered deeply on the matter for some moments. At length it said,

"If I'm satisfied with your tale I'll tell you mine whether they bury me or not. If they do, you'll simply have to listen twice as hard and I'll have to shout twice as hard - but with our combined efforts my words should rise above six feet of the densest earth and you will know everything of me living past. You may take that as a promise from beyond the grave, and there are no firmer guarantees available to mortal kind."

Sean was about to remark that he couldn't see how a comment could be delivered from beyond the grave by someone who wasn't yet in the grave, but thought better of it. Had he not been too lazy and shallow to think in proper depth about such things, he would have been terrified out of his wits by the strange, unearthly situation that confronted him.

"I was born in a fishing boat," he announced. "Me mother was overcome by fumes from the famous fire at Old Murphy's moonshine still as she was walking along the harbour's edge and fell head first into the boat's hold on the point of sailing. The shock of the fall caused me to drop the day before I was due. She was found safe and snoring with a new born babe in her arms after the boat had been twelve hours at sea. Fearing that I would die as a result of me long time in cold exposure, the skipper put me through a layman's christening and was faced with the grave embarrassment of having to name me Halibut."

"What?" the corpse spluttered incredulously. "If you're stretching me leg so far that the bells will ring in both me ears there'll be two deceased in this bar before the night is over!"

"I'm stretching no man's leg, or even his trousers," Sean said. "Me mother was so confused still as a result of the fumes they could get no sense out of her and the only name she'd give her new born child was Halibut. She thought it was unmatchably funny so I'm told."

"Then how is a man called Halibut called Sean?" the corpse asked, unconvinced.

"Because Halibut is me Christian name, if that's the right description, seeing as there were most certainly no St. Halibuts among the apostles, while Sean is me confirmation name. I used Sean from the date the bishop gave me the right - it was the only way to save meself from mockery and derision."

The corpse said,

"This is all very well, but is the story of a name you never use the most useful thing to tell when you have so little time for the tale? Aren't there more important things I should be hearing about?"

"I thought if I started at the beginning it would be easier to see that the middle is the middle and the end the end. To begin in the middle would leave you thinking it was the beginning and the end the middle and then we'd all be in a muddle."

"And that's the truth!" exclaimed Mary, spiritedly.

"What's the truth?" asked the second philosopher.

"The thing that just flew out of the window with its arse on fire!" a voice which appeared to belong to no one shouted.

Sean returned to his tale.

"When I was twelve me mother let slip that I was only eleven. A birthday present she said, but a considerable disappointment to meself, who'd long been living in the hope of a moustache and hairy knees. Sure, it's no fun finding you're only eleven when you want to be old enough to command the respect of a regiment."

"A regiment of what?" the second philosopher asked.

"Of divils most like," Mary Contrary replied.

"And then," Sean continued, "it got steadily worse. At every birthday me mother would tell me that I was a year younger than I thought, until I reached an age when I hadn't been born. According to her own true testimony I am now at a stage when I'm not due to enter her womb for another sixteen years."

"And that's assuming she doesn't turn into a celibate woman," Mary said. "You can hardly expect to be the second virgin birth. Why think of it man, you might never be born. And indeed, what a remarkable sight you are - a man who'll never exist talking to one who's ceased to exist."

"What does it mean to turn into a celibate woman?" the second philosopher asked.

"The same as if she turned into a priest," Mary said.

"Streuth," said the second philosopher, "now that'd be an amazing sight."

"Depends on where you're sitting and a woman priest would sit well with me," Mary replied.

The corpse roared,

"Is there not a single sane or sober person in the room?"

"There was, there was," wheezed the pugilist from the bar, "but he and his trousers were in some disarray and the two of them merged into one."

"What, the trousers turned into the man?" enquired Mary Contrary.

"No, the man turned into the trousers. The landlord's folded them up and put them under the bar out of sight to avoid distressing the relatives."

Sean suddenly laughed. Addressing the corpse he said,

"And that last tale and every one I've told you is nothing but a fantasy. If you were deceased you'd have known straight away - for don't the dead have eyes to see into the minds of the living? You're no more a corpse than I am, despite your terrible pong, which, I suspect is due more to a mortal fear of soap than anything else. Come on, come out of that pose and own up to whatever trickery it is you're playing."

"How dare you!" the corpse spluttered. "I've been called many things in me time but never a liar. Heavens knows why I chose you as the man to speak me mind to!"

"Come on, come on," Sean laughed, "the game's up my friend.

If you don't drop that rigor-mortis pose this very minute then I'll ask the landlord's daughter to stick a safety pin up your behind! That'll separate the living from the dead!"

"Aye, and bring more than a tear to your eyes!" Mary added. "I knew you were alive from the moment I thought you were dead."

"That's a contradiction in even the simplest of terms," the second philosopher protested from under the table. Noting that his head was now dry Mary poured some more beer over it, explaining in a kindly voice that her intention was to keep it from shrivelling.

The corpse that allegedly wasn't a corpse was mortally offended. It said,

"I'll not say another word to you or anyone else in this room until I receive a full apology for your most ill founded accusations. There's no rule in heaven that says the dead have to speak to the living."

Smiling quietly to himself, Sean slipped over to the bar and borrowed the threatened safety pin from the landlord's daughter. Then, with all the stealth of a hunter, he crept up on the corpse from behind and rammed the pin hard into its flesh. There was no reaction whatsoever. Simultaneously puzzled and disappointed, Sean repeated his effort with the same unproductive result.

Eyeing the situation thoughtfully, Mary said,

"I've a growing suspicion that no such test for separating the living and the dead can be valid without an element of comparison. It may be that that particular safety pin - or your unique way of thrusting it - has a strange and anaesth, anaesthut... numbing quality that keeps the victim unaware of the assault. You need to try the same thing out on yourself in order to be sure that a living man cannot display the same reaction as a corpse to the experiment you're so vigorously conducting."

"Why me?" Sean asked. "Why not volunteer yourself if you're so concerned for the proper application of the rules of science?"

"Because me own backside would not provide a true test," Mary replied. "By definition, as I am its owner and you are not, you would have no way of knowing that an appropriate yell on my part wasn't simply an act put on to hoodwink the innocent and the gullible."

“I can see the gullible,” the pugilist murmured, “but where in this holy of holies is the innocent?”

Ignoring this unwanted interjection, Mary continued,

“No, in the interests of true science you must use your own posterior as the guinea pig, if such a thing is possible given its non-possession of brains and ears.”

“Aye, but it has the guinea pig’s grin!” the pugilist yelled. “And half of its fur!”

“And how would you be knowing such a thing?” the landlord asked.

“In all me days I can’t ever remember seeing a guinea pig grin,” mused the second philosopher from under the table.

“Gentlemen,” Mary Contrary said majestically, “unusually for ourselves we are wandering slightly from the precise point under discussion.”

No sooner had she finished than a terrified sour faced man, who had only just exited himself and three quarters of his dog, came rushing back into the bar.

“The divil!” he screamed at the landlord. Checking momentarily in the mirror glass behind the whiskey bottles, the landlord calmly shook his head and said,

“No, still meself. I’m not even faintly related to the feller.”

“No, no! Outside! The divil’s outside threatening to come in!”

“He’s been in for hours,” Mary retorted, “he’s sitting at that table pretending to be a corpse.”

“No, no, no such thing! This is no time for the frivolities,” the sour faced man yelled shrilly, “it’s the corpse he wants. It’s either that or our souls instead.”

“Well, he can’t have mine,” the pugilist rasped, “I’ve been an atheist from the moment I was born, and a man who knows there’s no God knows also that there’s no divil, so there’s no one to come in to claim me.”

“If there’s no God then you can have no soul,” Mary observed.

“That’s the truth,” the pugilist replied.

“And if you have no soul in your body then by all Christian definitions you must be dead,” Mary said, “and by any understanding a man who’s dead is most certainly a corpse. I suggest we send you out to the divil as you clearly fit his requirements as much as the other feller. And being that you believe there's no such thing as a divil you'll have no objection."

"And indeed, indeed, that sounds a most reasonable proposition," sour face said with obvious relief. "Go forth me friend and save us all. And may God bless your trousers and all who sail in them!"

"So this is the kindness and charity of God-fearing Christians!" the pugilist said mockingly. "If a man's an atheist you'd give him to the divil at any price to save your own skins. Well if it's only me trousers that your God will bless, then it's only me trousers that shall go to the divil!"

With that, and to everyone's surprise, he pulled the said garments down with a vigour that instantly would have converted him from a bass to a soprano had any stray parts of his anatomy become entangled in the process. With a determined stride he marched over to the door and threw the things out into the street, without even looking to see if the alleged diabolical unpleasantness was on the outside as had been claimed. Striding back to the bar with a belligerent defiance in his gleaming eyes he had no sooner slid onto a stool than the door crashed open. The room suddenly was filled with a thick, sulphurous fog that seemed to burn and freeze the cheeks of everyone present. Even the trouserless pugilist trembled and stood up as a precautionary measure, in case he needed to make a quick scramble for safety over the top of the bar. A low, terrifying, rumbling roar echoed in from the dead street outside and bounced from the walls to the floor to the ceiling and all over again, boxing the ears of all but the oblivious corpse in so violent a manner that several cried out. And then, the unbelievable became the father of belief. The trousers, that only a minute earlier had been cast outside as if they were rags, strode angrily into the room of their own accord and marched straight over to the pugilist, who was too mortally afraid to take even the smallest peek over his own quivering shoulder. Stopping directly behind him, they took a well considered aim and then kicked him so hard that he flew in a perfect arc over the bar and landed, with a terrible cry, head first in the slops bucket. No sooner had this been done than the roar ceased, the fog disappeared and the trousers collapsed into a heap on the floor. As the trembling, ashen faced company crept fearfully to the bar to inspect the state of the victim, whose helpless legs were flailing wildly in the air, they saw that whatever phantom foot had kicked him had stamped - or rather burnt - a message on the seat of his underpants. Plain as the daylight that had gone down with the sun, it said simply,

"Send out the corpse."

Gently removing the man from the bucket and vice versa, they poured a large whisky down the gasping, gibbering throat of their now semi-deranged colleague. Then, satisfied that the unfortunate was at least half as restored to the possession of his senses as he was to his trousers, they turned as one towards the unmoving solitude of the corpse.

"He'll have to go as requested," said Mary Contrary. "We can't take any more of this. Heaven knows what might happen next. We'll throw him out into the street and leave the divil to do the cleaning up. He'll not be satisfied unless he gets his way."

Simultaneously, a determined look in every half-opened eye, they began to move towards their silent prey. Suddenly, Sean jumped out in front of them. Inspired to a wildly uncharacteristic gesture of selfless humanity by his accidental consumption of the pint of Legless O'Malley, so called because of his frequent inability to stand up after lacing his own drinks with legal and illegal highs, he said,

"No! Now we know the corpse is a truthful man. We have it written on the back of this eejit's knickers. Our ripe smelling friend is every bit as dead as he claims and hasn't been called to judgment yet. Only the Almighty has the power and right to allow a soul to be claimed by the divil, and I don't see any man here who might make even the slightest claim to being the Almighty in mortal form. The divil can say and do what he likes, but he'll have to wait to see what God and his angels decide to do with this feller, and so will we. Leave God's matters to God or you'll have far worse things than a pair of rampant trousers to worry about."

Mary sneered.

"A very courageous point Sean O'Riley - and to be sure, we'll all follow your advice, all to a man and meself, as soon as you go outside and explain matters to that fellow with the cloven hooves and the very unsympathetic reputation that's just looking for a chance to fry us all to a cinder. You go outside and do that Sean. If you come back in one piece we'll all be with you. But if you haven't a mind to take up me offer, perhaps you'd be good enough to stand aside and let the rest of us save our hides before it's too late."

"No," said Sean again, even more determinedly this time than the last. "On deeper consideration I'm afraid I have to modify me judgment. A proper thinking on the matter leads only to one thought - we still haven't proved that the corpse is dead. We have only the divil's word for that and he's the very definition of a liar. The final clinching test has to be performed by meself on me own anatomy. Act now, before I've resolved the matter beyond all doubt, and you could be condemning one of the innocent living to the fate of the evil dead. That, in any reasonable court, would be a crime akin to murder and a thousand other things besides."

"Very well," said Mary, ripping her hatpin from her apology for a hat that sat like a small furry creature on top of her head, "here's a pin, and there's your bum, now let's see how each reacts to a forcible union with the other!"

The vigour of her thrust was such that an equivalent attack launched on an elephant would have pinned it to the nearest wall. Sean's reaction was one of calm surprise. No sign of pain crossed his face, and no cry left his lips. His assembled audience was stupefied. Determined not to be frustrated in her purpose, Mary had another go, her hand this time following a gentler, more considered trajectory. Landing to the left of its predecessor, her well aimed stab produced exactly the same effect. Surveying her puzzled face calmly, Sean said,

"It seems, ladies and gentlemen, that we're a corpse short for the divil's needs. Unless anyone can produce an alternative test to distinguish the living from the dead, then we have no right to presume at all that the poor fellow over there is deceased."

"Nor that the eejit that is yourself is alive," said the sour faced man acidly. "I've never known a living man not to react to a pin in his bum."

Sean, whose combined wallet, diary and sensation-numbing consumption of O'Malley's cocktail of booze and drugs had been the true cause of his salvation, looked decidedly bemused. One word in his own defence would put paid to the corpse, towards whom O'Malley's potion was still inducing a strong humanitarian concern, but in protecting the deceased he could well put himself in the dock in its place. Mary Contrary eyed him thoughtfully for a moment and then said,

"It is indeed as our friend suggests. It seems we have a choice of corpses to feed to the divil. One always claimed it was deceased, and this one until now has pretended to be alive. One a man of truth, the other a liar. Gentlemen, it's clear which one is the divil's and which one will be claimed by the Almighty. I suggest we throw this fellow outside and give him to his rightful owner. Seize him!"

With that, the grizzled and spectacularly unfit company did the best imitation of a rush that it could manage, several, including the landlord, falling over their own or somebody else's feet in the process. Sean was grabbed roughly by both arms and dragged protesting to the door. At the very moment they were about to push him through it a loud cry came from behind,

"Stop! That man's as alive as a living man can be! Let him go!"

They all turned in shock to face the corpse, which could make no effort at all to face them.

"If this man's alive then prove it," Mary said. "All our tests have shown him to be as dead as yerself."

"His chest," the corpse said, "has none of you the wit to listen for his heart?"

Mary looked at the pugilist, who looked at sour face, who looked at the landlord, who looked at everyone else. As one they ripped open Sean's shirt, sending buttons flying everywhere. As one also they thrust their ears towards his chest, and in so doing, caused such a collision of heads that a passer by would have flung himself to the ground in the certain belief that a shot had been fired. The consequence, not unexpectedly, was that all bar Sean descended into an unconscious heap on the floor.

"Tell me," the corpse said, "is this place as full of morons on every occasion or is tonight a special event?"

"You've taken your time before deciding to speak," Sean said. "I could have been flung head first into hell if you'd waited a second longer. And that despite me risking me own life and soul to save your festering bacon."

"Now that's gratitude," the corpse replied. "And you, a man who only five minutes ago was calling me a liar and a trickster, expecting help from the honest dead. Had you not had such a spectacular change of heart, dubious as it is, sure I'd have been entitled to leave you to your fate."

"With the very divil at the door demanding your soul I could hardly do anything than change me mind – no matter what I said earlier, if a feller with all the supernatural powers that he has is convinced you're a stiff, then a stiff you are and I'm not going to risk being called to account by the Almighty for giving you to Beelzebub on a plate."

"Not as long as you've got the Dutch courage of O'Malley's cocktail inside you anyways," the corpse said. "I haven't the slightest doubt that it's that little mixture that's doing the thinking for you at the moment. I wonder if you'll be as kind towards me interests when the effects wear off."

"That's a terrible slander on me good name," Sean said. "But that as may be, there's still a problem that needs an immediate solution. You're a mortal danger to us all as long as the divil's on the outside thinking you're on the inside. We need to move you to safer ground."

"Safer for you or safer for me?" the corpse asked cynically.

"For us all," Sean replied. "If Beelzebub can unleash a pair of trousers upon an atheist in so violent a manner just think what he might do to a bunch of half-believers. I'll have to drag you down into the cellar and try and convince him you've bolted out the back."

"Such an innocent, touching soul," the corpse said. "Has it not occurred to you that there will be demons watching all the exits? And he's hardly going to believe his ears when you try and persuade him that a corpse has bolted now is he? 'Gone jogging with the other stiffs from the cemetery?' he'll ask with the full mockery of his diabolical wit. Can you imagine it?"

"Very well, I'll tell him you're not dead at all, there's been a mistake. That you're in a coma."

"No, no," the corpse said exhaustedly, "apart from the slight problem that coma victims separate themselves from the deceased by the act of breathing, the divil always hears when anyone dies. You can't fool the biggest liar of all time by telling him a whopper that wouldn't stand up even if you gave it a crutch and a place in the queue behind Lazarus. I appreciate your efforts, but none of what you've suggested will work."

"Then what's to be done?" Sean asked despairingly. "We've got to get rid of the feller somehow or we'll be prisoners in here for the rest of our lives - or in your case, the rest of your death."

"Send for Father Nolan," the corpse said. "Ask him to bring a crucifix and a drop of the old holy water. No, wait, considering that it's the divil himself we're dealing with you'd better tell him to bring a couple of bucketfuls of the holy stuff."

"Right," said Sean, relieved at the prospect of some positive action to deal with the terrifying unpleasantness that lay mercilessly in wait outside. Picking up the phone at the side of the bar, he began to dial the priest's number. Before he had registered even two of the necessary digits the pub doors were blasted open, felling instantly one of the previously unconscious eejits who had been in the process of trying to drag himself up from the floor. A scorching flame of white hot breath seared its way through the air and melted the telephone cable into a neat circular pool of molten plastic. The doors slammed shut again, a strong smell of sulphur lingering in the wake of the vanished flame.

"It doesn't look as though Father Nolan will be coming," the corpse said in a matter-of-fact voice. "As his parochial house is famously unable to get a mobile signal we've no alternative way of communicating with him other than you standing on the roof with a loud hailer in your mitts."

Dropping the telephone receiver from his singed and trembling fingers, Sean slowly poured himself a whiskey. He sat down at the bar, ashen faced, to wait for his hand to steady enough to raise the glass without pouring the contents down the front of his shirt.

He said, in a faltering monotone,

"I think we're going to need more than Father Nolan to get us out of this."

No sooner had he spoken than the bar was filled with a luminously glowing mist. It seemed to have at its heart a ball of pure and golden light, the rays of which cut through the surrounding vapours like knives. A strange and beautiful music, played on instruments so sublime in tone that they exceeded the perfection dreamed of by even the most demanding of composers, danced delicately around his ears and spun a web of aural crystals through his now singing consciousness. Sean truly felt that, at that moment, he had one foot in this world and the other in the next and that, strange as it may seem, heaven had dropped in for a drink.

This blissful visitation of supernatural light remained for a time that seemed immeasurable, neither long nor short, nor anything in between. Finally, at the point where Sean was beginning to wonder whether he had joined the corpse in death, the brilliantly lit vapours began to recede, revealing gradually his deceased companion from within the blanket of their concealment. But as the light faded from everything inside the bar, it remained within and on the corpse, giving it a glowing, angelic quality.

Suddenly, seeming to come from everywhere and nowhere at once, a fiddle struck up with a reel that would have caused even the most depressed soul in the world to burst instantly into a jig. No more than a few seconds later an invisible bodhranist joined in as well, the extraordinary speed and volume of his playing resonant with the pure joy of life's first breath. Without warning to itself or Sean, or the chair even in which it had been slumped, the corpse leapt to its feet and started jigging wildly around the empty tables of the half-lit, frowning bar. A fire that hadn't been ignited in three cold months suddenly roared into life beneath the grime-black stone of the mantelpiece. The corpse's high-stepping, un-tripping, flailing feet danced the dream of the singing sage, or so it claimed in the unnatural falsetto voice of its own song as it twirled and whirled and clapped its flying hands, as it jigged around the throbbing room. The bam-bam-bam and the thump of the drum banged out a rhythm on the walls to which the corpse's shadow also danced, like a slave to the flame-flickering, roaring glow of the fire. The drum and the dance and the fiddle got faster and faster, to the point where the corpse and its shadow seemed unable to keep up with each other, the latter tripping over both feet at once and disappearing headlong into the darkness below the fire-cast light. Finally, the corpse too lost its balance and crashed heavily into a coat stand which had never supported a coat in its life, but had proved extremely useful for propping up those no longer able to support themselves after prolonged imbibing of over-strong ales. The music ceased instantly, the strange light went from the dazed and now undancing corpse, and it collapsed into a lifeless heap on the floor.

Stunned to the point of disbelief, Sean went cautiously over to verify for himself the apparent decease of the already deceased. Having ascertained beyond doubt that no heart beat in the chest of the fallen dancer, he started to walk back to the bar with the firm intention of pouring himself another liver rotting, sanity-restoring whiskey. Before he had taken more than two halves joined of a full half step, the corpse cried out,

"And where do you think you're going Sean O'Riley? Are you intending to leave the dead to the fate of the drunk? Come back over here and pull me up into a decent chair."

Slowly and reluctantly, Sean did as instructed, then sat down himself to think. The corpse sighed contentedly.

"So, what was all that about?" Sean asked at length, as the effects of O'Malley's cocktail faded and he began to change his mind about the source of the strange supernatural occurrence to which he'd just been a witness. The more he thought about it, the more unlikely it seemed that such a pagan dance could have been in the slightest way heaven sent.

"I thought the deceased were supposed to be forbidden to dance. All the self-respecting corpses that I've ever known have been stretched firmly out on a mortuary slab by now."

"Most self-respecting corpses don't get a visit from the Archangel Sidney," the corpse replied. "He's Irish by adoption you know, but a lousy dancer. He wanted me to show him a jig or two."

"The Archangel Sidney?" Sean spluttered. "I've never heard of such a feller. Gabriel, Michael, yes, but Sidney? You're pulling so many legs there'll be none left for anyone to stand on."

"Surprising as it may seem, the fact that you haven't heard of one of the Archangels is no reason to doubt the feller's existence. He's number six in the ranks as the pecking order of Archangels goes, so you'd be a most unwise man to doubt or mock him."

"Would I indeed," said Sean. "And God gave this angel with the unlikely name permission to put on a light show and raise the stiff and the dead did He? Come off it friend, it's the divil you've been dancing with. Give you one last thrash at life before serving the final demand for your soul did he? You've been damned all along and simply kept mum about it, isn't that the case?"

"No, it surely isn't and the divil has markedly less claim to me soul than he has to yours, markedly less I can tell you. If you want to call me a liar then so be it, but Sidney and I know the truth of the matter."

"You're not honestly expecting me to believe that number six in the heavenly pecking order, the all-powerful Archangel Sidney as you'd have it, came all the way here just for a jig are you? And that seeing a corpse that is supposed to be parted from its soul still as firmly welded to the same as if it was alive, he didn't choose to rectify the situation while he was on the spot?"

The corpse tut-tutted impatiently. It said,

"What a fickle man you are Sean O'Riley, first saying I'm a living liar claiming to be dead, then defending me from those who say exactly the same thing on the surprising grounds that the opposite is true, then standing like a druggy hero to protect me from the very divil himself, and after all that, turning your coat inside out and accusing me of having been in the diabolical little feller's pocket all the time! You're a man who changes his mind more often than a beltless philosopher loses his trousers. Is there not even a drop of consistency lurking somewhere deep within your muddled mind?"

"Don't change the subject," Sean said, doing his utmost to remember what the subject was.

"Very well," said the corpse, "if you really want to know the heart of the matter that passed between the good Archangel and meself, then so you shall. But be warned - it'll strain your credulity just as much as any far fetched tale a less truthful man might be tempted to tell a doubter such as yerself."

"I have precious little credulity left to be stretched," Sean replied, "and what remains is now so unsure of the time of day that it's unlikely to register any contribution to the general processes of me mind's fine judgment. What hasn't been pickled by O'Malley's cocktail has been drowned in contemplation of the death that you've spent the whole of the evening parading as life. How can a man who has spent his one night out debating the finer points of fact and fiction with a corpse have anything left to be credulous about?"

"When you've finished your litany of complaints," the corpse said, "perhaps we could get down to business. You see, the fact of the matter is, the good Archangel was sent to reveal the full true purpose of me being kept in this strange suspension between the living and the dead."

"Was he indeed?" Sean said. "No doubt this grand purpose is to turn this most unholy of establishments into one more shrine to heavenly visitations that can be seen only by those who have sufficient grace, whiskey or fanciful imagination to conjure their immortal presence. It may be a cynical suspicion, but it does just occur to me that the 'Pig Breeders Bar' has something less of a charismatic resonance about it than the familiar and simple evocative ring of 'Knock'."

"If God was to turn your head into a bucket and your feet into cucumbers you'd still be too cynical to believe your own eyes in the mirror," the corpse replied.

"If me head had been turned into a bucket I'd be missing the eyes to see anything at all," Sean muttered. "And with cucumbers for feet the insufferable weight of me body would have squeezed them into a pulp before I made even the first step forwards to look for a mirror. You're the most impractical corpse I ever met."

There was a bitter silence. At length, albeit a short length, the corpse said,

"Well, do you want to know what Sidney told me or don't you? His message has implications for both of us."

"Does it indeed," said Sean disinterestedly, increasingly unable to determine whether all that had happened so far was even vaguely connected to reality. "And what about the feller with the horns outside," he continued, "what did old Sidney say about him? Does his message have 'implications' for him as well?"

"Indeed it does," said the corpse. "But I'm not sure that you are in a sufficiently receptive state of mind to treat the matter with appropriate respect."

"And how in a thousand blowing of the winds could I possibly be disrespectful to Sid the dancing archangel?" Sean asked. "If I mind me P's and Q's he might even teach me the steps he's learned from you."

"Your mockery of the good and the godly will be the undoing of you," the corpse replied acidly. "Given the declining quality of your conversation I'm beginning to suspect the Good Lord has already turned your head into a bucket, and deservedly so, most deservedly so."

"Get on with it and keep your insults for the cat and the flea in its ear," Sean muttered. "Amaze the already thrice amazed with your fantastical revelations."

"Very well," the corpse said, unconvinced that it had anything more than fifty per cent of its audience's attention, "Sidney told me that I'm the result of unbelief."

"Now that's an unbelievable statement if ever there was one," Sean murmured.

"The world is full of miracles," the corpse continued, undeterred, "the miracles of sight and colour and sound, the miracle of a bird that is nothing one year but the next bursts free from an egg and sits singing on a branch as if it had existed forever, the miracle of flowers, of light, of darkness, the huge diversity of everything that logic says should not exist, but which insists on the right to be - and that most amazing thing which everyone takes for granted - despite its stunning impossibility - the miracle of their own existence."

"I'm a great believer in the miracle of brevity," Sean said, untouched by the catalogue of wonderment that had danced from one to the other of his sceptical ears and then into oblivion. Pretending not to hear, the corpse continued,

"And yet," Sidney said, repeating the old complaint of all the angels since belief and unbelief began, "despite all these things, people remain at best half interested in the possibility of God. He told me that even in the good Irish Catholic there is as much of the unbelief as there is of the opposite. A terrible thing in the land of St. Patrick."

"If the unbelief and the belief balance themselves to so equal a degree, then every Catholic in the country who passes from this life into the next must have their head in heaven and their feet in purgatory or worse, is that not the case now?" Sean asked mischievously.

Ignoring him, the corpse continued,

"And so that's where I come in, me strange suspension between the living and the dead is for the convincing of the daft and the doubtful that death is but a transformation and something to which they ought to start giving some serious thought in terms of the need for a virtuous and God fearing life. Because if they don't - well that's where the divil stakes his claim to their souls, as has been so amply demonstrated tonight."

"Oh I see," said Sean. "So, putting you on one side for the minute and just looking at the role of the feller with the horns in all of this, you're suggesting that him, the divil, who was cast down into hell for the something less than minor sins of hate and pride, has suddenly changed his tune and agreed to play the symphony delivered to his ears by the command of Sidney the Archangel most high? To demand your soul on a platter in dramatic fashion, then growl and thump and strut just enough in the background to yourself to remind the forgetful of the penalties of unbelief, complacency and sin? Now that is a remarkable thing. I suppose that's why we haven't heard from him in the last few minutes - he's presumably too busy having a pint with St. Peter as a reward for his work in saving lost souls. I must say me dear, allegedly deceased feller, if ever there was anything or anyone to take the biscuit, then you indeed are King of all the biscuit takers."

"As usual me fickle friend," the corpse replied with considerable irritation, "you have both ends of the wrong stick. The divil is far too unpleasant a character to even dream of doing a virtuous thing. He is also, despite his pride, lacking the cunning and wisdom of the Almighty. And that, so Sidney tells me, is what makes things so easy."

"He's actually whisperin' directly into your ear is he, at this very minute like?" Sean asked. "If he's that close, and if I were you, I'd be terrible careful of them giant wings now, one rustle of the old celestial feathers and you could end up with a sneeze the size of a hurricane."

The corpse continued undeterred,

"You see, all Sidney had to do was spread it around within the divil's earshot that there was a soul on the loose down here - being meself of course - who hadn't been permitted to enter the pearly gates or moved sideways into purgatory, leaving hell as the only apparent alternative. As soon as he heard the news the cloven hoofed, power-crazed glutton was up here straight away, terrified for the sake of his pride that he'd actually missed out on a soul that should have been his. The feller's completely paranoiac where sinners are concerned - chalks each one up as a victory over the providential boot that kicked him down to hell."

"A paranoiac divil, now there's a thought," Sean mused. "Does the feller suffer from other of the medical disasters that afflict humanity - the odd bout of cramp in the tail perhaps, or a painful boil on the arse?"

The corpse continued as if nothing of any worth had been said, as of course it hadn't,

"But then, once he reached the doors of this sordid den of alcohol and other abuses, he had a bit of a problem. You see, half his success has been in convincing the gullible many that they needn't worry about him because he doesn't exist. Now if he were to make a personal appearance in here, face to face as it were, all pitchforks, sulphur and stamping hooves, he'd run the risk of spoiling all his own hard work and convincing the world's unconvinced of his own diabolical reality by the testimony of those here present and reliable."

"Of whom I see none," Sean observed tartly.

"Exactly," said the corpse, losing slightly the thread of his own logic in the complexity of the argument. "So he couldn't come in and had to insist on me being sent out. But in delivering the message, he still had to convince people of his terrible ability to enforce his command and thereby of the fact that he really exists. So, in staying outside the door and dim wittedly doing what he did with the trousers and the phone and other things, he gained nothing more than had he come inside, and fell straight into the trap the good Archangel had so cleverly set for him. He's provided enough evidence of his fearsome existence to convert every sinner in the pub instantly into a terrified saint – in theory at least. That's why we haven't heard from him for the past half hour, the poor diabolical little feller doesn't know which way to turn – in fact he may even have gone home to sulk."

"So let me get this straight," Sean said, taking a long draught of non-existent whiskey which, while ceasing in the context of his glass, had been accidentally tipped onto the lolling tongue of the landlord's spread-eagled cat, "the Archangel Sidney, besides wanting the somewhat surprising pleasure of a free lesson in the art of jigging, desired also to convince doubters and pagans of the existence of God and the divil alike through the agency of your humble personage, suspended as it allegedly is between the living and the dead, and having, thereby, the status of a miracle?"

"That's it in a nutshell, indeed it is," said the corpse, secretly surprised that his unpromising audience had been able to absorb so well all the complications he had been throwing at him.

"Then tell me," said Sean, "leaving the divil aside for a moment and concentratin' on you, what's the use of such an act? If, as you say, people have become so used to all the common miracles of everyday existence that they no longer can conceive of their miraculousness, then isn't exactly the same thing going to happen with you? The longer you stay around and the more familiar people become with your strange state, then the less miraculous it will seem, until they reach a point where you're regarded as being as commonplace as me own impossible existence, or the amazing sight of the flight of a fat-arsed magpie. Then what happens to the plan of your imaginary heavenly visitor? You'll have no more impact on the faithless humanity he's complaining about than a baby elephant's first fart."

At that point, the landlord's cat decided it was time for a change and attempted to transfer its fat bulk from the floor to the corpse's knee. It hauled itself unsteadily to the drunkenness of its feet, wistfully licked the remaining whiskey on its lips, raised its front paws in befuddled preparation for the necessary leap, and then did a perfect and completely unintended somersault. Looking confusedly back at the inexplicable path of its own trajectory, it hiccupped, allowed its paws to go where they most desired, which was in four different directions at once, all of them outwards, and promptly disappeared into a happily snoring oblivion. Watching it with incredulous bafflement, Sean continued,

"And look at Christ, and all the miracles he's said to have performed. Despite all of that, so many people remained unconvinced of his divinity that they killed him without so much as a murmur of protest from anyone but the odd apostle. If the feller claimed to be the Son of God himself was unable to convince the motley masses to believe and change their lives and all that stuff, despite being the greatest miracle worker of all time, then what chance has a one trick corpse? Your mad little dance was clearly a one-off and all you can do for the most part is talk, and that's hardly a startling feat, given the several billion other people who perform the same ordinary 'miracle' every second minute of their waking days. A true miracle needs to be something that will amaze and at the risk of being impolite, you look something considerably less than an amazing sight from where I'm sitting."

"Then perhaps you ought to sit in a different and rather more inspiring seat," the corpse retorted, while sliding helplessly out of the gradually collapsing chair in which Sean had dumped it. It continued from the floor as if nothing untoward had happened,

"Given that your eyes are still more closed than open from the after-effects of your idiotic accidental guzzling of O'Malley's cocktail I'm surprised you can see even as far as the end of your nose."

"To a man like me, insults, even from a corpse, are like mere ducks off a water's back. And to be absolutely fair, they make the man who hurls them seem a most unlikely recipient of so heavenly a message. A corpse who is visited by an angel of God should be expected to act like a servant of the Almighty and you, me friend, simply do not fit the bill. And even if you did, it would still be necessary to explain away a conundrum that is inexplicable – and that is why on earth would the alleged miracle of a living corpse be performed with only the semi-inebriate or the completely drunk as the first witnesses to tell the world?"

"Because the semi-inebriate, the drunk and the dubious are to be given the opportunity to become a miracle in themselves," the corpse replied. "They will have the chance to be turned amazingly into witnesses so sober and respectable that their word will be indisputable – once they spread the word the curious will come here in droves and be inspired, as Sidney intends, by the miracle that awaits them. Why shouldn't those least likely to be chosen for such a thing by a world obsessed with status be given such a chance? But it's all a matter of free will – not even an archangel imposes if people turn up their noses at what is asked of them."

"All very 'Christian' I'm sure," Sean said, "but I've yet to be convinced that a Christian is what you really are. In short, I am not in the slightest of all slight things convinced of the truth of any of your incredible claims."

"Is that the case now?" the corpse asked innocently.

"Indeed it is, most certainly it is," Sean replied.

"Well, presumably, you'll need another miracle than me to convince you of the veracity of me words."

"I will, and I'll need to know they're true as well," Sean said, not normally an ignorant man in the matter of meaning, but still not at his best after the accidental imbibing of an O'Malley special.

"Very well," said the corpse, "having seen the Thomas-like depths of your unbelieving, cynical pit of a withered mind, I've no doubt Sidney will be obliging in such a matter. But be aware, whatever happens is the power of heaven and nothing to do with the ill capacity of a humble servant like meself. I'm but a conduit for those above."

"Ha! An excellent preparation for a miracle that refuses to take place," Sean said, "whose surprise non-occurrence will no doubt be blamed on the good Sidney having decided that I am an unworthy witness and sufficient cause in meself for a sustained dose of non-performance: a bit like going to a show where the magician's bunny refuses to come out of the hat on the grounds that it doesn't like the look of the audience."

Ignoring this barrage of mockery the corpse was silent for a few moments, then said,

"Well, what shall we try? Sidney suggests two miracles - the raising of the fallen daft followed by the turning of the room upside down. If you're not convinced by all of that then you'll be convinced of nothin'."

At which point the entire collection of unconscious eejits lying in the doorway rose as one body and stared wide-eyed at everything around them with the wonder of infants.

Sean rubbed his eyes in disbelief, marvelling at the uncharacteristic steadiness with which the most hardened drinkers within the little company stood.

"You see," the corpse said, "even those who were completely sozzled are now sober – they have the choice and the chance that I said they would - now for the second miracle - and the test."

Before Sean was able to take in the profound wonder of the resurrection of the daft the second of the predicted miracles began. Without the slightest warning, the very room in which he was sitting spun upside down, himself and everything within it being thrown roughly first against the walls, and finally upon the ceiling, which to his and the amazement of all, had become the floor. Only the corpse remained where it had been before, laid obstinately out against the floor, which meant, given the new status of the latter as the ceiling, that it was performing a third miracle of defiance of the law of gravity.

"Now," it said, "the test begins. In the case of you all the Archangel Sydney has found that there's at least one thing of a kind and charitable nature that each needs to do urgently for either their friends or family - or both - rather than be sitting here killing time with a glass in your hands. He's going to give you a straight choice between the chance to do what the good and the just would do and put these things right where they should be put right, or the chance to ignore all of that, stay where you are and claim two tasty free pies and a pint at the bar. If you want to take the first option all you have to do is walk out of the pub and get on with whatever it is you have to do – if you don't know what it is Sydney will whisper it into your ears as you leave. If you want to disappoint him and go for the second, purely self-centred option, then head for the bar, although you'll find it a little more difficult to get there than normal, given the temporarily inverted nature of the building."

"He means everything is upside down – arse over elbow," the pugilist explained to the puzzled looking sour faced man.

"If you can pass the test you will be new people and fitting witnesses in the saintly service of Sidney's plan. Right, off you go!" the corpse said.

His words unleashed instantly a mad and frantic scrabbling up the wall behind the upturned bar as the entire company, except for Sean and the landlord, made the perilous ascent towards the promised land. Every fitting, from a picture rail to a serving hatch was used to gain a handhold or foothold. Once all were clinging by their finger tips to the upturned bar counter on the floor that was now the ceiling, their tongues outstretched in anticipation of the sizzling pies that magically hung upside down from it, the corpse shook its head in sorrowful desperation and said,

"A sorrier sight I have never seen – and given the impossibility of anyone hanging on long enough to claim their miserable prize, a more stupid bunch of eejits would be hard to imagine."

No sooner had he spoken than Mary Contrary lost her tenuous

grip on the counter and dropped with a heavy thud and an "Ouch!" onto the ceiling that was now the floor, followed rapidly by the pugilist and all the others. The entire pie and pint-less company ended up one piled on top of the other in a dishevelled heap.

"And these," Sean said to the corpse, "are to be your witless witnesses to the world of your own and the divil's strange existence?"

"That was the case," the corpse replied, "and indeed they couldn't have been given a fairer chance to live up to the requirements of their anointed office. This was to have been a chance for the sinful to be twice redeemed and become the messengers delivering Sidney's revelation to a disbelieving world. But in the face of so miserable a failure of will and spirit, I've no doubt the good Archangel will select instead persons made from sterner stuff."

"In that case," said Sean, still trying to come to grips with the inverted state of the room, "he'll have to move you to another place. You will admit that a pub such as this is a most unpromising source of the sane, the sober and the sinless. You'll not find any suitable witnesses coming between these doors."

"No doubt to you and me that seems a most logical proposition," the corpse replied, "but it must be remembered always that logic can be a poor tool for understanding the Divine purpose. It is, at best, a means for helping us deal with the mechanics of our own limited existence. If it's God's will, then I'll be moved, if not, then I'll stay in me strange position and that is simply that."

"And a strange position it certainly is," said Sean, eyeing with increasing incredulity and neck ache the spectacle of the corpse lying on the ceiling that had been the floor, despite the switched positions of the two. "And furthermore, if the Almighty sneezes, or otherwise loses concentration in the holding of your person up above, then there'll be a terrible mess down here. You'll drop straight onto this rusty old chandelier with a spike in the middle. You'll be the twice dead, two corpses in one and with none of this lot in a state to scrape you up."

"Or wantin' to do so," Mary Contrary added, having at last recovered enough from her own inglorious nose dive from the inverted heights of the bar counter to find her tongue. "Especially when it's all the work of the feller with the cloven arse. Now I've heard of statues moving on mountains and the sun doin' a dance at Fatima, all very respectable miracles that would seem impossible to have come from anywhere but above, if come from anywhere they did. I'm not much of a one for believing in such things, but if they were to be true they all sound innocent enough. But this is an entirely different matter. The corruption of the would-be innocent – particularly meself - with the distracting promise of two pies and a pint was an unsavoury episode that puts everything you've said in question. There's no doubt at all, that was the work of a tempter, not an angel or saint and it went straight for our Achilles' heels - it's the divil's work we're seeing and it's the divil that protects his own."

"That's a true and honest conclusion on the matter," the landlord said. "I couldn't have put things better meself."

"You ladies and gentlemen," the corpse replied, "if ladies and gentlemen you are, seem to have no trouble at all believing in the power and will of the angel of darkness. I wonder then, why it's so difficult for you to accept that what's happening here might be the will of his converse. You seem unwilling to credit him with anything."

"I've nothing against converts," the sour faced man said, "some of me best friends are converts."

"What the hell have convents to do with anything?" the second philosopher asked from under the one table that had landed on its feet in all the convulsions of the room.

"The holiness of nuns is a wonderful sight to see," sour face said. "There's many a nun who's brought tears to the eyes of a sinner."

"Usually through a swift clip across both ears if me schooldays were anything to go by," the pugilist added.

The corpse raised the eyes it couldn't raise in exasperation. It said,

"It's clear to me now that the good Lord has set as the final test of me soul the task of educating a bunch of half wits and eejits. Can none of yous here understand the simplest of English?"

"Only if it's translated into Welsh and hummed," Mary said.

Ignoring her, the corpse continued,

"The good Sidney tells me that, statistically, there's not more than half a man in this whole street that has a soul in sight of heaven."

"A half a man is a remarkable thing," the second philosopher said. "Would it be his legs that form the holy part, or the belly upwards?"

"And what about the women?" Mary Contrary asked the table, which strangely refused to reply. "If it's the likes of me sister that's under question then we'll be dealin' in quarters and eighths."

"You are the most literal and pedantic group of comedians that I've ever encountered," the corpse rasped.

"And you are the most unconvincing of liars we've ever come across," Mary replied. "A man who had conversed with the Archangel Sidney would not be attributin' daft words to the mouth of a servant of God."

"I was speaking, as was the good Sidney, purely illustratively, presuming a level of intelligence that exceeded that of a pumpkin."

"There you go again," Sean said, joining in the general attack, "on the one hand claiming to be a messenger of the Almighty, and on the other hurling insults at everyone in sight. How can you hope to persuade us of the truth of anything you say?"

"The fact I'm so clearly imperfect is a problem for you and for me, but not for God," the corpse replied. "If he chooses to communicate through so obvious a sinner, then he has his reasons. At least you're listening to me, even if you don't believe a word I say. Given that the nightly deserting of wives and husbands for the beloved and unholy elixir of the bottle is testimony to the lack of impact on some of your befuddled souls of all the priests and nuns in Ireland, then perhaps someone like me is the only one who possibly could get through to you."

"Oh, and of course you're right," Mary said, "there's no statement that can be more convincing than one from a man who uses a ceiling as a floor. There's no way that such a farcical act could possibly be the work of the divil now is there?"

The corpse sighed deeply. It said,

"Has it never occurred to any of you that the good Lord God has a sense of humour - that the reason for me strange position on the ceiling that was the floor, but no longer is, is God's inability to resist a joke - that in all your doubts and fantasies of the divil's work, you are merely demonstrating what humourless specimens you really are? Whatever was done as a miracle - serious, humorous or terrifying - you'd still find fault with it and revert immediately to your sinful ways. The Almighty wants you to become his virtuous friends, but he could make the world square and teach elephants to fly and you'd still continue in your old, pitiful ways. Is there not a man or woman among you who wants to be invited to the rich banquet of heaven?"

"A banquet would do me very nicely," the second philosopher said, "will there be any trifle there d'you think, I'm a man who can never say no to a bowl of trifle."

"I've heard of some strange relationships in me time, but a man and a trifle must be a first in anyone's book," Mary said.

"I think you're being very harsh on us," a previously quiet and almost unnoticed third philosopher said to the corpse. "We've been under threat of heaven knows what this evenin' - first the divil demanding you or us and now you're as good as tellin' us we're all on our way to hell just because of the way we live and drink. Have you and your Archangel friend never considered that there might be a kinder way to try and win the souls of the supposedly damned? We have, after all, been ill-treated in life, every one of us - and none of us has much more to rub together than we spend in here. Those one or two of us who almost drown themselves in drink don't do so to escape from a bed full of roses you know. I don't remember a lot of evidence in me own life of this God who wants to be me friend that you're talking about, so you can't expect me to start pretending that he exists just because I'm told I'm well on me way to being damned, or because of magical miraculous happenings that could come as easily from the divil. I've been damned since I was born and there can't be a divil who's worse than me wife or me father before her, a man of many blows and little mercy. I can believe in a God of Terror, or God the Bully - with that I have no problem, terrors and bullies and grim poverty have trampled all over me life and if God created everything they must have come from him. But if you want me to swallow the notion of God the Friend, then that'll take time. I'm sorry to have to say it, but you and this imaginary

Sidney feller are being most unreasonable in your expectations."

"So you think your attitudes would have been different if you'd fallen right side up in life do you?" said the corpse. "If your parents had been kind, your husbands and wives had been the loves of your dreams and the struggles of your existence had been replaced by silver spoons? If that had been the case then you'd all have been virtuous Christian souls? Alright me friends, we'll test this little theory. Sidney has asked that you each conjure up a picture of what your idea of heaven on earth would look like. Go on me friends, feel free to dream. Do as he asks."

"To dream, by chance to dream," responded the pugilist, misquoting a quote that he'd heard in turn misquoted outside a theatre whose name he couldn't remember.

"Go on," said the corpse to the author of the murdered quote, "do as you say and dream away, tell me what your greatest dream is."

"Me greatest dream?" the pugilist said. "Now that's an easy enough confession to make - to be me own boss, to be Lord of half the factories in Ireland and to be answerable to no-one but meself. To live like a king on the wealth of me industry and to have a wife who actually loves me. Now doesn't that sound a reasonable fate for a man so pronounced in talent as meself?"

"Go to the window," the corpse commanded, "and look outside."

"And what shall I do when I get there? Stand on me head to set the view the right way up? You're forgetting the blessed thing's upside down."

"Only the pub is upside down," the corpse replied, "everything outside it is as normal as it ever can be. Now please, do as I ask."

The pugilist did as instructed and looked out.

"Well, what do you see?" the corpse asked.

"Why, it's a magnificent house," the pugilist replied, "or rather a house that thinks it's a palace more like."

"And what do you see now?" the corpse asked.

"I don't believe it, it's the inside of the place. How on earth did you manage that?"

"And who's that sitting stuffing himself at the dinner table?" the corpse asked.

"Why, why it's me! Dressed in a suit that sings of wealth. All in white, with a wife in silk and smiling at me as if I were the joy of ages, served by a butler who fills me plate 'til it looks like a mountain, drinking wine that smells of roses, in a room that's panelled with oak and edged with gilt. It's me every dream come true - tell me, is this a promise, is this me future, can I hope to see all this take place?"

"This is what would have been had you had a more privileged birth," the corpse informed him, "not what was, is, or for you, might ever be. This is how you would have conducted yourself in a life of wealth."

The pugilist sighed wistfully, resting his chin upon his arms upon the top of the window frame that had become the bottom.

"And what do you see now?" asked the corpse. "Who's that knocking on the front door?"

"Him? Sadness incarnate, a feller dressed in the manner and quality of meself in me present state, a man of small means who's seen better times without ever having had the privilege of living them. He looks a strange visitor to a place like this."

"Indeed," said the corpse. "And what's he saying to the butler?"

"I can't hear too well. No, wait, he's pleading for his job, asking that the factory he depends on to feed his little ones won't be closed - if he can have a word with the man who's me, if you see what I mean."

"Do you think you'll see him?" the corpse asked.

"It would be a kind and charitable thing to do," the pugilist replied.

"I didn't ask about that," the corpse said, "I asked if you thought you'd see him. What are you saying to the butler now?"

"I can't quite hear properly," the pugilist replied, "there's a window between me and all of this you know."

"If I can hear from up here, then you can hear from down there. Shall I tell you what's being said?"

"Whatever you like," the pugilist said unenthusiastically.

"Well," said the corpse sarcastically, "all of this is a surprise. You've just told the butler to clear the impudent ruffian off your step and away from your house, to threaten him with trespass if necessary. And you're explaining to your wife that the clearly profitable nature of the factory is irrelevant, you've sold the land to a property developer and by so doing stand to add a fortune to your already considerable wealth."

"Is that the case now," said the pugilist disinterestedly.

"And what's this?" the corpse asked. "Is not the whole thing going back in time? Maybe you'll be a different man in a different century d'you not think? Sure now, isn't that you, all in nineteenth century dress. And that poor man in rags there, knocking at your door, doesn't he look like a feller racked by famine. Do you honestly believe he'll survive another day if he isn't fed by some kind soul? Now, do you think you'll be the one to feed him?"

"I can't see any of this," the pugilist lied, "either there's a blind been pulled over me eyes or you're imagining it all."

"Is that the truth?" said the corpse. "Well, as you say, it must be a blind that's fallen over your eyes, because I'm plagued with a very poor imagination. I'll have to tell you what I see... What's this, it looks like you've turned him away - and there's you with your table stuffed with grub. The poor feller can hardly walk now - it could be his death you've sent him to. And there's you and your wife in the house still stuffing yourselves and feeding your dog the scraps from the table, scraps that poor man would have given the shirt off his back for. Now does any of this suggest that wealth and plenty would have made you a more generous and God loving man than you are now in your drunken poverty?"

"It's all a trick," the pugilist said, sidling away from the window. "That was a man who looked like me and no more. Had it been really meself you would have seen a very different picture, a very different one."

"Would I indeed?" said the corpse. "I wish I or Sydney could share your certainty. You mightn't be able to see him, but he's right here beside me and he says it would only have been a different you had you purged your soul of all its selfishness – without first doing that wallet loads of wealth, beautiful wives and wonderful lives would not have altered you in the slightest. Now is there anyone else who'd like to have a glance at their dreams through our magical little window here?"

As one the assembled company shuffled two steps backwards, murmuring amongst themselves in a decidedly disgruntled manner.

"Nobody?" the corpse asked. "What a surprise. It couldn't be that, just like our friend here, you're all afraid you'd have been no better or even worse people had you been rich? What about you Sean O'Riley, you've had a lot to say for yourself, wouldn't you like to see how your life would have panned out had your dreams come true? You said earlier that you didn't know yourself – well this is your chance to change all of that and find out what you're really like. A man with everything he dreams of can be judged by how he helps those who have nothing can he not – would you like to see how you would have behaved towards the poor and deprived?"

Sean, who had gone as white as a spook's eyebrows at the thought of such a probing, pretended to be asleep and unhearing in a chair he'd sunk into. The corpse sighed and said,

"I'll take that as a no then. D'you know what Sidney's just said in me ear? 'What a bunch of negative noodles.' None of you wants to see the real you writ large and none certainly wants to be bothered with purging the poisons at the heart of your sozzled souls. So, as there's clearly no point in continuing his vain attempts to persuade the unpersuadable of the need for virtue and reform, my angelic friend tells me that the pub is about to be upended again, from wrong to right way up. With that he'll be on his way and leave you to your fates. You'll be able to get on with your sad and misguided existences as if nothing of a potentially life-changing nature happened at all tonight and I'll just mind me own business in the corner – you won't even know I'm here. The divil's gone off in a huff for reasons that I explained to the only man conscious after the mass cracking of heads, so you can all eat and drink to your heart's content without fear of the feller – until he comes knocking for your blighted souls when you kick the bucket that is. But then that's not something that anyone's going to be thinking about again until it's all too late, am I not right?"

No sooner had he spoken than, with a great jolt, the pub did exactly as predicted and began to swing in an uncomfortably jerking fashion from upside down to right way up. It made four complete rotations, each becoming uncomfortably faster than the last, until suddenly shuddering to a halt. Its occupants were slung in a great heap from the ceiling to the walls to the floor four times, finally lying groaning and grumbling in a daze – yet miraculously unhurt - when the dizzying motion ceased. Only the corpse was spared their fate, remaining glued to the same spot throughout the turning of the building.

"There must be a rational explanation for all of this," Sean said, having been 'awakened' from his feigned sleep by the rotation of the building. "All that rubbish about a non-existent Archangel Sidney and the spinning of the room - it's as though we've been the victims of some mass delusion. The more the effects of O'Malley's cocktail wear off me sad, thick head the more I know that all that's happened has either been the work of the divil or there's been some malicious tinkerin' with the drink in this place. Are you sure landlord that some irresponsible joker hasn't been concentratin' the alcohol in all yer booze?"

"Concentratin'?" the second philosopher asked incredulously. "You're addressing your question to a man who waters yer whiskey before he even puts the water in it."

Mary Contrary was looking extremely thoughtful. She said,

"I think, Sean O'Riley, that you're a man who's hit as nearly on the truth as truth can be hit. It seems to me that there's been an intoxicatin' substance at work alright, but I don't mean drink."

"Oh, so what do you mean?" Sean enquired.

"Well, I'm lookin' at that pie machine by the till, the one for keeping once hot things still faintly hot. You can see smoke coming from the thing and the plastic of the bar top where it touches. The device clearly is violently overheating and I reckon it's the vapours that have done for us, the gas the burning plastic has released. We've all been drugged and deceived to the point where we don't know right from left. Everything that's happened that we thought miraculous was simply the product of the vapours – it's an intoxication that has had the same effect on all of us and caused everyone present to imagine a speaking corpse and all his drivel about angels and sin and whatever. It's a most potent and unusual substance that's been at work and has, as you say, created a mass delusion."

"You know," Sean said, "you could have a point. That spinning we had just now - there was nothing it so much resembled as the effects of the anaesthetic at the dentists in the old days, when the gas mask was shoved over your face and your consciousness went round like a Catherine wheel. Everyone back then had the same experience of that did they not? The more I think on it the more certain I am that you're right."

"You poor, pathetic self-deluders," the corpse said. "Is there no end to the fantasies you'll try to sell yourselves in order to hide your simple souls from the pain of truth?"

"And he's the biggest fantasy of them all," Mary said. "Who's ever heard of a dead man speaking, especially one who's so incapable of moving his lips? Sure if we can unplug that heathen device and throw it outside our problems will disappear."

"They will, truly they will," Sean said. "For doesn't the thing smell sickly sulphurous and isn't that exactly the smell we got when we thought the divil and all his hordes of demons were camped upon the doorstep. It's all becoming as clear as clarity can make a thing. I'll unplug the faulty relic meself - there, done! And now, ladies and gentlemen if you please, a fire blanket!"

The landlord produced instantly a grey and reeking apology for a garment from under the bar.

"Hell's teeth! That's a bed blanket not a fire blanket!" Sean yelled. "I want to put the fire out not give the thing a good night's sleep! Have you not got anything more official and appropriate?"

The landlord shrugged and shook his head in an impressive display of certain uncertainty, trying hard to grapple with the unfamiliarity of the technicalities that separated a fire blanket from the wider family of bed blankets. Spotting the correct non-flammable item sitting idle and unrecognized on a shelf below the till Sean grabbed it and said,

"This will do the job. I'll wrap the thing thickly and well and chuck the lot out into the street. The sooner the air gets cleared in here, the sooner our heads will be back to normal."

Sean acted in line with his stated intentions and hurled the unpopular contraption into the street, an event that was accompanied by enormous clattering and a desperate squeal from a fleeing cat. The corpse said,

"So all you need now is for me to keep quiet and your little make-believe will be complete. Nothing will have happened other than your temporary intoxication and you can all get back to making the same mess of your lives as before. What a sad and shrunken monument to sinful humanity you are."

"It's clearing, me head's definitely clearing!" Mary said.

"And mine," volunteered the second philosopher, who was not entirely sure what a clear mind looked like in the first place.

"The pong's gone and me brain has come back from me arse to me head," the pugilist said. "I knew all that stuff about the Archangel Sidney was a load of bollix."

"Me trousers!" yelled the third philosopher with a panicky, urgent tone that would have raised a dozen Lazaruses and frightened the daylights out of the still unconceived.

"What about your trousers?" Mary enquired. "My God, you are without!"

"To be more accurate, I'm within and me trousers are without. It must have been that divilish spinning that did it. The room flew around so fast me pants must have shot off and up the chimney. Is there not a mountaineer in the house?"

"The spinning was in your head and nowhere else," Sean hissed sourly, "we've already established the cause of all the strangeness that has afflicted us tonight. You can't lose your trousers for real in a dream induced by a conspiracy of poison fumes. You must never have had them on in the first place."

"Never have had... do you think me wife would let me even get out of bed without me pants on first? She's such a prudish woman that she thinks the showing of a knee is equivalent to a belly dance in front of a bishop."

"'Tis awful strange," the pugilist said. "I know well the wife to whom the man refers and it's true indeed that she'd not consent to enter heaven unless she was sure first St. Peter was fully robed. And the parrot - how do you account for the parrot?"

"Thumper! Me poor little bird," the landlord wailed, conjuring up an instant and confusing vision of a parrot with paws and a vigorous woolly tail in the mind of all the assembly. Following his horrified gaze, they were confronted by a truly appalling sight. The poor little creature was pinned to the bottom of its cage by four stake-like pencils, a look of shock in its eyes that signified an instant and most unexpected end.

"Those are the pencils of Pencil O'Malley!" Mary said, turning accusingly to their owner, who when not being lampooned as 'Legless', was known by the name of the means by which he marked out the winners that would always be losers in the paper he nicked off the newsagent's stand.

“Is that the truth?” the landlord demanded. “Am I addressing now a perverted parrot murderer within the four walls of me own bar?”

“I’d never touch a perverted parrot or even go within spitting distance of such an oddity,” O’Malley replied.

“Don’t play with words you decadent deviant,” the landlord said, himself playing with words he was only half sure went together. “You’ve staked me poor little bird to the floor of its cage and now I’m going to stake yer balls to the ceiling!”

“I’ve done no such thing,” O’Malley replied. “If those are indeed O’Malley pencils then it was the force of the spinning that hurled them from me pocket and into the pure, soft feathers of your precious under-sized turkey.”

“Jaysis wept, how many times do I have to say it?” Sean rasped. “The only thing spinning was the inside of your head and half the cause of the spinning would be those pills you’re daft enough to buy from John the Con. Two of those in your beer and you’re a headless chicken at the best of times, so you could have murdered anyone or anything without hardly knowing it, never mind a parrot. If your pencils are embedded in the overfed belly of the little creature, then they must have travelled in the O’Malley hand. And as the hand is at the command of the brain, then the evidence against is overwhelming. We are indeed in the presence of a man who, when half in control of his mind and unable to murder anyone his own size, picked on a bird no bigger than his boots.”

“Imagining the little feller was his mother-in-law perhaps,” Mary added, “and doing to a defenceless bunch of feathers what he’d not even dare to half-do to her - the woman who punishes him for his idleness and indiscretions with an iron handbag and a tongue that can cut any man or woman in two from thirty yards.”

“Tell me Sean O’Riley and Mary Contrary,” the corpse roared, “if the great God almighty were to appear from out of a cloud of holy smoke right in front of your eyes, would you not tell him he was either a figment of his own imagination or an electrical fault and then soak the miraculous vision from head to foot with a fire extinguisher?”

“When the great God almighty comes I’ll know it’s the great God almighty,” Sean replied.

"Really?" said the corpse. "A man who doesn't even know his own mind would know such a thing? A man who one minute is arguing that I, a living corpse, am a fantasy and the next is holding a conversation with the same alleged fantasy? Tell me Sean, what are you going to do about this little problem of yours?"

"I'm going to fetch an undertaker and end this nonsense once and for all, that's what I'm going to do," Sean said.

"For the parrot or the corpse?" the second philosopher asked.

"To be sure that's the best thing," the corpse said. "A man who talks so freely with the dead but can't accept the evidence of his own ears can only conclude that his sanity is playing the fool. Or perhaps you're still afraid that I might put you in the same position I put our friend in there when looking at what he might have done had he been born with a silver spoon in his mouth – your pretence of being asleep when I invited you to take part didn't fool me for a minute. There's somethin' disturbing hidden deep within you isn't there – a potential for evil that frightens the living daylights out of you, that's what really at stake here isn't it? You're afraid that because it's so bad Sidney's going to come back and make it known through me, just as he did with your friend there – that whether you like it or not your real self will be shown to you and everyone here in another of Sidney's miraculous animations, simulations, whatever you might call the little virtual reality performances that he put on earlier. And that potential within you, your little secret, will be so appalling that not even this unholy crowd would want to speak to you again. So instead of heroically confronting the poison at the heart of your soul and purging it, you aim to take the less challenging and stressful option and bury it – and me – from view. Isn't that the truth now? For there are times when a corpse can read the minds of men and right now I'm reading you like a book. Yes, get me down, under the ground, that's the soundest course. Go on Sean, bury the truth as quick as you can before it gets out! The divil will be proud of you for keeping a bit of him in your head, safely preserved and potent, ready to swallow your soul! Strike another blow for the galloping forces of darkness!"

O'Riley did not look pleased and was starting to look as guilty as a man caught with his hand inside a policeman's wallet.

“Sean, if the man’s dead and devoid of conversation, how is it that we can all hear him still?” the pugilist asked worriedly.

“The lingering vapours from the pie machine,” O’Riley replied nervously as he strode over to the doors. Shouting with a desperate urgency until he was hoarse, he forced awake the slumbering undertaker and his assistant who, drunk and comatose after sharing a bottle of bootleg whiskey that was three times the strength on its label, had collapsed, one on and one under the same bed. Their shop and living quarters being directly opposite, they were stumbling bleary eyed into the bar in less than ten full minutes, their black regalia still damp from a puddle they had fallen face first into when crossing the road.

Nobody looked round or spoke as the corpse was dumped unceremoniously into an over-large coffin and carried out, the doors swinging hollowly behind the small entourage as it disappeared across the road.

“Well, that’s that then,” Mary Contrary said at length.

“Aye, that’s that,” Sean replied and each avoiding the eyes of the other, they slunk quietly home, taking the remnants of their drink-shrivelled livers to their beds.

Finale - The Judging

The end of Maggie's tale was greeted with loud and vigorous clapping, whistles and much banter between her and one or two she knew well in the audience. She took several bows and then walked calmly off stage and out through the back of the tent so that the judging could get underway. The applause followed her all the way out and didn't stop for a full minute after she had gone. Fierce Betty then took command, drowning out all competing conversations by using the microphone as if it was a loud hailer, causing several in the audience with hearing aids to rip them out of their ears to lessen the thunderous noise of her voice. She said,

"That's it everyone, the last tale of the competition has been told and the judges will now retire to consider their verdict. The winner will be announced in here at 10 o'clock prompt tomorrow morning and the prize of 3,000 euros and a hamper of cheese and hams and other produce of the county awarded. Make sure you arrive in good time – there will be no admission for latecomers so as not to disrupt proceedings."

With that she turned on her fiercely polished heels and left the audience to it.

"I'm in love with you Betty," a mischievous voice shouted

after her, “how could any mortal man resist such a charm offensive!”

“More like offensive charm,” Ben said to Sean with half a grin.

Sean smiled wryly. He said,

“Now then lads, the time has come. Dick McManus will be here now and open for bets – yes there he is at the back, sitting where all the judges were bunched. He’s put his sign up the cheeky owd sod, you’d think it was a day at the races. He’ll only stay for an hour or so then he’ll be off home for his supper, so you’d better make your minds up quickly as to who you’re going to bet on. Do you want to go and sit somewhere in the quiet end of the tent so you can hear yourselves think?”

“I’m alright where I am,” Ben said. “I’ve more or less made a decision. I’ll hang onto it for a few minutes more and if at the end of that no doubts have jumped into me head I’ll go and place my bet.”

“When both of you do I must come with you on each occasion,” Sean said. “I need to be the witness that confirms to the loser that the winner actually placed the bet that he claims. In a situation as critical as this betting stubs won’t be enough on their own.”

“That’s fine by me,” Liam said, a deep and dark undercurrent still running through his voice that suggested that all would be far from fine if he lost. “I’ll do as you suggest and go and sit in the quiet bit for a while – I don’t want to leave anything out of my calculations.”

Ben muttered “Loser” under his breath and Sean’s anxieties about what might happen in the morning doubled. He wandered over to the wily old book keeper to place his own bet, then sat down opposite to watch as a long queue of other hopefuls formed to do the same. He noted with interest how the various tales had gone down, with bets on all bar Declan’s shaggy dog story being regularly placed. That confirmed the fact that it was going to be a close run race with no easy way of predicting the winner. His own money had gone on the tale about the barmy prophetess, but she cropped up no more often than three of the other tales. He noticed suddenly that Ben was in the queue and would very soon be placing his bet, so got up to join him. As they waited for his turn

Sean noticed that Liam was still sitting at the far side of the tent, watching Ben with a dark, glowering look. Ben equally had grown tense and while never a man for much in the way of small talk, was saying even less now. Sean silently cursed himself for his naïve and unrealistic vision in thinking that this might be a peaceful and low cost way of bringing the land war between the two over-muscular chieftains to some kind of closure. His worry now was how on earth he could stop the loser trying to throttle the winner in the morning and the prospect of the long drive back home with the two irreconcilables filled him with drcad.

Finally Ben's turn arrived and he placed his bet, not on the barmy woman as had been Sean's preference, but on the professor's tale. Sean's heart sank into his boots. The more he had been thinking about it at the back of his mind the more he had become convinced that that was where his own money should have gone. It was too late now as owd Dick would only allow one bet per person. But that was not his main worry. If Ben had got it right then Liam looked likely to take it far worse than had the situation been the other way round. Looking eight places behind in the remaining queue Sean noticed that Liam had now joined the fray. He told Ben he would take both of them to the pub shortly and buy them pints of the best and went to stand with Liam, who grunted by way of greeting, but said little else. Sean tried to start some kind of a conversation but got nowhere, the tension that sat between his nephew's ears hissing and screaming like a pressure pot about to explode. When they eventually shuffled to the head of the remaining queue Liam finally revealed his hand. Like Sean he had plumped for the barmy woman.

Once the deed was done a weight seemed to roll off Liam's shoulders and he looked for a brief while more exhausted by the strain of it all than threatening to the peace. Sean called Ben over and then told each of them how the other had chosen in their betting. They both nodded but said little else. Liam thanked Sean for what he had done then said that he would give the pub a miss and was off to his bed.

The Oyster Bar begged a question and that was why did it have oysters in its name if it had nothing at all to do with them. A shellfish freak could search the place from top to bottom with sniffer dogs, but would find not even the smallest fragment of an oyster from the depths of its cellar to the top of its chimneys. When Sean and Ben walked through its doors it was heaving to the extent that if the whole of the crowd inside moved in the same direction at once they'd probably take the pub with them. Ben used his former rugby player skills to tunnel a way through to the bar and returned rewarded shortly afterwards with a pint for each of them. He then announced that he would be drinking his own alone in the beer garden outside if Sean didn't mind – he wanted to think how best to deal with the result of his bet in the morning, whichever way it went. A little disappointed but not surprised that neither one of his problematic nephews wanted to spend the evening with him Sean nodded his agreement and went to look for some familiar faces in the crowd. He found a couple of heartily drinking stewards who he knew from previous festivals and spent the night in their company, himself drinking rather more heartily than was wise. He looked once or twice through the window at Ben, still sitting alone in the garden as the last of the sun packed its bags and slipped out of view. He noticed on each occasion that his expression was as dark as the gathering gloom of dusk and that worried him. The morning was not going to be a happy time and he drank more than he should have done to forget about it as far as he could.

When eventually he awoke the following day it was nearly half past nine, leading to a mighty panic as he raced around to the showers and shaved himself so quickly that he was lucky not to have sliced an ear off. There was no sign of either Ben or Liam, who had both clearly gone already to await their fate at the feet of Fierce Betty and the judges. It had rained heavily overnight and he narrowly avoided going flat on his face in the mud as he careered over to the competition tent before Betty superglued shut its every flap and posted sentries with machine guns outside to prevent late entry. When he finally scrambled his way in, just in time, he found the two irreconcilables in exactly the same seats as they had sat in all of yesterday, with a space left for him in the middle. He hurried over and inserted himself between them, as tense as the two chieftains about the result and the possible horrendous consequences if the loser was not prepared to lose. They each nodded at him and Ben said,

"Sorry for not waking you uncle but you looked so much the

worse the wear for the owd drink when you got in last night that I thought you'd want to rest in a little longer."

"No problem, no problem, I got here and that's all that matters," Sean said. As soon as he had spoken Betty the Fierce advanced to the microphone, having noted on her ultra precise watch that the magic hour of ten had arrived. With her usual deafening, thunderous voice she said,

"We now have the results of the competition and the chair of the judging panel, Aidan Kilmartin, will announce the winner."

Aidan was a soft spoken academic of a man with a love of story telling and a nervous disposition. He had expected her introduction to take at least a minute or two, just long enough for him to compose himself for the announcement of what he felt to be an unsatisfactory result that would displease as many as it pleased. Betty's hurling of him straight off the cliff made him resemble a man who had just been electrocuted. He shuffled forwards as if ready to make a bolt for the exit and spent a good twenty seconds adjusting his glasses and rustling two pieces of paper that contained no relevant information, but served the same function as a teddy or a comfort blanket for a man who hated speaking in public. Gathering together his fleeing thoughts until they all sat in one place between his ears and in something resembling the right order he said,

"Ladies and gentlemen, it gives me great pleasure to announce the results of the 2017 Mullahy's Sock, sorry Rock, Storytelling competition. As you may know, in all previous years of the competition's existence there has been a single winner who has taken all of the prize. This year things are a little bit different. The panel was evenly split between two entries all the way through our deliberations until three in the morning, when finally it was decided there was only one solution to the deadlock, which was to use the chairman's casting vote. Unfortunately that did little to help because I supported each of the deadlocked stories equally, leaving us exactly where we were before."

Through the corner of his eyes Sean could see the jaws of both Liam and Ben beginning to drop in an equally measured fashion. The man unable to make a decision continued,

"So, in the end, the panel concluded there was only one decision it could make. For the first time ever in the history of the competition, the prize is to be shared equally between the tellers of two stories, which are: The Woman with a Man in her Hat and…" He didn't pause for effect, but rather as a result of temporary amnesia brought on by nerves. Fortunately it all came back within a few nail and shoe biting seconds and he said,

"The Grim Reaper's Apprentice."

There were gasps, cheers, some happy bunnies, others that appeared simply confused and the two curmudgeonly chieftains either side of Sean, who looked as if they'd just had pick axes plunged into the back of their heads. Instead of the clear cut victory that each had desperately hoped for, they had both won and in their own eyes, therefore, both lost. The bumbling Aidan Kilmartin welcomed the victorious storytellers onto the stage. They were simultaneously pleased and disappointed, given that their prize money had in effect been halved. As Aidan shook their hands Sean's brain raced while he struggled to find a means of dealing with this most unexpected of outcomes. Then it hit him, like lightning on ice – the almighty had delivered the one result that might finally free the two combatants from their unending battle. They had both agreed that no matter what, today's result would be the resolution to their dispute. They had previously refused point blank to even half consider any idea of sharing the land. But things had now moved on - they had both suffered two enormous emotional strains upon their warring brains from all that had happened at Mullahy's Rock. The first was the close shave with total loss - both had come closer than ever before to a moment when they could have found themselves suddenly bereft of all claim to that which they desired more than anything else on earth. The second was the knowledge that their one chance of an affordable means of getting sole ownership of the land had vaporized in front of their eyes. Should they now continue holding on to their sole claims they would be insanely choosing the path of financial ruin – the one thing that in coming here they had hoped to avoid. But the impact of these two strains was multiplied and supercharged by their obvious state of shock at the tied result. That had created an opportunity that deft diplomacy might seize, but it had to be grabbed now and at once, because it might never arise again. Sean took his chance and leapt off the cliff, blind faith giving him to believe that at some point in his plunge a parachute would open up and all would be well. He said,

"Now then lads, you both swore on everything sacred that no matter what, the results of your bets would be the final decider of everything to do with the land. The result is nowhere as good as you each wanted, but most crucially nowhere as bad as you feared in terms of losing, and the only alternative to it is the driving of yourselves to despair and destitution. Now I know you don't like it and before today you both said you wouldn't share even a single blade of grass or an ounce of sheep shit from the land, but the almighty has taken things into his own hands and given you a judgment of Solomon. If you're both real men and most certainly if you've any claim to be god fearing men, you'll accept the fate handed out to you and settle the matter in a manner that the almighty would call His own. The only dispute from today onwards will be as to which half of the land you each will farm and how you'll share all that goes with it. If you want to use legal men to settle all of that please do, but remember that if you're both bull headed over the matter then you'll end up as poor as you would have been otherwise. So use your common sense and a bit of give and take and then I'll be proud to call you me nephews. What do you say?"

Ben sighed in despair and put his head in his hands and Sean feared that all that had been won had been lost. But then, to his astonishment, the head that had sunk down into his nephew's boots rose up again. With a look of disappointment, resignation and weariness at the continual frustrations of the whole affair, Ben said,

"It's a solution that's no solution, more a defeat for both sides, but while I hate to admit it, what you say is the only thing that makes sense."

From seconds before having felt that his leap off the cliff was going to leave him splattered all over the rocks below, Sean suddenly heard the thwump of his parachute opening above him. Doing his best to hide his total astonishment at what he had just heard, he turned to Liam, who was looking like a man who had just been sentenced to be personally horse whipped by Vlad the Impaler. He said,

"And what about you Liam, how do you feel about the matter?"

There was a long pause in which Liam stared at the ground, seemingly focussed on a deep invisible chasm that had opened at his feet, threatening to suck him in. Finally he said,

"It's just like the bible isn't it, about this world being a vale of tears and all that stuff. There's nothing I can agree with him and nothing he can agree with me, but we've no choice but to agree on what you say. I can't afford to go on with this war and neither can he, that much is a fact. We'll have to do what you say uncle Sean, but I can't pretend that either of us will be a happy man as a result."

On that half-hearted but most definitely practical note the War of Bill's Will was finally ended and the two chieftains did not live happily ever after. But, every now and then, they had a bit of a go at doing so and that at least was something.

Other books by P.J. Anderson available in Nine Lives Editions UK

The Three Signs of the Serpent is now available in paperback and e-book versions.

Pre-release review and short synopsis:
"Well, what can I say – what a creation. ... Despite the several very scary episodes, some quite grisly too ... I think the most frightening elements are something else. One is the ordinariness of it all. There you are, for example, sitting in an ordinary coffee shop, with ordinary coffee shop noises around you from machines and customers drinking an ordinary cup of coffee, and the devil walks in. Or a man who thinks he's the devil. Or even a crossover, a man-devil. But you don't realise it's the devil or whoever/whatever because he/it is in the form of a man ... And you're not necessarily safe in what you suppose is the ultimate sanctuary: a church or its equivalent, because evil, the darkness ... can get in anywhere, even in your head, even in the heads of the supposedly incorruptible. That's the second most frightening element. It's like walking across Morecambe Bay without a guide: put a foot wrong and you don't know what you'll step into. Evil is to the side, at the front, behind, below, above... I do not remember breathing as I read the final chapter." A.B., a former book editor and previously of the Financial Times.

This is a unique and genuinely chilling book, a web of traditional ghost stories woven within a Faustian tale of evil at its most deadly and ambiguous. Christine O'Donnell is a teller of ghostly tales who finds herself being gradually ensnared by a diabolical master storyteller until, figuratively speaking, she is swallowed whole. She then engages in a desperate struggle to free herself from forces that systematically try to undermine her sanity and terrify her into becoming their servant. Her own fictional stories are frightening in themselves, but the real-life tale in which she finds herself cast in the lead role is more sinister and disturbing than anything she could have imagined.

Printed in Poland
by Amazon Fulfillment
Poland Sp. z o.o., Wrocław